Praise for
The Wattle Seed Inn

'Written with warmth, humour and sincerity, offering appealing characters and an engaging story, *The Wattle Seed Inn* is a lovely read, sure to satisfy fans of the genre.' **Book'd Out**

'Leonie Kelsall makes a welcome return that offers plenty of happiness, fun and heartbreak . . . With a wonderful message about letting go, seizing the day and embracing all experiences on offer, *The Wattle Seed Inn* is an encouraging read I highly recommend.' **Mrs B's Book Reviews**

'Heart-warming.' *Family Circle*

'Endearing and full of possibilities.' *Country Style*

'[*The Wattle Seed Inn*] is a meditation on the city/country divide, as well as a salutary tale about the importance of finding community. It's also a rollicking good read.' *Australian Country Magazine*

Praise for
The Farm at Peppertree Crossing

'Kelsall is a bold and fearless writer who is unafraid of presenting her readership with a plethora of darker style themes ... authentic, insightful and sensitive in the right places.' **Mrs B's Book Reviews**

'Léonie Kelsall's skilful portrayal of life on the land and the people who live it comes alive. An absolute gem of a book!' **Blue Wolf Reviews**

'... moves from foreboding, funny, breath-holding, sad and sweet. I loved the way Kelsall unwrapped the secrets slowly throughout the story—little teasers that kept me glued to the pages.' **The Burgeoning Bookshelf Blogspot**

'It's a mark of Kelsall's unique storytelling ability that she is able to combine both the dark and light elements of this story to create something so appealing.' **Jackie Smith Writes**

'A fantastic tale with relatable and loveable characters.' **Happy Valley BooksRead**

'... told with plenty of heart and humour ... a charming book full of strong, unforgettable characters that you'll fall in love with.' *Glam Adelaide Magazine*

Raised initially in a tiny, no-horse town on South Australia's Fleurieu coast, then in the slightly more populated wheat and sheep farming land in the Murraylands, Léonie Kelsall is a country girl through and through. Growing up without a television, she developed a love of reading before she reached primary school, swiftly followed by a desire to write. Pity the poor teachers who received chapters of creative writing instead of a single page!

Léonie entertained a brief fantasy of moving to the big city (well, Adelaide), but within months the lure of the open spaces and big sky country summoned her home. Now she splits her time between the stark, arid beauty of the family farm at Pallamana and her home and counselling practice in the lush Adelaide Hills.

Catch up with her on Facebook, Instagram or at www.leoniekelsall.com.

ALSO BY LÉONIE KELSALL
The Farm at Peppertree Crossing

LÉONIE KELSALL

The Wattle Seed Inn

ALLEN&UNWIN
SYDNEY · MELBOURNE · AUCKLAND · LONDON

This edition published in 2022
First published in 2021

Allen & Unwin
83 Alexander Street
Crows Nest NSW 2065
Australia
Phone: (61 2) 8425 0100
Email: info@allenandunwin.com
Web: www.allenandunwin.com

 A catalogue record for this
book is available from the
National Library of Australia

ISBN 978 1 76106 708 2

Set in Sabon LT Pro by Bookhouse, Sydney
Printed in Australia by McPherson's Printing Group

10 9 8 7 6 5 4 3 2 1

The paper in this book is FSC® certified.
FSC® promotes environmentally responsible,
socially beneficial and economically viable
management of the world's forests.

For Dad,
Who showed me that dreams deserve to be followed

And, as always, for Taylor,
Who takes that advice to heart

1

Gabrielle

'The place must be haunted,' the conveyancer said, shaking his head as Gabrielle signed the transfer paperwork.

'Why is that?' She underlined *Moreau* with a sweeping ink stroke.

The conveyancer tapped the original title, the document apparently a rarity since the Titles Office joined the twenty-first century and switched to computer-generated documentation. Gabrielle's ex-fiancé, Brendan, had splashed enough cash to somehow make the parchment appear when they purchased the hotel three years ago. Which was particularly ironic, given that he often accused her of buying her way through life.

'Fourth transfer in thirteen years. Unlucky number,' the conveyancer observed. 'Before that, the same family held it for over a hundred and thirty years.'

Gabrielle knew he was fishing for information, specifically about why this was the second transfer in three years, with the property being changed from joint ownership to hers alone. But she wasn't about to delve into the details of the demise of her decade-long relationship, to talk about the way she and Brendan had been drifting: not so much apart, as moored in a sticky morass of wealth and lack of expectation. Life was too easy, too familiar, too . . . perfect? But when Brendan accused her of lacking passion, her achievements and partnership in their marketing company a product of her parents' affluence and influence rather than her drive, she had finally woken from the daydream of wealth and privilege. Gabrielle had traded her share in their Adelaide apartment for Brendan's portion of the country hotel and now the Wurruldi Hotel was hers, as evidenced by the title deed, and it was here she planned to prove that her creativity trumped his supposed passion.

She set the pen down, pushing the papers back across the desk. 'I guess that family had the best of it, when Wurruldi was a paddle-steamer trading port. Progress—and, I suppose, roads—killed the town along with the trade. There's just the pub and a handful of cottages there now.'

'Looks like the river's going the same way,' the conveyancer muttered. 'Unless we get a bigger water allocation from upriver, it'll be ruined. Nothing but carp left in there.'

'Hopefully not,' Gabrielle said, refusing to let his doom and gloom sway her. 'In any case, I'm taking the premises in a different direction. Those roads that ruined the pub decades ago mean it's now perfectly placed for a bed-and-breakfast set-up.' She pointed in the general direction of the mountain range to the east of Adelaide, punctuating the air with her Chanel blush-nude nails. 'World-class wine regions within ninety minutes in three directions. The Barossa Valley pours a fortune into promotions and commands a massive tourist market. South, there's the Fleurieu Peninsula and McLaren Vale wineries, and the Adelaide Hills are also on the town's doorstep. So, Wurruldi is the perfect hub for holidaymakers. Backed up by the right marketing, a bed-and-breakfast there will be a guaranteed winner.'

'And that marketing is what Small & Sassy does, right?' the conveyancer asked, leaning forward, his eyebrows raised.

Gabrielle swallowed her irritation. *Small* was a nod to Brendan's surname, which unsurprisingly he despised and was hellbent on disproving; *Sassy* was for her role in the firm they'd started together straight out of uni. She knew that alliteration was a tool that should never be underestimated, and she could adopt the required personality at will. Or at Brendan's will: he was the one who viewed every interaction as a chance to network.

'I'm PR,' she said. 'I handle our clients' public persona, help shape the perception of their image.' She watched the conveyancer's eyes glaze over as he reached for his pen and rolled it between thumb and forefinger, though he kept his slightly unfocused gaze on her. 'Brendan does the marketing,' she wrapped up swiftly. It had taken her a bachelor's degree to realise that the unfamiliar necessity to stick to budgets and spreadsheets was never going

3

to sit well with her, but adding a postgrad in communications had been the perfect way to complement Brendan's indisputable skills and build their niche business. She had a practised talent for reinventing, camouflaging and selling—people, at least. Now, she had to hope her abilities would translate to revitalising an old hotel that had seen better days, so she could prove Brendan wrong: success didn't need passion, it needed a plan.

∽

Rather than take the main road through Settlers Bridge to the south, Gabrielle took a scenic route from the north, past the tiny wineries and through the gum-studded hills of Eden Valley. She hadn't paid much attention when Brendan drove them out to Wurruldi three years ago, and now she almost missed the unmarked turn-off that led from the bitumen onto a potholed dirt lane. It looked like the roads department had also missed it for quite some time.

The road wound for a couple of kilometres between paddocks filled with oatmeal-coloured grass and studded with granite boulders the size of caravans, then, without warning, it took a hard right. On Gabrielle's left was a breathtakingly sheer drop of hundreds of feet. Far below threaded the mighty Murray River, while directly opposite soared a vast apricot-toned cliff, the twin of the one she edged along. It was as though a rift had appeared in the earth, cracking the land apart as the khaki waters forced through the crevasse.

Yet another unmarked turn led her onto a series of tight switchbacks sliced into the cliff face. She took her time, her foot pressing on the brake until finally she reached the bottom of the steep descent and breathed a tremulous sigh of relief as the track levelled out onto a wide river flat. While her inexperience with country driving made the road seem particularly treacherous, Gabrielle recognised that the dirt track was part of the isolated, rural charm of the tiny, almost hidden town.

A forest of river red gums dwarfed her car, the leafy canopy making lacy dapples of the last of the day's light. The road wound across the broadening flats, the opposite side of the river still sharply defined by stark cliffs. Within a kilometre she was following a spit of land between the river and lagoons landscaped with the bleached skeletons of trees, victims of salinity caused by upriver locks interfering with the natural cycle of flood and drought.

Wurruldi might only be fifteen kilometres off the main road—according to her GPS, though she had doubts—but this stark, ominous beauty was a world away from her city life. For the right clientele, that could be turned into a selling point. Gabrielle would have to get on to the council about fixing up the road, though; there was a fine line between offering tranquillity and isolation, and being inaccessible in some banjo-playing backwater.

Her grip on the wheel eased as she reached the town-limit sign, an ancient, unofficial-looking piece of tin. *Wurruldi.* No population count.

She turned left, along the outside of the wattle-tree–lined boundary of her property. On the opposite side of the road was what constituted the township: a small, multiple-doored construction of stone and tin sat in the middle of a paddock. Low in one window was a faded sign: *South Australia's favourite. Amscol ice cream. 'It's a food, Not a fad.'* In the opposite corner a hand-painted poster, the curling, yellowed edges cradling decades' worth of fly husks, declared *Wurruldi Postal Agency.*

Almost on the river's edge, the road came to a junction. Gabrielle pulled up facing the rusting remnants of a massive pulley system. To the right, beyond the shop-cum-post office, four symmetrical sandstone cottages sat precariously close to the low banks of the river. To the left the road hooked, leading back up the inside boundary of her property.

Directly in front of her, a pair of pelicans floated across the olive satin towards a flat-bedded ferry moored among the moulting willows below the far cliff. The front of the punt drifted mesmerisingly from side to side, catching the sharp breeze—or perhaps swayed by invisible currents. She buzzed down her window, taking deep breaths of the rich, dank odour. The pelicans changed tack, effortlessly moving upstream, past an ancient timber dock, until they were hidden by the golden late-autumn willow fronds.

When they had disappeared, Gabrielle nodded decisively, put the car back into gear and made a sharp left U-turn onto a broad, crushed-limestone driveway. From here, this was her property. Thigh-high grass and weeds tangled in dying bushes almost hid the low drystone wall that separated the driveway from the public road.

Staring in appalled fascination, she let the car crawl two hundred metres, to where the driveway curved in a majestic swoop between the pub and a wooden horse trough, before running in a mirror image down the far side of the vast block. When Gabrielle had visited with Brendan to check out the potential investment, she'd told him she could imagine Shire horses clopping up the pristine concourse, pulling drays laden with trade goods—or perhaps barrels of beer—as women in long skirts reclined in lawn chairs on the soft grass beneath the lacy canopy of an imposing, multi-trunked jacaranda that stood proud in the centre of the area. Brendan had laughed and pointed out that dreaming didn't equate to passion. Maybe she should have seen the warning signs back then, but they had been together so long they were accustomed to one another. No, almost immune to one another. It had taken a long time for words, or even deeds, to burrow deep enough to hurt beyond a passing sting.

Pulling up, Gabrielle clambered slowly from the blue Audi S5 convertible, reluctant to face the magnitude of the task before her. Even Brendan's silver tongue would have trouble marketing this. Deep, crusted ruts scabbed the driveway, and rubble was scattered across the burr-covered yard. The century-old hitching rail and rough-hewn water trough that had fired her imagination were now a pile of splintered kindling.

She groaned, then recoiled as the noise startled a burst of rosellas from gums overhanging the stone wall. They shot skyward like fireworks, an explosion of colour in the drabness, and she turned to follow their flight above the high-peaked roof of the hotel. The Wurruldi Hotel.

Her hotel.

Resting her hands on narrow hips, Gabrielle slowed her slightly panicked breathing. Although the bones of the two-storey stone structure remained the same as when she and Brendan purchased it, the signs of insidious rot couldn't be overlooked. Unease wormed through her stomach. The best PR campaign in the world couldn't positively influence the impression this ruin would make on clients.

Beneath a hooded tin roof, three recessed doors were scarcely visible through the utilitarian square posts of the timber-railed balcony. Wooden-framed casement windows, softened only slightly by beige scrim netting, gazed sight-lessly at the river.

The deep balcony created a darkly shaded verandah over the lower level, but Gabrielle could make out *Gentlemen's Bar* and *Ladies' Lounge* stylishly rendered in peeling gold-leaf above two of the windows. Arching over the centrally placed door, *1884* was clearly legible but the name of the licensee had flaked away, becoming a few dots and dashes of glitter and the odd, almost indecipherable, letter. As though to invite customers, the doorway was generous, wide enough to fit a broad-shouldered farmer on his way in for a pint or two after tying his horse to the nearby hitching post.

Not that anyone would be tethering a horse anymore; Gabrielle waved a fly away as she tried to dispel the dis-illusionment that pulled her mouth into a tight line. Other than location, the place was nothing like she remembered, and the damage worse than she had imagined.

Slowly, her gaze travelled across the front of the building. Gabrielle recalled the property boasting stately, park-like gardens, a pleasing blend of form and function that appealed to her artistic nature. But now the rose bushes sticking out from the weeds bordering the pub were covered in mottled, mouldy leaves, the branches blackened with canker. The odd small, struggling flower clung to life well beyond its season.

The worst thing wasn't the sad state of the property, but the fact that much of it was her fault. Some time back, in a surge of manic creativity and without revisiting the property, Brendan had pushed through the required council approvals to remodel the upstairs space to fit his vision of a boutique ale house where they could occasionally weekend. But other than that, their development intentions had been buried beneath the demands of their business. Although the estate agent said a woman was available, they never managed to get around to hiring someone to maintain the property. Out of sight, out of mind, the best-laid plans, and all that stuff: living and working in the thriving urban heart of Adelaide, it was impossible to imagine the abandoned property would slowly turn in on itself, crumbling with neglect.

The earthquake, however, had not been her fault. South Australia had a history of small quakes, averaging around four on the Richter scale, but they rarely caused much beyond minor damage. Now she had to deal with the consequences of both her inaction and the fact that the world had rubbed up the tectonic plates the wrong way a few months earlier.

Gabrielle pinched the bridge of her nose, trying to ease the tension without messing up her eye make-up. 'Can't make plans until I see how bad the damage is,' she muttered, taking slight reassurance from the sound of a voice, even her own. She considered checking if anyone was home, over in the cottages, but decided the news that she planned on developing their graveyard-quiet village of four houses, one deserted multi-purpose shop and a derelict pub into a thriving tourist mecca might not go down well.

She snorted: they'd probably laugh her out of town.

Taking a deep breath, Gabrielle started along the tree-lined passage on the southern side of the building. 'Oh!' she yelped, thrusting a hand out to steady herself as the heel of the over-the-knee leather boots she'd picked up in Rome caught in a crack of the uneven slate. She swiped slime on her denim-clad thigh, glaring at the damp moss-covered stone wall, then wound a hand beneath her woollen layers to tug the vibrating mobile phone from her pocket. She scowled at the illuminated screen—it didn't matter how many public pronouncements they had made about staying friends over the past thirteen months, still Brendan's profile pic twisted her stomach with irrational annoyance.

With the Manawaiopuna Falls in the background, he was fully kitted out in hiking gear, a backpack over his shoulders, expensive carbon trekking poles in one hand. She wasn't sure how many years ago they had taken that trip— maybe four? It had been the Greek Islands last autumn,

10

Italy the year before that. What she did know was that the carefully cropped snap was, like all of Brendan's social media, a construct she had helped build; the image he currently required the world to have of him. The contrived outdoorsy theme was an indication he was wooing a client in the physical recreation field.

What the picture didn't reveal was the helicopter that dropped them at the Hawaiian waterfall, or the ubiquitous smoother tucked away in Brendan's pocket or palmed in his left hand, out of frame.

Last month, when he was chasing a corporate account, his profile had been a devastatingly handsome candid snap of him in a Tom Ford suit and open-necked shirt, his casually dishevelled hair cut in a fade above the AirPods permanently embedded in his ears.

Her own profile photo needed to be updated. Backlit by nightclub neon, cocktail in one hand, her French-polished nails caressing the hanging fronds of a potted bamboo, Gabrielle wore dramatic make-up and a black woven bamboo shirt dress, evocative of Audrey Hepburn. Small & Sassy had won the account for the clothing line and she handled their PR campaign with a heavy focus on the ecological sustainability of bamboo, environmental awareness and the innate ability of women to do good while looking good.

Like Brendan said, every point of contact was an opportunity to sell yourself.

The difference was that he enjoyed doing it.

'Hey, Brendan.' Gabrielle tried to keep the peevish sigh from her voice.

'Hi, Elle. How's it look?' Brendan's voice crackled down the line and she shifted the phone away from her ear, toggling it onto speaker.

'Like a crumbling ruin,' she exaggerated. Even without doing the loathed budget projections, Gabrielle knew that financially she had made a crap decision in taking this on. But emotionally? Finishing things with Brendan was the right call. They had a long history, and it would have been simple to stay with him, to tell herself she remained seduced by his urbane charm. But then life would have continued as it was, an endless loop of dissatisfied satisfaction.

'If it's too far gone, sell for land value. Recoup your losses and come back to work.'

The practised calm of Brendan's deep voice should be soothing, but instead he had her hackles up in an instant. After so many years together, how could he not realise how much his thinly veiled directions irritated her? Besides, quitting would be easy, she had the financial reserves to take the hit. But accepting a loss on the place would reinforce his accusation that she wasn't passionate, that she wasn't driven to see the project through.

Brendan didn't need proof that he was right, that instead of enhancing life, money was an anaesthetic. With everything so easily attainable, there was no edge, no fear of failure to spice a venture. And without fear of failure, it was impossible to cultivate passion.

Gabrielle tipped her head back, focusing on a lone gunmetal-grey cloud scudding overhead. The pelicans soared high above now, drifting in circles over the wetlands, their outstretched wings wider than the span of her arms. Tempted to lose herself in their hypnotic laziness, Gabrielle shook her head. *Focus.* At least she hadn't let her need to escape persuade her to sell her share of their business; rather, she had stepped back into a consultancy role.

As she strode from the passage into a brick-paved court-yard Gabrielle forced cheerfulness into her tone, as though a tight smile would evidence a positive attitude. If Brendan doubted her ability to follow through with her plan, that made her all the more determined. 'I'll work it out.'

'At least come back here after you've had a look around today, Elle. There's no point roughing it. You said you'd use the apartment as your base.'

The designer-furnished, fully serviced apartment in the city that was now all his. Just like this ruin was all hers. And, with the chill breeze gusting the musty odour of rotting vegetation from the river's edge, it didn't seem like such a fair trade. 'Actually, *you* said that.' Sharing the apartment hadn't been a problem for the first months post–break-up—after all, their relationship had never fallen into the hot-and-steamy category, they'd always been better suited as friends than lovers—but she was woman enough to feel irritation at the sight of the latest pocket-sized brunette or blonde draped all over her ex—and all over her bespoke handmade Molmic lounge suite.

Brendan's Molmic, now.

'I'm only going to have a quick look around the outside, then I'll head in to Settlers Bridge to pick up the key,' she said.

'You didn't go to the agent first?'

'I came the back way.'

By now he should know that she preferred a tactile approach to her job, getting to know her clients and their products before she calculated the best way to build and maintain their image. Today, she had needed to put herself in the place of her guests-to-be, and taking the scenic route had been mandatory to her process.

Brendan grunted. 'The agent will be closed now.' Gabrielle knew the rustle of fabric meant he'd turned his wrist to check his Tag Heuer. 'I said you'd left it too late to head down tonight.'

It had taken her a few years to recognise that Brendan's overbearing attitude wasn't one of protection, but of possession. 'And I told you that I needed to finish up the KPI report for Ormandes' campaign before I clocked off.' Collating data and statistics was her least favourite part of the job, and she'd dragged her heels. 'Anyway, the agent is leaving the keys in a lock box for me.' She crossed her fingers against the bad luck her lie could bring. 'Got to go.'

Brendan was right, though, she had left her run too late to make a decent assessment of the property. Already, purple dusk lay in plump pillows beneath the trees bordering the courtyard. But this was the first weekend she'd had clear for months. The PR business involved too many crazy hours, too many events, too many functions; all of which Brendan loved. He thrived on the stimulation of being constantly surrounded by people, always in the spotlight, putting on a performance. And he liked to party, even though he knew that drugs were her kryptonite. Had been since Amelie had hit a downward spiral and overdosed on a cocktail of prescriptions and illegals when they were seventeen.

Losing her sister had taught her to numb herself: without passion, there couldn't be pain. But there was no risk of pain in rescuing this ruin; she would only do it to prove to Brendan she could be successful in her own right, that she didn't need to fall back on the cushion of money. The cushion that had suffocated Amelie.

Gabrielle shook off her thoughts. It was time to add photos to the margin sketches and notes she had doodled. To create a brand for this property, she needed to connect with it, to clarify her vague ideas of what it could become.

Ideas that seemed more far-fetched by the second, she thought morosely as she kicked a clod of mud from the red-brick pavers. As though moving one lump of clay would make any appreciable difference to the derelict, forlorn look of the property. All it did was spray dirt across the fawn leather of her boots.

Gabrielle stepped back to look up at the rear of the building. While she had thought the front stark, the back had neither balcony nor verandah to soften the no-frills presentation. Snapping photos from various angles, she worked quickly in the dying light.

Across the courtyard, the building jutted out at a one-and-a-half storey right angle. A sloping verandah shaded narrow rectangular windows, while on the upper level, which must be a loft rather than another floor, small, square, uncurtained windows let in the light. At the end of the building, disappearing in the twilight, she could just make out a door in the same olive shade as the winter river. Although the barn style was different to the main building, the stonework was complimentary. She decided that the extension, which she recalled as being a large kitchen and new wet areas, had likely been commissioned by one of the recent owners; those who had been chased off by the ghosts of the conveyancer's imagination. A frisson rippled across her skin as the breeze billowed a dirty grey curtain from the window above, and she rubbed briskly at her arms through her sweater, huddling deeper into the alpaca wool afghan wrap.

Peering up, Gabrielle realised that the curtain fluttered where the window *had* been. While some of the mullioned panes reflected rainbows of the last of the muted ochre sun filtering through the hedge of wattles, others had exploded, leaving jagged shards of glass in twisted frames as the only deterrent to looters. Deep cracks creased the pale sandstone walls, and dark frown lines ran from above the central door to the forehead of the second storey. Dirty runnels gouged the mortar beneath the windows like tear stains, and the once-cheery trims were disjointed and splintered, held together with scabbed burgundy blood.

A sense of overwhelming desolation seized Gabrielle. An inanimate object couldn't die, yet it seemed that was exactly what had happened to the hotel.

She shook off the notion, looking around for something to relieve the oppression. The faded red-brick quoins on each corner of the building added a dash of colour in the face of the pervading grimness, and high above her, the second floor looked across the large courtyard to a vista of gum-studded wetlands beyond the wattle-tree hedge.

She set her jaw. The state of the property following the earthquake shouldn't come as a shock, but close up, the damage to the building looked far worse than it had in the photos the insurance company emailed a few months back. She and Brendan had taken the settlement in cash so they could rebuild to suit their needs—or at least, that had been the plan. Brendan had been in favour of modernising, capitalising on the property's location and outlook rather than on the dated infrastructure, but obviously she couldn't do that now. Gabrielle had to find something different, something *more*, to prove to Brendan that despite everything material in her life coming easily, she had vision and ability enough to not need his touted *passion*. She would find a point of difference, something to set the Wurruldi Hotel aside from the mundane bed-and-breakfast enterprises dotting the state. At the moment, she had a stellar location. And not much more.

Gabrielle wrapped her arms around herself, the enormity of the task suddenly daunting. What had she got herself into? With no real renovating experience, she'd signed up to prove her independence by making over a ruin? And why even bother? Brendan's interest, beyond his initial ego-driven taunt, would be limited, and Wurruldi was too far off the beaten track for any of her old crowd to visit. Siri's maps existed only to guide them to the nearest open bar.

A crow cawed in the tree overhead, echoed by more of his coven further along the river. Gabrielle shivered. The crumbling façade, undermined walls and missing windows vastly diminished any charm she had imagined in this venture. Realising she had been frowning unseeingly up at the building, Gabrielle snapped a few more pictures, then turned away. Against the wattle-tree hedge at the rear of the courtyard stood a row of stone outbuildings separated into pairs by five-metre spaces. Although she and Brendan hadn't bothered to investigate them when they had made their impromptu and unresearched decision to purchase the property, at her desk she had toyed with the notion of converting them into tiny cottages to house the overflow of tourists her campaign would attract. But now she saw that a combination of time and the earthquake had hit the smaller buildings hard. A pile of roofing iron created a funeral pyre alongside the corpse of a rusted vehicle in what the real-estate agent claimed had been a stable.

Gabrielle carefully navigated the mud-slicked pavers as she skirted fallen branches of the red gum that shaded the courtyard, the hardened amber sap shattering to release an earthy, resinous scent beneath her tread.

Orange bunting sectioned off one pair of buildings, a handwritten sign in a plastic sleeve reading, *Caution: Unstable.* She circled the sheds, stumbling through the scrubby saltbush at the rear. The back wall tilted outward, far enough that it would cast a shadow if the encroaching darkness hadn't already made the scene grim.

Rusted triangular hinge plates clutched at a wooden door that leaned drunkenly ajar. She edged closer and peered into the gloom beyond. Stone and mortar had tumbled from the rear wall, forming a pyramid on the dirt floor. The breach was plugged with a scrabble of twigs and twine and the odd piece of litter. The floor immediately below was centimetres-deep in bird mess.

Shit. Literally. Why had she imagined she could turn these feral hovels into accommodation? She flicked on her torch app and tentatively pushed at the final door. It gave reluctantly, creaking open.

'Oh!' She eased a step further into the room, peering around with renewed interest. With a ceiling of rusted pressed-metal tiles, each decorated with a stylised floral cross in the centre of an ornately curlicued border, and with papered walls, it seemed that, unlike the other sheds, this had once been inhabited. Under her feet, old lino cracked like bones, the pieces shifting to reveal a different layer beneath.

The iPhone's torch beam was too feeble to probe far into the gloom, but as Gabrielle's eyes adjusted, she could make out a few details. A plush armchair dwarfed a chequerboard cigar humidor, the spindly legs poised to dance across the room as soon as she turned her back. Against the side wall, almost consumed by the luscious darkness, stood a long sideboard. She couldn't see into it, but glass refracted her light in patchy flashes through the grime.

As Gabrielle took another step, something moved in the dim recesses and a chill rushed towards her. She lurched back across the stone hearth and into the last of the watery evening light. Gooseflesh prickled her arms as she clutched them tight across her chest and gave a nervous giggle. Prying around in the dusk made her feel like a trespasser, and if she was going to let a breeze and the rustle of a possum spook her, it was time to call it a night.

In daylight the project would seem more achievable, the property would look less abandoned.

It had to.

Otherwise, she had made the biggest mistake of her life.

2
Ilse

The thin net curtain on the dirty window drifted aside as Ilse approached it, her slow footfalls noiseless on the worn carpet. In her grandmother's day, the curtains had been of true lace, and neither the precious fabric nor the glass would ever have been allowed to become so filthy. Oma had ordered the bolts of material from Belgium, insisting the beautiful curtains adorn almost every window of the establishment she and her husband built upon their arrival in the young colony.

Ilse had learned her grandparents' stories at Opa's knee. Proudly twirling the waxed tips of his handlebar moustache, worn in defiance of the anti-German sentiment that had swept the land during the First World War, Opa was a natural orator. As he relived the years he had played to an enthusiastic audience of river traders and settlers,

21

he made Ilse feel she had seen the era of paddle-steamers towing huge barges laden with wool, tallow, station supplies, timber and farming equipment, plying the Murray. But by the time she, an end-of-war celebration baby— although perhaps her parents would have celebrated less, had they realised she would be their only child—was born, the network of roads and railways had claimed the bulk of the trade, though hawkers' boats still tied up on the long wooden dock in front of the hotel. Indeed, in her childhood, Wurruldi had briefly flourished. When Opa put in the ferry crossing, it encouraged an influx of the wheat and pig farmers, who tried to scrape a living from the arid Mallee soils on the eastern side of the river. Back then, the town boasted a general store, telephone exchange and tiny post office—all three housed in the same building.

The way Opa told it, the beautiful lace curtains had become something of a sore point when Ilse's headstrong mother married into the family. According to Oma, the lace should be carefully handwashed in the laundry trough every six weeks and then hung to dry out of the sun. Mother insisted on using Velvet soap, which she advocated for everything from her face to the saucepans. Arms folded across her ample bosom, Oma would staunchly declare the hard bar fit only for washing her hands of John Kitchen, the creator of the soap who had the audacity to desert the Methodist Church in favour of the Church of England.

Though Ilse's mother took over the hotel during the Great Depression, still she maintained Oma's routine—not that she really had a choice, with her mother-in-law sternly overseeing her every move from a wheelchair for many years. She was, however, swift to switch to Windex in place of the ash-and-vinegar Oma favoured for the windows.

Ilse chuckled as she recalled Mother's determination to own one of Herbert Hoover's Bakelite upright floor cleaners. Waving a tea towel at Father, she had insisted that, despite the outrageous seventy-pound expense, the new-age marvel would soon pay for itself, as they would no longer need house girls to hang the rugs over lines strung between the gum trees and beat the dust from them each week with a heavy paddle. As always, Father surrendered to her, happy as long as the three generations of women, all living under one roof, were able to get along in relative harmony.

Born in the hotel, Ilse had fallen in love here, birthed two sons here and, to the thrill of the local gossips, given birth to a third in the year her firstborn was lost to a point-less war waged in a rice field in a far-distant country. She pressed the heel of her hand to her chest, unsure whether the twinge was a remnant of the breath-stealing jolt of pain that occurred more frequently lately, or simply her unhealed heartbreak.

Reaching to wipe the grime blurring her view of the yard below, she thought better of it. Lips pursed, she shook her head in disapproval; clearly neither vinegar nor Windex had touched the glass in a long time. It was a shame, but when the hotel passed beyond the family, standards had slipped.

She couldn't lay all the blame on strangers, though; the changes had happened before then, when her son, Ivan, and then her grandson, Michael, managed the hotel. Yet, despite their shortcomings, the unmistakeably proprietorial stance of someone who was not her kin never failed to make her prickle with irritability—as she did now.

The narrow-hipped woman who stood in the courtyard below, one hand thrust into the rear pocket of her jeans, the other holding a phone pressed to her ear, had been here before. They hadn't met; Ilse had spied her when she and a handsome young man had inspected the building. The lack of space between the pair, their arms occasionally touching, and the casually familiar manner in which the man placed his hand on the woman's shoulder, made it apparent to a keen observer—or to Ilse, at least—that they shared more than the car in which they arrived. Shortly after, the real-estate agent confided in Ilse that, though the property was offered as a bank foreclosure, the couple had made a generous offer and would undoubtedly appreciate her assistance in maintaining the magnificent gardens, as she always had.

The woman's ash-blonde hair brushed her collarbones as she frowned up at the building. Perhaps she was wishing their offer had been a little less extravagant?

Ilse drew back, although she had no need to hide. Even after the hotel left the family, she had always been welcome here, though rarely did she trespass into the upstairs rooms, not since they had been ruined by startling avocado-green paintwork and burnt-orange bedspreads and curtains. She seldom set foot beyond the original kitchen, preferring the predictable familiarity of the gardens that her grandmother had planned and her mother had expanded during the Depression with the help of the raggedy men happy to work for a feed.

The woman below raked a hand through her hair, and Ilse caught the flash of dark nail polish. At least this one kept herself tidy. The previous owner had worn slacks that Ilse judged fit only for gardening, paired with cheap rubber thongs irrespective of the weather. Not that there was ever an acceptable excuse for that footwear. Ilse absently patted her short perm. She must call Leanne and arrange to pop into Settlers Bridge for a trim. It was important to keep oneself tidy.

Vaguely, Ilse recalled there was another appointment she must keep—but the thought vanished.

Despite her blue jeans, the new owner seemed well turned out, although somewhat hidden beneath a brown-toned wrap and high boots that made Ilse's breath catch with sudden desire. Ilse had, as Ronald liked to say, a good pair of pins, and knew exactly how to showcase them. When nylons were impossible to obtain during the war, she'd drawn seams up the back of her legs with an eyebrow pencil. The recollection brought a smile to her lips: Ronald had been so young, then. Handsome. He loved to tease that the line was crooked, and would offer to redraw it— and cheekily run his hand beneath her skirts as he did so.

Eyes closed, she sighed with the mixture of pleasure and pain her meandering reminiscences always awoke. Ronald had been her first love, her only love, her forever love. While all her memories, both the best and the worst, were tied to this place, those she most liked to relive involved her husband.

Her smile vanished and Ilse pressed trembling fingers to her temple, looking around in momentary confusion. Lost in her thoughts, she had wandered down the broad central flight of stairs and now stood in the small entry foyer, the frosted panels around the front door hazing the tessellated marble mosaics of the floor with faint splashes of the dying light. Here, as in all the public areas, Michael had hung televisions from the decorative cornices, despite her caution that they made conversation impossible. Perhaps because he and his wife didn't talk, he assumed all couples to be the same. Like her eldest grandson, the televisions were gone now, the bare ends of the disconnected wires poking like cockroach antennae from the plastic conduits that marred the papered walls.

Ilse shivered. Why did the hotel feel so . . . hollow? Undeniably, the spirit of the building had been slowly dying for years, but she had never before noticed this odd, pervasive chill that seemed to seep into her very marrow. Her puzzled gaze roamed to the glass panels framing the door. Broken. Why were they broken? It seemed she should know, yet it was as though she tried to dredge the memory from the muddy waters of the river.

Perhaps her mind was going? She worried about that on occasion, when she couldn't find her reading glasses, or the names of her great-grandchildren escaped her immediate recall. But those were minor inconveniences. This was . . . wrong. Deeply wrong.

Fear rippled inside her, the dread growing like rising flood waters, and she clutched at the heavy brass door handle, her hand and arm unaccountably numb and leaden, although pain shot into her jaw.

The water rose and the world went dark.

Yet there was familiarity in that darkness. Not comfort, nor peace; but horrid, bleak familiarity.

3
Hayden

'Sorry, mate.' Hayden reached beneath the table to scruff the dog's ears.

Trigger looked up at him, his brown eye glistening and the ice-blue one sparkling even in the dim light of the pub. His tail beat a tattoo against the grey carpet, but at Hayden's nod he dropped his chin down onto his neatly folded apricot-splotched paws.

'Talking to that dog more than to us again, Wheaty,' Taylor chided from across the table, tapping her glass with her fingernail.

Hayden shot her a grin. 'I can always thump you with my boot and then apologise, if that's what you consider a decent chat. Besides, it's hard for a bloke to get a word in around here, Doc.' He lifted his chin to indicate Taylor,

Luke and Sharna, who had already claimed a high bench table by the time he'd turned up with Justin.

As usual, The Settlers Bridge Hotel was Friday-night noisy. The preferred hangout for locals was packed with Rossi-booted farmers downing beers as though the end of the week meant they would actually get a couple of days off. The wall between the dining room and front bar had long ago been knocked out, creating one large, informal room, and the talk filling it was of crops and yields and weather and sheep.

For about the millionth time, Hayden was glad he'd chosen a trade over working the farm alongside his dad and brother. Not that running his own business excused him from lending a hand on the property; his parents often seemed to forget that he'd moved out years ago, but that was partly because his place was only a paddock away from the family home. He could guarantee that regardless of the time or day he turned up at the farmhouse, his mum would have enough Tupperware containers stacked in the fridge to feed him—and probably half of Settlers Bridge— and his dad would have a list of jobs that required 'an extra pair of hands', despite his four siblings still living at home.

Until last year, his brother, Rob, had been a prickly shit whenever Hayden turned up, as though he couldn't get it through his thick skull that Hayden didn't want to stake his claim. But Hayden had made up his mind about that long ago, before he even left school. Working a farm would never be for him. He didn't like the uncertainty, the fact that farmers were subject to the whims of weather and pests and the price-setting of grain-board contracts. While he'd never get rich in the building trade, at least he got to quote the job and get paid fairly for his effort. He had more control over his life than the poor buggers who couldn't write a business projection.

Or so he'd thought, until last year.

Trigger nudged his knee, and Hayden realised he'd been scraping his thumb up and down his thigh, the nail leaving a whitened trail in the faded denim. He glanced around their small group and caught Taylor watching him, her grey eyes far too observant. She'd obviously come straight from work and looked out of place in her black pants and soft pink blouse. Alongside her, Sharna was as cute as a dairy ad, with the Akubra hat she would never actually wear on the farm tipped to the back of her head, strawberry curls jostling for position around her freckled face.

'Okay over there, old man?' Sharna asked jokingly, though he could see her concern. Damn, he had to learn to get his tells under control; both women could read him far too easily.

'Fine,' he nodded. 'But a bit less of the old, okay?'

'You used to babysit me, remember?'

'I don't reckon being the one to pull your puking face out of a puddle of vomit really rates as babysitting. I know I sure didn't get paid for it.'

'You were the most adult-adult there.'

'Hey, hang on,' Taylor leaned forward to hear their exchange better. Unlike Sharna, she could put her feet on the floor while perched on the bar stools. 'What's the story?'

'I remember that one.' Juz lifted a lazy hand to wave as a couple of blokes cannoned through the double doors that led straight off the main street into the bar. 'Shearing shed, right?'

'Easy guess, mate,' Hayden said. Sharna's folks had thrown her the usual sixteenth: the neighbour's shearing shed decked out with pink and purple streamers and balloons, a chocolate fountain on the wool-sorting table and the smell of barbecued chops mixing with lanolin and sheep manure in what he now recognised was a pretty ironic full-circle kind of thing. He turned back to Taylor but jerked a thumb towards Justin. 'Not naming names, but *someone* spiked the punch at Sharna's sixteenth. She ended up puking in Technicolor all over the wool press.'

Juz knocked his schooner of beer as he jerked up his hands to form a halo over his head. 'Don't look at me, mate. I would've been, what, eighteen maybe? Pushing nineteen? Whatever, but too broke to afford my own beer, never mind donating to the girls' punchbowl.'

Sharna smacked a hand on the table. 'Yeah, well whoever did it killed my taste for anything stronger than Moscato, so thanks heaps, guys. Eight years down the track and even the smell of Bundy still makes me want to hurl. Plus, I ended up grounded for a month when my folks found out.'

'So, you had to miss what, three netball games?' Luke smirked.

'Screw the games. I missed the social. Twice!'

Hayden grinned at Sharna's aggrieved tone. The 'social' was drinks—though maybe not for her—and, after enough

31

liquid encouragement and with the music cranked up loud, a bit of dancing at the local clubrooms.

'Baby got put in a corner?' Luke suggested.

'Honey, you're showing your age,' Taylor groaned.

'Nothing to do with age. The drive-in at Murray Bridge was still open back when I was a kid and they'd play that movie every fortnight. I practically had shares in it.'

'Uh-huh. And have you ever actually *watched* it?' Taylor slanted her gaze up to meet his.

'Sprung, mate,' Hayden laughed, though jealousy twisted his gut. In his mid-thirties, Luke was only a few years older than him yet had been settled with Taylor forever. Which was kind of funny, given how wild Luke had been when they were teenagers. Actually, it wasn't funny; it was unfair. Though he would never let on to his mates, Hayden had always wanted what his mum and dad had: someone to come home to, to chew over his plans and dreams with. Maybe even to argue with about stupid things, knowing that, because they agreed on the important stuff, they would both be there for the long haul.

Though he'd had his share of girls, he never let anything get serious: he'd been holding out for the woman he would be happy to wake up alongside every morning for the rest of his life. The woman who would have his back when things got tough, have his children when the going was good, and have his nuts if he screwed up.

But now, there was no way in hell he'd find her.

Trigger whined, his wet nose insistently butting into Hayden's hand. Hayden hid his growl of frustration—at himself, not the animal. He tousled the dog's soft fur and dropped his other hand from where it had been reflexively massaging his left arm through the sleeve of his khaki shirt.

The door banged open and another noisy group bustled into the already crowded pub.

Juz shoved off his steel-framed bar stool. 'I'm grabbing a platter. Anyone want in?'

'Sure, yeah, go the wings for me, mate,' Luke said, reaching for his wallet.

Juz waved away the cash. 'My shout. Got a new job this week, so I'm flush. Ladies, what would you like? A little crayfish, perhaps? Cordon bleu? Caviar?' It was clear that he was stretching his repertoire of exotic dishes, and Sharna took pity on him. Not that she had much choice, considering the bar served only half-a-dozen dishes. Three of them were potatoes, in various forms: fries, wedges and fritters. The other three were meat: chicken wings, a smallgoods platter and meatballs. Everything came with a bowl of tomato sauce and a bit of limp lettuce on the side.

'Wedges will do fine.' Sharna smiled prettily and Hayden couldn't miss the sudden hope shining in Juz's face, though he tried to hide it by scrubbing a hand through the short blond bristles of his beard. Hayden knew that one day he was going to have to explain to the idiot that there was no point him holding out hope where Sharna was concerned; it didn't matter how nice the bloke was, he wasn't going to be what she was looking for.

'Get one of each, mate,' Hayden suggested. 'It looks like there'll be a load of us tonight. We'll split the cost. Skip the fritters, though.' He'd never quite been able to come at battered potato.

'No worries.'

With one foot on the brass rail, Juz leaned across the damp green-and-black Coopers Beer runner on the long hardwood bar to yell his order in the bartender's direction, then loped back to the table.

'So, this new job,' Hayden said. 'Another kitchen?' Even as the words left his mouth, he realised he was wrong. Juz was a cabinetmaker by trade, but the enthusiasm that creased his face in a broad grin could only be lit by his true passion. 'Wait: you're talking a commission piece?'

'Never thought I'd mentally link art and chainsaws, but there's no denying you've got the touch, mate.' Luke lifted his ale in salute.

'Come on, Juz,' Sharna said, leaning forward, her elbows on the table. 'Tell.'

Juz turned to face her, clearly more stoked by her interest than anyone else's. 'A winery near Hahndorf is bankrolling me to carve a pair of eagles for their entrance.'

'To mount on the gateposts?' Taylor asked.

Juz shook his head. 'Nope. These are massive mothers. We're talking fourteen foot apiece.'

'Wow,' Sharna said, her eyes wide. 'Awesome.'

'That includes a plinth they want styled as a tree.' Characteristically, Juz tried to downplay his achievement. 'Otherwise the birds' height would be out of scale with their width. You know the pelican carving at the start of the Coorong?'

'On the lake at Meningie? Sure.'

'About that big.'

'Wings folded?' Hayden asked, his own artistic bent already at work as he visualised the piece. He knew the magic Juz and his chainsaw could weave to reveal the life hidden in a tree trunk.

Juz threw his arms—as bulky as a wrestler's from wielding a chainsaw—up in a V-shape. 'Wings up, like he's coming in to land on the tree.'

Their food landed at the same moment, proof that the kitchen had the meals ready-cooked and just smashed the orders out onto serving platters. Still, it beat the baked beans Hayden would have heated through if he'd been home. He tried to resist his mum's attempts to load him up with food to take back from the farmhouse, in case she got to thinking he actually needed it. The last thing he wanted was to add to her workload, even though she reckoned she was okay now. Plus, he didn't need her on his case to move back home. Where he'd have no privacy. Where, when he woke up sweating with night terrors, he'd have to wonder who had heard him. No, the rundown old shearer's cottage suited him well enough. There, only Trigger could judge him.

'That'll be awesome, mate,' Luke said around a mouthful of potato. 'And the money's there, right? Or at least, here?' He waved at the mounds of fried food in front of them.

'Sure as heck is. I mean, I won't be retiring anytime soon, but . . .'

'As long as you don't turn up in the surgery,' Taylor cautioned, reaching for a wing.

Hayden always liked the way she dug in. She didn't put on airs and graces, never patronised the rest of the group, who were all blue collar. If he could find a woman like her, he'd be set.

Except, he would have needed to find her two years ago, before—

'Wheaty?' Taylor speared a potato wedge and held it towards him. He knew she wasn't worrying so much about his appetite, as his introspection. Knew it even before Trigger's hot tongue lapped the hand he had on his knee.

'Thanks.' He shoved the chip into his mouth, his eyes instantly watering. 'Shit, that's hot!'

Taylor grinned, carefully blowing on her own wedge before dunking it in chilli sauce then cream.

'Heathen!' Sharna said. 'It's supposed to be the other way around.'

'I'm putting my own spin on it,' Taylor said, feeding the chip to her husband. 'It's almost like I'm cooking for you, right Luke?'

'The safe version.' He grinned. 'Hey, look.' He lifted his chin towards the door, which admitted a cold gust each time it swung open.

Hayden took a long draught of his beer, still trying to cool his mouth, before twisting to look over his left shoulder.

Damn lucky he'd swallowed first. 'City,' he muttered. Could pick it from a mile off. The woman framed by the dark timber entryway had a carefully groomed look, her fingernails actually flashing burgundy as she raked them through shoulder-length blonde hair.

'That's a problem?' Taylor asked with assumed innocence.

'I can tell you firsthand it isn't,' Luke said, nipping at his wife's ear. 'You just have to train them right.'

Sharna snorted into her glass.

'Uh-huh, and how's that going for you, mate?' Juz scoffed good-naturedly. Luke was always the first to admit that he was punching well above his weight where Taylor was concerned.

'I only have to teach her the difference between wheat and barley, and we're about there,' Luke replied.

Hayden tuned out the banter, his attention on the woman.

She strode into the place like she owned it, her heels clicking loudly as she crossed the uncarpeted area surrounding the bar. She paused only to rethink the wisdom of placing her bag on the beer-sodden bar runner, slinging it over her shoulder instead. Despite the noise of the crowd, her voice carried clearly, an authoritative ring sending the pub's owner, Ant, into a stuttering, tongue-tied spiral.

'Do you sell Chateau Yaldara Reserve by the glass?'

'R-reserve?' Ant had apparently never heard the word before.

'Chardonnay. By the glass. Though I'll take the bottle.'

She wouldn't need it chilled, thought Hayden; her tone was glacial.

'No, I mean, yes, we've got a chardy by the glass,' Ant stammered.

37

Hayden didn't know much about wine, but he was pretty sure the house white Ant was about to pour wouldn't meet the mark.

'And you do meals?' The woman cast a brief glance around the pub, not long enough for her eyes to alight on anything.

'Yes,' Ant managed to get out.

'Salad plate, please.'

A long silence from Ant, as he evidently processed the wisdom of divulging what the salad plate included.

'Rescue her, Wheaty,' Taylor muttered.

'Hell, no,' Hayden said. 'Ant's the one who needs rescuing. But I wouldn't bail even him out, this is too good. Shame we don't have popcorn.'

The rest of his table had fallen silent, also transfixed by the interaction. The effect created a weird bubble around them; the noises of the customers, the TVs, the pokies on the far side only faintly intruding.

'Salad and a house white,' Ant finally nodded. 'I'll bring it over to you. You'd better take a table number, we're pretty busy.' He reached behind him to grab a chrome stand with a number forty-six taped to it, then smacked it down onto the bar.

'I never knew there were table numbers,' Juz said.

'Me neither,' Hayden agreed. It wasn't like Ant didn't know everyone in the place by name, business, and probably their last year's income too, given that the local accountant was also a regular.

'And your accommodation options?' The woman completed the triple.

Ant went even more brick red than his usual florid complexion. 'Rooms. We have rooms. Upstairs.' He jerked his thumb up to reinforce the direction.

'Ensuite?' the woman snapped.

'No, no, no,' Sharna giggled. 'This is excruciating.'

'Like watching a train wreck,' Juz agreed without dragging his gaze from the bar.

'Ensuite what? The dunny, you mean?' Ant said.

'Oh. My. God,' Taylor gasped.

'Nope. Shared facilities down the hall.' Ant jerked a thumb towards the door. 'Some of the rooms across the road have private dunnies, if that's your thing. Find yourself a seat, I'll bring your meal out.'

The woman picked up the table marker and turned to survey the crowded pub, not cracking a smile as her dark gaze glided over the mismatched, wet-ringed tables, the empty platters lined with chequered, laminated serviettes, and the bright red and yellow plastic sauce and mustard bottles stationed around the room—always at a two-to-one ratio, because Ant figured anyone in their right mind wanted extra sauce on their food.

Except maybe if it was salad, Hayden thought, suppressing a quick grin.

Apparently searching out a seat in some distant corner, the woman brushed past their table. A waft of something undoubtedly expensive made Hayden inhale more deeply than usual, and he blew the breath out with a snort of annoyance.

Trigger poked his nose out from beneath the table, and the woman jerked back, her drink splashing the front of the blanket thing she had wrapped around her shoulders. 'A dog? What on earth—?' She patted at the damp patch in brisk annoyance, glaring at the dog.

'Down, Trigg,' Hayden commanded, though the dog had barely moved.

'He's an assistance animal,' Taylor said hastily, like he needed her help.

'Oh!' The woman's icy composure momentarily deserted her. Her shoulders caved and she pressed a palm against her chest. Then she spoke directly to Hayden, loudly and slowly. 'I'm so sorry. I didn't realise you're vision-impaired.'

The assumption curled his hands into fists, but other than that, Hayden refused to react. Instead, he slid his gaze to meet the flicker of uncertainty in the woman's unusual river-brown eyes.

4
Gabrielle

He wasn't vision-impaired. He couldn't be: his gaze, as cold as the arctic green waters of the Fleurieu Coast, had her nailed to the spot. As nailed as she could be, considering she was melting into a puddle of humiliation.

'Ah, deaf?' she amended, then realised the hopeful tone of her voice was inappropriate. Not to mention that the sardonic quirk of one of his dark eyebrows made it clear she'd guessed incorrectly.

'Only selectively,' the guy drawled, his antagonism barely hidden.

'Well, I'm sorry.' Embarrassment clipped her tone. The dog had startled her but mistake made, apology offered, it was time to move on.

Instead of politely brushing aside her apology as unnecessary, the guy continued to stare at her as though she were some rare sub-species. The half-dozen friends he sat with had all fallen silent. Probably waiting for her to put her foot in it again.

A freckled strawberry-blonde woman darted a glance between her and the obnoxiously terse man. 'Chill, Wheaty,' she said finally. She shot Gabrielle a grin. 'Shame the selective deafness doesn't extend to the bits we want them to miss, hey?'

She was trying to break the tension, but Gabrielle could only manage a tight smile. Despite adopting her usual slick professional persona to step into the pub, the bartender's animosity had thrown her off-balance.

'Again, I'm sorry.' She didn't bother looking at 'Wheaty', who clearly carried a chip the size of a log on his shoulder. Instead, she directed her words to the pretty blonde. 'I'll get out of your way.' She lifted the disgustingly sticky table number she clutched, waving the evidence that she had a right to be there.

'Don't reckon you will.' One of the other men stood as he spoke, his arms straining the seams of his jersey. 'Fridays are always packed in The Settlers.' He nodded towards the vacant end of the table. 'Grab one of those seats or you'll have to eat your salad standing.'

She tried not to gape at his tacit admission of having eavesdropped on her order. 'No, that's fine—' she started, but a frantic glance around the dingy, crowded room backed up his words. She would get her salad to go. If the bartender even understood what that meant. Annoyance flashed through her. She hadn't wanted a bloody salad; she'd simply ordered it out of habit. Minimalist eating was basically a prerequisite of appearing professional. Young, eager, hungry only for success. She couldn't recall a lunch with female colleagues that had involved more than a half-tub of yoghurt, almost as though the admission of hunger were a weakness. Alcohol, though? The opposite. Long hours, and the constant need to maintain an image, nurtured functioning alcoholics, and plenty of the artistic designers she dealt with found their muse in illegal substances.

The guy waved at a stool opposite Wheaty, as though she hadn't spoken. 'I'm Justin. Juz, if you like.' He continued around the table, flicking long fingers at each person, as though she could possibly have a need to learn their names. 'Wheaty, Taylor, Luke—'

'Sharna,' the blonde cut in, smiling as she moved an enormous pleather bag from the stool alongside her. 'Here you go. Don't be shy. We don't bite.'

'I'm more afraid that she might,' Gabrielle nudged her chin at the dog who sat beneath the table, head resting on Wheaty's knee, still eyeballing her.

'You're scared of dogs?' Wheaty ground out, managing to sound incredulous despite his gravelly tone. 'He won't bite. *He's* well mannered.'

Gabrielle frowned. What the heck was his problem? She cast around for a coaster, then slid her glass of wine onto the naked table. From her taupe Kate Spade tote she withdrew an ornate silver compact, flipping it open and twisting it to reveal a weighted hook. She clipped the device on the edge of the table and hung her bag from the strap so it dangled above the floor.

And she didn't miss the raised eyebrows of her new companions.

'Ah.' Sharna reached over to drift her fingers across the crystal-encrusted silver shell. 'I've seen these online.'

The other woman, Taylor, nodded. 'That's beautiful. I checked some out in the Swarovski Boutique in Pitt Street, last time I was back in Sydney. I've never seen one actually used, though.'

'I guess it depends where you hang out,' Gabrielle replied, wincing as she caught the note of privilege in her reply. She had to remember where she was, that she was starting out fresh here.

The dog's tail brushed her knee as she perched uncomfortably on the edge of the stool. 'She—he—is the most colourful dog I've ever seen.' *Colourful* was polite: the dog was a messy patchwork of white, apricot, black and brown, and even had two different coloured eyes. 'Ha,' she flashed a grin at the table in general as a thought struck her. 'Guess you call him Afremov?' Her heart sank as the artist's name left her lips. No way would these farmers get her obscure reference.

After a moment of uncomprehending silence, Wheaty spoke. 'Nope. Trigger.' He looked down at the dog. 'Though I kind of wish I'd gone with Afremov, now. For the colours, right? Neat.'

44

Surprise loosened her shoulders, her breath out rippling the wine in her generously filled glass. She'd imagined his hostility. Relief lifted her tone. 'Correct. Why Trigger, though?'

The brief good humour dropped from Wheaty's face, his expression instantly hard and distant.

Sharna jumped in quickly, her hand moving from the bag hook to pat the back of Gabrielle's hand. 'Sorry, I missed your name. It's flipping hard to hear in here.'

'Gabrielle.'

Another moment of silence, as her new companions apparently digested that information.

'You're passing through Settlers?' Justin asked. 'Heard you ask Ant for a room.'

The statement brought an inexplicable snort of laughter from Luke, at the far end of the table. Taylor, who sat so close to him they had to be a couple, elbowed him.

Beer slopped from his glass and he grimaced. 'Aw, Tay, look what you made me do.'

'Serves you right,' Taylor responded, though she pressed closer to him.

'I reckon that makes it your wife's turn to buy the next round, Luke,' Justin said.

Taylor sighed, making to climb off her stool. 'Fine, fine. I know the penalty for spilling a man's beer.'

Luke stood quickly, huge behind Taylor, and placed his hands on her shoulders. 'I'll order. You've had a full-on day, babe. You can pay, though,' he added.

Taylor adopted a comical expression of disappointment. 'For a moment there I thought I was being rescued by a knight in shining armour.'

'You are. Just the slightly impoverished farming variety. Same again, all? What are you drinking, Gabby?'

'Gabrielle,' she corrected automatically. She looked at her glass and took another sip. 'I'm really not sure what it is. Certainly not what I'd hoped for.'

Alongside her, Sharna giggled. Looking up, Gabrielle realised her companions all seemed amused. She quickly replayed her words, then lifted one shoulder in silent question at Taylor, the only one who seemed prepared to catch her eye.

Taylor glanced at the others, as though seeking back-up, then shook her head, mischief in her gaze. 'It's just we couldn't miss how you put Ant on the back foot with your . . . requests.'

Laughter exploded around the group, but Gabrielle stared at her yellowish wine, a sense of isolation washing over her. Clearly, you had to be part of the in crowd to get the joke.

She startled as Sharna patted her thigh. 'Sorry, Gabs, we're being rude. Ant—the bartender—is a straight up and down kind of guy. If you order wine, you pretty much just say if you want white or red, it doesn't get any fancier than that. He'll have a bottle of each open behind the bar and in summer he'll serve them over ice.'

She must have looked horrified, because Taylor added: 'It's not as depraved as it sounds. When it's forty-plus out, the ice hits the spot.'

'As long as frozen water is the only kind of ice you have around here, I suppose it's okay,' Gabrielle said carefully, afraid her words would spark further condemnation or hilarity.

Taylor made a face. 'We have drugs, same as anywhere. Though I guess both supply and variety are more limited than in—where did you say you're from? The city, I'm guessing?'

'Only Adelaide.' Taylor's mention of Sydney had brought back Brendan's taunt that Gabrielle chose to stay in Adelaide because she got to be a big fish in a small pond, rather than trying to break into the more competitive interstate market. Irritating as he was, Brendon knew her well and on that point he was one hundred percent correct.

Sharna sighed, plopping her hand back onto the table, alongside her empty glass. 'I'm jelly. I'd love to live in the city. Melbourne, preferably, but Adelaide would do me.'

'Seriously?' Juz seemed shocked. 'I thought you were country through-and-through.'

'Country is where you're born, not a life sentence,' Sharna huffed.

'Nuh-uh,' Luke disagreed. 'It's a lifestyle. A choice. Example one: Taylor.' He showcased Taylor with his hands. 'City born and bred, now the perfect farmer's wife.'

'Oh, perfect now, am I?' Taylor laughed. 'So, my lack of cooking skills is excused all of a sudden?'

Wheaty shook his head. 'An appalling flaw, but you evidently have other talents that blind Luke to the fact.'

'Oh, she does, she does,' Luke said, winding his arms around his wife from behind.

Taylor reached back to swat at his face with one hand. 'My current talent is paying for those drinks, if you get them before we die of thirst. Hey, there's Matt and Roni. Get theirs, too.'

Luke smacked a kiss on top of her head, and shouldered towards the bar through the thickening throng.

Gabrielle studied the crowd. Mostly male, all were flannelette-collared and muddy-booted, aged anywhere between eighteen and eighty-eight, and either leaning against the bar or standing around high tables, similar to the one she had joined. A few women studded the room like potted flowers on the city footpath, comfortably bundled in enormous cardigans or primary-colour windcheaters decorated with bold prints of flowers or heavy beading. Or both.

If the other pub—situated directly across the road—attracted anywhere near the number of patrons as this one, it would be nice to infer that as promising for her plans. Yet the demographics were all wrong. Taylor was the only person here in semi-professional attire. As the establishment she intended to create would be vastly different to this noisy, grubby place, her target market wouldn't be found among this working-class clientele.

'Luke,' Taylor called. He turned back instantly. 'Soft, remember?'

He lifted a hand in acknowledgment, then continued towards the bar.

As another couple reached the table, Sharna leaned closer. 'Seriously, Gabs, if you're looking to stay over, you need to get a room in The Overland. The Settlers is the locals' pub. The rooms upstairs are only for when the guys have had too much and need to crash. Ant usually puts them up for free. Earns him plenty of goodwill, and I guess everyone drinks more, knowing they don't have to drive. In fact, the free rooms are the only reason Tay drinks here.' She waved a hand towards the end of the table, where Taylor had stood to wrap her arms around the tall woman who'd just entered.

'She has a drinking problem?' Gabrielle murmured, although, despite having moved closer to her, Sharna didn't seem to be keeping her voice circumspect.

Sharna giggled. 'Nuh-uh, not at all. More that she supports what she calls Ant's "well-calculated altruism" from a professional standpoint.'

As Gabrielle glanced towards Taylor, a ruddy man in half-mast jeans and an overly-tight grey work shirt made a beeline for them from the bar, his callused feet spilling over the rubber soles of his thongs. 'Doc, hey, Doc,' he bellowed. 'Didn't see ya here at first. Lukey had to steer me.'

Taylor's eyes darted towards her husband, but then she refocused on the man bearing down on her.

'Been meaning to come see you, Doc,' he continued at a volume that hinted he had a hearing problem. 'These damn piles are still giving me the gyp. Gotta do me spraying next week and don't see how I'm gonna handle sitting on the tractor for hours at a time.'

Taylor's smile didn't falter, but her fingertips whitened a little on the dewy glass before her. 'Shame, Neil. Did you get the cushion I suggested?'

Neil tipped his green, mesh-sided cap back, then scratched at his forehead. 'Truth to tell, Doc, clean forgot about that. But I can't come at carting some damn cushion around with me all day, y'know?'

'Of course,' Taylor said smoothly. 'Tell you what, I'm pretty booked out next week, but you ring Shirl at the clinic, and I'll tell her to find you a spot and we'll see what we can do, okay?'

'Priceless, Doc,' Neil beamed, smacking the black-and-yellow John Deere logo to shove his cap back into place, and raising his bottle as Luke edged past him. 'Yer got yerself a little ripper there, Hartmann.'

'I know it, mate,' Luke replied as he took his seat.

Neil turned back to the bar, loudly telling anyone nearby that the Doc was going to be taking damn good care of his arse, and Luke brushed his knuckles along Taylor's arm. 'Don't tell me you're not looking forward to work next week,' he muttered.

Taylor snorted. 'Can't say living this dream was quite the one I had in mind. Still, it has its compensations.' She smiled up at Luke.

'Gabby?' Justin seemed determined to make Gabrielle notice him. Not that she could have missed him. All three of the men around the table were astonishingly . . . present. Each larger-than-life, solid. 'This is the lesser known, rarely sighted variety of Krueger, aka Roni and Matt.' He indicated the couple who had joined their group.

The woman smiled at Gabrielle. Drops glittered like diamonds in her long brown curls, and Gabrielle realised the rain that had threatened all day must have arrived. 'Juz means we rarely escape the kids for a night out,' Roni explained.

'Twins,' Matt offered proudly, as though the number affected their escape opportunities.

Gabrielle hid her instinctive flinch behind a bright smile. 'Hi.' At the same moment, she caught the look Luke flashed at Taylor and the tightening of his grip on her hand. Why did the mention of twins affect them as it did her?

Beneath the table, the dog stirred and Gabrielle reflexively jerked back.

Wheaty noticed and glanced down. Although he didn't speak, he must have signalled the dog, because its warmth immediately shifted from her legs.

'He's fine,' she said, although relief washed through her. The urge to placate this man irritated her. It wasn't like her presence had caused him any hardship, yet she hadn't missed the fact that, unlike the rest of the group, he overtly excluded her from the conversations he continued with the far end of the table.

His gaze lingered on her for a moment—long enough to send heat prickling up her neck. He gave a slight nod, as though accepting her not-quite apology. 'It's just a bit crowded in here for him tonight.'

'I admit, I was expecting country-pub quiet.' She inwardly cringed at the over-engaged note in her voice.

'Bucolic? Smoky woodfire and muted conversation over a chessboard?' His lips quirked. 'Sounds like you're a Hallmark movie junkie.'

She wasn't sure whether he intended the observation as an insult. 'You're evidently an aficionado of the genre?'

'More that I have three sisters still at home who watch nothing but, during the Christmas season. They end up speaking with American accents. Drives Dad, Rob and me batshit. I swear they'll only be happy when Mum gives in and lets them do the whole cheesy Thanksgiving thing. Though I don't give much for her chances of organising the obligatory snow for the romantic scenes.'

'I don't give much for her chances of arranging any romantic scenes, period, around this place,' Sharna interjected. She twisted her lips wryly, one hand indicating the crowded pub, but seemed apparently oblivious to the two evidently loved-up couples at their table.

Justin leaned across the table. 'Hard-core cynical there, Sharn. I'm sure there's plenty of romance to be found round here.'

Gabrielle didn't miss the quick frown that swept Wheaty's face. She could see that he was interested in Sharna, but if Gabrielle knew anything about women, he wouldn't have a chance if he was still living with his mum and sisters. She tried not to scoff: he had to be in his thirties, same as her. But she'd left home as soon as she finished high school, moving into a beachside apartment her parents owned. They'd gone back to France when she graduated uni, supposedly for her dad's career, but she understood why they needed to run away. Still, even though her parents provided her flat, it wasn't like she lived *with* them. 'Well, I guess I can play the sister card, too,' she said. Not that Brigitte was a Hallmark-type.

'Three sisters, yet you can't set a friend up?' Justin gave Wheaty's arm a light punch, then jerked his hand back. Shock flashed across his face. 'Sorry, mate.'

Wheaty moved his hand in quick, irritated dismissal of the apology. 'Not happening. Told you that more times than I can count. Nothing's changed.'

'Aw, c'mon, mate. I'll learn to love Hallmark,' Justin wheedled.

Wheaty grinned. 'Loving chick flicks is entirely on you. But you're not loving on my sisters. In any case, you've got nearly ten years on Tara.'

'Tara's closer to my age, though, right?' Sharna piped up. 'I remember she was still in primary when I was in high school.'

Wheaty treated her to one of his long, silent appraisals. 'Yep. But she's not like you, Sharn.' His tone softened and he held her gaze for a long moment. 'She'll never leave the farm.'

'Well, there you go,' Juz slapped his palms on the table-top, apparently oblivious to whatever subtext was being shared by Wheaty and Sharna. 'Good ol' farm boy right here for her.'

Gabrielle frowned, trying to unpick the intriguing, tangled threads of conversation.

Her stomach rumbled loudly and Sharna shot her a commiserating grin. 'Your salad hasn't even turned up? The hot food comes out quicker than that.'

'I figure it must be super fresh; the kitchen is growing it from seed,' she said with a forced smile.

'Uh-huh. You believe in fairies and mermaids, too?' Justin chuckled.

Wheaty pushed one of the platters of fried food towards her. 'Dig in. If that salad ever comes, I can guarantee you won't like it anyway.'

Again, his words seemed judgmental. Yet if any of the others had uttered them, she would take them at face value. Why was she determined to read into everything he said? Was it simply because he'd embarrassed her?

A smile lit his dark features, and she did a double-take. Then she realised his gaze was focused behind her. In a flurry of movement, a petite woman towing a small child by the hand drew up to the table. She seemed a little shy as she cast a quick glance around the group. 'Hey, all. Sorry to crash your thing.'

'Not crashing. You're practically one of us now, Lucie,' Wheaty said, as though determined to point out that Gabrielle had no right to be there.

The child leaned against his solid thigh, holding her arms up to him. 'Up,' she commanded in a determined tone.

Great, he brought in his dog *and* his kid, Gabrielle thought with an unaccustomed wave of bitterness that she wasn't about to waste a second analysing. This was definitely a country pub, and not a style she would emulate in any facet once she got the Wurruldi Hotel up and running.

Wheaty swept the child up with his right arm and settled her on his lap.

The girl stroked pudgy fingers gently along his left sleeve. 'Mummy and me bringed you a present.'

'I thought you were my present, Princess,' Wheaty burred in an indulgent tone, totally different to the one he'd used all evening.

'Silly,' the child giggled. 'I not a present, I a girl.' She held her hand out to her mother. 'I give it him, Mummy,' she commanded.

'Who am I to argue?' Her mother laughingly rolled her eyes as she handed the brown paper bag to her daughter.

'Lucie, this is Gabby,' Sharna said. 'She's made the tragic mistake of setting foot in The Settlers on a Friday night.'

'Gabrielle,' she corrected, abruptly rising from her stool. Sharna might have got her name wrong, but her summation was accurate; coming here had been a huge mistake.

But at least this was one she could easily remedy.

5
Hayden

Even with his face pressed into Keeley's curls, he felt the burn of Gabrielle's hostile gaze as she shoved her stool back. To be fair, she probably had reason to be angry. Mum would have ripped into him for being such an obnoxious bastard.

He focused on another table, as though the single-mindedness with which old Cyril Jaensch was applying himself to his plate of fried crap, which would surely come back to haunt him in the shape of heartburn, was the most interesting thing he'd seen in weeks.

But it wasn't. This woman was. So much so, he'd barely been able to look at her, though he was sure the same couldn't be said for any other bloke in the room. With her unusual Nordic colouring—eyes of a deep, sepia-brown. and ash-blonde hair lying crisply against her smooth latte skin—she was doubtless accustomed to the interest that had stopped quite a few conversations the second she'd walked in.

He clenched his jaw, trying to dispel his irritation. Why was he even damn well looking? There wouldn't be one inch of her that was natural. The burgundy nails she tapped against her clearly disappointing glass of wine sure as crap weren't. Probably everything beneath the tight blue jeans and loose blanket draped around her was tuned and tucked, too.

Eighteen months ago, he would have made it his mission to find out. Hell, he would have had her phone number within minutes. Or at least had the balls to ask for it, not fazed by the possibility of being shot down.

Now, asking would be pointless because he would never follow through.

Could never follow through.

Sharna scooted off her seat, too. 'Here, take my stool, Lucie. Like I was saying a million interruptions ago, Gabby, The Settlers isn't really traveller-friendly, it's the locals' hangout. You want The Overland Corner Hotel, across the road. I'll show you.'

Gabrielle took her bag from the ridiculous clasp she'd hooked it on, like her shit was too good to touch the floor of the pub. 'That's okay, I'm sure I can find it.' She glanced around the table and he forced his gaze up, silently daring her to meet it.

She didn't.

'Thanks all for your company. Might see you around the place.'

Not deterred by the rejection, Sharna headed towards the door with her, her pale red curls a wild tangle alongside Gabrielle's sleek polish.

As Keeley stroked his upper chest, Hayden fought the urge to pull away, aware of what she could feel through the layers of fabric. It didn't bother her; she and Lucie had only been in town a short time and she'd never known him any different. But it bothered him.

'See us around?' Luke repeated Gabrielle's words. 'Did anyone catch what she's doing in town? I mean, it's not late, so no need to crash here on the way to anywhere.'

Juz shook his head. 'Nah, Wheaty had her buttoned down, too scared to speak. What the hell was with that, mate?'

Crap. He had hoped his surliness had gone unnoticed. He reached down to tug at Trigger's ears. 'Just got no time for chicks who act like they own the place.'

'Jeez,' Taylor said. She frowned, although her eyes questioned him. 'That's pretty harsh, Wheaty. She barely said five words.'

He scowled. Taylor was a good sort, and he didn't like to fall short in her estimation. Or in his own. He wouldn't usually derive satisfaction from making someone uncomfortable, but Gabrielle questioning Trigger's right to be there—and, by extension, his right—had hit a raw nerve. He shrugged. 'She read as fake to me.' Was that all that bothered him? Or was it the fact that the woman's innate confidence made him feel inferior, highlighting his defects?

'Wow, what did I miss?' Lucie gazed around the unusually silent table. As no one answered, she pointed at the paper bag Keeley was clutching. 'I made you a new pot, Hayden.'

'What's in this one?' Taylor asked.

'Mainly aloe. Coconut oil, frankincense, wheatgerm oil.' Lucie flicked up her fingers, counting the ingredients. 'Some lavender oil I distilled.' Her tone held a slightly defensive note, as though she expected the doctor to question her. 'It's not medically proven, but . . .'

Taylor waved a dismissive hand. 'Proof is in the pudding.'

'Lucky *you're* not cooking it, then,' Luke broke in, provoking a round of good-natured laughter at his wife's expense.

She pulled a face at him and continued. 'Okay, so proof is in the *result*, smartarse. And aloe—in fact, all those ingredients—are anecdotally and historically popular. I'd be interested to keep an eye on the results, Wheaty.'

He gave a slight shake of his head, uncomfortable with the attention, and lifted Keeley from his lap.

'I pat Trigg?' she asked hopefully.

'Sure can, Princess. Good girl for asking.'

As usual, Trigger looked to him for permission before giving himself over to the kid's pats and cuddles, seemingly oblivious to being poked and prodded as Keeley counted his eyes and ears.

'I'm going to call it early tonight, guys,' Hayden said, downing the last of his beer.

'Sure you're not nipping across the road to The Overland?' Luke asked.

'If Sharna's still there, tell her to get her arse back here,' Juz added. 'It's her shout.'

'Oh, sure, that's why,' Matt snorted. 'We've only been here ten minutes and you manage to work her into the conversation.'

'Every time,' Roni added with a grin. 'Something you want to tell us, Juz?'

'I'm going to the loo,' Taylor said, pushing up from the table.

Hayden hid his groan. He'd been hoping to make a clean escape amid the distraction of the new arrivals, but Taylor, as usual, was on to him.

As he expected, by the time he'd finished saying good-night and swearing to the blokes that he wasn't crossing the road to chase tail, Taylor had made the loop to the bathroom and was waiting to intercept him before he reached the door.

'All good, Hayden?'

She only called him by name when she was about to go doctor on him.

'All good, Tay. Just a bit loud in here tonight.' Damn, they were the wrong words, he could feel her instantly assessing him for signs of mounting anxiety. 'I mean, literally. Loud. Trigg and I are turning into grumpy old men; we prefer our own company.'

'Mmm,' Taylor said. 'But not too much of that loner stuff, all right?'

There had been a time, not that many months back, when he'd not left his house. He even had it figured with

Lynn at the IGA to deliver his groceries, which consisted of beans and pasta. 'Not much chance of that, when you've saddled me with a dog who eats his own body weight in kibble.' A dog who, without exaggeration, had probably saved his life. 'Even if I wanted to stay in, we have to hit the shop every couple of days.'

'He's a good pup,' Taylor said fondly, though she didn't touch the dog who, as usual, had his blue–brown gaze fixed firmly on Hayden.

'Yeah, he's getting the hang of staying in the ute when I'm working, too,' Hayden added, not so much to talk up the dog, but to let the doctor know that he was working. No matter how intuitive Taylor had proved, realising that medication wasn't cutting it as a solution for him, he didn't care to discuss his problems. Positive action seemed the best way to head off her concern. And it was, ironically, exactly what she demanded from him.

'I heard you were back on the tools,' she said, poking a hole in his fleeting belief that his business was his own.

'No secrets in this town, right?'

'Uh-uh.' A faint waft of perfume reached him as Taylor shook her head. 'Trust me, there're plenty of secrets. But this isn't something you need to keep hidden, Wheaty.'

At least the reversion to the nickname he'd carried since childhood meant he was off the hook; Taylor had scaled back her concern level.

'Also not something to advertise, Doc.'

She shook her head, heaving a sigh. 'You strong, silent types are the worst, you know that?'

'But you love us anyway, right?' Hayden jerked his thumb towards his cousin, Luke.

'I don't seem to have a choice. Are you coming for the barbie at Juz's on Sunday?'

He looked down at the muddy toe of his RMs. 'Might give it a miss this week.'

'This week?'

'Yeah. I know.' He found an excuse to avoid most of the social occasions that held their little group together. 'But, hey, I was here tonight, wasn't I?'

'Briefly. But I'll take it.' Taylor stood on her toes to plant a kiss on his cheek. 'I'd really like it if you came. There's going to be . . . something special.' A faint blush tinged her cheeks, and Hayden followed her glance across the room to where her husband's gaze hadn't left her.

'Special? As in, an announcement?'

She shook her head and backed away. 'If you don't come, you won't know.'

He groaned, shoving a hand through his hair, and Trigger immediately nosed at his leg. Knowing Taylor, she would lead him on just to get him out of his four walls and back into the community. She kept promising him that the more he pushed his boundaries, the easier it would get. But he dead-set adored her, and he and Luke were as close as brothers. If Taylor and Luke had something important to announce, he'd haul himself out of his comfort zone and be there for them. 'No promises,' he said.

'Just try. Okay, Wheaty?'

'Sure, Doc.'

'If you call me that, you have to pay me,' Taylor shot back with a grin as she headed into the depths of the pub.

As he walked out into the chill air and along the dark footpath splashed with the warm spill of light from The Settlers windows, he thought back to the gathering. Taylor had nursed the same drink all evening and, knowing her taste, he'd assumed it was gin-and-tonic. But it could just have easily have been straight lemonade. A grin broke across his face, lightening his tread. He had a fair idea what their announcement would be.

A lone car churned past, tyres hissing on the wet bitumen. Hayden looked directly across the wide road. Two lanes, then a middle strip planted with towering pots of some kind of flowering climber. Another two lanes, dark beneath the scattered streetlights, and The Overland loomed.

Sharna had gone over there. He could easily cross the road, see if she wanted a lift home.

See if Gabrielle had ended up checking in.

See how long she was staying.

See why she was here.

Except he had already screwed his chances there, and she wasn't his type anyway. Plus, he suspected he would have to deal with Sharna's wrath for treading on her toes.

'C'mon, Trigg,' he growled, clicking his fingers. Without another glance at the hotel, he turned left and strode towards the end of the block, where a narrow footpath led to the pub's rear carpark.

The signwriting on the door of his four-wheel-drive ute caught the flicker of the solitary light in the dirt yard, and he snorted disparagingly. Advertising his business on the car made the vehicle a tax write-off, but unless he actually produced an income this year, he'd have stuff-all to write off.

He needed to get off his lazy arse and force himself to work each day, instead of wallowing.

Hayden keyed the fob and wrenched open the door before the sidelight had even completed its acknowledging flash. 'In you get, Trigg.' He reached in to carefully place Lucie's package on the dash, then gripped the grab handle and swung up into the cab, wincing at the tug on his arm.

As he pulled out onto the main road, he shot another glance at The Overland. A single light was on in one of the top-floor bedrooms, and it was no stretch of the imagination to deduce that had to be Gabrielle's room.

Not that he cared, he told himself, beyond wishing Sharna luck with her new friend.

Yet he unnecessarily crossed all four lanes to drive in front of The Overland before continuing up the main drag, past the handful of cafes and the small supermarket, where he and Trigger had their standing order for dog biscuits and spaghetti. A hard right at the top of the street, and he was headed out of town, past the dairy flats and into the Mallee. He left the music off, preferring the soothing rhythm of his windscreen wipers chasing the rain. Waves on the beach for a country guy.

As always, his house was in darkness as he crossed the cattlegrid and bumped up the rough driveway, although across the paddocks he could see his mum's verandah light.

He really should get her a solar set-up: for the last year she'd refused to turn that light off, saying it was so he would always know where to find her, no matter how dark the night or his thoughts.

Stupid; it wasn't like he was a kid, afraid of monsters in the dark. What scared him was far more tangible, more painful. More real.

Despite laughing off his mum's idea, there had been many a night he'd turned on his side in the uncurtained bedroom of the shearer's cottage he'd moved back into after his convalescence, and stared across the darkness of the paddocks to where the light shone strong. He would focus on the butter-yellow glow, the beacon proof that he hadn't lost everything that mattered.

Hayden thrust open the unlocked door, kicking off his boots as he let the dog go in first. 'Going-out boots' his mum called his RMs, to distinguish them from the steel-capped Rossis he wore for work. Not that he'd needed to wear them much over the past few months, despite how he'd tried to make it sound to Taylor.

Padding across the dark kitchen, he picked up Trigger's food bowl and dipped it into the twenty-kilo sack of kibble alongside the fridge. After being out of the house for a few hours, he realised his mum was right: the place smelled of dog biscuits, a mixture of must and meat. Still, there were worse stinks.

Like smoke.

After a moment's hesitation, he opened the fridge and retrieved an egg, cracking it into the bowl. Matt, wearing his

65

cap as the local vet, had warned that too much egg wasn't good for the Australian Shepherd, but Trigger deserved a treat; he'd sat so patiently in the pub, despite being assailed by the smells of food and the well-intentioned interference of the locals.

And Gabrielle.

She hadn't tried to pat him, though, which was unusual. Even though everyone around here had at least one dog of their own, the novelty of seeing Trigger beneath the table or in a shop often led to inappropriate touching. People didn't seem to get what a companion dog did. Buggered if he really knew himself, except that when he was overwhelmed by the bleak darkness of his memories, the sights and smells of that bastard of a day threatening to engulf him, the knowledge that he was responsible for the dog forced him out of the funk. Before his nervous tells became apparent, even to himself, Trigger could sense his increasing anxiety and would demand to walk, or be fed, or play a rough-and-tumble game of tug-of-war; anything that would draw Hayden's subconscious away from his thoughts. And, when the nightmares and memories and pain ultimately won, when Hayden couldn't fight them any longer, Trigg would clamber up on the forbidden bed and curl beside him to lend warmth and comfort as he battled his demons.

With Trigger, despite what had been stolen from him, despite what he had endured, Hayden was never alone.

With the dog's nose happily buried in his feed bowl, Hayden took a deep breath, eyeing the doorway alongside the fridge. This was his least favourite part of the day.

He pulled the pot of ointment from Lucie's package. She'd provided an ingredient list, but he didn't care what herbal witchcraft she'd used. As long as the damn stuff worked. Not that the hospital medications hadn't, at least to an extent, but he needed more.

He crumpled the paper bag in one hand and tossed it towards the open bin. 'Shoots and scores,' he muttered. 'And that's the only kind of scoring I'll be doing.'

Still chomping noisily, Trigger cocked an ear in his direction. 'It's all right, mate, you keep eating,' Hayden said. That was the other thing about having a dog; at least he was no longer talking to himself. Not that his mum and sisters— or even, to a lesser extent, his dad—didn't encourage him to talk it through. But he would always imagine judgment in their attentive silence, so he kept his shit to himself.

He left the light off as he entered the bathroom. It wasn't like he didn't know the layout of the small, functional space by heart. And he sure as hell didn't want to see what the fly-spotted shaving-cabinet mirror would reveal.

He shucked his jeans and dropped his shirt to the floor, reaching back to grasp the neck of his T-shirt and draw it over his head. Even though he used his right arm, still the skin pulled tight in a large fan-shape across the left side of his chest. Challenging the flare of pain, he snapped his arm straight, bicep bulging as he tensed in anger, his knuckles grazing the wall. He dropped his T-shirt and then, rather than give in to the pain by moving towards the shower, he deliberately stretched to turn on the taps over the bathtub. Taylor had cautioned him against his self-loathing, his desire to punish his body for failing him. But she didn't realise that being able to tolerate the minor pains he inflicted on himself wasn't only a punishment; it was a test. A test of whether he was stronger today than he'd been yesterday. Both mentally and physically.

Above all, a test of whether he would ever be strong *enough*. Or if he would fail again.

Not that he planned on ever having anyone else to fail. His parents, his sisters, his brother—that was enough people to keep him tossing at night, imagining them in nightmare scenarios, wondering how he would save them.

Knowing that the evidence of his own history proved he couldn't.

He rolled the compression bandage down from his shoulder, then yanked it from his arm, his teeth gritted.

Stepping into the tub, the porcelain stained with iron stripes from the bore water, he allowed himself only a brief shower, keeping the water temperature well below what would be comfortably warming on the cold evening. Taylor had also counselled him against flogging himself for what wasn't his fault.

What she hadn't done was tell him how to cope with what *was* his fault.

He towelled roughly, picked up the pot of ointment, and then finally faced the mirror. If he presented his right shoulder, he would look normal, to himself and to the rest of the world.

Instead, he twisted, thrusting the left side of his torso and his arm close to the glass. His face puckered in distaste as he dabbed his fingers into Lucie's latest magic goop. He slapped the stuff on hard, smearing it thickly. His stomach tensed and heaved. His mouth squeezed into a thin line to contain the beer that threatened to find its way back up his gullet as he forced his fingers to touch the mangled, molten-plastic ridges of his flesh.

6

Ilse

Ilse blew out a sharp breath, then sucked it back in surprise. She couldn't recall seeing or hearing rain, yet the uneven pavers were puddled with what she had always told her children were fairy lakes. Jewelled drops spangled the pointed leaves of the golden wattles hedging the courtyard, and a pungent wash of eucalyptus tingled her sinuses. If she moved to the windows at the front of the hotel, she would look down the long, sloping lawn to where the redfin leaped in the watery, early-morning sun. Ronald always said the fish were confused, that they thought the splashes were caused by diving insects; but she knew better. The redfin frolicked in the rare luxury of rain.

The fish weren't the only ones confused: hadn't it been soft twilight only moments ago, when she was watching the new owner in the courtyard?

A willie wagtail chittered in the potted hydrangea outside the back door, and she shuffled towards it, wondering over the broken glass panel in this door, although it at least explained the strong smell of the damp trees. Quick as a blink, the immaculately suited wagtail flicked from branch to branch on the blue hydrangea, demanding she notice his antics. She smiled at his cheekiness, but the movement froze; the plant he danced upon was dead. Shocked, she creaked around to check the plant on the other side of the entrance, the one she regularly gave tiny doses of lime to turn it pink, the perfect contrast to the blue-flowered plant. Also dead.

Dread crept up Ilse's throat. She tended her hydrangeas—all of her garden—so lovingly, she was even aware when a caterpillar so much as nibbled a plant, although she weighed the loss against the prospect of the future butterfly's beauty. Yet these bushes were nothing more than lifeless sticks in pots of hard-baked soil.

Her hand moved down to her chest, clutching into a fist, as if she could somehow seize and regain control. If she had forgotten to water these pots when she passed them countless times every day, what of the seedlings she placed safe from the possums each night in the outbuilding Ronald called her castle?

He had always been a tease, that Ronald. With a wicked sense of humour, his broad, handsome face would light up the room a split-second before his chuckle boomed forth. Yet the castle had been entirely his idea. Originally a stable, the room was a mishmash: part cottage and part shed, with a lino-covered floor she could sweep clean. The walls were papered in creamy white, decorated with tiny sprigs of flowers and the plummy tones of bearded iris—wallpaper better suited to a bathroom, but she had been unable to resist the floral theme. And, as Ronald said, this room was entirely hers, to do with as she wished. If she couldn't allow a little whimsy here, then where? She had plundered furnishings from the hotel; two mismatched, comfortable lounge chairs, a chequerboard occasional table, a battered sideboard where she stacked her prized first editions of *Australian House & Garden* magazine behind the glass-fronted midsection. On top of the scratched mahogany was the gramophone Opa had so loved, along with a collection of records that spanned her grandparents' taste to her own. Along the back wall, her trowels, bulb dibbers, garden snips, shears and other implements hung from nails hammered directly into the mortared joints above the stone potting bench.

Ronald derived the same tactile pleasure from working with stone as she got from running her hands across the tight purple buds of the lavender she planted against the drystone wall he built around the yard. But when she laughed at the notion of a stone potting bench for the castle he promised to create something so beautiful she would want it in their riverfront cottage.

Over the course of months, finding time around his work on the hotel gardens and duties as ferry master, Ronald repeatedly loaded up the timber tray of their Dodge with granite, limestone and quartz from local farms. When he finally allowed her back in the castle, afternoon light from the solitary high window at the rear of the room reflected chips of mica and sparkling pink quartz in two plinths of neatly mortared rocks bridged by a glossy slab of fawn Monarto granite that was flecked with jet black and grey, almost-blue speckles. As Guy Lombardo sang 'It's Love-Love-Love', Ronald whirled her around the room like the record spinning on the turntable.

Ilse's eyes closed, and her memory danced. The castle Ronald created embodied every promise he had ever made. It had been her joy and her retreat, providing sanctuary during the grief of her son's death, and escape when the hotel changed hands, time and again. But more: it was her remaining connection to Ronald.

Because that much she hadn't forgotten; she had lost Ronald, even though she had believed their love would last forever.

No. That wasn't true: their love *would* last. It was just that Ronald was no longer here.

And, for the first time, maybe she didn't want to be, either.

She knew where to find him, though. With a glance up at the leaden sky to see if she needed to cover her hair, Ilse took wobbly, determined steps across the courtyard, avoiding the deepest puddles. She would put a record on the old gramophone, find her favourite pair of gardening gloves and potter for a while. Working in the castle always soothed her soul. And there, Ronald would come to her, he would ease the ache that weighted her heart and dulled her mind. Maybe he would be young and strong once more, the face she still saw each day . . .

Ilse stumbled to a halt, uncertainty tangling her feet. The face she saw where? How could she see Ronald's face each day, when he had been gone for so long? Lord, was she quite mad?

Panic surged; the memory, the wish, the dream, whatever it was, blocked by a wall of pain. Ilse moaned, fists clenched as she tried to force the lurking thought from the darkness. She almost had it . . . She gasped, crooning to ease the agony.

There, deep inside, she could sense the truth she fought to grasp.

There had been someone she cared a great deal about. Someone she hadn't seen in far too long.

But if not Ronald, her one love, for whom did her heart break?

7
Gabrielle

The early-afternoon light through the rain-washed window cast wavery patterns onto the mottled maroon-and-purple counterpane of the hotel bed. Despite having to stave off hunger pangs with a muesli bar rescued from the pocket of her bag, Gabrielle had managed a surprisingly decent night's sleep in the dated but cosy room at The Overland.

But now nothing was going according to plan. An entire morning with no progress.

Yesterday, that had been excusable; after all, she hadn't arrived at the property until late. But she had fully expected that today she would source numerous contractors and organise them to come out to Wurruldi and quote on the work she needed done. Unfortunately, it seemed tradies were phone-averse on Saturday mornings.

The bed creaked as she clambered off the high mattress. She shuffled across the room to tap the screen of her laptop, as though refreshing the search page would work some kind of magic. Twisting her signet ring around her pinkie, she stared at the list. It didn't help that she wasn't at all certain which trades she needed. A glazier, for sure. Painters. Electricians. Plumbers. But was there a certain order in which they should be contracted?

There was nothing like a baptism of fire to prove her ability.

She huffed and crossed to lean on the windowsill, staring out at the main street. To her right, the bridge for which the town was named spanned the broad river. Directly opposite, a regular flow of people braved the weather to scurry around the corner block and through the glass-panelled double doors of the front bar she'd been at last night. Hopefully they were headed in for a drink, because lunch didn't seem likely, considering she was still waiting for last night's salad.

She ran her tongue across her teeth, chasing the rich, nutty taste of the two coffees that had arrived with her room-service breakfast. On her short cruise down the main street yesterday, she had spied a bakery and planned to check it out for brunch, before heading out to Wurruldi. But waking late—and with a growling stomach—meant she ended up ringing down to see if she had missed breakfast.

Apparently, the dining room closed at nine, but the receptionist cheerfully offered to 'have the cook whack something on'.

That 'something' proved to be a good portion of pig, deliciously smoky and sliced into thick rashers with a crispy rind. Accompanying it were two of the most golden-yolked eggs she had ever seen, poached to runny perfection, and a huge serve of buttery fried mushrooms, all piled on slabs of toasted sourdough. It wasn't exactly the elegantly presented eggs benedict with a side of cured salmon she would have purchased and pushed around her plate in Unley, but she appreciated the card that showed each item was locally sourced. Not to mention absolutely delicious, and she had finished every morsel. Based on breakfast alone, she might have found a camp from which to conduct her initial renovations—if only she could find her renovators.

Rain drizzled down the window pane, washing the street in shades of grey and blue. Although the road was bitumen, rather than cobblestone, the pale sandstone buildings were darkened by the rain until they resembled brownstone, bringing to mind one of her favourite paintings, *Rainy Day, Boston*. Gabrielle used the edge of the curtain to wipe the steam of her breath from the glass. What was it that evoked the connection? Perhaps that, with the wide street between the two-storey pubs devoid of vehicles, the scene became timeless. Pushing back the gloom of the day, Victorian-styled lamps on tall, wrought-iron posts cast pools of custard-yellow light onto the road, and a horse-drawn carriage splashing through the puddles wouldn't seem the least bit out of place.

Her phone vibrated and she dashed to the bed to retrieve it, scanning the unfamiliar number. 'Gabrielle Moreau,' she said.

'Ah, this is Wayne Learman. You left a message on my phone?'

She moved quickly to her computer, scrolling to find his name and trade. 'Yes, yes, I did. Let me see, you're a ... painter?' It seemed a safe guess with the bulk of her calls being to painters, as her sole renovation experience had revolved around getting their apartment painted. Although they had purchased off-the-plan, neither she nor Brendan had particularly liked the brightly coloured feature wall in each room, and had employed a painter to redecorate in elegant shades of grey.

'You got it, mate,' he said.

She rolled her eyes, but pressed on. 'Terrific. Like I said in the message, I require an itemised quote for repainting a property.' She was quite proud of herself for not rushing in and employing him on the spot, which would have been far easier than evaluating quotes, but would not have proved to Brendan that careful planning could turn out a product every bit as dynamic and creative as his passion-infused projects.

'Sure, sure. Too easy. How many rooms are we looking at? Standard three-bedder, or plus an office?'

'Well, no. This is a sizeable job. A commercial premises. Are you able to handle that?'

There was a pause as Wayne took a swallow of something. Gabrielle would put money on it being Coke or Farmers

Union iced coffee. Or Red Bull. All had excellent targeted campaigns. 'Of course, mate,' he said finally. 'Give me the addy, and I'll swing by this week and have a look for you.'

'It's Wurruldi Hotel. In Wurruldi.'

'What's that? Wayville?'

'Wurruldi,' she enunciated.

'Ah, Walkley? Out at Salisbury? Bit far, but I'll take a look,' Wayne said.

'No, Wurruldi. W-U-R-R-U-L-D-I.'

Wayne grunted and she flicked the mobile to loudspeaker as a rustling noise had her picturing him scratching his head. 'Not heard of that one before. One of the new suburbs, is it? Give me two ticks, I'll just put her into maps.'

'No, not new.' Quite the opposite. 'Wurruldi is east of the city. Along the Murray River.'

'Ah. Well, that might be a bit tricky. Near Murray Bridge, is it?'

'Sort of. Closer to Settlers Bridge. Tricky, how?'

'Travel time,' Wayne said, his breathing laboured and the phone clicking as he apparently keyed the details into an app. 'We usually stick to local suburbs. There's no need for us to travel to find work. Price of fuel now, it's just not worth it. I'd have to add so much onto your quote to cover it, y'know? Besides, my teen is the next Greta Thunberg, and I don't need to stir up my ulcer with a lecture about carbon emissions or Amazon deforestation or whatever is causing the end of the world this week. So this hotel. How many rooms did you say?'

Gabrielle cast her mind back to the brief tour she and Brendan had made of the property, and the handful of photos the insurance assessor had sent. Her rose-coloured plans hadn't been concrete enough to actually quantify and design individual rooms, at this point she was working with an overall concept. Plus, she wasn't sure whether she should quote the original number of rooms, or the revised number according to the building permissions Brendan had pushed through local council. 'I'd say at least . . . ten? Twelve? I'm not sure.'

'Clearly,' the painter chuckled.

'But money is no object,' she added, and immediately regretted the words. She had been determined not to fall back on that—but she also needed to get this project started.

'Right you are, then.' Wayne suddenly sounded remarkably more positive about the job. 'You're all ready for the painting, then? Or do you need plasterwork and gyprock done first? I've got a top-notch gyprocker I can bring along. What are we talking, a freshen-up top coat or a colour change? What sort of timeframe are you looking at?'

'I, uh, well,' she stammered, thrown by his suddenly rapid-fire questions. 'I'm sure the plaster will need some smoothing.' An understatement, considering the outbuildings and the photos, but it seemed it wouldn't be a great idea to give Wayne further misgivings about the job. 'It's an old place. Had a few knocks, it's a bit rundown.' She twisted her ring guiltily. 'I'm definitely after a full colour change, something clean and neutral. And I want it done as soon as possible.'

'Uh-huh. How about I have a look at my calendar, see when I can get up there to eyeball the job? If the weather picks up a bit, I might bring the missus and kids for a day trip one weekend, and do you a quote then. I'll give you a call next week, let you know how it's looking.'

'Next week? That'll be great, thank you,' she said, hiding her disappointment behind the practised politeness drilled into her since childhood.

Disconnecting the call, she surveyed the dregs in her coffee cup morosely. She was tempted to ring down for another, but Wayne's questions had highlighted the fact that she really had to drive over to Wurruldi again. She needed to assess the property and get a firsthand idea of the renovations required, before the tradies started to inundate her with questions. And odds were her place didn't have a functioning loo, so more coffee now wasn't a great idea.

Resignedly, she slipped off her extra-tall sheepskin Ugg boots. They were probably considered perfectly appropriate outdoor footwear around here, but memories of the mud splattered across the courtyard meant a little less comfort was warranted.

Gabrielle flipped open the first suitcase, which Sharna had insisted on helping haul up the stairs last night. With the bulk of her clothes still at Brendan's apartment, she had packed for a week. A flurry of rain battered the single-glazed window and she shivered before pulling out her fleece-lined leggings and an oversized cable-knit jumper.

∾

In the watery daylight the tiny village seemed reassuringly closer to Settlers Bridge than it had yesterday. Only ten minutes on the bitumen, travelling inland through farming country, but still parallel to the Murray River much of the time. Then the slightly-less-daunting-today dirt track down the cliff face and across the river flats, and she was parked in front of the Wurruldi Hotel. Leaving the ignition on, she pressed the dashboard touchscreen to answer her ringing phone. 'Gabrielle Moreau.' She dug in the small Burberry rucksack she'd placed on the passenger seat to find her notepad. She always worked well on paper. Part of the whole tactile, artistic bent that helped her creativity.

Just not her passion.

'Hey, Gabs. It's Sharna. We met last night?' The woman sounded uncertain, as though she expected to have been forgotten.

'And you kindly walked me through the big, scary town to my hotel.' Gabrielle grinned.

'And then proceeded to leave you there without even making sure you had some dinner.' Sharna's tone was rueful.

'Hardly your responsibility.' Gabrielle turned the car off, quickly disconnecting the phone from Bluetooth and swiping it onto speaker. 'But in any case, I didn't starve. In fact, breakfast at The Overland has set me up for the day.'

'Oh.' Sharna sounded disappointed. 'That's kind of what I was ringing about. I didn't get a chance to ask if you're hanging around for the weekend. If you are, I was going to suggest we could catch up for dinner.'

'I'll actually be in town a bit longer than that,' Gabrielle said as she gazed at the forlorn exterior of her new venture. Although the mist over the Murray softened the rural outlook, wreathing the jacaranda tree in the centre of the paddock in front of the hotel like a soft bridal gown, it did nothing to improve the melancholy façade of the deserted building. Instead, the rain dripped tears from the upper balcony and she could hear a door bang again and again, the hollow, mournful toll echoing through the empty building. 'I've business in the area, so I'm thinking of basing myself at the hotel while I sort it.'

'Oh, you're on your own?'

Sharna's tone held a little too much interest, and Gabrielle cocked an eyebrow at her phone. 'Like I said, business trip, not pleasure.'

She caught herself on the too-professional tone of her voice. What was the point of being standoffish? She was new to the district and, though she liked to think she enjoyed her own company, in reality she had never been alone. Her parents' move overseas had coincided nicely with Brendan moving in. Loneliness wasn't a concept she had ever entertained—yet out here with nothing but the warble of a magpie in the century-old gum, the possibility suddenly seemed very real.

Gabrielle focused on injecting friendliness into her voice, which wasn't difficult when she thought of how welcoming the woman had been. 'But, yes, I am alone and some company for dinner would be terrific. Actually,

I could probably pick your brains about my project . . . if you're up for it?'

The warmth in Sharna's tone didn't sound the least forced. 'Awesome! I'll meet you downstairs in the dining room about six?'

Gabrielle glanced at the clock display. 'Better make it six-thirty. Is that okay? I really need to get some work done first.'

'Absolutely. I'll see you then.'

Gabrielle pocketed her phone and pulled an alpaca-wool beanie low on her forehead. As she clambered from the car, the wind caught the door, slamming it across her shins. 'Shit!' Though she cursed, the sharp pain couldn't dim her sudden cheerfulness. The quick exchange with Sharna had given her a much-needed boost. Daunted by the task she'd set herself, she had begun to second-guess the wisdom of abandoning her friends, along with her life.

Though, really, they were acquaintances, not friends. She had always kept them at a distance. Maybe that was a carryover from Amelie's death. A way to protect herself.

She had learned in the hardest possible way that there was no guarantee the people she cared for would always be there.

8

Hayden

Alerted to the approaching vehicle by Trigger's cocked ear and attentive stance, Hayden opened the door before the knock. Not that opening it was necessary; it was never locked and his friends merely gave a yell before entering uninvited.

'Hey, Dick,' Sharna said, using the toe of one foot to ease the heel of her rubber boot off the other and simultaneously thrusting a two-litre plastic bottle filled with milk towards him.

'Good afternoon to you, too,' Hayden replied, grabbing at her arm as she toppled on his doorstep. 'But, Dick?'

'Yup.' She succeeded in getting both boots off, the scent of manure rich and fertile in the damp air. 'You gonna try to tell me you weren't acting like one last night?'

'When?' He thumbed a smudge of something dairy-related off her freckled cheek.

'Last night. With Gabby. You were being a total arse.'

'Wow.' He cupped his hands over his crotch. 'Hitting both the front and rear biology insults already? You're in a fine mood.'

He tried to ignore the spike of irritation the mention of Gabrielle jolted through him. Or was it embarrassment? Because he'd lain for far too long last night torturing himself with thoughts of what he couldn't have. Which was ridiculous because even when he'd been on the prowl, city girls weren't for him. High maintenance, afraid to get their hands dirty. It would be a rare woman who, like Taylor Hartmann, managed to assimilate to the peculiarities of country life.

Sharna tossed an errant strand of curly hair back with a practised flourish, apparently oblivious to the fact that it was mud-spattered. She had probably been on the quad, moving the cows to a new paddock.

'As it so happens, I am in a very fine mood. Which will be improved even more if you add some coffee to that.' She tipped her head towards the milk bottle he clutched. Without waiting for an invitation, she slipped past him, turning left to enter the lounge room. 'Jeez, Wheaty, do you ever tidy this place up?'

He leaned against the door jamb with his arms folded across his chest as he surveyed the room. 'Any tidier, and I'd be doing a centrefold for *Australian House & Garden*.' Besides, the room was comfortable, not untidy.

'Oh, you could do a centrefold all right, dude.' Sharna laughed up at him as she shoved a pile of newspapers aside and plonked down onto one of the two under-stuffed, worn leather couches that faced off across a pine coffee table. 'I just don't think it'd be in that kind of magazine.'

His jaw tensed. Fifteen months ago, he would have played along with the joke. 'So, coffee?'

'Coffee. And make sure you skim the cream off, first. That's this morning's milk, so it'll have come to the top. I don't want any floaters.'

He hefted the bottle to his temple in salute. 'At least you didn't bring me the warm stuff. Can't stand that.'

'Don't I know it. But haven't you ever heard of not looking a gift horse?'

'Or a gift cow, in this case? Anyway, isn't it a bit late in the day for you to be drinking coffee?' It was only mid-afternoon, but Sharna would have been up since four a.m. for the first milking and, except for Friday nights, she usually headed to bed early.

She threw her head back against the couch, her eyes closed. 'Thanks for the concern, Dad. But I need the kick. Going out for dinner tonight.'

The only kick was in his chest. Because he had a sudden suspicion about where she was going. And who she was going with.

With Trigger shadowing him, Hayden headed to the small galley kitchen, filled the kettle and put it on to boil while he hunted for a couple of clean mugs. He forgot to skim the cream off the milk, so he grabbed a teaspoon from the drainer and scooped the clots from the top of Sharna's coffee, dropping them in the sink. Stirred the cream into his. In tea, he couldn't stand the lumps or the oily slick formed by the cream, but coffee was just fine.

He backed through the door, using his good shoulder to open it, but paused. The rhythmic rise and fall of Sharna's chest almost made him sneak back out, give her twenty minutes to rest. But it was already after four, so she would probably end up running late and would no doubt rip into him for letting her sleep.

'Wake up.' He nudged her leg with his knee and then placed her coffee on the table in front of her. 'Have you eaten?'

'You're a fine one to be asking that.' She yawned hugely and planted her hands on the seat cushion to wriggle upright. 'In any case, I don't suppose you have a bite in the house to offer a girl.'

'You know Mum keeps the place stocked given half a chance.' He tilted his head towards the kitchen. 'In any case, I've still got some of Roni's Anzacs in the tin.'

'I bet you have just as many as the day she dropped them off. How does she even find time to bake, with that horde of kids and animals?'

'I'm not sure the twins count as a horde.' The leather gave a soft woof as he dropped into his chair, and Trigger cocked an ear. He fondled the dog's head. 'But I'm with you on the animals.' Roni and Matt ran The Peaceful Paws, an animal retirement and rescue home. 'Want me to grab the biscuits or not?'

'Go on, then. Sugar has to help my energy level, right?'

'Stay, Trigg,' he said as he heaved to his feet again. In the kitchen he dug the old Arnott's tin out of the chipboard-fronted cupboard. He thought for a moment about unearthing a plate but decided against it, and dropped the tin on Sharna's lap as he re-entered the lounge.

She popped the lid and rummaged around before selecting a biscuit.

'Adding a bit of flavour, there?' He nodded at her grubby hands.

'Sure. Means more for me, if you're going to be a princess about it.' Dunking the biscuit in her coffee, she waited a moment to see if it was going to collapse, then snapped off half between her white teeth. She sighed with pleasure, speaking around a mouthful of oats and golden syrup. 'I vote that Roni shouldn't have any more kids. We don't want her to stop baking, right?' She chased a crumb from her flannelette shirt and transferred it to her mouth.

'I don't think Roni's going to be the next one announcing,' Hayden said.

'Taylor?' Sharna cocked an eyebrow at him.

'What makes you say that?'

'What makes you deflect my question?' She grinned back. 'So, Taylor?'

He shook his head. 'I'm not into *outing* anyone, Sharn. No gossip coming from this side.' He pretended to zip his lips closed, then watched her intently, wondering whether she'd read between the lines and realise this was no longer about pregnancy.

She stilled, her face suddenly tight.

Hayden held her gaze. Would she share?

Sharna frowned, then grabbed another biscuit before tossing the tin onto the table with a rattle that made Trigger jerk around. 'Guess we'll find out tomorrow, huh?'

'You're coming to Juz's barbie, then?'

'Wouldn't miss it,' she said brightly. 'For once my day off falls on the get-together, so I have great plans. I'm going to sleep until just before it's time to feed. Then I'll grace you lot with my company, eat myself stupid and sink back into a coma.'

'Speaking of eating . . .'

Damn it, why was he even asking? Taylor would say it was like he deliberately picked off a scab to expose the raw wound beneath so that he could rub salt into it. And she'd be right. He did it because the pain meant he remembered. And, although remembering hurt, it was better than the alternative. He wouldn't risk ever forgetting. Couldn't risk believing that life was safe and secure, that those he loved were immune to harm, that he was big enough, strong enough, brave enough, to save them all. Because he had already proved that he wasn't.

Ripping at his scars, both emotional and physical, helped him remember that.

Trigger nudged his knee, gave a heavy sigh, then rested his chin on Hayden's thigh, gazing up at him. Hayden took a deep breath. His knuckles gleamed as white as polished marble against his black coffee mug. It took a conscious effort to ease his grip on the cup. 'Where are you headed for dinner?' he said. 'Going down to the city?' Suddenly, he very badly wanted Sharna to be going to Adelaide. If she was further away, anywhere but here, he wouldn't have to think about what he was missing out on.

Sharna shook her head. 'Nah. The Overland. Why?'

He leaned forward to take a biscuit, using it as an excuse to break from Sharna's too-intent gaze. 'I'll head down the pub and let Ant know that you've betrayed him.'

'Yeah, right,' Sharna scoffed. 'Like you'd go out twice in a week.'

He kicked back on the lounge, putting his bare feet up on the coffee table. 'I'm going to Juz's tomorrow. I'd have to count it on my fingers, but I'm pretty sure that makes twice.'

'Smartarse,' Sharna shot back. 'Sunday is the start of a week, not the end. So, that makes once.'

'Fair call. Anyway, this dinner?' Despite his casual façade, his guts tensed. For Christ's sake, why couldn't he leave it alone? Why was he worrying at the question like a terrier with a dead rat? What the hell did it matter who she was going with? 'What's it in aid of?'

Sharna fiddled with a strand of hair, winding it around her fingertips. 'Not in aid of anything. I thought Gabby might like a bit of company if she was stuck here.'

Gabrielle. 'She's stuck?' he repeated, with far too much interest in his tone.

'Wow, it was just a random word choice, Wheaty. Calm your farm.' Sharna narrowed her eyes at him. 'I got the impression Gabby was staying in town, so I called her this afternoon to see if she wanted to do dinner. Turns out she's here on business, and was eager for company. Well, sort of eager,' she corrected with her trademark forthrightness. 'I probably didn't give her much of a chance to say no.'

He winced at the sudden self-doubt in Sharna's voice. 'I'm sure if Gabrielle—' Damn, had he ever spat out a prettier name? There had been a couple of Melissas, a Sophie, a Sarah, but nothing as exotic as *Gabrielle*.

Nor would there be.

He cleared his throat, as if the harsh scraping would yank his errant thoughts back into line. 'I'm sure if she wanted to say no, she would be more than capable. She didn't come across as someone who would mince her words.'

Sharna chuckled at him over the rim of her mug. 'Wow, she really got you offside, didn't she?'

Hayden shrugged, flinching as the movement tugged at his shoulder. 'Struck me as kind of judgmental. You might want to tread carefully around her.'

Sharna's face crumpled in sympathy and she sat forward, placing her mug on the scorched table. 'Ah, Wheaty, she didn't mean anything. It would have sucked walking into a pub full of locals on a Friday night. I'm sure she just blurted without thinking.'

'Yeah, that's the truth.' And the issue. The woman had instantly assessed him as handicapped and unworthy. She hadn't even needed to *see* to recognise his damage; the fact that he had an assistance dog already marked him in her eyes. Her only mistake had been in not hiding her judgment, as his friends did so carefully.

Sharna wrinkled her snub nose, and he knew she was about to disagree, or worse, insist he needed to talk it through. He didn't care to share his pathetic vulnerability with anyone, so he continued hurriedly, 'Anyway, what kind of business is she here on?'

'No idea. I mean, she looks like she should be in the fashion industry or acting or something, right? But I'm not sure how that works in with Settlers Bridge. Guess I'll find out tonight. Speaking of—' She picked up her mug and tipped her head back to drain it in one go. Then she shoved the cup back on the table and stood with a groan. 'I suppose I'd better go shower some of this stink off.'

'Oh, so it's fine to have your pong permeate my furniture, but you'll hose off for strangers?' Hayden teased as he also stood, towering over Sharna.

She squinted up at him. 'I tell you what, how about you come along, Wheaty, and we'll pretend that I showered just for you?'

He couldn't miss the sudden entreaty in her words. But he also couldn't give the answer that she wanted. He shook his head. 'Much as the thought of seeing you scrubbed up and halfway decent for once is a major drawcard, that'd break my one-outing-a-week allowance, wouldn't it? Reckon I'd better save myself for the barbie tomorrow.'

'Aw, come on, Wheaty. You know conversation will be easier if there's a few of us.'

'Never known you to be short of words, Sharn,' he said as they headed to the door. 'You'll be just fine.' Yet, even as he spoke, he was tempted. He could go along as wingman for Sharna. Check Gabrielle out a bit more. God knows, she was easy enough on the eye; it would be no hardship.

Yeah, and then what? he snarled at himself. Chat her up? If history was any predictor, there would be a schnitzel, a couple of extra drinks, a bit of flirting, some making out, and then he'd take her home.

But that was where the comfortable predictability would end. He would be in uncharted territory. There had been no one since . . . His hand instinctively moved to his shoulder, but he snatched it away. They would get to his place and, even if he kept the lights off, it would be only minutes before she would run, as if were one of Frankenstein's creations. If he couldn't bear to look at himself, he couldn't expect anyone else to.

Hayden shook his head decisively. 'Why don't you hit up one of the others, Sharna? Juz would be all over the invite.'

Sharna surveyed him soberly for a long moment. She didn't say anything, but he could read the accusation in her stare.

She was right, that had been a bastard move. He knew the invitation would get Juz's hopes up for nothing and leave Sharna trying to fend off the lovesick bloke all night.

'Fuck, Sharn.' He groaned, running a hand around the back of his neck. 'All right. I'll meet you early. Buy you a Moscato, then I'm out of there, okay?'

She dimpled at him, standing on tiptoe to press a quick kiss on his cheek. 'Your sisters don't know how lucky they are, Wheaty. I'll see you at six, then.'

He leaned against the door jamb, absently fondling Trigger's ears as he watched Sharna's beat-up Holden ute jounce along the driveway and out onto the main road.

Damn it. Why the hell was he such an easy touch? He knew Sharna was doing it tough, trying to work her life out, but he couldn't afford to add friends to his list of responsibilities.

God knows, he didn't need someone else to lie awake at night worrying about.

9
Ilse

This was one of the worst depredations of age, Ilse decided with a brisk click of her tongue against the roof of her mouth; the terrible memory fog that made it seem she viewed her recollections through the hops-blurred dregs of a butchers of beer.

As she peered across the foyer—little more than a grandly named passage between the front and rear entrance, with an archway leading to the bar on the left, and a smaller one to the Ladies' Lounge on the right—the vaguely familiar woman reached through the jagged shards of the frosted-glass door to fiddle with the latch.

The door opened and she blew into the public area on a flurry of wind-driven leaves. She entered something in a notebook, then shoved it in her back pocket, and swept a mottled grey beanie from her blonde hair. Ilse tutted again. The woman was particularly distinctive, and had been wandering about the courtyard only—when? Last week? Yesterday? Never mind. Forgetfulness was no excuse for poor manners now.

She stepped from the broad sweep of stairs, her hand outstretched. 'Good afternoon. You're the new owner, I understand? I'm Ilse. We never formalised the arrangement, but the estate agent intimated you would like me to continue to oversee the gardens.' Although the grounds were increasingly hard to manage, having her value recognised made it worthwhile. It seemed that as she grew older, her focus became narrower, the world ever-diminishing until it was a conveniently contained bubble of time and place. Now the beautiful gardens she and Ronald had laboured over together were her world.

'Gabrielle Moreau.' The woman's chocolate-dark eyes met Ilse's gaze, but then she turned to look around the dusty, webbed room. 'What the heck have you done?'

Ilse faltered. So much for manners. 'The property has been somewhat neglected,' she shot back. 'But the suggestion was that I assist in the gardens, not the interior.' Indeed, she had been meaning to take up with the real-estate agent the fact that the escalating expense was still coming out of her own purse.

Gabrielle clutched the knitted cap like a shield as she surveyed the entry hall and beyond. 'What am I supposed to do with this mess?'

Ilse's mouth tightened. The last two generations had been born with an increasing sense of entitlement and a corresponding diminishing sense of responsibility. The roll-up-your-sleeves work ethic of Ilse's youth had disappeared along with morals and personal accountability. 'I'm certain it's nothing that can't be fixed.' She waved towards the walls, although she felt rather less confident than she sounded. 'My grandfather built this place on solid foundations and the structure is certainly sound.' Guilt drifted through her, a dark wraith that clutched at her insides. She could all too easily imagine Oma's outrage, peppered with Teutonic expressions and a steadily thickening accent, at the deplorable shabbiness of the property in which she had taken such pride.

With one hand on her hip, Gabrielle puffed her cheeks, then blew out a long, considering breath. 'I suppose at least it hasn't been vandalised.'

'Well, yes, there is that.' Good, the girl had her emotions under control. Ilse had no patience for overt displays of any sort.

The younger woman wandered towards the Ladies' Lounge, frequently pausing as though trying to absorb the layout of every nook and cranny in the recessed hollows of the entry hall. She pulled a mobile telephone from the pocket of her chunky-knit jumper, and Ilse startled as the flash went off.

'Oh!' Ilse patted at her chest. 'That was a heart starter.'

'Let's hope I don't scare any rats out of their hiding places,' Gabrielle muttered.

Ilse drew herself up to her full less-than-impressive height. Of course, there were vermin issues from time to time—each particularly wet season, greeted with thirsty glee by the farmers, saw rodents invade the houses and outbuildings, looking for protected spots to build their nests of stolen fabric and paper—but they were dealt with promptly, and not so much as a cockroach had ever been spied by a customer.

'I certainly doubt you'll have any such issue.' A breeze almost as chilly as Ilse's tone rushed through one of the shattered window panes, tangling the curtain. The billowing fabric gave off a distinct odour of mildew, and an ominous semi-circle darkened the carpet beneath the rattling window frame.

'I just . . .' Gabrielle shook her head, sounding woebegone. 'Where do I even start?'

Ilse took a couple of steps sideways, peering out of a filthy window. 'Is your young man not joining us?' She should count how many windows needed to be replaced; it seemed that protecting the property from further damage would be an obvious point from which to commence repairs. One that, really, anyone with an iota of common sense should see. She tutted irritably beneath her breath, her dentures loosening a little. Honestly, it would have been far easier if the property had remained within the family, so she wouldn't need to carefully mask her suggestions and couch her opinions within social niceties. But it wouldn't do to be too overt about directing Gabrielle, not this early in their relationship. *Sie werden mehr Fliegen mit Honig als mit Essig fangen*, as Oma would say. You catch more flies with honey than with vinegar.

On the gravel driveway sat a peacock-blue convertible, but there was no sign of Gabrielle's partner. 'Or should I say, your husband?' Ilse angled for a little more information. She could only hope that he possessed the necessary common sense. And a rake and some brawn, she thought as she surveyed the gravel scattered across the withered, patchy grass at the front of the hotel. Though it was years since she had wielded tools, she directed the man who came to do the heavy labour each fortnight—her thoughts stalled as she stared at the grounds. Their appalling state suggested the labourer had not been for some time, but why? A terrifying darkness existed where the memory should lie. Had she taken a spill and bumped her head?

It must be that. Oma, Opa, Mother, Father, Ronald—the addition of his name to the list of those departed caused a tight twinge in her heart—had all retained their faculties until the very last. She simply refused to be the one to let the family down.

Gabrielle ignored her question, pinching at her lower lip. 'Maybe I should ring Brendan?'

'Perhaps a good idea,' Ilse replied waspishly. Not that men inherently possessed the solution to all of life's problems—although Ronald had been something of a gem in that respect—but right now Ilse needed to focus on her own concerns.

'No, I can't,' Gabrielle groaned. She stared through the doorway into the gloom of the Ladies' Lounge. 'I just don't remember it looking this bad.'

Ilse cringed. The desecration of this room had been her son's doing. With women finally permitted in the front bar, he had turned the redundant Ladies' Lounge into a discotheque, installing an ugly floor of plastic cubes that lit up and vibrated beneath the dancers' feet. A mirrored orb reflected neon lights that flashed bright colours on the glossy black walls. The wallpapered grace of Oma's dreams had disappeared in a herb-infused haze, and Ilse had been relieved when subsequent owners at least removed the deplorable floor, though it was arguable that the stained burgundy carpet was any kind of improvement.

As though retreating from the darkness, Gabrielle spun quickly and strode across the foyer to the main bar. The room had an air of neglect, with overturned tables and broken chairs creating skeletal mountains among the dust. Winding swiftly between the discarded furniture, Gabrielle ran her hand along the mirror-tiled bar. 'What on earth is this supposed to be?'

'Quite,' Ilse agreed, tapping her fingers on the ugly black-veined tiles. At least Gabrielle's apparent taste extended beyond her fashion sense.

Placing her hat on the counter, Gabrielle dropped to a squat with a flexibility Ilse barely remembered and certainly coveted. Age brought with it aches and ailments that the young could never imagine. Indeed they would never want to imagine, or they would put far less effort into prolonging their lives, and more into enjoying the moment.

'Oh, my goodness, what do we have here?' Gabrielle said in a tone of wonder as she investigated beneath the overhanging lip of the counter.

A burst of pride warmed through Ilse. She could still recall exactly how the bar had looked, gleaming red beneath the mellow, mustard-yellow of the pendant lights. 'Red gum. Opa—my grandfather—had it brought downriver by paddle-steamer from Echuca.'

'Red gum?' Gabrielle squinted up at the underside from where she crouched. 'Yes, I'm pretty sure it is.'

'As I just said.' *Steady girl*. Flies and honey and all that.

Gabrielle stood and pulled at the edge of one of the tiles. 'Surely I could get these stripped. Restore the bar to what it was back in . . .'

'Eighteen eighty-four,' Ilse supplied, almost tripping over the date in her eagerness. After decades of deterioration, had the hotel finally found the right owner?

Not that Gabrielle, with her long nails tapping a quick rhythm on the tiles, looked any more capable of hard work than the previous owners. Though, truth be told, the rich burgundy ovals, glistening like wine droplets on the bar, did rather remind Ilse of how she had worn her own nails many years earlier, when appearance had been paramount. 'I do like that colour,' she murmured. 'I have a lipstick tucked away somewhere in that precise shade.' Not that she had worn anything that racy for a very long time. Old ladies didn't do red well. 'Although, we always left the moon of our cuticles revealed. It makes hands look more elegant, fingers longer.' Of course, that snippet of fashion advice

102

belonged in the forties. She tapped a finger on Gabrielle's hand. 'This is—oh!' She jerked back. Her own hands were as dry and brittle as crepe tissue, blotched with freckles and sunspots and roped with raised veins, her knuckles swollen with arthritis. 'Goodness, I don't recall when I last had a manicure,' she said, trying to hide her embarrassment. 'I suppose it was decades ago. A lovely nail polish and a passion for gardening make for poor partners.'

Gabrielle shivered and twitched her hand away, politely ignoring Ilse's discomfort. 'Definitely restoring this. It'll be the centrepiece of the room.'

The thought thrilled Ilse. Opa's bar was intrinsically tied to her favourite memories when, even on the precipice of war, the world had seemed full of possibility and adventure. When she and Ronald had been young together.

It was behind that bar that she had met Ronald. Beyond handsome in his light brown, neatly creased pants, a matching open vest over an unbuttoned white shirt, with his hat tipped rakishly to the back of his head, he had ordered more drinks than he could possibly consume. Eventually, she felt the need to point out the still-full glasses arranged along the bar in front of him. He grinned. 'Ordering a drink is the only way I can make sure the prettiest girl in the room will speak to me,' he said. Of course, with women not permitted to drink in the bar, she was the only girl in the room, but his intent, and his roguish charm, had been clear from the outset.

Ilse sighed. She had been devastated when the bar disappeared beneath the tiles, but had at least been able to trust her mind to hold her memories close. Now she yearned for a more tactile reminder. Longing made her fingers tremble . . . the touch of the grainy, oiled surface of the wood would somehow bring everything back, she knew it with a certainty that consumed her soul. The music of conversation and laughter in the smoky recesses of the crowded bar would again fill her ears, the clink of glasses and scrape of chairs replacing the thready whisper of the wind through the tomb-like rooms. Hidden beneath pomade and aftershave, the yeasty smell of beer and hard-worked bodies would overtake the mould and damp of desertion. Ronald's spatulate fingers splayed on the counter, nails blackened where they'd been crushed between stones, he would shove aside the ashtray and hoist himself up, his muscular arms bulging in his shirtsleeves as he craned forward, laughingly begging her for a kiss. A kiss she would always bestow, no matter her mood.

She pushed away the silly fantasy. 'Knowing Ivan, the tiles probably aren't even properly attached.' Of course, she shouldn't speak ill of her own son, but he had proved a disappointment in so many ways. Unlike . . . she pressed trembling fingertips to her lips, searching for the name that had suddenly disappeared. A rush of sadness and fear swirled dark and ominous, and she struggled to draw breath. She clawed at her blouse, although the pain that crushed her chest wasn't physical; it was deep within her, an aching loss that made no sense. Names often eluded her now, so why did this one make her panic?

Sorrow pierced her heart but there was more than that. Anger? Yes, anger.

10

Gabrielle

Gabrielle pulled the straightener through her hair with quick, irritated strokes. It was beginning to seem like she would never make any progress on the bed-and-breakfast.

She had only been at Wurruldi for a short time, procrastinating by searching for remnants of the beautiful gardens she recalled bordering the stone fences before summoning the nerve to face the damage inside. Though she hadn't yet collected the keys, the shattered door panels made it easy for her to reach inside and turn the latch on the deadbolt to let herself in.

As though she were trespassing, the thrill of imminent discovery had tingled up her spine and pricked the hairs at the base of her neck. She scribbled *Locksmith* on her notes as she moved into the main rooms off the foyer. The paintwork was horrendous, the carpets rotted and there were more broken windows than anyone could count. But, other than some cracks she could slide a hand into, there seemed remarkably little damage from the earthquake. The newer kitchen, laundry and bathroom facilities in the extended slate-tiled, barn-like wing, brightly lit by the small, square windows below the vaulted ceiling, appeared surprisingly functional despite the layer of filth.

She had been inside for less than an hour, snapping photos and making sketches, when the real-estate agent rang. Clearly disappointed that Gabrielle's business hadn't manifested into a lucrative property management opportunity, she insisted the keys be collected. When Gabrielle directed they be tossed in the trash, as the building was unsecured anyway, the agent maintained she had a legal obligation to have them signed off her register before she headed overseas for a month. Gabrielle had taken a few more photos, then reluctantly closed up and rushed back to Settlers Bridge.

Now back in her room at The Overland, with the useless keys tucked safely in her bag, Gabrielle tweaked the V-neck of her fitted sweater a little higher, adjusting the collar detail that circled her throat like a choker. She added a narrow leather belt to match her fawn suede boots. It was amazing what the right choice in clothes could hide; even her distressed pale denim jeans had the slashes across the thighs placed just so.

She surveyed her reflection critically, leaning close to the steamed mirror, looking for the tell-tale signs. Even though nothing had changed for years, still she was hypervigilant.

Behind her, the beige shower curtain hung in damp folds. Despite the somewhat less-than-salubrious presentation, the shower was one of the best she'd ever had: hot, with such pressure she wondered if the hotel pumped directly from the river, which was only a few metres down the hill. She would have to look into whether it was possible to get a licence for that. Great showers went a long way to enhancing guest satisfaction.

She pulled a wry face at herself; before she got carried away with water pressure, she needed new bathrooms at Wurruldi. According to Brendan's plans, there were only two upstairs, and one down. That hadn't mattered when they had intended to run the premises as a brewhouse, but now she would need to renovate to take into account accommodation options. Exclusivity offered a better guest experience, but would be impossible unless she considered the income irrelevant, as she would only ever be able to let a couple of rooms. Which, realistically, suited her fine; she had lucrative investments and could always fall back on her PR consultancy. Yet she hesitated: where was the challenge if she simply threw money at the project and didn't at least try to get it to a point where it produced a positive income? Maybe she needed to make decisions as though she depended on the money the property earned. The unfamiliar notion was somewhat disconcerting.

She checked the time on her phone and added a last quick flick of mascara to her dark lashes. She was running a little late, but it wasn't like she needed to travel to a different suburb to meet Sharna. If brunch—which suddenly seemed a long time ago—was anything to go by, the prospect of dinner was enticing.

Taking the narrow flight of stairs swiftly, Gabrielle paused to take a deep, steadying breath as she surveyed the dining room. The crowded space hit the shabby-without-chic restaurant vibe perfectly. Berber-covered chairs and square tables, each set with a triangular napkin holder and chrome-topped salt and pepper shakers, suggested that freshly ground black pepper and Himalayan rock salt were sadly unlikely to be the norm here.

Sharna's distinctive pale-red curls were easy to spot alongside the silver bain-marie counter. Gabrielle started forward eagerly, but then pulled up. Sharna was not alone. In fact, Gabrielle was surprised Sharna's companion wasn't the first thing she noticed. His brooding Heathcliff-type dourness should cast a pall of darkness around him.

He glanced up, catching her eye. Didn't politely look away, nor did he smile. Instead, he said something to Sharna, then jerked his square chin in Gabrielle's direction.

Sharna spun around and waved eagerly, mouthing, 'Over here.'

Gabrielle's stomach coiled with nerves at the thought of another evening spent in the company of the one person from last night who had been less than friendly.

Yet her hands reflexively smoothed her sweater over her hips, a quiver of excitement tingling through her as Wheaty stood. Towering over the table he leaned towards Sharna, then crossed the room, gaining ground before Gabrielle had a chance to compose herself.

'Gabrielle,' he rumbled.

The knot in her gut released, her stomach flipping in a dizzying rush. She took a quick step back, as though the distance would allow her time to organise her response.

Because her visceral reaction to his nearness was not acceptable. Not at all.

She would have to ask Brigitte what on earth that was about. Her sister loved any excuse to revisit her psych training.

Except she didn't really need to ask; her sister would trot out some long-winded explanation that could be boiled down to Gabrielle's innate need to have everyone like her. Wheaty had spent the previous evening either ignoring her or barely hiding his antagonism. Now he was a challenge. But not one she cared to take on.

Gabrielle drew back further, partly because he filled a ridiculous amount of the entranceway, and partly because his dog was close on his heels. 'Whea—hi,' she stammered, not knowing what to call him.

Without another word, he strode past.

She puffed out a long breath, then pulled her shoulders back and ran her fingers through her hair to bring it in line with her collarbone. The combination of movements was habitual, a ritual she used to help centre herself before presentations. Brendan teased her about it, said it bordered on obsessive–compulsive, but she had trained her brain to become calm and self-assured with the action. It was failsafe.

Usually.

But Wheaty swung back towards her, and her composure evaporated beneath his gaze. He tilted his head towards the seat he'd vacated. 'Sharna's over there. She's a good kid.'

'O-okay?' she said, lifting an eyebrow as she waited for some explanation of the odd statement. Wheaty's stern inflection made the words seem almost a warning.

He stared at her a moment longer. Then he nodded once, turned and strode away.

'What the heck?' she muttered, her clenched fists sweaty. The man was bizarre. And, unsettlingly, intriguing. No, just bizarre. She had to stick with bizarre.

Sharna had half-stood. 'Hi. I wasn't sure if you'd remember me.'

'Couldn't miss that gorgeous hair,' Gabrielle said as she slid into her seat. 'Do you mind if I ask, is it natural? My hairdresser would kill for the name of that shade.'

'Oh.' Sharna's cheeks coloured, her hand distractedly tangling in her curls. 'Yes. Natural. To be honest, I've never been to a hairdresser. Mum gives it a trim once in a while.' She licked her lightly glossed lips. 'And now this is kind of awkward, because I was going to say how gorgeous your hair looks, but that sounds dumb now that you beat me to it.' She laughed self-consciously.

Gabrielle shifted the thick white china side plate a little further to the left. 'Not awkward. We'll just form a mutual admiration society. Membership—' she held up two fingers '—two.'

'We could,' Sharna said tentatively, a crease forming between her fair eyebrows. 'If you like?' Her question seemed to hold far more weight than Gabrielle's flippant line warranted, but then Sharna seemed to flick aside whatever thought had momentarily bothered her. She indicated the room with a wave. 'I've not eaten here for a while, I can't believe how busy it is.'

'I guess it's all your fan club turning out,' Gabrielle said, thinking back to the loud greetings in The Settlers pub last night, where everyone seemed to know one another.

'Nope. Definitely not. This place is crazy popular with locals, but it even gets the out-of-towners in now.'

'Proof.' Gabrielle pointed at herself.

'Can't say it's a bad thing, given present company. I reckon there'd be an eighty–twenty split tonight, farmers to visitors.' Sharna held up her hands, palms out, displaying ingrained dirt. 'Guess which side I fall on?'

'Pretty easy, given the math,' Gabrielle grinned. But it wasn't only the math, there was something about Sharna's sun-kissed skin, her freshness and easy, outgoing nature that spoke of being country.

Sharna flipped her hands over. 'Milk might make your nails grow long and strong, but I can assure you that working in the dairy has the opposite effect,' she said ruefully, then tucked her hands under the table.

'Are most of the eighty percent into dairying, then?' Gabrielle asked, feigning nonchalance. Why did she care what Wheaty did for a living?

Sharna shook her head, curls jostling. 'Nope. Lot of sheep and cereal farmers out this way. But we won't hold that against them,' she added with a wink. 'We even let them on the footy team.'

Now Gabrielle wanted to know if Wheaty played football, and that was bloody ridiculous, she'd never even watched a game. 'What else do you do for fun around here?' she forged on. 'I mean, other than football?' Research. That's really what she was doing, checking out local entertainment for her future guests.

'You're after some fun?' Sharna said, one eyebrow lifting. 'Your options are going to be pretty limited. Most of the guys are in the footy team and play lawn bowls in the off season. Girls are into netball—or breeding,' she added as a young woman cradling a sobbing infant passed the table. 'So, unless that fits your definition of fun, you'd be better off in the city. I sure know where I'd rather be.'

'Really? I thought country people kind of always stayed in the country.' Again she caught herself, this time at her sweeping generalisation. The last thing she wanted was to get Sharna offside. It was nice having someone to chat with.

'I guess plenty are happy enough to hang here. But not me. This town is small. And gossipy and judgmental.' Sharna's frown had returned, and she shredded a thin white serviette she pulled from the holder.

Gabrielle toyed with the diamond-studded 'G' pendant than hung below her choker. So, there were skeletons in Sharna's past? Perhaps that tied in with Wheaty's statement about her. Were they an item? At a glance, he seemed older than Sharna, probably closer to Gabrielle's own age—but that wasn't enough of a gap to explain the gossip. 'Wow, you're not selling it. I may have to rethink my plans.'

'Sorry.' Sharna flashed a shamefaced grin at her. 'That's just me being whiny. Settlers Bridge is a nice place, just quiet. Wheaty reckons I have a grass-is-greener thing happening and would hate the city, really. Anyway, plans? You said you were here on business. What is it you do?'

'I'm in PR, but I'm taking a break. Or trying to.' She paused as an older man doddered past their table, his plate piled dangerously high with cauliflower cheese, rice and roast potatoes. 'Oh, that smells so good. Shall we order? I'm starving. It must be all this fresh air; I'll end up looking like the side of a house soon.'

'I doubt that.' Sharna stood, her sky-blue eyes darting down Gabrielle's body. 'Anyway, there's no point looking at the menu. The specials are on the board near the register and pretty much anything you choose from the menu will be unavailable. Alex likes to have only a handful of different dishes to cook each night, so he keeps about three blackboards with a different selection on each, and sticks one of them up.'

'Is that the same chef who does the breakfast?'

'He's the only chef. Well, he's the cook. I don't suppose he's actually qualified. So, anyway, yup,' Sharna gabbled as though suddenly nervous, taking a couple of steps towards the silver bain-marie unit. She stumbled and Gabrielle stood swiftly, reflexively reaching to steady her.

'Thanks.' Sharna looked down at Gabrielle's hand on her arm and a small smile played across the slightly irregular bow of her lips. 'Guess I shouldn't have had that warm-up drink with Wheaty. This way.'

Gabrielle hid her frown. If Wheaty had been there for a drink with Sharna, why hadn't he joined them for dinner? Because of her?

Sharna led the way across the room to a bar with a register at one end, and as Gabrielle followed she noted the stiff-legged, baby-giraffe awkwardness of the younger woman. Though the strappy heels she wore beneath her tight blue jeans weren't particularly high, it seemed more probable Sharna was unfamiliar with walking in them, than unstable because she'd had too many drinks.

'Schnitzel is always the best bet in a country pub,' Sharna said. 'But The Overland does a great surf 'n' turf, too.'

Gabrielle chewed on her bottom lip as she read the board behind the register. The rainbow of chalk was more varied than the food selections, which were all basically meat-and-veg combinations. 'Well, I think I'll put my trust in you and try that, then.'

Sharna darted forward. 'Hi, Lynn. Two surf specials, thanks,' she said to the burgundy-haired woman behind the register. 'No.' She held up her hand as Gabrielle dug in her bag for her wallet. 'My treat.'

'Oh, no, you don't have to do that,' Gabrielle said, slightly shocked.

'Don't worry, I get locals' discount.' Sharna grinned, handing her credit card to Lynn.

'I'll get drinks, then,' Gabrielle said, hoping Sharna would also be up for dessert, so she could even the account. 'What are you having?'

'Always Moscato for Sharn,' Lynn butted in. 'What's your poison, lovey?'

Gabrielle hesitated, unwilling to repeat the previous night's debacle. 'Um. Just make that two, please.' She handed over her card.

'Take a table number,' Lynn directed. 'I'll bring the drinks when I get a minute.'

'So,' Gabrielle said as they took their seats again, 'how long do I need to be here to get locals' discount?'

'How long are you thinking of being here?' Sharna countered, toying with her hair.

'In Settlers Bridge? As short a time as possible.'

'Oh.' Disappointment flashed across the younger woman's face. 'That's a shame. We don't get many new people through.'

Gabrielle paused as Lynn delivered their brimming glasses. 'Thank you.' She turned back to Sharna. 'I mean I'm only here a short time because I've bought property in the area. I'll move in there as soon as I get it renovated.' There, she'd committed herself now, even though she had been avoiding facing the fact that, logically, she would have to move into her own place sometime.

Sharna seemed incapable of masking her reactions, and now she perked up. 'Cheers.' She tipped her glass to clink with Gabrielle's. 'So, is there a Mister Gabs following you here anytime soon?'

Gabrielle couldn't stifle a giggle at the thought of Brendan's reaction to being referred to by any variation of her name. 'Nope. Trust me, I have absolutely zero interest in any of that.'

'Oh?' The single syllable vibrated with interest. 'I'm sure Juz and Wheaty will be sad to hear that.'

'Wheaty? He's the guy with the dog, right? The one who just left?' She snatched at a lock of her hair, pretending to inspect the blunt-cut tips for split ends as she avoided Sharna's suddenly penetrating gaze. Damn, she should have asked after the other guy first, hidden the interest that flared within her at the realisation that Sharna could dish the dirt on the brooding hulk who had managed to both intrigue and irritate her within minutes of their meeting.

Both emotions were easy to explain. He intrigued her precisely because he was dark and brooding, the polar opposite of blond, gregarious Brendan. And he irritated her because . . . Gabrielle screwed up her nose. In truth, it was more embarrassment than irritation. She had plonked her size-seven Manolos fair in it the first time they crossed paths, with her clumsy comments about his dog. Then she had allowed her mortification to manifest as annoyance, and, as Brigitte would point out, Wheaty had pretty much reflected the behaviour right back at her.

'Yeah, Trigger.' Sharna ran her finger around the top of her thick glass, as though expecting it to sing like crystal.

'And Wheaty is his surname, I guess?' Crap, she really had to stop asking questions. But surely Sharna, who seemed so ingenuous, wouldn't read anything into it?

'No, he's a Paech. It's Wheaty because his name's Hayden.' Sharna paused, her eyebrows raised as she waited for Gabrielle to make the connection.

Gabrielle lifted one hand in question, her tennis bracelet tinkling against her silver bangle. 'Wheaty?'

'Yeah,' Sharna grinned, her eyes sparkling in the glow of the cheap, battery-operated candle on the table. '*Hay*-den. *Wheat*-y. Get it? Hay and wheat.'

'Ah,' Gabrielle nodded, taking a sip of Moscato. 'Okay. Got it. Bit of a dad joke.'

'More like a farmer joke.'

'Yeah. So, Hayden.' She had no reason to repeat his name, other than that she suddenly wanted to feel it in her mouth. 'And the two of you . . .'

'Us?' Sharna seemed shocked. 'Oh, god, no. I mean, he's like a cross between a big brother and a friend, you know?'

Gabrielle shook her head. 'Can't say that I do.' And, given Wheaty's reactions, she wasn't entirely sure he did, either. Although he had also been overly friendly with the other woman at the pub, Lucie.

'No brothers, then?' Sharna asked.

'Only sisters. A sister.'

Sharna looked confused. 'So . . . sisters in the solidarity sense, and one in the biological sense?'

Gabrielle didn't want to rehash the trauma of Amelie's death. 'Yeah, that's about it.'

'Excellent,' Sharna smiled with inexplicable enthusiasm. 'I was—oh.' She broke off as their meals arrived.

Gabrielle had assumed the surf 'n' turf would be a variation on a schnitzel topped with deep-fried prawns and squid. To her surprise, the plate a jeans-clad waitress slid in front of her held a thick, juicy fillet steak in a moat of pale pink jus. Crowning the meat were medallions of delicate white crayfish propped on an angle by a mound of barely golden, finely cut calamari rings.

Sharna grinned, enjoying her surprise. 'Told you Alex does a nice job. The vegies are in the warmer, grab whatever you fancy. There's usually a great chowder over there that you can use as a sauce. The bread's too good to miss, make sure you take a couple of rolls.'

Gabrielle groaned. 'I wasn't joking about that side-of-a-house thing. How am I going to work all this off?'

'I can always find you a job in the dairy,' Sharna laughed, collecting her side plate and heading towards the bain-marie. 'These plates are small,' she called back over her shoulder, 'but you can go up as many times as you like.'

'Oh my god,' Gabrielle moaned a few minutes later, speaking around a mouthful of meat.

'I know, right?' Sharna said.

Gabrielle waved her fork at her plate. 'This is amazing. I'm not a big meat eater, but if I hang around here, I could be turned.'

Sharna frowned. 'Not quite the way I imagined the conversation going . . .'

'The crayfish is unbelievable, too. I would never have expected to find good seafood in the country.'

Sharna lifted one shoulder. 'Kingston is only a couple of hundred k's down the road. Story is, Alex's brother has a cray licence and a boat. He gets his quota and does a swap with Alex.'

'What on earth could be good enough to swap for this?' Gabrielle flaked off a morsel of delicate flesh, savouring it.

Sharna took a huge mouthful of her steak, chewing with relish. 'That's where it gets more complicated. Alex also swaps the local butcher for sides of prime grass-fed Coorong beef. His brother gets the beef, Alex gets the cray, we get dinner.'

Gabrielle held her fork in the air, using it to count the points. 'Okay, so most importantly, you and I are in glutton's heaven. But, working back: Alex is happy, Alex's brother is happy . . . what about the butcher? What does he trade Alex for?'

Sharna grinned. 'He is a she. And Alex is *very* good looking.'

'Ah, quid pro quo, huh?'

Sharna looked a little uncertain. 'I'm not sure about that, but there's definitely a lot of trading goes on around here. That, and we just help mates out, you know?' She warmed to the topic, her elbow on the table as she leaned forward. 'Tay only ever bulk bills, so we don't pay a cent at the docs. Roni takes in animals if people can't care for them. Lucie's pretty new around here, but she knocks up this great hand cream for me, and I give her milk for her kid.' She seemed to realise how fast she'd been talking, and sat back. 'Well, anyway, we look out for each other. You know what I mean, right?'

So, if there was nothing between Sharna and Wheaty, what about Lucie, whose daughter had seemed comfortable enough to crawl all over him? 'Sure,' she lied, although she did not *know*. On the spot, Gabrielle couldn't think of one instance in her life when she had been 'helped out'. Nor, more mortifyingly, could she recall when she had helped out. It wasn't that altruism wasn't in her nature—she donated to the Salvos like everyone else. It was just that city living didn't offer opportunities for the kind of thing Sharna was talking about, she assured herself, trying to ignore the niggling little voice that suggested the fault was hers: perhaps she simply hadn't bothered to look for opportunities. But it was different here, helping each other would be second nature to people who had spent their entire lives together. They would be like an extended family—and helping out family *was* something she could conceive.

Although she hadn't done as well there as she should, either. She made an effort to displace the melancholy that memories and thoughts of her family, more than sixteen thousand kilometres away, always brought. 'It must be kind of cool to know everyone you pass in the street.'

Sharna twisted her mouth. 'Maybe. In some ways. But, like I said, it's hard around here if what you want isn't the norm. Anyway, another drink?'

'Sure,' Gabrielle agreed, downing the last of her oversweet wine. She wondered if Sharna usually drank so much— this would be at least her third glass. And she seemed unaccountably nervous; one moment cheerfully engaged, the next a slight frown on her pretty face as though trying to analyse Gabrielle's words. 'Actually, I might get a juice. Need a clear head for my planning.'

'Good call,' Sharna agreed. 'I'll go.'

Gabrielle fished out her card and handed it to Sharna. 'My buy.'

Sharna ran her thumb over the card. 'Moreau? That's a pretty fancy name.'

'Not if you're French,' Gabrielle chuckled. 'It's kind of like Smith.'

Sharna had started to rise, but now sank back down onto one knee on the chair. 'You're from France?' she said breathlessly, her eyes huge.

'Sadly, nothing that interesting. I'm Adelaide through and through. But my parents are French.'

'That's still amazing,' Sharna said, settling back into her seat. 'Do you plan on ever going to France?'

Gabrielle spun the stem of her wineglass between her fingers. 'I've been several times, and I'll be in Saint-Germain-en-Laye for Christmas because my family are over there.' As she spoke, Sharna's face clouded over, and guilt prickled through Gabrielle. There she went again, taking her privilege for granted. It was clear Sharna dreamed of escaping her country lifestyle.

'This Saint . . . wherever. Is it close to Paris? That's really the only thing I know about France,' Sharna asked wistfully.

'About half an hour on the rail. But, honestly, history aside, South Australia has almost everything France offers.

I mean, an hour from here and you can be at beautiful chateaux in the Barossa. You've got Central Market down in the city if you want to go a bit cosmopolitan with your food—not that there's anything wrong with Alex's cooking.' She tapped her knife on the steak. 'Or you can do a river cruise right off your own doorstep. And the beaches here are so much better—' She broke off with a grin. 'Really, South Australian Tourism should have given me their PR gig. Anyway, what I mean is, travel's not really that big a deal. You don't need to go far to get a great experience.' She realised she sounded hopeful, rather than persuasive, mainly because she was waffling, trying to downplay the advantages that came with her birth. It was moments like this that Brendan's accusations rang true; she did tend to take for granted the benefits life bestowed on her.

Sharna shook her head doubtfully. 'I don't know. I suspect being able to travel overseas is like getting married and having babies and all those other "milestones".' She air-quoted the last word. 'They're no big deal when you're one of the people they just happen for.'

The girl with the baby passed them again, her cheeks flushed, her movements flustered as she desperately jiggled the child, who was screaming more loudly by the second. Gabrielle quirked an eyebrow. 'At least two of those things I'm quite happy to not have on my list of milestones,' she joked.

Sharna's countenance brightened. 'Me too. Anyway, tell me about this place you're doing up.'

'There's not much to tell, at the moment. I just got the keys from the agent this afternoon, as apparently she's—'

'Going to Bali?' Sharna finished with a giggle. 'Told you no one's allowed secrets in this town.'

'Wow. You weren't kidding. Anyway, I only got to have a quick look around today. I'll go and take some more pictures tomorrow, before I head back to Adelaide.'

'I thought you were staying here longer?'

Gabrielle sighed. 'I was planning to, but the office has called me back in to sort a new account. Once that's done, I should be able to work from here while the renovations are finished. I'll keep my room, though, save you hauling my cases back down the stairs tomorrow,' she added with a grin.

'You mean you already have tradies organised? You must have some pull, if you can get them to come out here. Mum had a bathroom reno done last year, and she had to drop a grand on a shower screen before they'd even come out from the city to measure up. Generally, there's no such thing as free-measure-and-quote once you get this far out.'

Gabrielle forked the last of her meat into her mouth. 'Don't tell me that. I'm already getting cold sweats because contractors aren't returning my calls. Though I do have one guy organised for the end of the week. Well, loosely organised, anyway.'

'If you're stuck, the local guys will muck in. I'm sure we can all hold a paintbrush, get your place freshened up in no time.'

With a start, Gabrielle realised that Sharna thought she was moving in to a regular house. Which wasn't really surprising: not many people would take on a derelict pub. But if she corrected the assumption, would it sound like she was flaunting her privilege? 'It's going to need a bit more than a coat of paint. Last year's earthquake shook it up.'

'And you still bought it?' Sharna seemed surprised. 'No shortage of places for sale out here, you should have picked one with no damage. The quake was pretty localised. We got cracks in the dairy, but the house was fine. Which was a pain; the house we could have lived with, but the dairy Dad had to have fixed, pronto.'

'I bought it before the damage. So, I'm stuck with it now. Who did your dad get to do your repairs? Maybe I'll have to look them up if I can't get anyone from the city.'

'There're a few locals. You won't find them listed—most probably aren't even licensed. But their work is good, so no one cares.' Sharna shrugged off the blatant flouting of regulations. 'I can put you on to someone, if you like.'

'I might take you up on that,' Gabrielle said, without meaning it. No way was she having an unlicensed cowboy work on her project.

Sharna pushed away her plate with a satisfied groan. 'Darn it, I got side-tracked and didn't get that drink. Not sure I can fit it in now.'

'I was hoping you'd be up for dessert,' Gabrielle said.

Sharna gave her a quick glance, her freckled cheeks colouring. 'I'd normally jump on that offer. But how about a raincheck? In fact,' she looked down, tracing the bleached heat rings on the table top, 'if you want to get on-side with the local tradies, there's a barbie at Juz's place tomorrow.

You met him last night. The blond guy with a crap sense of humour.'

'No, that's okay, I—' Gabrielle started to trot out the usual litany of excuses, perfected in the face of Brendan's insatiable need to socialise. Then she checked herself. New start, new life. Even though her place was a few kilometres out of Settlers Bridge, this was the nearest town and was obviously going to become her local centre. She knew the importance of building brand trust, and that would be enhanced if the locals knew and liked her. She pressed a hand against her chest, subconsciously checking her V-neck hadn't slipped.

Clearly Sharna mistook her reluctance for nerves. 'Come on, you've met most of the gang. They're all real chill. And, speaking of chill, Juz has a pool. It's heated. Last chance for a swim before it gets really cold.'

'I consider it plenty cold enough already.' Gabrielle couldn't help but smile back. Sharna's enthusiasm was contagious, though there was nothing that could persuade her to don a bathing suit.

She'd sworn off anything that revealing more than a decade ago, when Amelie's death scarred her body and soul.

11
Hayden

What the hell was she doing here?

Hayden's hand tightened around the neck of his beer bottle.

Sharna waved across the shed at him. The unusual excitement lighting her face would normally leave him stoked, but the company she kept immediately put him on guard: Gabrielle.

As usual, she was overdressed—although even Sharna had done herself up again. He'd been amused last night to see her in heels. Hadn't even known she owned any. Usually she'd show up at a barbie wearing jeans straight from the dairy, yet today she wore a tight blue pair with suspiciously even slashes above the knees, which didn't quite emulate the artfully ragged gashes on Gabrielle's undoubtedly expensive pair. Sharna wore a tight jumper with a ribbon tied around her throat, which he couldn't help but compare with the fitted top Gabrielle had worn the previous evening.

'Wheaty!' Sharna bounced over and gave him a one-armed hug as he lumbered to his feet. 'Look who I found.'

'Not hard finding someone in a town this size,' he said dryly, offering Gabrielle a tight smile. Damn, no matter how he wanted to downplay it, she looked good—but in an artificial, calculated manner. He had no time for that; he liked his women real. Though he probably should get used to liking them online, because that was the only outlet left for someone like him.

'Hey.' Gabrielle's smile was as tight as his. 'Hey, Trigger.'

'Oh!' Sharna blurted. 'You're not supposed to speak to service animals.'

He scowled at her. At least Gabrielle had made the effort to remember the dog's name. And, though she would look more comfortable if she had parked her tight butt on a box of chisels, she wasn't backing away from Trigg. Probably only because she considered Juz's shed close enough to being outdoors to meet her expectations of where animals were permitted.

'It's okay. Not like Trigg's doing anything,' he said, trying to minimise the dog's importance to him. 'Didn't realise you were staying on in Settlers.'

Gabrielle tilted her head down at Sharna, who was hovering close to her. 'Sharna has a persuasive tongue.'

'Is that so?' He quirked an eyebrow, glancing from her to Sharna, who was looking very pleased with herself. For her sake, he could make the effort not to be a total turd. 'I'm sure there are worse places to be.'

Sharna slapped playfully at Gabrielle's arm. 'Sadly, Gabs' presence has nothing to do with my tongue. She's doing up a place here. Right, Gabs?'

'Something along those lines.'

Gabrielle's responses struck him as more uptight than Sharna's excited babble, but each to their own. 'Get you a drink, ladies? I'm pretty sure there won't be any Yaldara Reserve in the tub, but there might be some pear cider lurking towards the bottom.'

Sharna scrunched her face. 'Soft for me, thanks, Wheaty.'

'A cider would be great. Thank you.' Gabrielle's cultured tone invested the words with a believable gratitude.

And Sharna was right; he was a total arse. Hayden aimed a kick at the icebox as he flipped the top open. Even if there had been nothing wrong with him, Gabrielle was now strictly off-limits.

He passed a can to Sharna, then wiped the dew from the cider bottle on his shirt. 'Slippery,' he excused his chivalry, twisting off the metal cap before passing it to Gabrielle. 'Sorry, no glasses.'

'That's fine, thanks.' Gabrielle clinked her bottle against Sharna's can. 'Bottoms up.'

He had to tear his gaze away as Gabrielle tipped her neck back, the graceful golden column worthy of a sculpture.

Sharna didn't bother looking away. When she finally noticed his eyes on her, Hayden gave her a grin. She blushed and spoke hurriedly. 'Well, I'm going to hit the pool. Still sure I can't persuade you, Gabs?'

'Positive,' Gabrielle said vehemently. 'But where is this pool?' She glanced around the shed.

Their group had been using Juz's place to hang at since primary school, but for the first time Hayden viewed the setting as an outsider.

It was a shed.

Sure, it was a large shed, solid stone, nicely whitewashed inside. But still a shed. Old vinyl benches, ripped from a school bus one of their mates had found in the wrecker's yard in Murray Bridge, were strewn around, facing one another in groups of two or three. On one wall, beneath strings of multi-coloured fairy lights the girls had put up was a rank of eskies, a fridge that had at least a decade up on him, a long, flat barbecue of questionable cleanliness, and a couple of rusted drums filled with empties. Juz would eventually return the bottles and cans to the recycling yard and reinvest the ten cents he got back on each in gas for the barbie. Down the far end of the shed, as far from Hayden as he could make it, there was a fire blazing in a forty-four–gallon drum. Juz, Luke, Taylor and a couple of others were chatting down there, but he knew they would take turns circulating up to this end, where the fresh air blew in through the open doorway, cool and sweet.

Another wall had a long, heavy metal sliding door, suspended on flywheels. He could see by the look on Sharna's face that she was glad the door was closed, so that she got to do a big reveal with the pool. And his heart cramped.

While they all rated Juz's pool—it was a darn sight warmer than the river at this time of year, and had none of the filthy carp, which stirred up the mud—he could imagine how it would look to a city chick.

Despite the chill, Sharna ripped her jumper over her head, revealing a milk-pale body in a tiny yellow bikini, instead of her usual shorts and T-shirt. Hell, she was going to give Juz a coronary.

She toed off her Rossis, then yanked off her jeans. From the old school-logoed backpack she had dropped near his feet when she hugged him, she pulled a frayed bath towel. 'This way.' She flitted, as light as a butterfly, towards the door.

Shit. It was like watching someone stumble in slow motion, knowing the impact was inevitable. There was no way a woman like Gabrielle would react to their pool in the way Sharna expected.

Gabrielle glanced at him as they followed Sharna. 'Not swimming?'

He shook his head. 'Not my thing.' Not anymore.

'Good.' She shot him a grin in answer to his questioning look. Perfect lips, predictably perfect teeth. 'I won't look like the lifeguard sitting out by myself.'

'Well, I guess a couple of us have to act like the grown-ups, right?' he said, rubbing at his chest. The sudden lightness there surprised him. Why the heck should he care that maybe she actually had a sense of the ridiculous?

'Hey, ladies,' Juz called as he intercepted them. Sharna danced ahead, her feet no doubt freezing on the cement. 'Cover's off, Sharn. I take it you're not game, Gabrielle?'

'Someone has to be the cheer squad,' she said.

'I offered to lend Gabs a cozzie,' Sharna piped up, 'but she has a list of excuses for not swimming. C'mon, it's out here.'

As Sharna dragged Gabrielle forward, Juz slowed his pace, dropping back next to Hayden. 'Wish she'd taken Sharna up on that offer, huh?' he muttered.

'Those togs would never fit the body she's rocking,' he agreed. Not that he was looking. The response was a habit. 'What's the water like?'

Juz grinned. 'Cold enough to freeze the nips on a seal.'

'You're welcome to it, then,' he said. But the truth was, he missed swimming. Or rather, he missed the freedom of being able to strip off and swim if he felt like it. Today though, he decided as Sharna tried to drag the heavy door open, today wouldn't be so bad. At least Trigger wouldn't be his only company.

Juz moved in to lend his strength, shoving the door along an unlubricated rail, and Hayden watched for Gabrielle's reaction as it screeched open.

A tiny frown creased between her eyes, then she turned her molten-chocolate gaze on him. 'A water tank? Or a well?'

'Or a swimming pool,' he said. At least she recognised the huge stone structure.

'Heated, you said?' Gabrielle lifted her voice as Sharna stepped ahead of them.

Hayden snorted. 'That might be overselling it, Sharn. Juz chucks a solar blanket over it at night,' he added to Gabrielle.

Gabrielle walked to the tank and tilted her head back to look up at it. 'That's freaking awesome. Who has a stone swimming pool? And it's, what, about three metres high?' Her eyes huge with interest, she didn't seem to be faking her curiosity at all—but it would have sat far better with him if she'd been contemptuous of their country-style swimming pool. That way she would fit neatly into the opinion he had formed of her.

As Sharna darted to the ladder and platform Juz had built, Hayden reached down to fondle Trigger's ears, as though the contact would remind him of Gabrielle's haughty demeanour a couple of days earlier. 'It's far deeper than that. This was the catchment tank for all the sheds on the property. From before mains water connections, so it had to hold a summer's worth of water. It goes well into the ground.'

'In-ground, stone and deep? Wouldn't it be like, absolutely freezing, then?' She pulled an appalled face and he struggled against the realisation that, even when she was deliberately distorting her features, she was gorgeous.

'Guess there's only one way to find out.'

Sharna called back, 'He's right. And better you do it now, Gabs. Skinny-dipping comes in three drinks' time.'

'What a shame I can only have one drink before I head back to the city,' Gabrielle said dryly.

'I thought Sharna said you were hanging around?' Damn, why did he even ask? He sure as hell didn't care, beyond wanting Sharna to be happy.

'Coming and going.' Gabrielle pointed up to where Sharna had reached the platform and was silhouetted in a burst of sunlight that darted golden shafts between threatening banks of dark clouds. 'Wow, that could be a Constable, don't you think?'

It took him a moment to switch gears. 'The painter?' he hazarded. 'I don't know much about him.'

Her head was still tipped back, her face in profile as she admired the sky. 'John Constable. He was really into clouds, but I bet he never got to see anything as spectacular as the skies out here.'

Sharna squealed as Juz grabbed her around the waist, threatening to throw her into the tank, and Gabrielle hesitated, her fingers curled around the wooden ladder. 'Is it safe?'

'Juz knows how to nail a couple of planks together. You'll be right.'

'I meant more along the lines of, am I going to get soaked? I don't know how Sharna isn't blue.'

'No promises.'

To his surprise, Gabrielle started to climb, balancing on the balls of her feet with the narrow heels of her boots hanging off each tread.

'Stay, Trigg.' He took a hold of a rung, sucking in a breath as he prepared for the tug in his shoulder. But as he glanced up, the view was enough to take his mind from the pain for the first time in months.

Hell. He clenched his teeth, dropping his gaze to stare stonily at the rock wall inches in front of him. It would do him no good to look up. It didn't matter how tantalising that tight arse was, bobbing up the ladder ahead of him—Gabrielle wasn't interested. And he wasn't able.

'Oh my god. This is amazing!' Gabrielle said.

The realisation that Juz was there with her got Hayden up the ladder faster than a ferret down a burrow.

Gabrielle glanced back at him as he topped the ladder. 'This is awesome. The walls are so wide I could lie on them and sunbathe.'

With more than half a metre of stone, she could spread out like a starfish. He grunted at the mental image.

Juz whooped as he tossed Sharna in, then wrapped his arms around his knees and cannonballed after her.

'Oh!' Gabrielle squealed, whirling away as the water erupted in a geyser over her. Her heel caught between the rocks and she lurched towards him.

He reflexively took a stride forward, wrapping his arms around her and easily holding both of them steady. 'Okay there?' Did he ask only so he had an excuse to breathe in the perfume of her hair as her head tucked neatly beneath his chin, her hands pressed to his chest?

She didn't pull away, merely leaned her head back, her eyes dancing as she laughed. 'Oh my god, I should have made you promise! That water is bloody freezing! And I'm soaked.' She twisted to face the pool, but stayed within the circle of his arms. 'Sharna, how can you? You're nuts!'

She had her balance now. He should let her go. But he hadn't had a woman in his arms for . . . longer than he cared to think about. And, regardless of why she was there, it felt damn good.

Until, as she twisted further in his embrace to catch Sharna's giggled answer, Gabrielle clutched his arm to keep her balance, digging her talons in.

His left arm.

He smashed his eyes closed, clamping his teeth together.

He wasn't even certain that her touch hurt, or whether it was the memory of pain, or the fear of pain. Or the terror that she would feel something beneath the thick compression bandage. But, fuck, he felt like he'd been kicked in the guts.

Still laughing at Sharna, Gabrielle didn't notice his reaction. Her soft blonde hair whispered across his face, cool and silky as she turned back to him. 'How good is your fireman's lift? I'm not sure I'm game to let go.'

What the hell? Had Sharna told her? He snatched his hands back abruptly. 'I'll go down first. If you fall, you'll land on me.'

Confusion at his terse tone flashed across Gabrielle's face, and he suddenly doubted whether Sharna had said a word. Still, he needed to back off. Gabrielle was taken. And in any case, she would never have been his type. Maybe his brief flare of interest was because not only was she unattainable but it was safe to fantasise about something he didn't truly want. It saved him from having to invest any effort or risk rejection. Gabrielle was about as far from

being the type of woman he would ever be interested in—
would ever *have been* interested in—as granite was from
sandstone.

Still, as she navigated down the ladder in those stupid
boots, he reached up to grasp her waist.

As though she read his mind, Gabrielle pulled a wry
face as she reached the ground. 'That's the second time I've
tripped in these this weekend. I'm going to have to get some
work boots.'

He refused to wonder who had caught her the first time.
'Sharn will be able to steer you clear on that.' He glanced
at her shoes. 'Depends on how long you're hanging around,
but one of my sisters might have something you can use.'

'Spangled and fit for dancing in the snow?' she shot back.

He allowed himself a brief smile. 'Glass slippers will give
you the same trouble you're having right now.'

'But there's always a handsome prince attached to them,
right? Fair pay-off.'

Sharna had followed them down the ladder. She tow-
elled her dripping hair, a scowl flitting across her face.
'Didn't think a prince was on your wish list?' she said to
Gabrielle, a querulous note in her voice.

Gabrielle unwound her wide, soft scarf and draped it
around Sharna. 'You're making me feel cold.'

All her animosity instantly disappearing, the glow that
came off Sharna was enough to warm all of them.

And, damn, he was jealous. Jealous that yet another
of his friends was going to disappear into that halcyon
cocoon of a new relationship, jealous that it was never

going to happen to him. And jealous that Gabrielle would always be unobtainable, at least to him. Which was ridiculous because he'd already assessed her—a habit from when he had choice and standards and dreams—and found her wanting. Even when he had been in the market, he'd been set on the type of woman he wanted. Someone who wasn't afraid of hard work and getting dirty, someone who would stick up for their beliefs, had their own dreams and wasn't just riding life.

Gabrielle had an air of being pampered and cossetted. She was the type who put on a show, lapping up the adulation. She wasn't real.

Still, she was real enough to have Sharna bubbling with happiness, and that's what he should be focused on. 'Gabrielle said she's heading back to the city today,' he said carefully, hoping it wasn't news to Sharna.

Sharna pulled a face, but looked less disappointed than he felt. 'Yep. But only to finish up some stuff. Right, Gabs?'

'Yeah, I—'

'Oh,' Sharna butted in excitedly, snatching at Gabrielle's forearm. 'Wheaty would be able to help you out with your reno. He's a builder.'

His stomach turned to concrete. The last thing he needed was to hang around Gabrielle's house.

Evidently, she agreed. She gave another of her tight smiles. 'Ah, I've already made some calls. Hopefully, I'll have the contractors I need organised by the end of the week.'

'Sure. Give me a yell if you fall short,' he said, without meaning a word of it.

'Aw, yeah. Sorry, Wheaty. I wasn't thinking,' Sharna said as they walked back inside the shed. 'You're still limiting what you do, right?'

He glared at her. She made it sound like there was something wrong with him. 'No. Full on at the moment,' he replied shortly. Now he'd have to take on the jobs he'd been putting off, just to make his words true. Which meant getting out of the comfortable little bubble he'd created of only seeing the same dozen-or-so people. If he ventured beyond his group, he'd be hit with a new wave of commiseration and far-too-interested questions from the well-meaning community who all knew his story but would be hanging for a firsthand recount. Hospital had been bad enough. He'd been a goldfish in a bowl: constantly watched, fed on schedule, bathed on schedule, as far from master of his own destiny as it was possible to be. On discharge, he had become pretty much a recluse until Taylor dragged him out of it. But the last thing he needed now was to return to that oppressive level of observation and hungry interest in his private business.

Gabrielle glanced uncertainly from him to Sharna. 'Well, I'll keep that in mind. Anyway, I think I'll head off now. I want to get a few more photos while it's still light.'

'Oh, already?' Sharna practically pouted. 'You're not staying for lunch?'

'Last night set me up for a good while,' Gabrielle smiled, and Hayden wondered if he imagined the subtext. 'I'll see you on the weekend.'

'Feel free to call during the week. You know, if I can do anything to help.' Sharna's attempt at being nonchalant fell flat, and Hayden dropped an arm across her shoulders.

'C'mon, Sharn, get your gear on. That barbie is smelling mighty good.' He directed a nod towards Gabrielle. 'Catch you next weekend, then.'

What the hell was he talking about? She'd made no mention of seeing him, wasn't part of their group.

And it wasn't like he wanted to see her again.

Except, he did.

12

Ilse

It was rather nice to have the young woman's company again, Ilse thought as Gabrielle strode towards the Ladies' Lounge, notebook in hand.

'Okay, take two.' Gabrielle's fist slammed onto her hip, and she huffed out a frustrated breath. 'What on earth were they thinking?' She stared at the glistening walls. 'Can this even *be* painted over? It's so . . . black.'

Ilse tottered after her as fast as she could. 'I assume it would need an undercoat. Or three. But we—oh, wait!' A flash of memory surprised her . . . She was dancing with Ronald after hours, when she was supposed to be cleaning the tables and collecting the odd teacup that had found a home in one of the large pots of aspidistra Mother had placed around the elegant room. With Jimmie Davis crooning 'You Are My Sunshine' on Opa's gramophone and her cheek against Ronald's shoulder, they circled more slowly than the music warranted, until Ronald manoeuvred her into a corner alongside the plants. As he pressed her back, she placed her palms against the solid coolness of the wall behind her, seeking some kind of grounding as his handsome face, unusually serious, moved close enough that she could smell the Brylcreem he used to slick his dark hair. Every inch of her skin awake to his presence, she was achingly aware of his warm breath against her cheek, the dimples of the textured wallpaper beneath her fingertips and the coarseness of the brush of his trousers against her naked calf as he crushed the red plaid A-line skirt she wore. His ice-blue eyes were intent as his hands slid up her arms to the puffed short sleeves of her white button-down blouse.

And then, for the very first time, he kissed her.

His lips, oh she remembered the firmness of his lips. And, though he was clean shaven, the surprising roughness of his strong jaw when she dared reach to trace a finger along his cheek.

There had been so many kisses since that first one. Their relationship wasn't perfect; there were fights and arguments, disagreements and squabbles, where she would refuse to speak to him for a day or two. But never had they stopped loving one another.

As she had not allowed death to steal those memories, dementia had no chance. However, she did need to force her mind to the task at hand.

'Perhaps . . .' she began tentatively—after all, Gabrielle might have her own ideas for redecorating. But what harm could there be in making a suggestion? 'Perhaps we could have it wallpapered instead?'

'Would wallpaper work?' Gabrielle asked.

Ilse hunched one shoulder, her cracking vertebra supporting her mother's caution: *Ladies Do Not Hunch*. 'I don't see why not.'

'But what colour? There would need to be a theme, something that ties the rooms together.' Gabrielle tapped a fingernail against her teeth. 'And I suppose that would depend on exactly what I'm using each room for.'

'A tea lounge, perhaps? Not all women are comfortable in the front bar, even now.' Ilse had never been particularly keen, herself. 'During the fifties it was quite the thing for the farmers' wives to take afternoon tea in their best frocks, the children scrubbed as though they were on their way to church. I suppose we all like to play make-believe on occasion.'

Gabrielle tilted her head to one side. 'I don't know . . .' she said doubtfully.

'Well, I presume if you are fortunate to be born into a certain lifestyle, imagination becomes somewhat less necessary,' Ilse snapped, then remembered she should pull her horns in. Gabrielle was including her far more than the previous owners had. 'Anyway, the children would run off to play in the willows along the riverbank while the women practised their elegance, sipping tea and chatting over cake. Oma had the most beautiful tiered cake stands.' She tutted, glancing around as though she would spy the china lurking in the gloom. 'I'm certain they must be packed away somewhere. Nothing ever leaves this place. Perhaps in the cellar? I seem to recall there being wooden packing crates and boxes down there, along with all sorts of furniture.' Years ago, she had regularly raided the cellar to furnish her castle.

Gabrielle moved across the room, investigating the far wall as though the dark paint might be a tad less bleak close up.

'Oh, I do know where the scone plates are, though!' Ilse called, welcoming the sudden clarity. 'Mother always put out scones, as well. But they were more for the children. The women would never admit to fancying something as mundane as a scone when there were delicacies to enjoy. I suppose, if you think about it, the farmers' wives were themselves enjoying the chance to pretend to be an eclair rather than a scone.' She laughed self-consciously. 'Well, that is a rather ridiculous analogy, isn't it?'

'I think it could work,' Gabrielle said, her lovely blonde hair swishing gracefully as she nodded. Although she didn't turn towards Ilse, an appreciative smile curved her lips.

For all that Gabrielle kept her own counsel and her reactions conservative, she was a good listener, Ilse decided. It was rather nice to guide someone along the winding paths of her memories. But perhaps that was why young people—herself included, when she had been among them—were abrupt with the elderly? The trip down memory lane could take almost as long as the original journey, travelled, as was requisite, at a more sedate pace. Each recollection discovered hidden among the autumn leaves and windfalls unlocked a new path, and memory meandered at whim. Young people had no patience for that kind of thing. Except for Gabrielle, who seemed able to bide her time and bite her tongue.

'Maybe this could be a breakfast room?' Gabrielle asked. 'Or even a morning room. If it was wallpapered with something light and pretty to evoke a sense of springtime gardens . . .' She formed her stretched fingers into a square, holding them before her face as though framing a photograph in her mind.

'Yes!' Ilse barked a little too eagerly as Gabrielle tugged the notebook and pencil from her pocket.

'And we could source some funky little occasional tables and mismatched lounges covered in beautiful fabrics, where customers could curl up and read. If that fireplace still works . . .'

Ilse grimaced dubiously. She couldn't remember the last time any of the fires had been lit, superseded as they had been by gas heaters and then by air conditioning, but she didn't have the heart to ruin Gabrielle's enthusiasm. 'I'm sure the chimneys could be swept.'

'Then in winter we could have a log fire. Vases of seasonal flowers to make it fresh and inviting—does anything flower in winter?'

'Jonquils, daffodils, hyacinth, lavender,' Ilse supplied quickly. They were all available for the picking in her gardens.

'It would smell divine. The perfect winter weekend getaway, cosy inside while watching the rain pound against the windows and lash the river.' Gabrielle smiled, her hair shifting like quicksilver as she moved animatedly around the room. 'The trick is to find the points of difference that make staying here an experience, rather than simply an accommodation option. Oh!' She whirled around, pointing with her pencil. 'A library. Or, at least, bookshelves. On that wall, there.'

Ilse cocked an eyebrow. The young woman's notions were a little on the whimsical side, probably in keeping with her age and lack of life experience. A library didn't belong in a pub. She stared at the recessed wall Gabrielle indicated, mulling the idea in her mind. A library would be odd . . . yet, surely, fanciful was preferable to those revolting poker machines her grandson had wanted in here?

Gabrielle's enthusiasm was contagious. In her mind Ilse could envisage the setting the younger woman proposed. Maybe somewhere in the cellar were the waterfall side-boards they had used in the Ladies' Lounge. 'Perhaps if we placed nesting tables alongside the chairs?' She cringed as she realised she had used 'we', but Gabrielle pretended not to notice, so she rushed on. 'They could be decorated, but "use-fully". I have a wonderful collection of gardening magazines that would look quite lovely displayed. And perhaps a nice fountain pen and a newspaper folded open to the cross-word—far too few people tackle the crossword, nowadays.' Too lazy, in too much of a hurry, and possibly not intelligent enough, she supposed. 'Oh, and how about music? Not the radio. I have a Glenn Miller collection that would be just perfect.' The LPs retained the richness of the day they were recorded. Her grandchildren had tried to persuade her that their devices produced sound almost as good—and had, indeed, given her a ridiculously tiny electronic gadget—but nothing matched Opa's gramophone. Almost giddy with excitement, Ilse fanned herself with one hand. The atmosphere in the new Ladies' Lounge—or Morning Lounge, if Gabrielle preferred—would be genteel; sophisticated in a way Oma could only ever have dreamed of.

Gabrielle crossed to one of the unbroken windows, easing the latch to open it. Wrapping her arms around her slight frame, she stared across the withered grey grass towards the lake-like expanse of the river. 'With that soft fringe of green and gold willows, it's like stepping into a Monet. Oh!' She clapped a hand across her mouth and whirled back to Ilse, her eyes huge with excitement. 'I have it! The verandah is deep enough to be an alfresco area . . . and I can market the experience as a living art gallery.'

Enthusiasm bubbled in her voice, but Gabrielle wasn't being practical.

'It gets terribly cold in winter,' Ilse cautioned.

Gabrielle pointed thoughtfully towards the back of the building. 'The rear courtyard is quite protected. No view, of course, other than all the stunning stonework, but it has kind of a nurturing, country vibe. Perhaps if I have it roofed?'

Ilse shook her head doubtfully. 'There's the big river gum out there . . .'

The fine golden triangle of her earring brushed her shoulder as Gabrielle considered the issue. 'Or only partially covered? In something sympathetic, like huge rustic beams, maybe shingles. A couple of fire pits, so the area is useable year-round, and encourages people to linger. Would that offer another experience?'

'Absolutely,' Ilse agreed. It was rather odd to be so included in the plans for the hotel after so many years, but it certainly was not unpleasant. Although, she did wish away Gabrielle's tendency to mumble.

Gabrielle stared up at the ornate ceiling rose above them, as though she could see through it. 'But is that really creating an experience, or simply a nice setting?' She scowled, her elation dropping like a chiffon scarf. 'I suppose I need to find out if there are any rooms I can rescue for accommodation, before I get carried away.'

'Ah, yes.' Ilse rubbed at her forehead. All this planning was exhausting. 'You go ahead and have a look. I'll pop the kettle on.' And perhaps have a sit down for a moment, although there was no need to dampen Gabrielle's enthusiasm with her fatigue. 'I'll be up in a minute,' she said to Gabrielle's back as the young woman took the stairs two at a time.

Ilse sighed in envy. It had been so long since she had been youthful enough to dash up the stairs like that. Her boys had done the same, and their children ... Again the shadow darkened her mind, but she shook it aside and headed towards the kitchen, humming softly.

13
Gabrielle

It was almost three weeks before she managed to get back to Wurruldi—or, at least, as far as Settlers Bridge. It took sixteen days of that time for her to realise that, while Brendan needed her help creating an upbeat new profile for an artisan cheesemaker, he was manufacturing reasons for her to stay faster than the cheesemaker was manufacturing triple-cream brie.

That realisation saw her slapping a fat sum on a storage unit and a pile of new luggage. The Overland would do just fine for a few days while she did a rush job of getting a couple of rooms at her property to a basic degree of liveability.

Or it would be a rush job if she could find anyone to actually work on it. Despite leaving messages with a dozen more contractors, only four had returned her calls; two to say that Wurruldi was well beyond the radius they were prepared to travel. In desperation she called Wayne Learman again, only to get a repeat of his story about coming for a drive out there 'one day'. She had, however, succeeded in arranging a glazier and locksmith, though she'd had to pay through the nose for their mileage from the city.

Now, with every kilometre she travelled towards Settlers Bridge, the constriction in her chest eased. Although renovating the hotel was a daunting task, she'd had time to dwell on it, to consider how best to make it over. It was problematic, difficult and challenging, yet she felt enthused. She would actually get to create something from scratch, rather than put a spin on someone else's concept, and that offered such scope that unfamiliar eagerness bubbled within her.

Eagerness—or passion? Could Brendan be right? Was this what had been missing all her life?

She shook the thought away, cracking open her window. The air was fresh and crisp, hints of cypress pine and eucalyptus filling the car as she whipped along the narrow bitumen roads between fields of green crop that were punctuated every so often by a paddock of sheep wrapped in their winter woollies as they browsed the low vegetation.

As she crested the hill overlooking the valley that cocooned Settlers Bridge, she couldn't help her gaze straying towards the end of the main street and The Settlers pub, where she had met Wheaty.

She hadn't spared a thought for him over the past few weeks.

Well, not many.

Though she had left her suitcases at The Overland earlier in the month, the receptionist wouldn't take extra payment. 'I'm sure your bags weren't using any power or water. And it's not like we needed the room. At least, not in winter. Things pick up, come summer,' she said, waving away Gabrielle's credit card.

'Are you sure, Lynn?' Gabrielle asked, reasonably certain she remembered the woman who had taken her dinner order weeks earlier. 'I don't want to get you in trouble with your boss.'

Lynn chuckled. 'My boss? No worries there, lovey. Go on, up you go.' Her burgundy hair trembled towards the stairs.

'I'm making a habit of this,' Gabrielle said as Sharna helped lug cases up the hotel's carpeted stairs fifteen minutes later.

'Of what?' Sharna gasped, hair straggling in wild wisps around her face. 'Winning over the female population of Settlers Bridge?'

'I meant of getting you to haul my gear around. Though that receptionist is super nice.'

'Lynn? She's okay.' Sharna sounded a little short.

'Do you think her boss will kick up?'

'Her boss?' Sharna heaved the case up another step, then looked at Gabrielle. 'You don't want to judge a book, Gabs.'

Gabrielle smiled as a comforting sense of familiarity warmed through her. 'Let me guess: Lynn has some sort of trade deal going with the mysterious Chef Alex, too?'

'No need: Alex works for her. Lynn owns this place, plus the IGA. Not that you'd ever know it from looking at her. She puts in hours at both. Used to do a bit of house-keeping in her downtime, too.'

'Downtime?' Gabrielle said incredulously. She blew side-ways to move sticky hair from her cheek.

Sharna laughed. 'If you didn't know her, you'd think she needed the money. But she reckons she just likes to keep busy.' She groaned in exaggerated relief as she reached Gabrielle's room. 'Travelling light really isn't your thing, is it?'

Gabrielle paused to catch her breath, leaning on the extended handle of her hard-shell case. Her backpack threatened to topple her down the steep stairs. 'You should see how much I put into storage.'

Sharna turned the key and elbowed open the door. 'You are joking, right?'

'Not even smiling.'

'Wow.' Sharna surveyed the room, already crowded with cases Gabrielle had hauled up. 'How do you wear so many clothes?'

Gabrielle sighed. 'I'm sure I don't know. What I do know is that I'd better add a cabinetmaker to my list of tradies-who-don't-bother-coming. The bedrooms at my place are really basic, no built-in robes.'

Sharna flopped onto the bed, screwing her hair into a messy bun and snapping a tie from around her wrist to secure it. 'Well, I can fix you up there easily enough. Remember Juz? The pool guy? He's a cabinetmaker. And I keep telling you, Wheaty is your guy for anything else you need doing.'

'He really didn't seem too keen on the job.' It appeared she had a knack for ticking him off—although . . . she had thought they had a moment, there on top of the water tank. Years of yoga guaranteed she could have caught her balance without his assistance. Failing that, she could have extricated herself from his arms instantly. But his grip had tightened as he tugged her against his chest and, for a few seconds, she had luxuriated in the contact, the feeling of taking shelter, of being protected.

Brigitte would insist that her stumble had been deliberate, albeit subconscious, a symptom of her search for validation. Even if that were the case, surely she was entitled to gloat a little, considering Hayden had seemed equally loath to end the embrace? Until he'd pushed her away as though she'd electrocuted him. Talk about mixed messages. Why did men have to be so complicated?

Sharna bounced up and down on the bed a couple of times. 'Nah, that's Wheaty being Wheaty. He'll help you, for sure. He's just a keep-it-to-himself kind of guy nowadays.'

'Nowadays?' She hiked an eyebrow.

Sharna yawned hugely, covering her face with both hands. 'Ugh, sorry, Gabs. Cows are such early risers. I'm glad you're back, but is it okay if I wait until tomorrow to hit the guys up to get your house sorted? I'm kind of crashing right now.'

'Of course! You didn't need to stay up just to haul my bags around. I could have managed just fine.' She'd said as much when Sharna texted to check on her arrival time, but Sharna had been insistent.

'Well, that's obviously not the only reason I wanted to be here when you arrived.' Sharna suddenly looked wide awake, playing with the faded maroon tassels of the bedspread, the colour high on her freckled cheeks.

Gabrielle shot her a distracted smile, her fingertips tingling with an ill-timed remembrance of the feel of Hayden's chest beneath them. 'But there's really no need to bother Juz and Wheat—' No, she couldn't bring herself to use the nickname, as though he were something more than a passing acquaintance. Even though her fingertips insisted otherwise. 'And Hayden. I managed to get a locksmith and a glazier in last week, so I guess that's some progress and proof I'll get there eventually. And I'd rather pay a contractor full tote than ask for any level of favour.' She gestured at her bag collection. 'As you can see, mixing business and friendship ends up messy when guys are involved.'

Sharna straightened slowly, sitting determinedly erect. 'This lot has to do with a guy?' She waved towards the luggage, her tone oddly accusatory.

Gabrielle snorted. 'Well, my partner. Not that that makes him less of a guy, but you know what I mean.'

A deep frown creased Sharna's forehead, her gaze intent. 'I'm not sure that I do. You said you weren't into guys.'

Gabrielle unshouldered her backpack, confused by Sharna's sudden change in attitude. Was she angry because Gabrielle refused to use Wheaty and Juz for the renovation? If that were the case, they had the job, no questions asked. Over the past three weeks she had enjoyed the relaxed friendship she and Sharna had fallen into. The short messages and quirky farm videos—like the one of cows galloping after Sharna's quad bike down a muddy road, which was funny enough to go viral—had become a highlight of her day. Each time her phone buzzed with the promise that she could escape her desk and into the countryside for a few minutes, her heart lifted in anticipation. And maybe it also beat a little faster because each message from Sharna flicked her thoughts to the enigmatic Hayden Paech.

Gabrielle forced her focus back to Sharna. 'Sorry, I can't imagine why I would say that.' Because she was definitely interested in guys. One in particular.

She had spent hours at her desk compiling portfolios of the photos she had taken of her property, expanding on them with pencil and ink mark-ups of her planned improvements. As always, she doodled in the margins of her notes. But now the sketches were of a face.

Which was ridiculous, she reprimanded herself each time she caught her pencil betraying her subconscious. She wasn't a teen, enjoying the pleasurable pain of yearning for the unattainable. Yet Hayden's initial reserve and subsequent inscrutability made him strangely thrilling and completely intriguing.

Sharna nodded assertively. 'You definitely did. You said you had zero interest in there being a Mr Gabs.'

'Oh,' Gabrielle dropped the bag, relief lightening her tone as the misunderstanding made sense. 'Yeah. That's because my ex is being a dick. We were supposed to have made an adult break—you know, where you keep acting nice to the other person's face while secretly judging everything they do.' She grinned at Sharna, inviting her to the comfortable solidarity of dishing the dirt on men in general.

'Ex?' Sharna barked the word, her eyes huge. 'I thought you meant you're a lesbian.'

'No,' Gabrielle chortled. 'Mind you, Brendan's got me tempted to consider swapping sides,' she added, unzipping her vanity case and starting to lay the bottles on the laminated chest of drawers. 'Do you reckon the light is better in here for doing make-up, or the bathroom? I hate not having natural light; I'm always afraid I'll head out looking like Trump.'

'Consider?' Sharna hissed. She thrust up from the bed and slammed her arms across her chest.

Estée Lauder pump in hand, Gabrielle froze. 'Consider what?'

Sharna's beautiful pale skin was marred by two spots of angry colour on her cheeks and her narrowed eyes flashed with fury. 'You'd *consider* being a lesbian? Let me guess: you didn't have to *consider* whether to be hetero, right?'

Gabrielle gaped at her as she slowly connected the dots and understanding dawned. 'No, no, I didn't mean—' she eventually stammered.

'What *is* it with people?' Sharna stormed. 'You don't *think* about being gay. It's not like a dress you try on and then toss to Goodwill when it doesn't fit right, or a new perfume you wash off because you change your mind about the smell. You either are, or you aren't. It's fucking simple.'

'Hey, calm down.' Gabrielle dumped the make-up and patted the air with her hands, trying to placate her friend.

155

'I didn't mean it like that. It was just a stupid word choice. I'm used to joking around with my sister-in-law—'

'Oh, fan-fucking-tastic,' Sharna sneered, tears shining in her blue eyes. 'So there are two of you *Karens* having a laugh about it? That makes me feel so much better.'

'No!' Gabrielle's stomach knotted in dismay. How could she, of all people, have screwed this up? 'Let me explain. Please.' She edged between the cases, grabbing at Sharna's hand. 'What I said was inexcusable—'

'You understand inexcusable generally means that you're not going to try to come up with some lame-arse excuse?' Sharna said, her chin trembling, although Gabrielle didn't know whether it was with fury or hurt.

'Sharna, you have every right to be angry with me. I was out of line and said something really stupid. It's just how my sister and I used to joke around. I guess it was my way of trying to empathise.'

Sharna dragged her hand from Gabrielle's grip. 'Bullshit. You said *sister-in-law* before. Can't you even get your excuse straight? And why the hell would I want your *empathy*?' She spat the word like an insult.

'Not you. I meant I was trying to get a handle on my sister *and* sister-in-law's perspective.'

Sharna's eyes widened, but her tone was cautious. 'Your brother's wife?'

'No brother, remember? But for three years I've had the most amazing sister-in-law. Sharna, I'm so sorry. I screwed up.' She knew her tone was wheedling, but this vivacious young woman had become important to her. Perhaps it was because she represented an escape from the world in which Gabrielle had always existed—or maybe, lacking artifice, Sharna was the embodiment of what Gabrielle truly wanted to be. Whatever the basis of their bond, Sharna's pain was a result of Gabrielle's thoughtlessness.

And the worst thing was the realisation that, if it had been Hayden throwing out hints and tentative feelers, she would have been all over them. But, self-absorbed as usual, she had been oblivious to Sharna's overtures. Even when Sharna mentioned that what she wanted from life wasn't considered the norm in the tiny community, Gabrielle had naively assumed she referred only to her desire to move to the city.

She closed her eyes for a second, sick at her ignorance. How the heck did she fix this? She groaned. 'Sharn, sometimes I say inappropriate, ridiculous things without even thinking. Foot in mouth, you know?' Or silver spoon in mouth, maybe. With money came popularity, so she had never needed to learn to be careful with her words.

She looked beseechingly at Sharna, who stared back stonily. 'Look,' she continued, 'I know it's juvenile and crass, but making jokes with Brigitte and Caroline about my sexuality seemed like a way of acknowledging what they were going through. I realise that it isn't, that it can't be, but I don't know what else to do. There's no way I can put myself in their—your—shoes.' Like Brendan said, she was privileged; everything came easily to her.

At least, everything had. Until now. When it finally mattered.

'No. You're dead right you can't.' Sharna's shoulder hit Gabrielle's arm as the redhead stormed towards the door, shoving suitcases out of her way. She paused, her fingers bleached white on the door jamb, hurt and betrayal clear in her wounded blue gaze as she glanced back at Gabrielle.

'Sharna, I'm so sorry. I don't know what I can say.'

'Nothing,' Sharna whispered.

The slam of the door trembled through the sunset print on the wall.

14

Hayden

The rough stone grazed his palm as he hefted it but, as always, the friction felt almost like a caress, gratitude from deep within the rock as he placed it where it would rest for the next couple of hundred years.

'Are you finished, then?' Nan asked.

He startled. For an old bird, Nan had a hell of a stealth mode going. Or, more likely, he'd been too absorbed in his task to hear her shuffling approach. He dusted his hands against his jeans and nodded towards the final topper he'd placed, a large piece of rough-hewn sandstone as deep as the wall was wide. The slab would help tie the construction in place, the weight and width acting as an anchor and cementing the smaller rocks interlocked like a jigsaw beneath it. 'I reckon that'll do, but you're the boss. What do you think?'

Nan had a mean eye and a sharp tongue when it came to judging his work. She stood back, critically surveying the knee-high drystone wall. Then she shuffled forward and hunched slightly as she sighted along it, apparently ascertaining whether the border he had built was straight.

Hayden started to gesture towards his string line and levels, but checked himself; Nan would be satisfied when Nan was satisfied. No amount of attempted persuasion would win him any accolades. She'd done the same with each side of the ten-metre square garden, and he'd resigned himself to only moving on to the next wall when he'd finally got her tick of approval. Nan wasn't above telling him she didn't care for the colour or form of a particular rock, even if it was in the middle of the wall. He could try to persuade her it fit perfectly, but it was better he saved his breath and rebuilt it the way she wanted.

'Where are the bulbs you dug out?' she asked. The ground had been hard-packed with years' worth of corms that had gradually failed to flower in the shade of the jacaranda.

He tipped his head from side to side to release the crick in his neck, then gestured across the grassy expanse. 'In the shed. Dry, single layers, in hessian sacks, ready for you to divide,' he added, forestalling what he knew would be her next questions, particularly given that she had already asked them multiple times. Over the past year or two, Nan had developed a habit of repeating herself. 'Once you're happy with the wall, I'll put them back in for you.'

Carefully. There would be hell to pay if he damaged one of her precious plants.

Nan tutted with exasperation. 'You can put in the bearded iris, but the Dutch will have to wait a month or two until it's cooler, now.'

'Sorry. The job took longer than I expected.' *To be fair, he hadn't rushed it. There was something cathartic in the process of creation, especially with stone. Maybe because he knew it would endure. He'd spent months on the project, selecting each rock carefully, slightly tapering the wall from the base to the top, placing a tie stone through the width of it every metre or so. Every few rocks, he would stand back to assess the construction for form, strength and colour, making sure the mottled patchwork of cream, rust and grey sandstone was visually appealing. Unless Nan changed her mind about where she wanted it, the forty metres of hard labour would outlast them both.* 'Work's been kind of crazy. Plus, you know, Mum . . .' *He let the sentence trail off. Certain words shouldn't be spoken; it was as though his breath would give the disease life.*

Nan's steely grey eyes pierced him. 'How is she?'

He hunched one shoulder, sliding his gaze past her to stare at the graphite slick of the river.

'Hayden?' *Nan said, her tone sharp.*

'Dealing with it,' *he muttered.*

'And your father?'

'Also dealing. In his own way.'

Nan snorted. 'Which I take to mean he's still acting like an ass?'

He shot Nan a grateful grin. She always told it how it was. No fake little-old-lady sweetness in her. 'You know it.'

'Stupid man. He'd be lost without Susan. He'd do well to appreciate that.'

'Oh, he knows it, right enough. It's all an act.' When Mum had found Thing, as she called the lump, seven months back, Dad had lost his shit. Slammed out of the house as though it were her fault. He'd come back a couple of hours later, of course—he and Mum never spent time apart. At least, not until she'd gone into hospital for the mastectomy. But even though the Old Man still demanded his dinner on the table at six sharp so he could watch the news while he ate, even though he still traipsed into the lounge room in his filthy boots, despite thirty-odd years of Mum's nagging, even though he still complained when Mum and the girls got giggly over some TV show, he'd changed. Now, for all his grumbling, Dad would often go quiet. More than once, Hayden had caught the Old Man staring at Mum, as though he were trying to fill his memories. Just in case.

And that scared the shit out of Hayden. Mum and Dad were supposed to be as solid as the rock walls he created. They might not always fit together perfectly, but by supporting one another they were sound, their foundation unshakeable.

'They'll be just fine, Hayden.' As frequently happened, Nan knew his concern ran deeper than the obvious. 'Life isn't supposed to be a straight path. Imagine how very boring that would be. Anyway, speaking of straight . . .' She

gestured at his wall. Maybe it was a generational thing, but Nan had never been one for sentimentality. It wasn't that she didn't love; more that she was damn sure where she stood and expected others to follow suit without needing to wear their hearts on their sleeves. 'Some things are worth waiting for.'

Like it had since he was a kid, his chest swelled at Nan's sparse praise. 'Good-oh, then,' he said gruffly. 'I'll start getting the topsoil into the bed this afternoon.'

Nan twisted her arm to look at the watch encircling her thin, liver-spotted wrist. He was pretty sure she couldn't see it, but she clucked her tongue. 'It's early. Come into the house for some morning tea, and then you'll have time to get the soil in before lunch.'

'Slave-driver,' he grumbled. 'It'd better be wattle-seed cake.'

'Of course,' Nan replied, as though there had never been room for doubt.

'And coffee,' he called after her as she started to pick her way across the summer-wilted grass towards the river.

'Tea,' she called back without turning around. 'Wash your hands.'

He grinned. She would make him coffee, but serve it in a teacup. Nan always won.

∾

She peered intently at his hands as he took a seat at the glass dining table in her small cottage. He held them up for her inspection, and she gave a tight-lipped nod. Then *she coughed, a dry bark. Hayden frowned. 'Have you been in to Settlers to see Taylor about that yet?'*

She gave him a withering glare. 'If I went to your lady-doctor friend every time I coughed or sniffled, she would be one wealthy young woman. You worry too much.' With painstaking concentration, she placed a cup in front of him. 'Your great-grandmother's china, so be careful.' She supplied the same admonishment each time, as though he were still a kid. Although lately she had begun to drop one of the 'greats' from the title, as though time had leaped a generation. 'Speaking of lady friends, you need to bring in some manure to layer with the soil. Though not where the iris are to go.'

He cocked an eyebrow. 'Am I missing the connection?'

'Manure.' Nan snapped her fingers testily. 'Cows. Perhaps go and see that lovely little redhead you're sweet on over at the dairy.'

'Sharna?' He shook his head. 'Nothing happening there, Nan.' Despite her age, Nan's observation skills were some-times too sharp.

'Well, be that as it may, she can still get you some manure, right?' Nan wielded a knife to slice a large slab from the domed ring cake.

He frowned as her hand trembled, the cake shuddering precariously as she used the flat blade to lift it onto a tiny, floral-bordered plate.

She snorted with exasperation, passing him the plate and drawing her cardigan closer. 'It really is too chilly today. If it continues this cold, those bulbs will be able to go in before March.'

His frown deepened; she had only just remarked on it being too warm for the plants. And it was hot: normally he would work shirtless, but that offended Nan.

She coughed again, the harsh bark deep and phlegmy now, not the dry tickle he'd noticed a week earlier.

He blew out a long breath, knowing she would argue. 'I'm going to call Taylor, see if she can get you in this afternoon.'

Nan observed him for a long moment, then she nodded. 'All right, then.'

Her acquiescence shook him. He would far rather she had argued, insisted that she was fine.

'Eat your cake,' she directed. Nan wasn't much of a cook, preferring to spend her time in the garden, but there were a few dishes she had perfected. 'Your great-gran's recipe,' she said, as though he didn't know—and again skipping a generation.

'Perfect,' he mumbled around a mouthful, realising his mistake as he spoke.

Yet she didn't chip him on the breach in manners, seeming distracted, her gaze wandering to the small-paned window. 'Dad should be in soon, I'd best boil the kettle again,' she murmured.

'Dad's coming by?' he said, then drained his cup. 'Good. He can help me manoeuvre a couple of big rocks into place to make steps up into the garden.' He didn't dare mention it was because he doubted Nan would be able to climb *over the low wall. 'I'll go put in some dirt. The first layer, that is, then fetch manure,' he qualified, knowing the raised grey brows meant he was about to cop a lecture.*

∾

His stomach was growling by the time Nan made her way outside again. He'd wheelbarrowed enough loads of dark, rich loam from the mountain she'd had delivered to mound near the base of the tree and had replanted the gnarled bearded iris corms. Sharna would be up from her nap to do the afternoon milking, soon. He'd catch her at the dairy and organise to load his ute with cow dung.

'Very good. I'll trim the leaves back on the iris this afternoon—' Nan broke off with a tut as a chime sounded from his jeans pocket. 'Those telephones . . .'

'Not a phone, Nan. CFS pager.' He pulled it from his pocket and checked the small screen. 'Hang on, Nan.' He dashed across to his ute and grabbed the portable VHS unit. 'Settlers Bridge Brigade Captain responding to pager. All members to station.' As he gave his title, his chest swelled with pride. It was new, and it sure as heck wasn't going to get old anytime soon.

Nan shuffled over to join him.

'Gotta go check this grass fire out, Nan.'

'Is it close by?' She squinted towards the river, although the rust-coloured cliffs blocked any view.

'No, it's the plains on the far side of Settlers. I've called Taylor; she'll get you in at four today. I shouldn't be too long, but I'll text Dad to take you when he gets here, okay?'

Nan looked confused. 'Your father's coming?'

Hayden had been folding his tall frame into the ute, but paused. 'You said he is.'

Her grey curls bobbed as Nan shook her head. 'No, I've not heard from Mark in ages.' Then she smiled. 'But your grandfather will be here in a moment. As soon as his shift finishes.' She gestured towards the river, and a chill rippled through Hayden.

Nan pointed at his radio. 'You'd better go, Hayden. Fire service captain, and all that.' His recent appointment had been one of the rare moments she had shown her pride in him. Yet it was disconcerting that she could remember that, but not that her husband had been dead for a decade, the ferry he had operated rotting on the far side of the river.

'Yeah. Look, I don't have to go, Nan. It's voluntary . . .' Still he hovered uncertainly. Static crackled through the two-way, and he knew the other members were calling in. Part of him itched to lean into the car and tune the radio; another part of him keened towards his grandmother. She was definitely scattier than usual.

She coughed again, reeling unsteadily and gasping as though she were short of breath.

Right, that was it. He was taking her to Taylor.

Chatter broke through on the CB, discordant voices from different units, their tones betraying a mixture of alarm, adrenaline and excitement: '. . . big . . . five resources . . . got in behind plantation . . .'

'Go,' Nan urged, her hands pushing against his biceps without making an impression.

'Okay,' he grunted reluctantly. 'But I'll be back as soon as I can. Make sure you're ready to head into Settlers.'

By the time he reached the fire station base, he'd already called through and had the fully-crewed Isuzu tanker head out. Donning his two-piece yellow overalls and black boots, he grabbed his yellow helmet, rubbing his thumb over the red panel that marked him as the captain, even though it already glistened like blood, given that he'd damn near polished it off after training.

'Flip you for the keys,' Simmo called over the bonnet of the white LandCruiser.

'Support trailer hitched? Good job.'

A contract worker at one of the piggeries over the river, Simmo was relatively new to the brigade. As the aging population of the district made fresh volunteers few and far between, Hayden had been stoked to see him turn up at training every Tuesday night for the past couple of months.

This was the first multiple-appliance call-out the unit had got since Simmo joined, and it was obvious the guy was wired. Hayden headed for the passenger side of the Quick Response Vehicle. 'All yours then, mate.' In any case, he needed to think about Nan some more.

A while back, he'd talked about moving closer to her. For all she treated him with a mixture of caustic indifference and occasional pride, Hayden knew he was her firm favourite. And he sure had a soft spot for the old battle-axe. He saw a lot of himself in her impatience, her inability to tolerate fools, offset by a consuming passion for her interests. But, all things considered, it would be better if *she moved in with him. That way she would be closer to Dad, her youngest son—and maybe the girls would find time to come over and keep her company when they only had to cross a handful of paddocks.*

Of course, tearing Nan away from her beloved garden would cause a drama of epic proportions.

He refocused on the dirt road unravelling before them. With less than five-hundred litres on board the Toyota, they would soon catch up to the tanker hauling a three-thousand-litre water tank.

'Hit it,' he ordered Simmo.

∽

Hayden tossed restlessly, thumping his pillow into submission. The flashback sent him into a cold sweat. Not only because he knew what the next instalment would be—the nightmares always took the same pattern—but because seeing Nan gouged at his insides, the shame raking through him like the licking tongues of fire.

'Yeah, Trigg, come on up,' he said in response to the dog's nosing. He shifted his bulk across the bed, flinching as he rolled to his left. When was this ever going to end? The anger, the guilt, the difficulty sleeping. At least he'd been spared the daytime flashbacks. He could take the meds Taylor prescribed, but they would just give the nightmares a surreal edge, they didn't actually block the damn things. Besides, after sixteen months, he should be able to deal with this shit himself. He'd thought about looking it up on the internet, seeing if there was an end date, but that would mean typing in the words. *Post-Traumatic Stress Disorder.* And that was all kinds of damn wrong: he was no soldier, no war hero. It had been bad enough claiming the condition so he could get the dog—though really, that had all come down to Taylor, he'd just added a signature wherever she indicated.

Trigger nuzzled a wet nose into his armpit, taking full advantage of being permitted on the bed.

As he rubbed his thumb hard on the furrow between the dog's eyes, Trigger relaxed against him with a comfortable sigh. Hayden gave a rueful chuckle. 'Jeez, mate, thought you were supposed to make *me* feel calm?' Funny how the dog had come to mean so much to him. He'd grown up with more animals than he could count, but he'd never been this invested in one before. Part of him fought the attachment: the average lifespan of an Australian Shepherd was nine years. Even with the best of care, Trigger wouldn't see out the decade. But, while the thought ripped at his guts, the dog's death wouldn't be his fault.

It was strange how Gabrielle had shied away from Trigger. He'd never met anyone who had a fear of dogs—well, of any animal other than snakes or spiders.

Gabrielle. He stared up at the ceiling, the web of cracks in the plasterboard invisible in the dim ambient light filtering through the dusty window. If it wasn't for the side serve of guilt, he could quite happily lose himself in thoughts of that woman for a while. Why couldn't his dreams be about her? He would hurt no one that way, and he'd spent so much time reimagining the moment she had been in his arms, it only seemed fair she should take over his subconscious. It took everything in him not to ask after her each time he saw Sharna.

He closed his eyes, blowing out a long breath. Dreaming about Gabrielle would bring pain, but only when he woke to find it wasn't true. Surely that was preferable to the never-ending hell of his memories?

∞

'Hey, slow it down, mate,' he said as the Toyota barrelled through the ash-laden smoke. He swiped the stinging grit from his eyes. For over four hours, they'd battled the flames that swept through Talbot's scrub, exploding the spindly gums into instant charcoal and raging underground through the Mallee roots so each dragging, exhausted step of their heavy boots threatened to plunge them into a burning, subterranean hell.

'Where's that bloody airdrop?' Simmo grunted, hunching closer to the wheel, though he didn't ease his foot from the accelerator. The wipers whipped from side to side, fighting against the cinders that pelted the screen. The wind had turned just as they seemed to be making headway against the fire, and now the flames raced parallel to them, across the paddocks towards the homestead, invisible through the choking smoke. Focused on asset protection, Hayden had deployed the main unit to the far side of the fire, but he and Simmo were aiming to get ahead of it. Talbot had a tractor with a blade he used for grading his rubble driveway. If they could get enough of a lead on the

flames, Hayden would grab the equipment and carve a break between the paddocks and the farm yard. He knew the property well; in his mind, he had already drawn the grid he would scrape clear.

He flicked a finger at the two-way. 'Coming in. But a light load because of the heat.' The halfway-decent morning had turned breezy but, feeding on the thick undergrowth of the ungrazed scrub, the fire created its own unpredictable weather patterns. The wind whirled, forming tornados that sucked the flames up in a cone before spurting them free in a volcano of ash and burning debris.

'Ease up, mate.' He snatched at the grab handle above the door. Simmo didn't seem exhausted: in fact, the guy was pumped. They all got an adrenaline kick when they were out fighting the fire, but Simmo had something else going on. Hayden frowned. Simmo was eager. Not only keen to get on top of the fire; he was admiring the damn thing.

As they jolted and bounced along the rough dirt track, Simmo whooped. 'Man, look at it go! The bloody thing's getting away from us!'

'Talbot's driveway should be coming up on the left,' Hayden warned, unease prickling sudden cold down his spine. 'Fuck, slow it down, man. She's jumping the road!' The fire swept in suddenly from their right, only a hundred metres ahead. The tongues of flame stretched to lick eagerly at the thin scrub that lined the left side of the road. 'Slow down!' he yelled again, as they barrelled towards the centre of a whirling furnace.

'Oh man, oh man, oh man,' Simmo chanted. Hayden tore his gaze from the road. The flickering of the flames danced across Simmo's gleeful face as he leaned eagerly towards the inferno. 'We're gonna be heroes, mate. We're gonna put this sucker out and be goddamn heroes!'

Holy shit, the guy was baked. 'Jesus, this is a QRV unit, Simmo! We're not equipped to go in. Pull off. Pull off now!'

He caught one more flash of Simmo's elated expression before the darkness enveloped them with a suffocating totality relieved only by the tiny glowing-red demons whipping by the windows.

The dash buckled.

The heat sucked the oxygen from the air.

Flesh melted.

And Simmo's insane laughter filled his ears.

15
Ilse

It was a shame her old legs couldn't match the pace of her over-excited heartbeat, Ilse thought as she shuffled from room to room, seeking a new vantage point. Though she couldn't recall their conversations, she knew she had carefully overseen the locksmith, and had been relieved beyond measure to find that Gabrielle had instructed the glazier to replace not only the breakages, but every one of the windows. In place of glass scratched by decades of polishing gleamed panes clearer than rainwater, each separated by half-inch wide timber bars painted burgundy to match the freshened exterior surrounds.

The inside sills were still peeling, and the carpets, littered with leaves and dirt, smelled of mould, but things were finally happening. The building already felt more . . . solid. She gave a sharp nod of satisfaction. It didn't matter how many years had passed since the pub had belonged to her family, still she felt a sense of responsibility that extended beyond her garden domain.

That garden, though. She wound the chain of the locket Ronald had given her decades ago around her fingers as she looked down at the paddock reaching for the glisten of the winter river beyond the lacy-leafed jacaranda. She couldn't understand how the acreage was getting away from her. Though it was certainly a long time since she had been able to manage the grounds by herself, she had hired help. There was a man to do the hedges and mow the grass, and one to dig new garden beds or plant trees, always under her direction.

But there had been another, someone who did the work for ... duty? For love?

Her fingers tightened on the gold heart. Someone who had failed her when she needed him most.

16
Gabrielle

After Sharna slammed from the room, Gabrielle sat on the bed, slightly stunned. How the heck could she backpedal from this mess? And why was it that no one in this town was what they seemed? She'd had a somewhat derogatory opinion of country folk, expecting them to be a little simple, bland and predictable; she certainly hadn't anticipated this spider's web of twisted dualities. There was the wealthy Lynn working menial positions, Sharna hiding her sexuality even while the local guys were obviously panting after her, and Hayden ... well, Hayden. What was his story? It seemed he knew something about Sharna, yet he was oddly protective. And Sharna knew something about him, too. What secret was he hiding?

Gabrielle angrily thrust that thought aside; she had no right to mull on what amounted to a fantasy. What she needed to do was find a way to make good on her self-centred ignorance. She texted an apology—another—to Sharna, and waited for a reply as the room grew dim around her. None came.

Eventually, leaving her cases still packed, she went downstairs and stepped out onto the deserted footpath. She let her gaze travel slowly along both sides of the darkening street, probing the shadows as though she might find Sharna sheltering beneath the hooded verandah of one of the shops. There wasn't a soul to be seen. Belting her khaki Isabel Marant trench coat tightly as the wind tried to push her down the road towards the bridge spanning the inky river, she crossed two lanes. On the centre island, great arching stems of bougainvillea whipped and swayed wildly where they escaped the top of three-metre–high sculpted iron cages. She swerved around them and scuttled across the next two lanes and up the steps into The Settlers.

Maybe she would find one of Sharna's friends here, check if Sharna was okay.

Apparently, The Settlers was not the place to be on a Wednesday evening. In stark contrast to the Friday night three weeks ago, it was almost deserted. An elderly man hunched over his beer on the long counter.

Ant stood behind the bar, his arms crossed. 'What'll it be, Miss Reserve?' he greeted her.

She sighed. Her drink choice was hardly what she wanted to be remembered for, yet here she had no reputation to fall back on; she had accomplished nothing worthy of note other than being the stranger who ordered an unusual drink. So much for her grand plan of making her solo mark on the world. Still, it had been less than a month since she'd struck out alone. She had always been impatient, but this was clearly the wrong part of the world to exercise that trait.

'House white, please,' she said, though she would rather have dashed back across the stormy street to what now seemed the warm welcome of her room in The Overland.

Ant nodded with something that could have been approval. Either that, or his jerky movement was to reinforce his direction to her to sit. 'Coming up. Take a pew next to Young Eric.'

She eased onto the bar stool.

The old man twisted with arthritic slowness to look at her, giving a toothless smile. 'Missy,' he lisped.

'Gabby,' she corrected. In a town full of nicknames, using her full name suddenly seemed pretentious.

Ant slid the brimming glass of wine in front of her. Apparently, the serving line etched a third of the way up the glass was irrelevant.

She unclasped her bag and took out her wallet.

The negative movement of Ant's shiny head reflected the overhead light. 'On the house. I hear you're about to be a local.'

'Well, actually I'm quite a way out of town . . .'

Ant shrugged, his neck disappearing like a turtle's. 'Being in the district makes you local. Don't have to live in the town.'

'Okay,' she nodded. The idea of being considered a local somewhere held a surprising amount of appeal. Even though she had favourite coffee shops and restaurants in the city, she was a regular, not a local. She had always found the notion of a life spent in one place where your every moment—every secret—from cradle to the grave, was known, bizarre. But her brief glimpse of Sharna's relationship with her group of friends revealed the flipside of that intimacy: loyalty. That contrasted strongly with her experience where everything, from clothes to holidays to work, was a cause for rivalry among her peers.

'Cheers.' She lifted her drink to Ant, and Young Eric laboriously reached across to clink his bottle against her glass. 'Where you at?' he said.

'I, uh . . .' She glanced down towards her stool. 'Here?'

Ant shook his head. 'He means where are you living. Right, my man?'

Young Eric nodded vigorously.

'I, well, I'm staying over the road at The Overland.' She darted a glance up at Ant, feeling a little guilty.

'Good call,' he grunted, pulling a towel from his shoulder to polish a glass.

'And I bought a property out at Wurruldi, which I'm planning to restore.' Simply speaking the words aloud gave her an unexpected burst of enthusiasm. Tomorrow, she would head out to Wurruldi and check how the place looked with the new windows. A thrill of ownership and potential ran through her. Although she had co-owned the apartment with Brendan, the possession had never truly excited her. The purchase hadn't been made because they had loved the floorplan or desperately wanted a home, but more because it had seemed the appropriate time in their relationship for them to act like adults. The original purchase of the hotel had been for much the same reason: an investment. But the property had begun to call to her, encouraging her dreams.

'Wurruldi, ya say?' Young Eric asked, cupping his ear.

'Yes. It's up the river a little.'

'Yup, I know right enough where it is. Sad place, that.'

'What?' She put her glass down in a rush. 'Why?'

'That's enough, Young Eric,' Ant said. 'Past is past. No point getting in Gabby's ear about it.'

'Past is never past. Not until it's finished. Not while some are still living it. Or not living it,' Young Eric said, his pragmatic tone at odds with his mysterious words.

'Don't pay him any attention,' Ant said. 'I should've put two and two together. Had some guy from the city in here last week saying he'd been doing some security work upriver. Top up your drink?'

Gabrielle put her palm flat over the top of the glass. 'No. I mean, no, thank you.' She turned to Eric. 'What's sad about Wurruldi? I mean, it's a little rundown, but not . . . sad?' Yet, as she said the words, she realised that was exactly what the place was: sad. Sad and unloved, yet it seemed that there was so much more beneath the surface, that the façade was a pause, a brief hiatus, as though the hotel waited for something. Or someone.

A shiver ran up her spine, and she lay her hand on Young Eric's arm. 'What can you tell me about Wurruldi?'

'About where, now?' Young Eric turned bleary eyes on her.

'Wurruldi. Where I've bought a property.'

'Wurruldi?' Young Eric said slowly, considering, as though he'd never heard the name.

Gabrielle looked up at Ant, hoping he'd help. He shook his head. 'He's done for the night.'

She lifted her glass and raised her eyebrows at the bartender. 'Too much?'

'Nah. Not that,' Ant said. 'Old-timer's.'

'Oh. I'm sorry.' She mashed her lips together, not sure what she should say.

'No need. We take care of our own in Settlers. Speaking of, are you all right by yourself here for five minutes, while I run him home?'

'Is that even legal?' she asked in surprise, but then held up her hand. 'Actually, it doesn't matter. You do what you have to, I'd better head—' she gestured towards the door '—you know, across the road.'

'All right, then,' Ant said, dropping his chequered tea towel on the bar. 'Quiet night, anyway. I might as well close up. I'll see you home.'

'I-er-I'm only staying at The Overland,' she reminded him. Perhaps Young Eric wasn't the only one afflicted with an unreliable memory.

'I heard you. But we're heading out the door, so we'll see you to yours. Right?'

The trip back across the rain-swept road, hampered by Young Eric's shuffling steps, was slow enough that the tips of her hair were dripping onto her collar by the time they reached the frosted glass door labelled *Accommodation* at

The Overland. 'You'll be right now, Gabby?' Ant asked, his large hand holding the door open.

'Fine. Thank you,' she said, still bemused. There had been neither a car nor a person in the main street. 'Do you have much trouble round here?'

'Trouble?' Ant's face creased in a ferocious scowl. 'No. Why?'

'Just you . . . walked me across the road.'

Ant's neck did the disappearing-in-his-shoulders trick again. 'Yup.'

'But if it's not dangerous . . .'

'It's the right thing to do,' Young Eric announced with sudden startling clarity. 'We look out for our own round here.'

'Until you give us a reason not to,' Ant added ominously. 'Night, then.'

She leaned out of the doorway, watching as the tall man matched his stride to the shuffling older man and they slowly made their way up the street. For a short time, they had taken her mind off the mess she'd made of her friendship with Sharna, but now she had a whole lot more to keep her awake all night.

∾

As she expected, she slept poorly, her mind churning with thoughts of her screw-up with Sharna, but flitting to Young Eric's strange hints. And Hayden. As always, she couldn't shake thoughts of the enigmatic man who seemed to command both friendship and something else . . . maybe a quiet concern, as though his friends were watching out for him? Exactly as Ant had said. Her thoughts drifted to his parting words, which had sounded like either a challenge or a warning. Lying on her back, staring up at the ceiling, Gabrielle huffed out a long breath. There was definitely something odd about Settlers Bridge, as though layers of secrets lay beneath the façade of a simple, friendly country town.

The knock on the door jerked her out of bed, and she rushed across to it, raking her fingers through her hair. She was sure she hadn't ordered room service, but perhaps Lynn had decided to duplicate her order from her previous stay.

Sharna leaned against the door jamb, a look of wry amusement on her face. 'I should have known you'd look good even when you've clearly just crawled out of bed. How come you're not up and out at your place yet? Thought you needed to check whether the locksmith has finished up? You should have used Sully's from Murray Bridge. Always pays to go local, least you can get them back easy enough.'

As she spoke, Sharna leaned in for a hug. Instinctively, Gabrielle stiffened, over-cautious about sending the wrong message. Again.

Sharna jerked back, slamming a hand on her hip. 'Oh, for Pete's sake, get over yourself, Gabs. I'm not going to jump your scrawny bones.'

Gabrielle felt the colour flood her cheeks. 'Sorry. I'm an idiot. You'd think I'd know how to act, right?'

Sharna scowled. 'Of course you should,' she snapped. 'Because it's like, "This is my token lesbian friend. She's queer, so she will say *this*, think *this*, do *this*."' She took a step back. 'Except I'm actually a person, you know. Not a sexuality. There's no way to *act* around me. And no bloody need to act.'

Gabrielle felt sick as a wave of embarrassment washed through her. 'Oh my god. Again. You're right. I wish Brigitte had told me to pull my head in years ago.'

Sharna thrust a hand through her long, spiralled curls. 'Just stop tiptoeing around me like you're in a paddock full of cow shit. If I was some guy you'd told to screw off, you wouldn't be the least bit worried about how I'm handling it. Do me a favour and treat me the same as you would all of the blokes you've blown off.'

Gabrielle closed her eyes for a second, trying to re-centre. 'You're right. Except for the multiple guys bit, anyway. It's just I know this is a much harder gig you've ch—'

'If you say "chosen", I'm going to slap your face.'

'I know,' Gabrielle pulled a wry expression. 'And I'm trying really hard to think of another word that starts with *ch* to cover my arse.'

Sharna gave a flash of her old grin. '*Ch*ugged,' she supplied. 'You owe me a chug of Moscato by way of apology. And don't worry, I won't make a move on you. Guide's honour.'

'Is that even a thing?'

Sharna rolled her eyes. 'Like I'd know. Here girls have a choice of the CWA or netball when it comes to social outlets.' She must have caught Gabrielle's over-concerned look, because she groaned. 'Jeez, Gabs. Settlers is only an hour and a half from the big bad city. And we actually do have phone signal and internet, even out here, you know. I'm not exactly alone and desperate.'

Gabrielle scrubbed her face with both hands. 'Okay. Do you think we could just wind back a day and pretend I'm not such a huge idiot?'

'We can. But do me a favour.' Sharna looked suddenly nervous, chewing at her lower lip. 'Just keep it on the down-low, okay? Not everyone knows.'

'I'd figured there are a few who don't. Justin springs to mind.'

'Yeah, him. And, well—' Sharna stared down at her muddy boots, knocking the toe of one against the carpet. 'Well, technically, no one knows.'

So much for her assumption that the residents of the small town lived in each other's pockets.

'Except Wheaty. He doesn't officially know, but I'm pretty sure he *knows*, you know?' Sharna grinned at her own words. 'He's got kind of this thing, where he deflects his own problems by worrying about the rest of us.'

'He seems . . . nice,' Gabrielle said carefully, ignoring the ridiculous way her heart beat a little faster at his name, as if she were suddenly sixteen again.

Sharna rolled her eyes. 'Oh, so that's the way it's gonna be? I'm going to lose my new best friend to my old best friend?'

'Hardly. I didn't come here to find a man. More to escape one.' And to find herself.

Oblivious to her dirty jeans, Sharna dropped onto the mussed bed, lying on her stomach. 'Tell me more,' she said, her chin propped on her hands, her feet waggling behind her. 'But get ready while you're doing it. The guys are waiting downstairs.'

Gabrielle had started to laugh at Sharna's demand, but almost choked. 'The guys?'

'Yeah. Juz and Wheaty. I told you they'd come to help out. And, adorable as your bedhead is, I suspect you're not going to be quick getting ready. So, shift it.'

'Oh, but I don't even know what I need done. That's half the problem,' Gabrielle stammered.

Sharna slapped at the bedcover. 'Well, they'll be able to set you straight.'

'No offence, but that's about the last thing I need from a man,' Gabrielle said, tugging blue jeans, a turtle-necked black bodysuit and a cable-knit cardigan from her case. The tight bodysuit would give her a nice silhouette beneath the loosely-belted, chunky woollen.

'Do tell,' Sharna prompted, her eyes alight with a wicked gleam. 'Who has driven the lovely Gabrielle to desert all her friends, flee the big city and end up square in the middle of nowhere?'

Her back turned as she slid into a bra and pulled on the turtleneck, Gabrielle thought that over for a moment. 'Not so much a who, as a what. I figured it was time for a change from the whole scene.'

She turned to catch Sharna's frown. 'A sea change I get,' Sharna said. 'But this place is barely even a tree change. What the heck is the attraction?'

Gabrielle pulled on the cardigan and used it as a screen as she snapped the bodysuit then wriggled into her Levi's. 'No, a change of scene, not scenery. Everything back in the city seems . . . superficial, I guess.' Maybe her growing dissatisfaction with the phoniness of her lifestyle, the shallowness of her friendships, was why she'd seized on Brendan's taunt that she lacked passion, using it to shock herself from a numb existence. 'Everyone I know there is focused only on what money can buy. Even our achievements are purchased. In fact—promise not to laugh?' She paused, waiting for Sharna's nod. 'It's like we're all playing at being grown-ups, we never really have to be accountable.' She didn't want to make it sound as though she moved in wealthy circles, but that was the truth of the matter. And part of her issue. 'I needed to get out, to breathe, to find a challenge where there was actually a risk. Because if there's no chance of failure, there's no true success.' She shot Sharna a sheepish grin. 'Whack, huh?'

'Well,' Sharna said dubiously, 'if the short version is that you wanted to find a place where there's zero money and a good chance you'll screw up, you sure chose well. But you're kind of the most-together person I know. I mean . . .' She waved a hand at Gabrielle's quick change, then at her suitcases.

Gabrielle rolled her eyes. 'Trust me, a lot can be hidden behind a few nice pieces of clothing.'

'You call this a few?' Sharna teased with a grin. 'Oh, hang on,' she added as her phone buzzed. She rolled onto her side to tug it from her pocket and then checked the screen. 'The guys are getting antsy. Are you ready?'

Gabrielle jerked a thumb towards the bathroom. 'Got to brush my teeth and stuff.'

With a groan, Sharna rolled off the bed and pushed herself upright. 'I'll go down and delay them with another coffee, but they're already baconed up; I can only buy you so long. And I've got to be back for afternoon milking, so don't dawdle, okay?'

'Sure,' Gabrielle said. 'And hey, Sharn?' As the younger woman paused at the door, Gabrielle shot her a smile. 'Thanks for the do-over. And for organising the guys.'

'No worries,' Sharna called back sunnily. 'I just hope you know that friendships are harder than relationships. No chance of make-up sex to fix your screw-ups.'

Gabrielle only managed a half-laugh. Sharna was right; she would have to tread carefully because she certainly had a talent for creating those screw-ups. She strode into the bathroom. She had ten minutes, tops, to make herself look as hot as possible.

Because Hayden was downstairs. Waiting for her.

Butterflies flitted in her stomach but she assured herself that it was excitement at the prospect of finally getting the renovations at Wurruldi properly underway. Nothing more.

17
Hayden

Hayden traced circles in the spilled coffee on the table, ever larger and faster, as though he were winding up his own emotions.

'You're wired, Wheaty,' Sharna remarked. 'What's up?'

He bit back a sarcastic laugh. 'Nothing.' Just because he had spent the past three weeks wondering when—and if—Gabrielle was coming back to Settlers, there was no reason for him to be nervous now, knowing she was only minutes away. Hell, a few nights he'd even dreamed about her, dreams that were hot enough to make him break a sweat now, just at the memory. They had been a welcome change from the damn nightmares, but he couldn't avoid the thought that he was doing wrong by Sharna.

He'd expected daylight and company would help him shake the fantasy, but if he'd realised it would be so hard to get a grip, he would have shot down Sharna's request for help today. The two women didn't need him: Sharna could easily point Gabrielle towards a builder in Murray Bridge.

Aware of Sharna's inquisitive gaze, he made an effort to control his fidgeting hand, and when he couldn't, he snatched a serviette from the holder and swiped at the coffee spill. If only he could wipe his thoughts so easily.

'Closest you've got to cleaning in a while,' Sharna teased.

'Looks like you've been doing a bit of scrubbing up yourself, lately,' he shot back. Though Sharna wore her regular boots and Akubra, the chequered red shirt tucked into her jeans was unusually clean, considering she had already done the morning milking and shifted the cows to a fresh pasture.

'This old rag?' She ran her hands over her breasts. 'Didn't win me any fans.' She pulled a disappointed face, and his eyebrow hiked in silent, surprised question.

'I wouldn't say that,' Justin mumbled from the other side of the table.

Sharna shot him her sunniest smile. 'Hey, Juz, could you do me a favour?'

'Sure.' He perked up as if she had offered him a gift.

'Could you ask Lynn if there are a couple of pieces of toast or something left over from the buffet, so Gabs can eat on the way? She's taking so long to get ready, it's all going to be cleared off.'

Hayden shook his head as Justin bolted towards the purple-haired cashier almost before Sharna had finished speaking. 'Cruel. You're gonna have to let him off the hook sometime, you know.' He speared Sharna with his gaze, willing her to share. He knew what she hid, knew she did it because she was scared. And he also knew how fear could eat at you during the dark hours of the night so that you were left doubting your right to exist.

Sharna plucked agitatedly at the sleeve of her shirt. 'I know. I should. But—' she lifted one shoulder '—it's Settlers; you don't get to tell just one person here your secrets, you know?'

'You do if it's me,' he said gently. 'In case you haven't noticed, I'm a bit of a loner nowadays. Except when you drag me out of bed to sit here waiting on your . . . *friend*.'

Sharna levelled her gaze. 'Seems she'd rather be *your* friend, Wheaty.'

His heart fair stopped, his hand fisting on the table. 'I thought you two . . .'

'Nope. I was just acting as wingman for you.' Sharna shot him a grin, but it wobbled a little.

Shit, shit, shit. She couldn't be right. Because he needed his attraction to Gabrielle to be completely one-sided.

Sharna pulled forward a strand of her hair, curling it around her finger. 'My guess is that redheads don't do it for Gabs; I reckon she prefers them tall, dark and handsome.' Her smile became more natural, her usual infectious grin as she teased him. 'At least you've got the tall and dark covered. You can always try your luck.'

Panic squeezed at his guts and his hand moved instinctively to his left shoulder. 'Can't.'

Sharna tutted as if she were the one ten years older. 'Come on, Wheaty. You've got to dip your toe—or whatever part of your anatomy you prefer—back in the water sometime.'

He could feel the sour twist to his lips that matched the acrid churn of his stomach. 'What the hell's the point, Sharna, when there's no way I'm going to risk revealing the fucking truth to anyone?'

Sharna's blue eyes flashed with sudden anger. 'Jesus, Wheaty, don't you reckon every single time I get up the guts to talk to someone, I'm shit scared? I have to *reveal* myself,' she thumped her fist on her chest, 'every time. Wondering if I'm going to be shot down, knowing that if I share with the wrong person, my business will be all over town. You're worried about exposing a physical imperfection: I'm worried about exposing *me*.'

The anguish in her tone made him wince. He wished he could make things easier for her. For all that he loved the small-town community, he could see that it was stifling Sharna.

'Vegemite on the toast, love?' Lynn's voice rang across the room.

'Wow, what sort of monster spreads someone else's Vegemite?' Sharna muttered. She craned to see beyond him. 'Maybe a couple of jams, too, Lynn,' she bellowed back at a volume that would bring the cows up from three paddocks away. 'Do you still use Tracey's?'

'Wouldn't touch anything else,' Lynn called back.

Hayden leaned towards Sharna. He had to speak quickly, before Justin reappeared. 'The difference is, there's nothing wrong with you, Sharn.'

'Well, of course there isn't,' Sharna drawled, rolling her eyes and evidently trying to lighten the mood. 'But there's nothing wrong with you either, Wheaty.' She nudged her chin at his shoulder. 'So you've got a burn. I've got a mole shaped like a cowpat. Checkmate.'

'Jesus,' he snorted, torn between genuine amusement and despair. 'You want to see my burns?' Not giving her chance to reply—being Sharna, she would probably say yes—he rushed on. 'Because it's not something you'll ever forget. It's the kind of shit that'd give kids nightmares.' God knew, it gave him nightmares.

Sharna waved aside his words. 'Well, Gabs doesn't look much like a kid to me, so maybe you'd best let her decide.'

He swirled the last of the coffee in his mug. 'Not happening. Anyway, you're forgetting. City chick: not my type.'

Sharna tilted her head, as though awarding him a point. 'If the writing in the loos at the footy club is anything to go by, I know you've sure as heck put plenty of effort into researching all the different types.' She waggled her eyebrows meaningfully but then leaned forward, pushing the remnants of her huge breakfast aside. 'But do you reckon you're overthinking this one? I mean, what do you actually know about Gabs?'

'She's up herself.' He knew he had no right to judge Gabrielle, but tallying up the points against her seemed the only way to protect himself from his pathetic interest. It would have been better if she'd been into Sharna; then she would have been truly untouchable.

Sharna knew what he was doing. 'You can be such a tosser, Wheaty. Yeah, she's from the city, but up herself?'

He slammed his mug onto the table, anger at himself translating into annoyance at Sharna. 'Damn, Sharn, you nag more than all my sisters put together. Yeah, up herself. You forget that whole scene where she had the shits up about Trigger being in the pub?'

Sharna looked at him open-mouthed for a moment and his insides shrivelled with self-loathing. He'd moved on from Gabrielle's blunder, but now he'd dived back in to cling to it like a life raft. '*Whole scene?*' Sharna said. 'All I remember is she was surprised to see a dog there and made a couple of guesses at the reason.'

'Wrong guesses,' he muttered, as if it were a defence.

'Yeah. She made wrong guesses. God forbid any of us should ever assess someone wrongly.'

Simmo's open, friendly personality flashed into his mind. They'd all fallen for the labourer's lines, taken him at face value, judged him likable, trustworthy, one of them. Without exception, they had assessed that lying, psychopathic, arsonist bastard wrongly. It had nearly cost him his life. And the eventual cost—the tragedy Simmo had unintentionally created—was far worse.

Hayden had learned that each goodbye could truly be the last.

Sharna wasn't done. 'You know, recognising a PTSD dog is probably a bit of a learning curve for the general public. You see someone with a white cane, maybe you assume they're blind. You see someone with a service dog, you assume they're blind or deaf. Big deal.' Sharna leaned closer, jabbing one grimy-nailed finger at him. 'You might be doing a bang-up job of fooling yourself, Wheaty, but you're not fooling me. You're making up bullshit excuses just so you don't have to find out anything about her. And I totally get why you're doing it. But you're wrong; you can't live the rest of your life pushing people away because you're afraid of getting hurt. Trust me, it's about the one damn thing I do know.'

She didn't have it completely correct: it wasn't about pushing people away so he wouldn't get hurt, it was about not getting close to those he couldn't save. He forced a short laugh. 'So young to be so wise.'

'Just call me Yoda,' Sharna said, sitting back.

'Pretty sure Yoda was ancient.'

Sharna's eyes widened, but she was looking past him, towards the stairs that led from the first-floor accommodation. 'And I'm pretty sure Gabrielle isn't turning this on for me,' she murmured. 'Wow.'

He didn't want to turn. Knew he shouldn't. He should just get up from the table, walk out of the hotel without even looking. The woman was trouble; she was nothing he wanted, nothing he needed.

Sweet perfume wafted gently over him, as though it could chase away the reek of charred flesh that permanently seared his sinuses, and he was intimately, undeniably aware of Gabrielle standing slightly behind him.

'Sorry I took so long.'

How had he forgotten what Gabrielle's voice did to him, how the soft, cultured lilt seemed to speak to something wounded inside him, as though she could soothe the beast that raged in his subconscious?

Sharna looked at Hayden, clearly waiting for him to reply, but he couldn't.

'Guess you had to find the right shoes to fit into, huh?' Sharna leaned sideways, apparently checking out Gabrielle's feet.

Gabrielle's voice held a laugh, as though the two women shared a joke. 'I figure I'll work my way through everything I have, until you tell me I've finally got it right. But I was actually held up by a work call.'

Hayden cleared his throat. 'What is it that you do, Gabrielle?' It was going to be something in fashion, he'd put money on it. Or maybe the make-up counter somewhere fancy, like David Jones.

'I'm in PR.' He turned, flicking a brief glance towards her, but Gabrielle's eyes were on Sharna. 'But I'm taking a break for a while.'

'Obviously not such a great break, seeing as you've already been called back,' Sharna noted.

Gabrielle screwed up her nose. Adorably, he couldn't help but notice. Then she ducked her chin, as though her announcement embarrassed her. 'Actually, I co-own the company, so it's proving impossible to pull right back. I guess I'll just have to get better at it, though.'

He grunted. There went his preconceptions.

'Hey, Gabby. How're you going?' Juz boomed as he reached them, a brown paper bag dwarfed by his fist.

Hayden let his shoulders cave with relief as his mate interrupted—but then jerked upright as Juz patted Gabrielle's back, as though she were a member of their group. Hayden dragged his glare away, but scowled as he caught Sharna laughing at him.

Gabrielle turned her smile on Juz, looking up at him. 'Hi, Justin. Thanks for turning up. Sharna said you're a top-notch cabinetmaker and, as she'll confirm, I'm going to need a whole lot of wardrobes.'

Juz puffed his chest out at the second-hand compliment, his delighted gaze straying to Sharna. The fact that Gabrielle didn't use the nicknames the group had honed over years of friendship placated Hayden a little. At least she wasn't muscling in with an assumed right to be there.

'Right, then, let's go see what needs doing, shall we?' He made a play at taking control of the situation.

'Juz can come with me,' Sharna said quickly.

Hayden lifted an eyebrow in surprise. Sharna usually tried to avoid the awkwardness of being alone with Juz since he'd developed an infatuation with her. 'How about we take one car?'

She shook her head. 'I need to bend Juz's ear about something.' She played with the buttons of her shirt, seeming suddenly nervous, and Hayden had an inkling that she was going to tell Justin that she wasn't interested. 'You take Gabs.'

'I can drive,' Gabrielle jumped in.

He thrust up from the table. 'Nah. I've got the dog. I'll drive.'

'Trigger's fine. I'll throw a blanket on the back seat.' Gabrielle seemed determined to prove her acceptance of the dog.

His chest tightened. 'No,' he snapped. The last time he had allowed someone he didn't know to drive—

'Oh!' Shocked realisation flashed across Sharna's face. 'Sorry, Wheaty, I didn't think. We'll all go in my car.'

The fact that she felt it necessary to baby him grated. Damn it, he had to get over himself. Taylor liked to say that he should give himself time, but how the hell would he ever claw his way back to normality if he didn't make an effort? Or if everyone insisted on pussy-footing around him? He needed to man up: the physical scars were healing and the mental scars should be bloody well hidden. 'It's fine. If you're sure you're good to drive, Gabrielle?'

'Absolutely.' She darted a smile at him, the first time she'd allowed their eyes to connect that morning. The first time he'd allowed it, too. And his heart stuttered. To cover the moment of weakness, he snatched his wallet and phone from the table, stuffing them into his jeans pocket as he unnecessarily clicked his fingers for Trigger, who had uncurled and clambered to his feet the moment Hayden stood.

'But—' Sharna's distress showed clear on her open face.

He shook his head. 'We'll see you both there.' He strode towards the door, belatedly realising that he had no idea where 'there' was.

'I'm parked out the front,' Gabrielle said from near his shoulder.

'Definitely not a local, then,' he muttered, before realising he sounded churlish. The nerves churning in his gut made it hard to focus on finding words. 'Not yet, anyway,' he forced himself to add.

Gabrielle gave a soft snort of laughter. 'I imagine that title takes decades to earn in a country town. Did you all grow up together?'

'Those of us who grew up,' Sharna called from behind them. 'I'm out the back. Give me a minute to pull round, and we'll follow you.'

'Sure,' Gabrielle said. 'It's not all that far out of town.'

Right now, he didn't care how far out of town her place was: travelling a single kilometre in a stranger's car seemed a stupid risk. His entire focus was on making himself get into the car rather than running for the safety of his house where he could at least try to suffocate the memories beneath the bedcovers.

'This one,' Gabrielle waved a hand towards a blue Audi. 'I'll just grab a blanket for Trigger from the boot.'

He stood silently, unable to unclench his fists despite the thrust of the dog's wet nose against his hand.

Gabrielle flipped forward the front seat and bent to spread a soft blanket, far too good for any dog—even Trigger—over the leather of the back seat.

He realised with a start that he was staring at her denim-clad backside, and managed to avert his eyes just before she turned.

'Okay, that should be all good. If you want to lift him in?'

'No need,' he said curtly. 'Trigg. Up.' He flicked a finger, and Trigger obediently bounded into the car. Gabrielle flinched as the dog brushed past her. 'You really don't like dogs? Any dogs?'

'It's not so much dislike.' She shot him a shamefaced look. 'They scare me.' One elegant hand waved him towards the passenger seat.

He pulled the belt across his chest, feeling the fear rise up his gullet. He had to keep talking to ward off the panic. 'Scare you?' he said, as she slid behind the wheel and cranked the ignition. 'Why is that?'

She kept her eyes on the rear-vision mirror. 'Sharna has a white ute?'

'Along with two-thirds of the population of Settlers.'

She flicked him a quick, nervous smile, then indicated and pulled smoothly onto the road. 'I got bitten.'

He felt instantly guilty. He was the last person who should judge someone for their fear. 'I'm sorry. That must have been terrifying.' He had visions of a pit bull savaging her lithe, tanned limbs.

She reached to turn on the windscreen wipers, sluicing rain and the odd gum leaf from the glass. 'It was years ago.'

'Still, nightmare stuff.' Okay, so he had to swap out the somewhat tantalising vision of golden flesh for a kid, but at least it was forcing his mind from the fact that the vehicle was accelerating through the outskirts of the town. On the left side of the road were large, comfortable stone houses sprawled across ample blocks studded with fruit trees and vegetable gardens, recreations of the farmhouses the owners had retired from. On the opposite side, swamps and lagoons shone grey in the sheeting silver of rain. Low reeds and saltbush fringed each pond across the plain to where a line of willows bordered the mercury ooze of the Murray.

Gabrielle hunched closer to the wheel, as though she had trouble seeing through the misted windscreen. She flipped the vent to outside air and a familiar gust of the distinctive, earthy smell of wet mud mixed with her soft, sweet fragrance. The side of her mouth twitched up a little, but she kept her tone neutral. 'It was a chihuahua.'

It took him a moment to picture the dog. 'Ah. Didn't take a large chunk out of you, then?'

The smile curved her generous lips now, and even if he was about to run full-tilt into the flames, he couldn't drag his eyes away.

'A teacup chihuahua,' she said. He shook his head, but then she turned to face him, her eyes dancing. Taking one hand from the wheel, she curled her fingers to form a bowl. Her nails were a pale pink, the tips whiter than could be natural. He couldn't stop himself wondering if her hands were as soft as they looked. 'They're about this big.'

'Ah.' Why the heck was he so stuck for words? She would think he was an idiot. He dug deep. 'Like the dog that Kahlo always painted?'

Gabrielle concentrated as she took a couple of corners, but switched her attention back to him the moment she hit a straight. 'I could be wrong, but I think that was some sort of rare ancient Aztec dog. But, yeah, the same size, at least.' She pressed her lips together, her focus on the slick black bitumen. A tiny vertical frown line appeared above her nose, the thick lashes hiding the eyes he didn't need to see to recall the exact shade of chocolate. 'You're interested in art?'

Hayden shook his head, although her attention was now on navigating the road between wind-lashed trees as they headed out of town. 'Only by osmosis; Mum's always been really into it. She would have studied art at uni, if she hadn't got knocked up young.' He tapped his chest, indicating he was the cause of her abandoned dreams. 'So, what happened to this monster that ripped a piece out of you, Gabrielle?' That name, though: why was it that every time he used it, a flush of juvenile excitement radiated through him as though he'd been crushing on her for a year? He'd never had to do the chasing, but it couldn't be any worse than his current pathetic state. Because, for the first time, he was both intrigued and intimidated by a woman.

He wanted to tell himself that wasn't possible; it didn't make any kind of sense to be fascinated by a woman he'd barely spoken with—though he had spent countless hours fantasising about her, about what could have happened if he'd never trusted Simmo with the car.

It wasn't credible that a woman who was the exact opposite of everything he wanted should take up so much of his thoughts. And the irony was that even if every one of his assumptions about Gabrielle proved wrong, even if she was, inconceivably, every damn thing he could want in a woman, his injuries meant he could never make a move on her.

Yet, even as he ground his teeth together, staring unseeingly out the window, Nan's matter-of-fact pronouncement kept running through his brain: *Life isn't supposed to be a straight path. Imagine how very boring that would be.*

18

Gabrielle

Hayden was so close to her, she was subconsciously mirroring his every breath.

She had to get a grip, and not only of the steering wheel she clutched as though she didn't trust her hands not to wander towards him.

She had already tested him once, letting go of the wheel to describe Amelie's dog, stupidly hoping he would seize the chance to take her hand.

Of course, he hadn't. There was nothing between them, other than those few seconds at the water tank, and now, as usual, he was unreadable. And given the way she had totally misinterpreted Sharna's overtures, perhaps she shouldn't even be trying to discern something behind his distant gaze as he focused on the rain-lashed windscreen. His left hand never relaxed its white-knuckled grip on the armrest, as though he didn't trust her driving.

She eased her foot off the accelerator, searching the unfamiliar roadside for landmarks so she didn't miss the turn to Wurruldi. 'What happened to the dog? Nothing that I recall. He belonged to one of my sisters, and she was crazy about him.' Sudden loss pierced her, as it had a habit of doing at the oddest moments. She would take any number of bites from the savage little beast if it meant having Amelie back.

'You have more than one sister, then?'

She pressed her palm against her chest, below where sorrow swelled her throat in a hard lump. It shouldn't be like this, not after more than a dozen years but, god, it still hurt. 'Not anymore.' She forced the words out, grazing her throat. Her tone was harsh, but she couldn't risk softening it or the tears would come.

Hayden was silent for a moment and she kept her eyes straight ahead, aware of the rise of his chest before he spoke. 'I'm sorry. Losing someone is hard.'

'It was a long time ago,' she said dismissively, fending off his empathy.

He gave a soft grunt, almost a despairing laugh. 'I was hoping time makes it better.'

She frowned: Hayden sounded grief-stricken. 'Not really,' she said. 'It doesn't hurt quite the same way, but it still hurts. Time lets guilt creep in; you get to feel guilty about wallowing in your misery of missing them, then you get to feel guilty about the rare moments you forget to miss them. You feel guilty having any experience you know

205

they'll never have, and you feel guilty for resenting them for making you feel guilty.'

'Wow,' he said after a moment. 'You'd better not go into the counselling business. You're painting a pretty bleak picture.'

'Sorry. I'll shut up.'

'No. Don't do that.' His words were forceful, and she glanced at him in surprise. He kept his eyes ahead, though a rueful smile curled the corner of his mouth. 'Your voice is unusual; you have the slightest accent. What is it? Something Nordic?'

She shook her head. 'French parents. My sisters and I—' Again, the jab of pain that momentarily stole her breath with the memory of togetherness, completeness. 'We grew up speaking only French until we started school. Then we had to play crazy catch-up.'

'I like it.'

Now it wasn't sorrow that stole her breath. She swallowed hard, needing to reroute the conversation. 'Anyway, I've told you my hairy dog story, what about yours?' She lifted her chin to the rear-view mirror. Trigger sat stiffly erect on the small back seat, his gaze fixed on Hayden. 'I take it he doesn't like cars?'

'Usually loves them, but he's on duty.' Hayden's mouth twisted self-deprecatingly. 'I don't give the poor bugger much down time.'

'Can I . . .' she started hesitantly.

'Pat him? Sure. When we stop. Right now, he's focused.'

'No, I was going to say, can I ask what sort of service dog he is? I mean, rather than make more awkward, embarrassing guesses that leave me looking like an idiot.'

'Ha.' Hayden grunted. 'I kind of like seeing you wrong-footed and flustered.' He was silent for a long moment, again staring straight ahead, as though something other than the road played out before him. 'He's a trauma dog.' The strong column of his throat moved jerkily, and he thrust a hand aggressively through his short hair. 'For PTSD. And, no, before you ask, I didn't serve.'

She lifted one shoulder. 'I wasn't going to ask. There are plenty of reasons for having PTSD. Maybe if Amelie had a decent dog, instead of the Chihorror, she would have . . .' She let the sentence trail off with her thoughts. The demons Amelie fought had been caused by her PTSD, but she had been psychologically damaged long before that. 'Does having him help?'

Warmth seared through her at the brush of Hayden's hazel eyes. 'You mean, would I be even more of a dick without him? Impossible as that seems, probably.'

'So, you think there's a chance of winning against PTSD?' She shouldn't keep pushing him, but for Amelie's sake, she needed to know.

'*Winning* just means I get a tomorrow.'

She understood, because that was exactly what Amelie hadn't got.

Hayden turned to scruff the dog's head, as though he couldn't stand the intimacy of their locked gaze. But the movement brought him closer, and the mixture of male musk and aftershave trembled through her senses. She couldn't comprehend why she was so drawn to him, particularly when he was one of very few men to disregard her. And the feeling was so damn pointless: getting naked in front of Brendan for the first time had been a drunken moment of youthful bravado she could never replicate.

Hayden was still angled backward, between the leather bucket seats, fondling the dog's ears.

Even though she slowed to a crawl to take the turn off the main road onto the dirt track, the lean of the vehicle forced his shoulder to brush hers. Struggling to find somewhere to plant his hand to push himself back upright, Hayden grinned. 'Sorry, I'm not built for small cars.'

He was so close to her. As his breath washed across her cheek, she could smell the rich, dark coffee he'd had while waiting for her to get ready. He made no move to jerk away, and she breathed unsteadily, her eyes on his, only centimetres away.

Flicking his gaze away for only a second, he reached to run a finger over her signet ring, then across the ridges of her knuckles to the white, crescent-shaped scar between her thumb and forefinger as she clutched the wheel. His hands were work hardened, the fingertips unusually broad and slightly flattened. 'This is where the dog got you?'

'Uh-huh.' She couldn't manage more. Her heart was pounding more unsteadily than the wheels churning slowly along the rutted road, which she prayed remained straight, as she had no intention of taking her eyes from this man.

Hayden evidently thought one of them should be watching the road. His eyes crinkled at the corners, and he glanced forward, not taking his hand from hers.

His fingers clenched.

His head swung from side to side as he checked their surroundings.

His jaw spasmed.

His eyes flashed fury.

'Where the hell are you going?' he snarled.

'To . . . to my place,' she stammered, shocked at his tone.

'There have never been houses for sale here.' His voice was too loud for the small confines, and Trigger whined in consternation.

'It's not a house. It's a hotel.'

'Pull over. Fucking pull over!' he yelled, gargantuan and threatening in the small car.

She slammed the brakes, not bothering to edge to the side of the track.

Hayden wrenched open the door, spilling out. The dog scrambled across the centre console to follow him.

Stunned, Gabrielle stared at the rear-view mirror.

Hayden stumbled from the car, bending double, his hands on his knees at the muddy roadside. Sharna flew from her car as it skidded to a halt behind them. She ran to Hayden, throwing her arms around him. Justin followed only seconds later, glancing from her car to Hayden, before placing one hand protectively on his mate's shoulder.

Gabrielle swiped a hand over the mirror, now misted with her panicked breathing. She didn't dare get out, didn't dare approach the group of tightknit friends, who seemed oblivious to the pelting rain.

Hayden slowly straightened, shaking his head. He looked beyond her, across to the cliff that lay just before them. Then he pressed the heel of his hand to his forehead, his features contorted with pain.

Justin dropped an arm around Hayden's hunched shoulders, drawing him closer.

Hayden shrugged him off, stared down the road again, then dropped to his haunches, his face buried in his hands.

What the heck was going on?

Lurching to his feet, Hayden staggered towards Sharna's ute, the dog glued to his leg. Gabrielle felt a sharp pang of loss as she realised he was leaving her. What had she done wrong this time? She had barely uttered a word, only answered his questions.

As Hayden clambered into Sharna's car, Justin slammed the door on him and then strode towards Gabrielle. She shrank back as he dropped heavily into the seat. He glanced across. 'It's okay, Gabby. Just drive.'

'But, what . . .' She was shaking.

Justin frowned at her hand trembling on the wheel, then covered it with his. Just like Hayden had. 'Are you all right to drive? Or do you want me to? It's Wurruldi we're headed to, right?'

'I'm–I'm okay. Just . . . what was all that?'

Justin lifted his chin at the road and she put the car into gear. He waited until she had turned the sharp corner and was travelling parallel to the sheer cliff before he spoke.

'Wheaty's got some history with the place. I guess he was just blindsided that you brought us out here.'

'How could you not all know that I bought the place— oh.' Even as she spoke, she realised why: it had been more than three years since the property was on the market. Their original purchase would be old news and, with the real-estate agent away on holidays, no one had any reason to associate her moving into the district with the hotel. 'Is this history related to whatever caused his PTSD?'

Justin did a double-take that would have been comical in other circumstances. 'He told you about that?'

'Shouldn't he?'

Justin rubbed a scarred hand across his jaw, the rasp of stubble audible over the rain. 'No reason not to, I'm just surprised. We're all pretty tight, and I guess we don't generally share much outside our group. Though, considering what Sharna just laid on me, maybe we don't share enough.' He shook his head, seeming despondent, but then pulled himself upright. 'Anyway, thing is, I thought it was a house you needed fixing up.'

'I never said that,' she whimpered.

'No, no, that's fine,' he said. 'My bad. I just assumed that was the case. So, tell me what needs doing there.'

She suspected he was asking to distract her from constantly checking the rear-view mirror, making sure Sharna was following them on the steep descent through the tight switchbacks. 'Loads of stuff,' she started tremulously. 'The place was damaged in the earthquake a few months back, but I'm hoping it's more cosmetic than structural.'

'Yeah, that was a decent shake. You're looking to fix up what, just enough to live in?'

'Initially.' She changed up a gear as the road levelled out and threaded between the trees. Sharna's headlights danced blurrily on her back windscreen.

'And Sharn said you needed some cabinet work?'

She managed a grin. 'She seems to think I have too many clothes. And that's based only on my suitcases. But, yes, I want to make some of the rooms more functional by adding built-ins, though I'm wondering if maybe I can include some stand-alone pieces from different periods downstairs.'

'Which decades?'

She had to give Justin credit; if he was trying to deflect her thoughts from Hayden, he did a good job of sounding interested in her project. 'I'm not sure. For some reason the fifties keep popping into my head and I've ended up with an entire Pinterest Board dedicated to it. But the forties seem evocative of real old-school glamour.'

'Forties and fifties, huh?' Justin squinted through the trees as they crossed the spit of land between the lagoon and the river. Two long-legged egrets wading in the shallows turned to watch their passage. 'So . . . retro, vintage stuff. You could lean into some art deco for the forties. Sharp geometrics, clean lines, lots of layered woods, contrasting grains. Interesting sideboards and bedroom pieces. Then you'd be moving into the Scandinavian influence for the fifties.'

'You really know your stuff. I thought cabinetmakers were, you know . . . about cabinets.'

Justin tugged at his ear. 'A bit like Wheaty, the trade is my bread and butter, but the craft is my passion.'

'Like Wheaty?' The confusion must have been apparent in her voice, because the seat leather squeaked against Justin's wet jeans as he twisted to look at her.

'He's a builder, and a damn fine one when he's on the tools. But stonemasonry is his passion.'

'Oh.' She digested the information for a moment. 'And yours?'

'Wood carving.'

'So, like, bespoke stuff?'

'Exactly,' he nodded. 'If you ever need a giant sculpture, I'm your guy.'

'I can't think of a need for any sculptures off the top of my head, but what about restoration work? I mean, I know it's not carving, but there was this beautiful water trough at the hotel that I'd love to see restored.'

'The one next to the hitching rail out the front?' Justin cracked his window as his damp body steamed up the interior.

'Oh, you know it?' She asked in surprise.

'Sure. Been here with Wheaty a few years back, and kind of make it my business to notice nice woodwork. We'll see what I can do.' As they pulled into Wurruldi, his face tightened. He looked around with a frown. 'Wow, this place has really gone to the dogs.' He grimaced. 'Sorry. That was a bit harsh. Wasn't thinking.'

She chuckled, though the sound was mirthless. 'That's generally my gig around here. In any case, I only own the pub. I've no idea who owns the cottages, but it looks like they're deserted.' She cornered the property and slowly crunched up the long driveway before stopping near the water trough.

Behind them, Sharna pulled up the ute. The rain had almost stopped, and her headlights shone hazy through the drizzle.

Justin glanced over his shoulder. 'How about we give Wheaty a moment alone? We'll go inside and have a look around.'

'Sure. Will he be okay, though? I mean, is something here likely to trigger him? Oh! Trigger!' She belatedly understood the significance of the dog's name.

'He'll work through it. Come on, let's run before the rain starts again.'

Unlocking the building and going inside without Hayden diminished the thrill she had been anticipating. Still, even though the day was grey, already the inside of the hotel appeared brighter with the curtains removed and the windows gleaming.

'The bedrooms are all upstairs.' She gestured at the staircase opposite the main entrance.

'Let's start there, then,' Justin agreed, his gaze darting around the interior. 'Oh, man.' He hadn't made it two steps up the staircase before he squatted, examining the railing. 'These spindles are all hand-turned.' He stood and ran a hand along the smooth handrail. 'And I'm willing to bet this is hand carved, too.'

'You do this kind of work?' she asked.

He nodded, his attention fully on the woodwork as he continued climbing. 'I can. This is the kind of thing I love.'

'In that case, remind me to show you the upstairs balcony. It's basically really boring straight up and down slats with a flat piece of wood sitting on top.'

He looked at her and grinned. 'And you want something fancier? Like maybe custom-turned balusters?'

'As far as I'm concerned, you're no longer speaking English. But something nice, yes,' she said as they reached the head of the stairs and turned into the first of the bedrooms. Although the walls were still the lime green of avocado flesh, the room seemed light and airy without the heavy drapes and grimy windows. Leaves littered the beige carpet and she had an urge to start cleaning, but instead she crossed quickly to the window, pressing her fingertips against the new pane as she craned to see the driveway below.

Hayden had emerged from Sharna's car. He stood, hands thrust deep into his pockets, facing the river. Beyond him, Sharna was dwarfed beneath the umbrella of a massive jacaranda.

There was no welcome in Hayden's stance, yet she longed to run to him, to apologise for inadvertently causing his pain.

'And you want built-in robes in here?' Justin said, surveying the blank walls.

'In all the bedrooms,' she said absently, still focused on Hayden.

'All? How many are there?'

'Ten, currently, but I'm deciding whether to take out a couple of walls between the rooms overlooking the river to turn them into luxury suites. And the same with my room, at the back. If I do, there will be two guest suites and four standard rooms, plus mine.'

Justin pulled a steel tape measure from the pocket of his thick flannelette shirt. 'These are fourteen-foot ceilings. That's a whole heap of storage space, you know.'

'There's nothing worse than paying for a room and finding you have to leave all your clothes in your suitcases,' she said. Giving in to the impulse, she bent and picked up some leaves from the carpet.

'You're eventually going to run the place as a pub, then?' Justin was entering measurements into his phone.

'No, the last couple of owners proved pretty conclusively that there's just not enough passing trade here to make that viable. I'm going for a guesthouse set-up.'

'I see.' He rubbed at his chin. 'Not really a change of use, so you shouldn't fall foul of council. Have you thought about finding some original robes? People staying over won't need much storage. In fact, they'd need a ladder to access the top of built-in robes. If you got second-hand gear we could refinish it, and it'll match your theme better. Plus, it'll keep your costs well down.'

She chewed on her lip, looking at him thoughtfully. 'You're dead right. If I could source decent pieces, that'd be cool. Oh!' She gasped excitedly, 'Instead of having random pieces scattered around, I could dress each room with a different theme, depending on the furniture. Like, this room could be all art deco, the next could be fifties retro, with the Scandinavian stuff you mentioned.' Eagerness seized her. 'Justin, you've got it! I've been racking my brain for a niche to make the property more marketable, all the time thinking I need to make it quirky. But that's not it: I need to take it *back*. Back to the elegance and grandeur, recapture a time when days were slower and life was simpler. A nostalgic taste of yesteryear.' She cupped her hands over her nose, barely able to breathe in her excitement. It was always like this when she hit on the perfect branding for a client. 'People need to take a *break* on their break, instead of filling their lives with the rush to get somewhere, to be somewhere, to be seen to be doing something for their social media posts. If we go retro, we could even make the premises device-free. No TV. No phone. No wi-fi. Oh my god, why didn't I see this? I had all these haphazard ideas about furniture and wallpaper and stuff knocking around in my head.' She was babbling but she couldn't contain her enthusiasm. 'I was even considering dinner settings, but I just couldn't pull the whole look together. And then you just . . . How did you do that?'

'Not sure I did a thing, but as you're happy, I'll take it,' Justin said, looking slightly bemused. 'If you're going to live here, you'll still want full-height robes in your room, though? May as well maximise storage in there.'

She shook her head. 'This is why I told Sharna I've no idea where to start; it depends whether I extend my room into the next, perhaps use it as an ensuite dressing room. I've got the building approvals, but I need to know whether it's actually feasible.'

Justin rapped his knuckles against the stone wall. 'That'd be Wheaty's area of expertise. I don't mess with structural alterations; you'd have to ask him.'

The mention of Wheaty quelled her excitement and she nervously twisted Amelie's signet ring, which she never removed. 'I'm not sure he's going to take any requests from me very well.'

'Wheaty's cool. He'll do right by you.' Justin's tone was solidly certain.

She turned back to the window. Hayden still faced the river, as immobile as a statue.

She wished he would do right by her.

19

Hayden

Even from a distance, he could hear the wind soughing through the branches of the century old jacaranda, a sorrow-laden sigh. He couldn't keep staring beyond it, towards the river. Besides, the rotting timbers of the dock held their own memories, and he didn't want to revisit them, either. But refusing to look at the building wasn't going to change a damn thing. And Gabrielle was going to think he'd lost it.

Well, she'd be bloody right. The panic that had welled up inside him as he realised where she was driving them had almost made him throw up. He'd needed to get his head down low, before he blacked out.

He rubbed roughly at his shoulder, deliberately causing pain to punish himself for ignoring the danger. He should have known better than to get into a car with someone who wasn't a friend. How had he not learned his lesson?

'Hayden?'

The tentative sound of his name on Gabrielle's lips immediately eased his anger, though no one could ever make it disappear. He forced himself to turn, keeping his eyes strictly on Gabrielle's face, not allowing them to stray to the building behind her. It was no hardship: Gabrielle was gorgeous, made even more so by the new hesitancy curbing her businesslike attitude.

'Yeah?' he said.

'I'm sorry,' she said softly. 'I didn't know this place would be an . . . issue for you.'

He shook his head. 'Not an issue. Just a shitload of memories.'

'I'll get someone else in to do the work. Sharna said there are tradies in Murray Bridge.'

For a second, he was tempted to agree. But then some other guy would get to spend those hours with Gabrielle. Besides, this way he could keep an eye on what she planned to do with the place.

The place.

He forced his gaze to move beyond her.

The building looked worse for wear and sadder than the last time he had seen it, but still basically the same as it had always been. The grounds shocked him, though. If he had ever allowed his thoughts to wander here, maybe he would have anticipated the gardens being overgrown. They'd been heading that way even when Nan was here, using her own funds to try to shore up what had once been the magnificence of her labours. He'd helped out as much as he could, but still the place had been steadily getting away from her. This tangle of death and neglect reinforced all he had lost that day.

'Don't bother,' he said. 'You've had insurance assessors through?'

She nodded earnestly. 'Claim settled, no major structural damage. At least, not to the main building. So, I'm thinking it's more a cosmetic fix, mostly repainting and refinishing floors, that kind of stuff. But I do have council approval to reconfigure the rooms, if we choose to go that way.'

He rubbed at his shoulder again, cautioning himself. 'You're taking the floors back to timber?'

'Except for the tessellated marble in the original kitchen and the entryway. I want to keep the essence.'

He forced himself to hold her gaze. Damn, she had to stop doing that wrinkling her nose thing; it made her look vulnerable and just plain adorable.

'"The essence,"' she mocked herself. 'Listen to me; what a poser. It's just . . .' She toyed with her necklace, her knuckles pressed to her chest as she looked back at the hotel. Then she glanced up at him. 'I get the sense that under this damaged exterior, there's something . . . special. No, wait.' She shook her head vehemently, her white-blonde hair shifting in a silky wave. 'That's the wrong word. I feel like there's something *real* about the place.' Her elegant fingers stretched and flexed as she searched for the words, a frown of concentration between her eyes. 'A soul.'

He startled, unable to contain his grunt of shock.

She mistook it for laughter, pulling a rueful face. 'I know. Now I sound like some marketing tosser trying to sell you my vision.'

He placed a hand in the small of her back, on the pretext of guiding her to the building as a sudden squall blew in off the river, scattering the last of the lacy yellow leaves of the willow trees along the banks.

'Not at all,' he said. 'In fact, I wish you were right: I wish the place had a soul.' Maybe then he would get a chance to apologise.

He turned back to Sharna, who was lurking in the scant shelter of the jacaranda as though she didn't want to intrude on them. Or maybe she was avoiding Justin. After they'd swapped cars, she'd tried to distract Hayden's panic as they headed into Wurruldi by telling him what she'd shared with Juz.

He took a deep breath and forced a cheerful tone. 'Come on, Sharn. It's freezing out here.' He'd be a dick to cling to his own problems, which all belonged in the past, when his friends had their own shit going down.

As the three of them reached the front of the hotel, the timber door slammed in their faces, the noise echoing from the river cliffs like a gunshot.

'Crap,' Gabrielle gasped. 'I should have shut that. Lucky the glass panels didn't break again. I would have thought it too heavy to catch the wind, but I guess either the locksmith or the glazier oiled the hinges.'

Hayden took a tight grip on the large, round brass handle, and the door swung open.

20
Ilse

Two cars today!

Ilse patted her hair into place and smoothed down the neat blouse she wore tucked into her slacks.

It was getting positively busy around here, although she'd been careful to stay out of everyone's way, aware that she had no real place in the hotel and was only there by Gabrielle's good grace. But Ilse had been certain to complete a thorough inspection each time the tradesmen left, to make sure Gabrielle would be happy with the work and hadn't wasted her money.

As though her thoughts conjured the woman, Gabrielle stepped from the car, dressed with her usual elegance. Ilse was surprised by the jolt of happiness that flashed through her. Gabrielle had become familiar, her visits welcome, even though Ilse frequently couldn't recall them after the event.

Ilse glanced towards the hall, wondering whether she should cross to the bathroom to check her face. She no longer wore make-up, but it never hurt to check that one was presentable. Reluctantly, she decided that considering her lack of speed these days, she wouldn't have time.

Instead, she determinedly plodded towards the head of the stairs, each step taking what seemed an eternity, as though time were mired in the mud of the river's edge.

Puffing with exertion, she reached the stairs. Glanced down. For the briefest moment, she knew the man who stood on the threshold with Gabrielle.

Anger and betrayal flashed through her.

Then the glass-panelled front door slammed shut, amputating the odd emotion.

Shaking her head, Ilse took a few more steps down.

The door swung open again, leaf confetti surrounding the couple haloed by a burst of wintry sunshine.

Ilse stared. Her hand clutched the pendant at her neck.

No. The tall, dark man who stood alongside Gabrielle couldn't be . . .

She shook her head, anxiety clawing up her throat as she fought against the memory.

That couldn't be him. He had been just a boy, such a sweet boy.

Then a teenager, cheeky and gregarious, the only one who had never grown away from her.

Then a dashing young man who still made time for her, even when her softness and patience had been whittled away by age and aches.

She teetered at the head of the stairs, snatching desperately at the bannister rail. Time whirled in a kaleidoscope, past meeting present. And, her recollection suddenly perfect, she knew . . .

No! It wasn't possible. Dry sobs of terror spasmed her chest, the convulsions choking her, robbing her of oxygen.

Except, that didn't matter. Because she was already . . . *No!*

The blackness crowded in and she thrust out a hand, but she was plummeting, knowing there would never be an impact: instead she would spiral endlessly in the void of despair.

Because she *knew*.

She remembered it all.

Including the surge of betrayal and grief that had literally ripped her heart apart.

21
Hayden

Entering wasn't as bad as he'd feared. After all, his memories had never belonged inside the hotel. He hadn't even been in there since his uncle sold it more than a decade ago. His shoulders eased, and he rolled his neck to release the tension.

'Wow, cool place,' Sharna murmured as she scooted past them into a room on the left.

Trigger took a few steps ahead, snuffling his interest. Then he stopped and looked back, waiting for permission. 'Is it okay for him to come through?' Hayden asked Gabrielle.

'Sure,' she said. Her words were easy enough, but he felt her lean into him as the dog brushed past. That dog was worth his weight in gold.

'Trigg. Here.' He snapped his fingers. The dog instantly came and sat on the floor, gazing up expectantly. 'If you want to make friends with him, I promise you he won't bite,' he assured Gabrielle. Why was it suddenly important that Gabrielle accept his constant companion?

Gabrielle's even white teeth worried at her lip. 'I . . . want to,' she said hesitantly. 'And I know I'm being stupid, but . . .'

'Everyone's scared of something.' He tried to make the words sound generalised, a throwaway placation, but he knew the truth better than anyone. He put his hand down and Trigger thrust his rubbery nose against it. 'Do you want to try?'

Gabrielle nodded, but fear darkened her eyes.

He took her trembling hand and guided it towards Trigger's head. She flinched, her fingers instinctively grasping at his. Their upper arms brushed, and he felt the tension vibrate through her taut frame. 'It's okay,' he murmured.

But perhaps the words weren't so much for her, as to calm himself. While the nerves that stiffened Gabrielle's body and shortened her breath came from fear, his own reacted to something entirely different. A wave of longing and desire. Emotions that were as far from being okay as was possible.

Safely encased in his grip, Gabrielle stretched one finger towards the dog. As though he recognised her uncertainty, Trigger nosed it gently, rather than give her his usual over-enthusiastic head butt.

Gabrielle's hair brushed against Hayden's sleeve as she leaned forward and he had to force back the urge to touch, to discover whether it was as silky as it appeared.

She twisted to look back at him, delight dancing across her face as she rubbed a finger on Trigger's velvety muzzle. The spill of her hair slid like satin across the back of his hand, the sensation everything he could have imagined.

'Here,' he said gruffly, trying to find control. 'Rub the furrow between his eyes. That's his favourite spot.'

'How funny,' she murmured.

'Why's that?'

She straightened. Trigger stretched towards her, understandably eager for more of her caress. 'When we were kids, Mum used to soothe us by stroking our foreheads. Much like that.'

'My Nan did that too. Must be some old-school trick.' He realised with a start that it was the first time he'd mentioned Nan since . . . 'Anyway, let's get on with this assessment, shall we?'

'Sure.' Gabrielle straightened, but made no move to pull her right hand from his, using her left to gesture at the stairs. 'Justin has some good ideas for upstairs, he's already measuring . . . stuff.' A faint flush mounted her high cheekbones beneath her golden tan.

Damn, he really had to let go of her hand. He had no excuse not to. 'Are the stairs sound?' he said, trying to mute the hopeful note in his voice. If they were white-anted, he would be justified in holding her hand as a safety measure.

'They're cool, man. Not so much as a squeak.' Juz boomed from somewhere out of sight above them.

'Great,' Hayden muttered.

Gabrielle slid her hand from his but gave him a quick, shy smile. 'I admit, I need a lot of input into this project. I was just explaining to Justin that I plan to convert this into a guesthouse, but beyond knowing that it needs a coat of paint and new carpets, I'm kind of lost, especially on the structural stuff.'

'Altering the structure will depend on how many rooms you want to end up with,' he said as they mounted the stairs. 'And on your council approvals.' Although the carpet was frayed on the edges and worn through in patches in the centre of the treads, Justin was right: there wasn't so much as a squeak.

'Well, that's what I'm trying to work out. There are currently ten rooms upstairs, and two main areas downstairs. Plus a galley kitchen, the foyer, and a newer wing with a more modern kitchen and wet areas, which are in pretty good nick. But there are approved plans to enlarge some of the bedrooms, which will make the accommodation more luxurious. Set it apart from places like The Overland. Not that there's anything wrong with the pub,' she added quickly, and he realised that she was anxious not to upset him with a misplaced word. Which proved what a prick he'd been. But it also proved that she actually cared what he thought—surely that could only be good?

Hand clenched on the bannister, he paused. Of course it wasn't good: he had to remember, he couldn't take this further than few loaded glances, a stolen touch of her hand or her hair.

Gabrielle smiled at him, her expression tentative and uncertain and . . . hopeful? Sudden anticipation surged in his chest. Christ, he wasn't a complete idiot, he could still read a woman's interest. Perhaps he could risk taking things just a little further. Because he sure as hell wanted to get to know this woman better. What harm could there be in a bit of making out, if that's what she wanted? He could pull the pin before things got too heavy. Before she discovered what lay beneath his clothes.

Maybe a taste of her soft lips would be enough.

The tightness of the new skin across his shoulder and chest tugged like a leash. Would a kiss be enough to get him through the lifetime of monk-like denial that stretched before him?

More like enough to drive him mad.

He tried to focus on her plans. 'How many bathrooms?'

'Only two upstairs.' She gave that nose wrinkle again.

Jesus. It was hard to force out words without croaking. 'Might make it tough to have more than a couple of bedrooms up here.'

'I know. But I do have some thoughts about that.' They turned to the right at the top of the stairs and Gabrielle pushed down the lever-style brass handle on a solid timber door.

Two walls were mustard, the third burgundy. Inexplicably, the fourth, framing the window, was wallpapered in large splashes and drips of colours. 'Guess there's a Jackson Pollock autograph scrawled somewhere in here, huh?' Hayden murmured as he stepped into the room.

'You should have seen it when the curtains were still up.' Gabrielle's eyes sparkled, as though the art reference were a shared joke. He sure owed his mum one for indoctrinating him with that stuff. 'They were masterpieces in their own right.'

'Shame I missed it.' He crossed over to the window.

'I think they're in the dumpster. You could retrieve them if you really wanted.'

He barely heard her. His gut clenched. The room overlooked the courtyard at the back of the hotel.

Facing the wattle-tree–bordered outbuildings.

Loss seared through him, hotter than the tongues of fire that had stolen his flesh. He gripped the windowsill, his fingers denting timber as he fought for control.

Gabrielle moved to stand beside him. 'See those buildings?'

Of course he bloody saw them.

'I was thinking of converting them into accommodation to make up the shortfall if I enlarge the upstairs rooms. One of them looks as though it was used as a retreat or study or something.'

'The castle,' Hayden grated out, his heart threatening to tear from his throat. *Her* castle.

He felt Gabrielle look up at him, the movement accompanied by a faint waft of gardenia, although he'd not placed the perfume before. One of Nan's favourite flowers.

'Oh, of course, if you know the history of this place, you'd know what it was,' she said.

231

He forced air in through his nose, out through his mouth. Tried to tear his eyes away from the outbuildings, look beyond the courtyard to the wetlands. 'Even at mates' rates, those buildings would be too expensive to do up. They don't have any plumbing, and the electrics will be basic.' And the castle shouldn't be touched. It should be preserved, exactly as it was when . . .

Gabrielle leaned against his left shoulder to look out of the window. He recoiled at the contact, but it wasn't because of the pain. 'I figured they wouldn't be self-contained,' she said. 'More a detached bedroom, with the facilities indoors in the kitchen wing. In any case, the cost isn't an issue. And you don't have to do me a special deal. I appreciate that you're willing to make time to take on the work.'

Was that her way of saying she wanted nothing from him? Or at least, nothing beyond his labour.

He seized on his disappointment, using irritation to disguise a far more dangerous emotion. 'Clearly, you're not country. Out here, money is always an issue. But we can't be bought. We help out, take on jobs because it's the right thing to do. Not because someone throws cash at us.'

A frown creased her forehead at his tone. 'That's not what I meant. Just that I don't want to undervalue your labour.' Gabrielle moved away from him, pointing towards the doorway in the mustard wall, as though she could see beyond the room directly opposite. 'But I was also thinking that if it's not feasible to get those buildings up to scratch, I'll get my broker to find out who owns the cottages and that funny shop on the riverfront. They'd be perfect for self-contained accommodation.'

His skin prickled at her assumption. 'They may not be for sale.'

She tilted her head disbelievingly. 'Everything has a price.'

'Perhaps you can't afford it.'

She laughed softly, as though the notion were absurd. 'Oh, I can.'

He scowled. 'You'll find it hard to fit in here if you believe everything's for sale.'

'Lynn seems to do all right. I hear she owns half the town.'

'She does. But you won't hear it from her.'

He heard her gasp behind him as he strode across the room.

'Wow, what did I say to deserve that?'

As though his anger required more room to pass, he slammed back the door, letting it shiver on its hinges. Was it just his bruised ego that provoked his temper? He couldn't pin it on Gabrielle's plan to renovate the outbuildings; she had been willing to give that one up without a fight. Although maybe that was what truly irritated him; like her fleeting interest in him, there was no passion in her decision. No necessity, no drive. She planned to destroy his memories to fill her grasping desire to have what she wanted in that instant. He snarled without bothering to turn back to her, 'Not everything has a purely monetary value.'

'I don't think I said that it has?' She sounded uncertain.

'That's exactly what you said. "Everything has a price."'

'And it does. But I didn't say that was its *only* worth.'

'You inferred that.' Certain things had immeasurable value, for the memories they held, the love and pain they evoked. But grief robbed him of the words to explain any of that.

'Hayden, I'm sorry.' Gabrielle had stopped behind him and, a product of Nan's wooden-spoon enforcement of manners, he turned reluctantly to face her. Her hands were on her hips, her expression fierce. 'That's certainly not what I meant. I was only thinking that this whole place is decrepit. If I buy the properties, I can renovate the entire town. Create something from scratch, a tourist destination.'

She emphasised *destination* in the pretentious manner corporate millennials used and—to hell with Nan's rules— his anger erupted. 'Doesn't it occur to you that maybe this was more than a destination? That it was someone's home, their life? That you can't just flounce in here, splashing cash around and making history vanish?'

Fuck. He was out of line. But seeing the castle had woken the anguish and the guilt and it ballooned inside him, dark and evil and painful. He had to get the hell out of there, away from Gabrielle's wounded expression, before he made things worse.

'Wheaty?' Sharna stood at the top of the stairs. 'Are you okay?'

'Gotta get outside.' He shouldered past her, thundered down the steps and shoved open the back door. Pulled up short as the courtyard caged him.

Jesus, why the hell had he thought escape lay in this direction? He was trapped, as surely as if he faced a wall of flame, the retreat behind him cut off, the advance—towards the castle—impossible.

Panic crushed his chest. His vision narrowed to a tunnel, bounded by darkness. He bent double, hands on his knees as he gasped for breath.

Sharna's hand appeared, reaching for his. He knew she was speaking, but for long seconds he couldn't hear anything over the rush of blood in his ears.

'Wheaty? Wheaty? Do you have something you can take?'

He tried to shake his head, but dizziness overwhelmed him.

'Tay gave you something, didn't she? Something to calm you down?'

Something to prove he was less than a man, that he couldn't control himself. 'Fuck Tay. She doesn't know everything,' he spat. Jesus, please don't let Gabrielle be there, watching him fall to pieces.

'Hayden.' Gabrielle's voice penetrated his panic, and he groaned. 'Hayden, I'm going to need your help with the hotel. I don't know whether I should pull out the carpet or get the painters in first. And do plumbers or electricians take precedence? I've got a ton of plans and sketches, but no idea what order I'm supposed to do things in.'

Her tone was smooth, soothing, as though they hadn't argued.

'Does the council approval I already have cover everything I need?'

Her questions forced him to concentrate.

'And is there a way to get the pipework checked to make sure the place isn't going to flood? I've been down into the cellar, and that definitely looks like it's been water damaged at some stage.'

'Floods, back in fifty-six,' he managed.

'So, not a leak? Do you think we can get the pipes tested, or is it just a case of seeing if something leaks? Or I guess, given the age of the place, waiting *until* it leaks.'

He could make out Sharna on her knees, her face white as she looked up at him, but Gabrielle was still out of sight, her voice unfailingly calm. His erratic pulse was gradually returning to normal, the nausea-inducing racing of his heart decelerating.

He straightened slowly, trying to force in deep breaths.

'Wheaty?' Sharna whispered. 'Are you okay?'

'He's all right,' Gabrielle answered, somehow knowing that questions about his condition, unlike questions that forced him to think beyond the panic, would spiral him down again. 'Could you get some water, though, Sharna?'

'Sure.' Sharna's boots slapped on the wet pavers as she raced towards the kitchen wing.

Hayden groaned again, but this time he forced himself to turn, blinking back the tears of weakness the attacks induced. 'How . . . how did you know?'

'Amelie. The sister I told you about?' she said quietly. 'She used to have panic attacks.'

Sharna dashed back, water spilling over the edges of the flowered teacup she carried. 'Sorry, it's all I could find.' She thrust the china into his hand.

'Fuck,' he moaned as water slopped from the shaking cup. 'Sharn, what I said about Tay . . . I didn't mean it.'

236

'I know,' she said simply.

Hell, he wanted to find a rock to crawl under. Quickly, before his legs gave out.

'The wind has dropped,' Gabrielle said. 'I've got a load of floor plans and vision boards, in the car. If you can find somewhere to spread them out, maybe you can go through them and see what's going to be feasible and what's a pipe dream.'

If she laid her plans on the saturated table beneath the big gum they would be ruined; but she was clearly giving him an excuse to sit without emasculating him. At least, no more than he'd already emasculated himself.

He wanted to argue, to insist they go and knock down a wall, or start ripping out the bathroom or something physical. Something to prove he was a man. But the fact was, he would have enough trouble making it over to the bench. Something to do with the after-effects of an adrenaline spike, Taylor had explained to him, but he didn't give a damn. All he knew was it made him look weak.

22
Gabrielle

'He's trying to avoid me, you know.'

Gabrielle morosely pushed the piece of cake around her plate, although it was a bit of an act; she was definitely going to eat it. She had discovered that one of the two cafes in the main street, Ploughs and Pies, not only did awesome coffee but also had a stellar line of baked goods. Over the course of the past three weeks, she had steadily worked through the menu and was about to start over.

Sharna took a huge bite of her lamington, speaking around it. 'No. That's just Wheaty. He's the strong silent type.'

'Say that again and you'll be using twice as many words as he's spoken to me in nearly a month. I get texts telling me who I should try for a quote, or asking me to leave the keys hidden so he has access, but other than that, I swear he must race out the back door every time I turn up at Wurruldi.'

She was only half-joking. More than once she'd had the feeling that someone was watching her. And she knew for sure it wasn't the tradies; they were few and far between, with progress much slower than she would have liked. For every one who turned up, two either said it was too far or were simply a no-show. Now she had her vision, she was eager to see it come to life, but the mundanities of plumbing and plastering didn't do much to nurture the anticipation that drove her.

Sharna spluttered and then took a swallow of her cappuccino. 'I swear I'm allergic to coconut, but these lamingtons are too good to resist. I doubt he's avoiding you. More likely he's working at night.'

'Ah,' she said guiltily. Was she ever going to learn not to focus solely on herself? 'Too much on at work?'

Sharna tipped her head to one side, appraising Gabrielle for a long moment before she spoke. 'I guess there's no harm in telling you. He doesn't sleep well. So he tries to keep busy at night.'

'Because of the PTSD?'

Sharna nodded.

'Nightmares?'

The long breath Sharna blew out was enough to cool both their drinks. 'I wouldn't know. Like you said, he doesn't talk much. But that'd be my guess.'

'Shit. I should have figured that.' Nightmares were one of the factors that had driven Amelie to seek refuge in drugs.

'I guess that explains why it is that whenever I turn up, there's been more done to the place. The cracks have all been fixed and the wiring is chased into the walls. Plus, two of the walls between bedrooms have disappeared. If it weren't for the text updates, I'd think maybe I have a ghost working on the place.'

'How handy would that be? If your ghost gets tired of renovating, send him over to do a couple of my shifts at the dairy, okay? I'm a bit over that place.' Sharna rubbed wearily at her face. 'But, yeah, if you were there at night, you'd likely catch him. If it's any consolation, I've barely seen him either.' She eyed Gabrielle for a long moment, then giggled. 'That was no consolation at all, was it? Ah, you've got it bad, Gabs!'

Gabrielle could feel the instant blush rise up her chest. 'It's just bizarre to never see the person who's working on my property, is all.'

'Uh-huh,' Sharna snorted. 'Bet you didn't feel like that about the glaziers. The electrician. Did you keep an eye on the plumbers? Nope? Well, you're excused that one because plumbers' crack—ugh, no one needs that in their life. Anyway, our Wheaty is far more worth watching, right?'

Gabrielle instinctively started to deny her attraction, but then remembered: this was her new life, the new Gabby. Maybe one who dared allow herself to feel passion. So, perhaps a little honesty was in order. 'I guess he's pretty easy on the eye . . . if dark and brooding is your thing.'

'Obviously not my thing.' Sharna folded one leg beneath her on the chair, leaning forward over the table conspiratorially.

'But he didn't used to do the brooding bit. You've noticed that thousand-mile stare?'

'Where he looks off into forever, as though he's on an entirely different planet? And you wonder whether what you just said was excruciatingly boring or simply inane?'

Sharna snorted. 'Yeah. You've noticed it. That only started after the thing the other year. Like, don't get me wrong, Wheaty's always been a nice guy, but he pretty much used to be the life of the party. Now he's more . . . serious.'

Gabrielle straightened. This was her chance to discover what had caused Hayden's PTSD, and why it was that his friends seemed solicitous of him, despite his deliberate distancing.

'Or maybe that's just how he keeps a lid on the pain,' Sharna continued.

'Pain? You mean psychological?' Maybe Brigitte could give her a few pointers on how to help Hayden through it. Although she had arced up, ready to fight back when he verbally attacked her at the hotel, by the time he got down the stairs she had recognised his panic attack . . . thanks to Amelie. Even though Gabrielle had been scared, she had known how to deal with it, and to expect the subsequent crash when his fight-or-flight reflex gave way to adrenaline depletion. But beyond dealing with the immediate physical presentation, she didn't know much about PTSD. She rubbed at her chest, forcing the fine silk of her blouse against her skin, although the friction could never erase the evidence of the outcome of Amelie's terminal aloneness.

Sharna tucked her ringlets behind her left ear. 'No. Well, yes, I guess, but also—'

'Auntie Sharna!' a demanding voice interrupted.

'Rug-rat one! And Rug-rat two.' A grin lit Sharna's face as she turned to greet a little boy about three or four years old, his blond hair mussed in errant spikes. His sister, obviously a twin, stood a little behind him, a finger in her mouth, enormous blue eyes fixed on Gabrielle.

Her heart tightened. Would she ever be able to see twins without a fresh sense of loss and guilt spearing through her?

'Where's your mumma?' Sharna asked.

'Chasing the whirlwinds,' a woman called from near the counter where she was talking with Samantha, the cafe owner. Gabrielle recognised her as Roni who, according to Sharna's intel, owned the best animal boarding house ever conceived. It had given Gabrielle an idea about offering her guests a package deal: while they relaxed at her guesthouse, their furry friend could enjoy luxurious accommodation at The Peaceful Paws. Definitely a concept that invited some exploration with Roni when the time was right.

Sharna scooped up the boy, placing him on her lap. 'Hey there, little dude. Do you want some of my cake?'

The girl sidled closer, her gaze still on Gabrielle. 'Pretty.' She pointed at the mulberry cashmere pashmina Gabrielle had draped around her shoulders.

'It is, isn't it?' Gabrielle said. The child stretched a tentative finger towards the fabric.

'No!' Roni dashed over, intercepting her daughter's hand. 'I can't guarantee where that grubby little mitt has been, but I can imagine. I'm sure you don't want it all over your scarf.'

'It's fine,' Gabrielle said, unwinding the fabric while making sure the neck of her blouse was tweaked together. 'Would you like to try it on . . . ?' She glanced questioningly at Roni.

'Marian,' Roni supplied. 'But let me at least wipe her hands first. That wrap looks like it would have cost a fortune.'

'It's only money,' Gabrielle said, draping the fabric around the child's shoulders.

Sharna snorted. 'You are literally the only person to ever say that around here, Gabs.'

Gabrielle grimaced. 'So Hayden told me. Well, maybe a little less gently.'

'Uh-oh,' Roni said. 'I've learned that even in good years, farmers don't take money for granted. Not that Wheaty's a farmer, but like Matt he's from farming stock.'

'Learned? You're not from around here?'

Roni shook her head, then re-ponytailed her golden-streaked brown hair. 'No. I'm from Sydney, like Taylor.'

Sharna sighed loudly, stirring the blond mess of the boy's hair. 'Along with you, Gabs, there's something of an influx of city girls hitting on the guys in Settlers Bridge. Shame the relocation isn't on an exchange basis.'

She sounded glum and Gabrielle gave her a sympathetic smile before switching her attention back to Roni.

'I thought moving from Adelaide was a big deal. How does a Sydneysider end up transplanted here?'

Roni looked a little embarrassed. 'I inherited a property from my aunt. I'd planned to sell it, but—' she spread her hands wide, apparently indicating far more than the sun-filled cafe '—here I still am, five years later.'

'Sharna said you've built a successful business?'

Roni grinned. 'Success is in the eye of the beholder. Or the wallet of the owner, I guess. According to Matt, I home almost as many animals for free as we charge for stays. But, oh well. We might never be rich, but it's a lifestyle. A damn good one,' she added, suddenly serious, as though it were important that Gabrielle understand.

The child on Sharna's knee looked up at her, his icy-blue eyes intent. 'More,' he demanded.

'Simon!' Roni said. 'Manners, remember?'

'He only had a few crumbs,' Sharna said. 'I'll get him a jelly cake.'

'No, we're meeting Tracey shortly, and you know how she loves to fatten up these little monsters.' Roni affectionately scruffed Simon's hair and the boy scowled. 'I heard that you own a pub out along the river somewhere, Gabby?'

'Wurruldi,' Gabrielle nodded.

Roni screwed up her face, thinking. 'I'm not entirely sure where that is. I mean, I've heard it mentioned, but never found the time to go. What's it like?'

Sudden pride filled Gabrielle. 'It's a gorgeous old stone place, two storeys with what were once magnificent gardens around it, stretching down to a dock at the riverfront.'

'Sounds impressive. And there's a town nearby?'

'Looks like there was at some point, but it's deserted now. They must be holiday homes.'

'Do you think you'll get much business through there?' Roni broke off, glancing up as the cafe owner approached with a coffee and two plastic beakers of juice. 'Thanks, Sam. I'll grab the window seat, near the playpen.'

'No, sit with us,' Sharna urged, burying her face in Simon's hair. 'We never seem to find time for a girls' catch-up.'

'You're right,' Roni said. 'We should arrange to meet sometime. And work it around Taylor, when she's taking a break.'

'I guess she'll finally slow down a bit now,' Sharna said, turning to Gabrielle. 'Taylor's preggers. Due in five months.' She grinned at Roni. 'So, the way you two are going, the regional population will be doubled in a few years.'

'Don't look at me,' Roni protested. 'With the twins and animals and Matt, my hands are full. I'd be screwed if it wasn't for Tracey helping out. Anyway,' she continued, deftly turning the focus back to Gabrielle, who had been happy to sit absorbing the snippets of information, 'we were talking about Wurruldi. When are you planning to open the pub? In time for spring?'

Still wearing the wrap, Marian crawled into Gabrielle's lap, apparently not the least fazed by her unfamiliarity. Roni pulled a face. 'Sorry. They're so used to knowing everyone. My kids are definitely being raised by the village.'

'No worries.' Gabrielle settled the toddler more comfortably. 'I'm not reopening as a pub, but as a luxury guesthouse. Hayden's helping me remodel.' She caught the look that flashed between the two women and realised it was the second time she'd mentioned him in the space of minutes. 'And Justin,' she added, trying for balance. 'He's sourcing antique furniture from farm clearances, and doing some cabinetmaking. He's already stripped back the staircase and added fancy new carved post-things.' Justin had made a feature of the staircase, oiling the timber so that it glowed a deep, rich red, and adding a slight, sensuous curve to the bannister that slid as smoothly as silk beneath her hand. 'He's going to restore the original red-gum bar, too, but I have to find the time to strip off some really gross mirror tiles first.'

'Gabs is still running her old business as well. She's a PR exec,' Sharna said, with something near pride in her voice.

Gabrielle waved off the accolade. 'Supposedly I'm just on call for existing clients. But by the time I do a bit of work for that, then drive out to Wurruldi, it's too late to do anything there.'

Except hope to run into Hayden.

Roni stirred her coffee, then took a sip. 'Wow, it's a treat to get a hot drink. I usually have a kid on my lap,' she said, although Gabrielle felt she'd never heard a woman sound happier about usually having to put up with cold coffee. 'So, you don't live out at Wurruldi, Gabby?'

'No. It's, um . . .' Gabrielle hesitated, embarrassed. 'It's kind of lonely. I know it's not far as the crow flies, but it's off the main track and somewhat secluded. It'd be different if the other houses were occupied, and obviously it'll be fine once I have guests there, but at the moment it feels very isolated.'

'I know *exactly* what you mean,' Roni said. 'When I first moved here, I was stuck at the farm alone for days on end. Took me a while to appreciate the seclusion wasn't oppressive.'

Sharna looked thoughtful, leaning her chin on Simon's head as she gazed at Gabrielle. 'But you'd rather be living at Wurruldi than here?' she said slowly.

'Well, I guess I have to man up sooner or later, and I'd certainly be getting more done if I pulled myself together and moved out there. The guys tackled the upstairs renovations first, so I really only need to get some paint in the main bedroom, and then I'm out of excuses. It's perfectly liveable, just kind of . . . vast.'

'Have you thought about renting out rooms now?' Sharna asked.

'Oh, it's nowhere near guest standard,' Gabrielle said. 'The electrical and plumbing are almost done, but the rest is really basic. I've got so much to do before I can even start marketing it.' She laughed ruefully. 'Yet here I am, taking tea like a lady of leisure.'

'I didn't mean guests. More like tenants,' Sharna said. Simon scrambled off her knee and crawled onto his mum's. 'Missed your hot-coffee opportunity, there, Roni.' She turned back to Gabrielle, spots of colour highlighting her freckles. 'I was just thinking, I'm looking for somewhere to live. If company means you could move out there and get on with your renos, maybe it's something to consider? Of course,' she added slyly, 'we'd have to warn Wheaty that he no longer has the place to himself at night.'

Even without the bonus of Hayden not being able to avoid her, Sharna's proposal held instant appeal. 'But won't that be too far for you to travel in to the dairy? I know you keep crazy hours.'

Sharna fiddled with a ringlet. 'I'm kind of over that place. In any case, my brother came home from ag college last week, and the old man wants him to knuckle down and do a bit of work, remember what it's like to get his hands dirty instead of just reading about it. The business can't really afford both of us. Besides, if I bail while he's there, Dad and Mum might get used to the idea of me moving away. Like, to the city,' she added wistfully.

Gabrielle stared at her, absently massaging her upper chest as she thought. 'I can't rent you a room, Sharna,' she said gently.

Sharna flushed more deeply, picking at the skin around her nails. 'Of course. No, that's fine, I understand.'

'I can't rent you a room,' Gabrielle repeated, 'particularly if you're about to lose your job at the dairy.'

Sharna stared at her hands, a glassy sheen in her eyes.

'But what I can do—no, what I *want* to do—is offer you bed and board in exchange for your labour.'

'What?' The word came out as a gasp.

Gabrielle sat forward eagerly. 'Like I said, I've got so much to do out there. Not only could I use your company, but I could sure use your muscle. If your dad can spare you, I'd get so much more done if I was actually out at Wurruldi. But you know me: city girl. I'm way too chicken to be alone out there. This could be a win–win.'

'Oh, I'm pretty sure you wouldn't be alone for long,' Sharna chortled, and Roni smiled as though she were in on the joke.

Gabrielle raised her brows, looking from one to the other. Sharna glanced at Roni as though deciding whether they could share. Then she grinned. 'Last weekend, when you said you were too busy doing that storybook thing to hang with us—'

'Storyboard,' Gabrielle corrected breathlessly.

'Yeah, that. Wheaty turned up at Juz's barbie. Reckon he'd expected to see you there. Anyway, Juz made it clear— in boy speak, if that can ever be considered clear—that if Wheaty's not in the running, he's keen. Seems he's not languishing with a broken heart after I turned him down,' she added dryly.

'Oh. Oh!' Gabrielle said, fighting the urge to fan her face. She'd never had a problem attracting guys, but there had always been safety in the fact that everyone knew she was taken, that she and Brendan had been an item for over a decade. Knowing someone was making a play for her was flattering, but also a little terrifying. The tall, muscular woodworker was super nice, but the thought that he might scare Hayden off was . . . untenable. Without being too obvious, she needed to know what Hayden had replied. 'I, ah . . . so, Hayden told him to go for it?'

Roni giggled. 'Hardly that. Wheaty can be a man of few words, but he chooses them carefully. I sure hope you like him, because Juz is going to be behaving himself very well around you.'

Gabrielle gaped in surprise. 'But, like I was telling Sharna, Hayden's been avoiding me for the last three weeks.'

The metal bell over the cafe door jangled and Roni waved towards an older woman, her hair a nimbus of curls threaded through with fine, multicoloured leather strips. 'Here's Tracey. And that trick must run in the family, then, Gabby. Matt ran hot and cold for weeks, and I thought he couldn't stand the sight of me. Now look at us.' She gestured at her children.

'In the family? You mean Matt and Hayden are related?'

'Uh-huh. And Luke Hartmann, and about half the district,' Sharna said wryly. 'They call each other cousins, but they're probably second cousins, or cousins twice removed, or something like that.'

'But you're not related to any of them?' Gabrielle said curiously. 'You said your family has been here forever.'

'Oh, I'm for sure related to people around here,' Sharna said airily. 'But as I don't plan to breed with any of them, I reckon I don't have to figure out who or how.'

Roni shouldered a large satchel, which had a fluffy purple dog sticking out of one side, wet wipes out of the other. 'I guess that's why everyone gets so excited when new blood moves into the district. I'll catch you girls later. Send me a message when you want to do coffee.'

'Sure, sure,' Sharna said, pulling out her phone.

'Bye,' Gabrielle added, then turned back to Sharna. 'So, supposing you decide that you are interested in my proposition, how much notice would you have to give your dad?'

'Hang on two seconds,' Sharna muttered, tapping at her screen. Then she held up her phone. 'About this much. Done and dusted. When shall we move?'

23
Hayden

'Wait there, Taylor!' Hayden bellowed. 'Road, Trigg.' He glanced down the nearly empty street, strode to the pedestrian island, then had to wait for a solitary car to idle past. With Trigger at his side, he jogged across the remaining two lanes and took the shopping bags from Taylor. 'You're not supposed to carry heavy stuff, remember?'

'You're going to tell me that's doctor's orders?' she laughed. 'I'm knocked up, Wheaty, not knocked out.'

'But *I'll* be knocked out if Luke hears that I saw you hauling these and didn't grab them. Are you buying the whole IGA?' How she'd even managed to grasp all the carriers was a bit of a mystery. Luke always said she was stronger than she looked.

'Ready meals. And desserts. Apparently, pregnancy is not a cure-all for having zero cooking skills.'

'Guess Lukey's sad to discover that.'

'Lucky Gran still bakes for us once a week,' she replied as he hoisted the bags into the rear of her silver RAV4. 'Though I have a horrible fear she's going to expect me to suddenly become all domestic.' She ran a hand through her hair, the mist crystallising in tiny droplets. 'I'll be glad to see the end of this rain, even if it means the season is about to heat up.' He knew she was referring to the farming workload, rather than the actual temperature. 'Though from what I hear, you're keeping yourself pretty busy day and night. Rob told Luke you've been helping out on the farm, but Juz reckons you've got a ton done at Gabby's place.' She walked to the front of her car. 'Just take it a bit easy, okay, Wheaty? You don't have to push yourself.'

He slammed the boot. 'Weren't you chasing me up only weeks ago, making sure I wasn't drinking myself into oblivion in a pit of self-loathing?' He tried to make the words sound like a joke, but the wounds were too fresh. At least pushing himself physically, day and night, was having a numbing effect on his memories. Too tired for nightmares and too busy for reminiscing made a pleasant change. 'Thought you'd have enough on your plate now, without worrying about me.'

Taylor caressed her belly with a tiny smile, and jealousy bloomed within him. He wanted what Taylor and Luke had: each other, security. And now, family. But with all those things came risk. If he had nothing, loved nothing, nothing could be taken from him. He had to remember that.

'I've got plenty on my plate, but still room to worry about you.'

'No need. I'm big enough and ugly enough to take care of myself.'

'And I'm small enough and annoying enough that I'm just going to hang around, nagging at you,' she grinned. 'Anyway, you disappeared from Juz's so fast on Sunday, I didn't get a chance to talk to you.'

'Third-degree me, you mean,' he muttered as the door of Ploughs and Pies jangled open, the gust of hot pastry reminding him that he hadn't had lunch.

'Whatever you want to call it,' Taylor dimpled at him sweetly. 'But anyway, I did hear a bit of what went down with Juz.'

'Nothing went down,' he said, feeling the back of his neck heat up despite the chilly air.

She merely raised an eyebrow. 'So, the gorgeous Gabrielle is getting a guernsey?'

'I don't know about getting a guernsey,' he growled.

'But you're not going to argue the first part of my statement?' she teased. '*Gorgeous* Gabrielle?'

'Can't argue with the facts.' A car swished past, the tyres squelching on the bitumen. Thank god it had started to rain a bit heavier; Taylor would have to cut him some slack now.

'And what do you plan to do about those facts?' she asked, immediately proving him wrong.

He sighed, defeat sitting heavy in his gut. It had been nice to fantasise for a while. That was part of the reason he'd been avoiding Gabrielle: without her presence, there was no opportunity for ugly reality to manifest. 'Nothing at all. I fucked up, Tay.'

She frowned. 'How so?'

He stared over her head, at the far side of the street, though in reality he was looking back, to the previous month. 'I lost it. In front of her. Couldn't hold it in. Couldn't hold it back.'

'Flashbacks?' Taylor said, the teasing vanished from her tone.

He shook his head. 'Not just that. Guilt.'

'Is working out at Wurruldi too hard? Too confronting?' Her forehead wrinkled in consternation.

'It was before that.' Which made it ridiculous that he'd chased Juz off only a week ago, when he'd actually been relieved Gabrielle wasn't at the barbecue, despite a longing to see her. He rubbed a thumb against his shoulder, pressing hard. Physical pain was preferable to emotional. 'No. Actually, working there is kind of good. I feel . . . feel *her* there, sometimes. And it's good to be fixing the place up, anyway. It shouldn't have been let go so bad.'

'So, how is it that you've messed up with Gabby?' Taylor probed.

'Told you. I had a total fucking meltdown.'

'And how did she react?'

He eyed her suspiciously. 'C'mon, Tay. This is Settlers Bridge. Love Juz and Sharna with all my heart, but there's no way you've not already heard the story.'

She nodded. 'I have. But the way I heard it, Gabby took your panic attack in her stride.'

'She was pretty awesome,' he admitted.

Taylor merely watched him in calm, slightly unnerving silence.

He slumped back against the wet car, rubbing both hands through his hair. Sighed. 'Yeah. Okay. You don't have to say it. Gabrielle handled it fine, I just don't have the balls to face her. Like, she already knows that I'm a mess here,' he smacked a palm, wet from the car, against his forehead. 'But there's no way I can let it go any further. She can't know I'm a mess *here*.' He slammed the same hand against his shoulder.

Taylor snatched his hand away. 'You're not giving her much credit, Wheaty.'

'Have you *seen* her? She's so perfect, she should be a damn model. And what am I? Fucking Quasimodo.'

Taylor's eyes filled with tears, but he put that down to pregnancy hormones. She usually maintained professional decorum. 'Hayden—'

'Uh-oh, first-name terms. You gonna get serious on me, Doc?' he interrupted, trying to deflect her.

She wouldn't be deterred. 'You know everyone has something to hide, right? We all have secrets in our past, flaws and faults. That's life. That's what creates forward momentum; the constant search to do better, to be better.'

He shook his head. 'I can't risk that forward momentum, Tay. It's not just this.' He was gentler as he smacked his hand into his shoulder this time. The scar tissue could only take so much abuse. 'I can't risk caring about anyone else. There are too many already. And now you're adding to that list.' He nodded at the slight curve of her belly.

'You think I'm not scared too, Wheaty?' she said softly. 'I'm scared literally every single day, worrying about what I could lose, what could be stolen from me. The more perfect my life is, the more there is to fear. But if I let myself fall into the trap of denying the risk, avoiding the danger, refusing to take the chances, then I've already lost. Because a life half-lived is a life half-wasted. Life should be seized and relished, not feared, no matter what your experiences.'

'But it wasn't only my life, Taylor,' he reminded her.

She nodded. 'I know, Hayden. And I also know that it doesn't matter how many times I tell you that it wasn't your fault, you're going to have to find that forgiveness in yourself.'

A thunderclap rolled overhead, the echo cracking like a whip through the valley, and she tried to lighten the mood. 'I do love it when my wise words are backed by celestial applause.'

He gave her a grin. 'Got tickets on yourself, Doc. Come on, get in your car before it starts pouring.'

She clambered in and buzzed down the window as he closed the door. 'So, what are you up to today? Besides helping maidens in distress with their shopping.'

'Not so sure you can make claim to being much of a maiden, when you've got a bun in the oven.' His chest felt less constricted now they were back on more casual ground. Taylor had helped him through some tough times, but he wasn't one for talking it out. 'Dad doesn't need me today, so I might head out to Wurruldi.'

'No other work booked in?'

'Not today.' He'd knocked back jobs, keeping time free to do Gabrielle's renovation.

'Looks like you'll have some company out there, then.'

'How so?' Even as the town doctor, it was unlikely Taylor would know if the painters had finally decided to put in an appearance.

'Sharna moved out there a few days ago.'

'She what?' Why did jealousy instantly spike through him?

Taylor started the car. 'Is Trigg off the road?'

He pointed at the footpath. The dog had only needed a twitch of his finger to know to stay on the side, his brown and blue eyes unblinkingly trained on his master.

'Tim's come back from ag college to help his dad,' Taylor said. 'So, Sharna was at a bit of a loose end. She's helping Gabby out with stuff at the hotel.'

'Cool,' he nodded, trying to process the information. Maybe he should stick to working at Wurruldi at night— although if Sharna was out there, Gabrielle might hang around later.

At some stage, he would have to see her again. Had it been long enough for her to forget he'd made an idiot of himself?

❧

'Hayden!'

He could almost persuade himself that Gabrielle's surprised greeting held nothing but pleasure.

With a rumbling stomach he'd left Taylor and driven straight out to Wurruldi. He knew that if he gave himself time to think he'd find excuses not to go if there was any chance of Gabrielle being there.

Coward.

He had to front her, anyway, to discuss the next stage of the renovations. Surely it would be better to do it with Sharna present, use her as a buffer against awkward conversations or silence.

Yet Gabrielle made it seem that there was no issue. She set down the cardboard box she'd lifted from her car, and walked quickly towards him. Damn, she looked good. Her blonde hair was up in some kind of knot on top of her head, with pieces escaping to frame her face. A face that no man would ever tire of looking at.

'Hey, Gabrielle,' he finally managed. 'Wasn't sure if I'd time it right to catch up with you.'

'I was beginning to think you were avoiding me,' she said with a devastating lack of artifice. 'The highlight of my day has been getting your texts.'

The words hit him with a physical resonance, impermissible hope suddenly soaring high, but then she blushed and added, 'To see what you'd got done overnight.'

Yeah, that made a hell of a lot more sense.

As she reached him, Gabby stretched up on tiptoe and planted a kiss on his cheek.

He stood as still as a monolith, unable to either act or react.

She dropped down onto the balls of her feet and shot him a devastating smile. 'I just wanted to say thank you for all the work you've been doing. You're kind of like Batman, appearing in the dark of night and setting things to rights.'

Jesus, he wanted to seize hold of her, crush her slight frame against him, feel her pliable softness in his arms. 'I'm probably more of a Bruce Banner,' he managed to mumble. 'The Hulk.'

She pressed her lips together, her dark eyes compassionate. 'The traumatised superhero who changes personality when he's stressed.'

Evidently, they weren't going to politely pretend his meltdown had never happened. He held up his paint-speckled hand. 'More because the undercoat I'm slapping on those dark walls is supposed to be grey, but looks kind of green in this light.' At a stretch.

She took his hand, tipping the palm up to the watery sun as though she needed to inspect it more closely. 'Oh, that was you? I thought the painter must have finally turned up. I was kind of surprised he didn't quote first but, hey, I'll settle for just having the job done.'

'I'd keep that a bit quiet,' he cautioned, 'or you'll end up paying through the nose. Anyway, I figured while I was waiting to catch up with you to discuss taking out another wall, I could be getting some undercoat on now that I've plastered the cracks. The foundation needs to be perfect and a good undercoat is your most effective way of getting that.'

'Don't I know it,' Gabrielle muttered.

He snapped the fingers on his free hand. 'Trigg, out you get.' The dog was still sitting in the car, keeping an eye on

Hayden from the warmth of the vehicle. 'Can't blame him for not wanting to get out. I need to get some work done outside, but that's going to have to wait for better weather.' And until he could steel himself against constantly looking for *her* in the gardens.

'Well, I have a surprise for you inside,' she said, tugging his hand.

Thanks to Taylor, he had a fair idea what—or rather, who—that was, but he was more than happy to play along if it gave him an excuse to hold Gabrielle's hand a little longer. It was juvenile and pathetic, but so what? If it was all he could have, he'd take it.

The door slammed in front of them as they headed towards the hotel. 'I swear this place is haunted,' Gabrielle said.

Her glib words stopped him in his tracks. 'Because the door catches the wind off the river?' he forced out.

'Legit, that only happens when you're here,' she said, letting them into the foyer. Even with the patched plaster-work and grime, the glow of the chandelier made the marble-floored entryway welcoming. 'But, no, not that. There's a small door from the original kitchen that leads down into the cellar. Anyway, Justin and I were talking—'

'Juz?' he said, a little too quickly.

Gabrielle darted a curious look up at him, but then something distracted her. 'And here's your surprise.'

He followed her gaze as Sharna hurtled down the ruby-hued glow of the restored timber staircase.

'Wheaty! What do you think of my new place?'

He reluctantly let go of Gabrielle's hand to halt the younger woman's headlong flight. 'What do you mean, new place?' he played along.

She stepped back and pouted up at him. He noticed she wore the same slightly pink sheer lip gloss as Gabrielle. 'Ack. Shit poker face, Wheaty. You totally knew, didn't you? That's why I hate bloody Settlers; no one can have a secret.'

'I wouldn't say that,' Gabrielle muttered.

'I heard you'd moved over here,' he admitted. 'What's the deal?'

'Labour for bed and board,' Gabrielle supplied. 'And as payment for keeping me company out here.'

'Sounds sweet.' He hadn't realised that Gabrielle was also moving out, and his shearer's cottage seemed suddenly very unappealing.

'You want in on it?' Sharna asked, her eyes dancing. 'I'm sure Gabs can find somewhere to put you up. The linen she's bought is ah-mazing, but only two of the bedrooms are liveable at the moment, so you'd have to share . . .' she trailed off meaningfully.

'Wouldn't want to cramp your style, Sharn,' he said dryly. 'Anyway, you don't like my housekeeping, remember?'

'Wouldn't be me it affects,' she grinned, refusing to back down.

Gabrielle moved towards the room on the left, looking embarrassed. 'I left that last lot of your boxes out the front, Sharna.'

'I'll grab them,' he said.

Sharna rolled her eyes. 'Don't bother. I know when I've been given the arse. Go on, then, you two, go check out those bedrooms.'

Hayden frowned. Sometimes Sharna took it too far. Shit, what if Gabrielle thought he'd put Sharna up to it? 'Actually, I've got to get the paint from the back of the ute. I bought a few more trade buckets while I was over in Murray Bridge. Hope that's okay, Gabrielle? It's cheaper in bulk.'

'That's great. If Wayne Learman ever shows up, he won't need to bring paint.'

'I reckon you can cross him off your Christmas-card list,' Hayden said. 'You've been chasing him for what, a couple of months?' As though he didn't know exactly when Gabrielle had first shown up in Settlers Bridge. 'He's not coming.'

'Then who do I try now?' Gabrielle twisted the ring she wore on her little finger. 'Nobody else in Adelaide will touch it, and it seems everyone closer is booked out.'

'Don't worry about it. Your electrics are all certified now, right? And plumbing is done in the first bathroom, booked in for the others. There's a tiler in Murray Bridge who owes me a favour, if you still want to upgrade them, but other than that, there's not much we can't take care of ourselves.'

'I can't ask you to put in even more work here. I hired you for the actual building stuff, not window dressing. And I know those couple of invoices I've managed to drag out of you were nowhere near full tote.'

'Told you way back, friends help friends around here.' He gave a mock scowl. 'But I'm sure as hell not helping you choose any curtains, if that's what you mean by window dressing. I saw your vision boards; you've got it all covered.'

Gabrielle crossed into the front bar. The room was empty now, its original purpose hinted at by a couple of dated wall prints and the partially tiled bar and shelves. 'It was more a figure of speech than a reference to actual curtains. But, see, that's my problem. I have this dream, but when it comes to turning a fantasy into reality, I have zero experience. I don't know what I have to do to make it happen.'

He met her gaze. Was she talking about more than a fairly simple renovation? How could a woman who looked like she did possibly be as inexperienced as she hinted? 'Take it step by step, I guess,' he ventured tentatively.

She moved closer, a trace of gardenia wafting over him. 'And the first step would be?' she murmured.

Christ, the first step would be pulling her into his arms and never letting her go. The second would be working out how he was going to make love to her without her ever seeing his ruined body. 'Maybe discussing your . . . dream,' he croaked.

'Or I could show you?' She was so close to him now he could feel the warmth radiating from her body. His clenched knuckles brushed her forearm.

'That would work.' He opened his hand, deliberately slid it up to her shoulder.

'Shit!' They both jumped as one of the prints slammed to the floor. 'Lucky I didn't like that one,' Gabrielle gasped. She didn't pull away from him, but the moment was lost.

Or perhaps he had imagined it to begin with.

'Not much to like in a still life,' he agreed.

'You have no idea how right you are,' Gabrielle agreed fervently, as though he spoke about more than the tacky print.

'Anyway, work. I'll strip all your old floor coverings before I do any more undercoating, otherwise the skirting boards will get a ridge of paint and need scraping back. Once they're tossed, I'll knuckle down and get the undercoating done throughout, while you pick out final colours and finishes. And the curtains,' he added with a grin.

'No, that's what I was trying to say before I got . . . distracted,' she protested. 'I can't have you doing all the work for me.' She extracted herself from the hand he still had loosely on her upper arm, and wandered over to the print, propping it against the wall.

'Dodgy nail,' he said, moving to investigate the reason for it falling. 'Anyway, why not have me do the work? I don't have anything else on at the moment.'

She shook her head, scrubbing at the carpet with the toe of her shoe. Not high heels for once, he noticed, but a fancy leather work boot that wouldn't be out of place in a shopping mall.

'It makes sense for me to complete the job, instead of just being the middleman and chasing up contractors for you,' he pressed.

'I kind of had this plan that I'd actually achieve something myself.' Her tone was despondent, as though she were failing some imaginary test.

'Achieve something? Seems to me you're pretty accomplished in your professional field. And, yes, I did google you.' Complete with pictures, although his burst of honesty didn't extend to admitting that aloud.

She darted him a glance and a wry smile. 'Professional achievement isn't the same as personal accomplishment. Just like education doesn't necessarily equate to intelligence. Anyway, I promised myself I was going to do this alone. As it is, I've barely even managed to get contractors to show up, no matter how much money I throw in their direction. And, yes, I know you warned me that not everything is for sale around here.' She forestalled the comment she obviously thought he'd make. He hadn't been about to. 'In fact, pretty much the only tradies who turn up are the ones you've strongarmed into coming. And now you're stuck here doing absolutely everything else for me. I'm not sure where my input is, other than financial.'

'So, help me.'

'What?'

'Help me do the work. Prove to yourself that you can achieve your dream, but do it by being proactive, instead of hiring tradies. Roll up your sleeves and grab a paintbrush.'

She stared at him for a long moment, as though the idea were mad. Then a slow, delighted smile lit her face. 'But I thought you said the floor coverings had to come up first, boss?'

24
Gabrielle

Near the river, the winter chill wasn't evident, particularly in the lull of dawn. As the sun broke through the cloud cover the cliffs came alive, patched in ochre stripes of red, orange and yellow. Ripples spread through the reflected pink and purple sky as the occasional leap of a redfin created a third dimension on the natural still-life canvas. The haunting cry of bush stone-curlews echoed along the river valley, while egrets and spoonbills noisily puddled through the shallow water around the reeds, searching for breakfast.

Gabrielle took a deep breath, trying to absorb the tranquillity in an effort to slow her racing heart. She'd spent last night replaying the events of the previous day in her mind, and there had been an unhealthy but delightful amount of pulse-pounding going on.

She had taken the biggest gamble of her life, putting every ounce of her professionally cultivated acting ability on the line when she dashed outside to greet Hayden. He could have rejected her. He could have been sullen or angry or just plain withdrawn. Instead, he had kept a tight hold of her hand. And he had quickly picked up on her innuendo and gone along with it.

The thrill of the chase shivered through her. She couldn't put her finger on what it was about Hayden that had piqued her interest from the moment she had, quite literally, stumbled across him and Trigger. Now, a hint of his approval or the tiniest gleam of what she interpreted as interest in his green eyes stirred a primeval need to be noticed, to be desired.

As the weather blew in, she dashed back up the overgrown paddock, through the long, tangled grass and into the foyer in a bluster of cold wind and leaves. The hotel was still quiet, so she headed for the luxury of a long, hot shower, to feel the fierce needles of water tingling her chilled skin.

'Gabs?' Sharna knocked on the door as Gabrielle was pulling her jeans back on.

'Ten minutes,' she called back. Over the past few days she had tried to discover more about Hayden's PTSD from Sharna. But her friend, perhaps because of her own issues with secrecy, was surprisingly tight-lipped. Still, slowly discovering Hayden's layers was as tantalising as unwrapping a gift.

She grimaced wryly at her reflection as she applied tawny eyeshadow: the unwrapping analogy was unfortunate, given that she could never reveal herself. It had been a very long time since she'd felt this level of all-consuming interest in a man—actually, in anything—and spending yesterday wandering the house with him and Sharna as they made notes of what still needed to be done had been sweet torture.

Sharna banged on the bathroom door for the second time. 'Gabs?' she called. 'I'm sure you look divine. Come on out. I need to clean my teeth before lunchtime.'

Gabrielle fluffed her lavender mohair midriff jumper and folded down the high cowl neck of her bodysuit over it. Her hands paused on the stretchy black fabric. It seemed unlikely Hayden would be the kind of guy to agree to getting it on in a dark room, and the only operator she trusted to do her spray tan, after years of perfecting the subtle layering needed to match her natural colouring, was on an extended European trip. And a flawless tan wasn't a long-term solution, anyway. Hayden would eventually see her for what she was. And that, she knew, would be a PR disaster. Loss of consumer confidence and trust.

Her bubble of happiness deflated, she slammed shut her large make-up case and opened the door.

'I knew it. Stunning.' Making the most of not keeping dairy hours, Sharna still wore her pyjamas, her feet stuffed into fluffy socks.

'You know, you're really good for morale. I might have to keep you around.'

'Happy to be of service,' Sharna grinned. 'Though I know who else would be happy to give you a boost—among other things.'

'I hope you're right. He's kind of . . . intriguing.'

'I'm going to assume that's city speak for "Wheaty's hot-as",' Sharna teased, scooting past Gabrielle and into the blue-tiled room.

'You assume correctly,' she said after only a second of hesitation. Since Amelie died and Brigitte moved overseas, she'd had no one to gossip and giggle with. And her relationship with Brendan had never been the type of affair that invited secrets shared with girlfriends. But this was her new life.

'Speaking of,' Sharna continued, toothbrush in her mouth, 'he's already got a skip delivered and is downstairs demolishing something in a manly chest-beating fashion.'

'He's here?' she gasped. There was little chance of looking effortlessly attractive if Hayden had been working for an hour while she was primping.

She dashed down the stairs and into the Ladies' Lounge, following the sound of ripping fabric. Hayden had already made inroads on pulling up the thin, flat carpet, slicing it into squares and placing it in towering stacks. The motes of centuries floated in the sun coming through the sparkly new windows and the early-morning sun glinted enticingly off the river at the bottom of the long block.

'Morning, Sleeping Beauty,' Hayden smiled as he clambered up from his knees. 'I grabbed you a coffee from The Overland. You mentioned you liked theirs, and Ploughs and Pies isn't open yet. Skim milk no sugar, right? Might be a bit cold by now.'

She reached for the disposable cup. Sleeping Beauty had been a throwaway line, but the fact that he remembered her coffee order? It was on par with bringing her flowers.

Their fingers touched as she took the coffee. She almost dropped it.

'Careful. Double cupped to keep it at least a bit warm.'

They were both still holding the cup. Hayden brushed a strand of hair from her face with his other hand. 'I like your hair like that. Cute.'

'It's just a ponytail,' she said, resisting the urge to toss her head to make the tresses bounce. It had taken an age to iron out any hint of frizz and hide the elastic tie by winding a strand of her hair over it.

'Well, you look very workmanlike.'

'Must be an interesting crew you hang out with,' she replied with a grin. Fully clothed and made-up, she had boundless confidence. Much like her sketches and designs, her presentation was a form of artistry, her face and body the canvas. She could paint it fresh each day, put a marketing spin on the product; but never would she allow a naked canvas to be displayed.

'Ugh, get a room, you two,' Sharna chirped from behind Gabrielle. 'Oh, wait. We have a whole heap of them. Half of which need to have the floors stripped today, right? Well then, as I was under the impression I had quit the dairy, I would like to see less cow-eyes and more *moooving* of floor coverings.'

'It's far too early for you,' Hayden grumbled. 'Not that your so-called humour improves later in the day. Here. Coffee. Gloves. Box cutter. Start in that corner, pull as hard as you can. What doesn't lift off the floor, cut away. I'll come along behind you and pull the staples and punch in the nails. There are masks in the box over there; you might want to put one on. There's probably fifty years' worth of beer and dust soaked into this stuff.'

'I was looking through the title last night,' Gabrielle said as she kneeled at the edge of the room, carefully levering the knife under the carpet. She'd sat up in bed, the new Garnier-Thiebaut sateen linen smooth against her skin as she paged through paperwork, trying not to think about Hayden. 'And there's definitely decades' worth of beer in the carpet. Maybe not so much in here, but next door in the main bar. Apparently, the original building is over a hundred and thirty years old. It was in the one family until two thousand and seven.'

Hayden had squatted to take hold of the manky carpet next to her. His shoulders tensed. 'Yep.'

She looked across him to Sharna, lifting a questioning eyebrow.

Sharna shook her head quickly, as though signalling her not to pursue the conversation. 'I'll put some music on,' she suggested, shoving to her feet and crossing to prop her phone on the windowsill.

With the music blasting, they worked in companionable silence for an hour, Gabrielle and Sharna slicing the carpet, Hayden carting armloads of the heavy fabric and underlay out to the skip. The edge of the floor was painted with a black border half a metre wide, but inside that the boards glowed a rich gold.

As they pulled up the last strips of carpet, Sharna lifted her voice over the eighties soundtrack she had selected. 'What are you going to use this room for, Gabs?'

Gabrielle wriggled her fingers, trying to find room for her long nails in the gloves. She needed to have her gels removed; she adored the elegance, but they were definitely not designed for labourers. A quiver of excitement ran through her, because it finally seemed that not only was her project feasible, the culmination was imminent. With the original timber revealed, the room looked brighter and more inviting. 'I have kind of an interim plan because, considering I can only overnight a handful of guests, there's a ridiculous amount of space downstairs. At least until I can figure out how to make extra bedrooms from the outbuildings or . . .' she trailed off, watching Hayden's back for signs of anger as he shifted the equipment into the main bar. 'Anyway, for the time being, I'm using this one as a morning room with a cafe-style setting on the verandah for the nicer weather. The bar will be more of a multi-purpose area. I won't need much seating for dining, so I'm seeing it as a sitting room and a library.'

As they carried their tools across the foyer and into the larger room, she pointed towards the boarded-up fireplace in the far corner. 'I'm going to get the fireplaces operational again, make sure they draw.' She pulled a wry face at Hayden. 'That's one trade I've actually managed to get booked in.' She had been planning to surprise him with that achievement, hoping for his approval.

His face tightened. 'You've got gas bayonets down here, you don't want to use heaters? And the air-con throughout has been serviced, right?'

Sharna put her phone on the bar, suddenly watching him anxiously.

Catching her stare, Hayden gave a short shake of his head. 'Not earning your keep over there, Sharna. Come on, put in some muscle.'

'Slave driver,' she said, picking up her box cutter and heading into a corner.

'I'm having the air-con updated, but the charm of a wood fire is hard to beat,' Gabrielle said.

'If you say so,' Hayden muttered darkly. 'Can be dangerous, though.'

'What else you got planned, Gabs?' Sharna called over her shoulder.

Gabrielle rubbed her nose with the back of her hand. The amount of dust she had inhaled, despite the mask, should have made it impossible to smell anything, but compared to the slightly piney tinge of the floorboards they had revealed in the lounge, the carpet she kneeled on definitely held the aroma of a pub: beer, spirits, fried food and cigarettes.

'I'm having Juz make bookcases to line the two walls around the fireplace,' she said. 'Then we'll furnish it with some fifties-era lounges and side-tables. Maybe a retro stereo set up with a stack of old vinyls that residents can go through.' As she spoke, the room came to life in her imagination, enthusiasm firing her descriptions. She wanted her friends to understand her vision, to share her passion. Living in a beautiful apartment, still she had felt homeless and displaced. She swivelled on her knees to point. 'The area over there, overlooking the river, will be for intimate dining—tiny tables with just two seats for romantic lunches. In the centre of the room, I'll put a couple of larger tables, in case we have families stay. Although that's not really the demographic I'm targeting, but I guess we can't have a no-kids rule.'

'Or no dogs,' Hayden said, watching as Trigger padded towards her. 'Are you okay, Gabrielle?' His posture suggested he was ready to surge forward, although she knew he only needed to click his fingers to control his dog.

She nodded and held a timid hand towards the animal.

Trigger swung his head to look at Hayden, requesting permission to approach.

'Okay, Trigg. Lie down,' Hayden said.

The dog sank to the ground with his chin on his paws, but rolled his eyes up to watch Gabrielle.

She wished Hayden would hold her hand again, but she really didn't need him to. She put her palm to the dog's nose, holding her breath as he sniffed at it. His tongue flicked out, far smoother—and much wetter—than a cat's lick. With one finger, Gabrielle rubbed between his eyes, like Hayden had instructed. The dog gave a huge sigh, as though she'd hit just the right spot, and she laughed in delight. She wouldn't be approaching strange dogs anytime soon, but Trigger seemed an extension of Hayden, like a permanent shadow. He felt safe.

Hayden grinned. 'Ah, see? He's in love with you already.'

'If I'd known he was so easy to win over, I wouldn't have wasted any time.' Her words were dangerous, she knew it. But Hayden could easily pretend she was truly talking about the dog, if he chose to. Yet she didn't believe he would. Every time their glances met, the tension in the room was almost tangible. It had to be evident, even to Sharna, loudly singing along with her awful Spotify list, that there was something going on.

Hayden sat back on his haunches, looking at her levelly. 'Maybe he shouldn't have played hard to get.'

Sharna snorted. 'Since when do dogs play hard to get? Give them one glance and they roll on their backs with their paws in the air. Even when you're a cat person.'

Gabrielle shot her a sympathetic glance, but Sharna didn't notice. 'Anyway, you were telling us about the room plans?'

'Uh, yeah,' she said. As much as she loved Sharna, a little privacy might be nice.

Evidently, Hayden thought the same thing. 'Hey, Sharn, when we're finished in here, how about you take my ute into Settlers and grab us lunch? My shout, but I know Sam always looks after you.'

'Like there's anyone she doesn't look after,' Sharna muttered. 'But, yeah, I get the message.'

So did Gabrielle. Her heart beat way too fast, and she tugged hard at the carpet, trying to mask her sudden nervousness. 'So, anyway, this will be a secondary lounge room, for when I close the breakfast room for cleaning.'

'Aren't both rooms essentially the same thing, then?' Hayden asked.

Sharna snorted. 'Men.' Then she grinned. 'But feel free to explain the difference, Gabs. Grab your storybooks again.'

'Boards,' she corrected automatically. 'But I don't need them. The difference will really only be in the furnishings, at this stage. Because the other room was originally the Ladies' Lounge, I'm thinking of making it pretty, with floral wallpaper and soft colours. Sumptuous fabrics. Kind of going for a genteel air. This room will have more of a retro, masculine vibe.' She stood, stretching her calves, which had cramped while she worked on the floor, then ran her hand across the underside of the bar. 'Justin reckons we can strip this back to the original red-gum slab, which will make a fantastic feature. If I've got my head around it right, even though I don't have a liquor licence I can still provide drinks. I just can't sell them. So, service will be all: "Would you care for a complimentary snifter of port, sir, as you recline before the fire with your book? A sherry with your novel, ma'am?"'

'Ma'am?' Sharna gurgled. 'When did we turn American?'

Hayden had returned to levering out nails with the claw of his hammer, but shoved back onto his haunches with a grunt. 'Seriously? That's your only problem with that visual?'

'That and the lack of Moscato,' Sharna said. 'What's your beef?'

'All these guys hanging around for free drinks. And the sightseeing,' he added, lifting his chin towards Gabrielle to indicate she would be the sight.

'With the market I'm targeting, I don't think pervy Mervs will be an issue,' she laughed.

'Just so you know, I'm with Wheaty on that one,' Sharna said. 'But I figure you're going to have staff out here, right? That'll make it safer.'

Gabrielle shook her head. 'It's not really where I'm going at the moment. I plan to get the guesthouse side running first, and because I have so few rooms, it'll start out quite exclusive. But with all this downstairs space, I'd love to eventually offer something more.'

She straightened to point out through the paned windows. 'You couldn't put a price on that view—uninterrupted, tranquil water frontage with that huge old tree in the middle of the grounds. My dream is to add high teas indoors in winter near the open fire, light lunches in spring in the courtyard, gourmet picnics or something similar beneath the beautiful purple jacaranda in summer, where you'll catch the breeze off the river. And perhaps rustic farm fare during autumn, something like pumpkin soups and organic sourdough, all using local, seasonal produce. Some kind of unique experience, value adding that will cater to day visitors, not just the overnight B&Bers. If I ever get that sorted, then I'll need staff. But, until then, I'll be on my own.'

'Only if you throw me out,' Sharna said, apparently oblivious to the fact that she was residing in one of the limited bedrooms. Not that Gabrielle cared; she only needed to source enough paying visitors to prove she was capable of conceiving and building a functioning business by herself. If that took a little longer because a couple of the rooms were unrentable, it didn't matter; Sharna's company was well worth the delay.

'That won't be happening,' she said. 'I mean, I kind of don't want to rush it. I'd rather build the business organically. Does that even make any sense? It's like I want to feel out what fits here, rather than force the property to fit my ideas, which could turn out to be way off base.'

'Sounds good to me,' Hayden said.

'But dumb, because that's really not the way to do business, is it?' she said reluctantly. 'I really need to decide whether I'm trying to create a business that proves to the world that I'm capable, or whether I want something that . . . nurtures me.' Gabrielle rolled her eyes. 'Seriously, a few weeks away from the city and I'm channelling my inner hippie. I should probably have bought a property in Byron.'

'Glad you didn't,' Hayden said, his gaze level. 'This place needs someone to love it.'

'Glad you didn't,' Sharna echoed, grinning wickedly. 'It's not only the place that needs some love.'

The front door slammed, causing all three of them to jump. Hayden frowned. 'I'm positive I closed that when I came through. Have you been out, Sharn?'

The strawberry-blonde shook her head. 'I don't care if I never see another early morning as long as I live.'

'Told you, it's my resident ghost,' Gabrielle joked.

'Ah—' Sharna cautioned, screwing up her face.

Hayden gave a shake of his head, a communication that seemed to frequently pass between the friends. Then he glanced at Gabrielle, but allowed his gaze to slide away, his face suddenly tight. 'I sure as hell hope not. My nan lived here all her life.'

'Oh?' she said. Why hadn't he mentioned that before? Then she gasped, choking back her sudden realisation. 'Oh. All her life? Do you mean she also . . .'

He nodded grimly. 'She also died here.'

25
Ilse

Ilse moved back into the centre of the foyer and fisted her hands on her hips as she glared at the trio in the bar. Her heart thumped erratically as her gaze steadied on Hayden. She had loved him so very much. But now she felt only pain: he had deserted her, and that was a betrayal from which she could never recover.

She gave a short, sharp laugh, unsurprised when none of the group paid her any attention. She would never recover from anything again, but neither would she be harmed or hurt. Her entire existence was now not only in this place, but in memory.

And that memory was suddenly all too clear. As her temperature had increased the cough worsened and the chest pains began, but still she waited for him. Of course, she could easily have picked up the telephone, called her son, or one of the other grandchildren. But Hayden had made a promise, and she had faith he would honour it. And, in a way, it suited her to be frailer by the time he arrived; that way she wouldn't have to admit how much she relied on him, and his innate guilt would work in favour of her grand plan.

Hayden had always been her favourite grandchild, and she was old enough—*had been* old enough, she corrected herself acidly—that she didn't find it necessary to hide behind the pretence of loving them all equally. When his mother needed help, Ilse had been taken by the opportunity of raising a toddler who increasingly reminded her of his uncle, lost to the Vietnam war. As Hayden matured, his charming roguishness and self-assurance were also comfortingly reminiscent of his grandfather.

Growing old was unimaginably hard. Although anticipating a few aches and pains as she drifted inexorably towards old age, she had expected to remain fiercely independent. She had been unprepared for the humiliation of being forced to rely on others.

But Hayden had made it easier, though she never told him.

She scowled now as he mentioned her name. Gabrielle gazed at him, her lovely face soft with sympathy. Ilse looked for something to push to the floor. How dare he invoke her as a means to win Gabrielle over? What was he even doing here, when he hadn't bothered to come the one time she truly needed him?

She hesitated: the thought was a little unjust. Hayden often seemed to anticipate her needs, the frustrating, menial tasks she could no longer complete alone. Those that he didn't foresee he would laughingly trade for a slice of cake. In fact, he spent so much time with her that she had secretly hoped he would move from the ramshackle quarters on his father's farm, and come to live in the riverfront cottage alongside hers. She had been certain her prompting had him leaning that way, too, until his parents got tied up in his mother's illness. Hayden had been exhausted, running both his construction business and mucking in on the farm to help his brother, who didn't always seem to appreciate his input. Not as much as she had, anyway. Yet, still, he made time for her.

After the chemo, his mum had finally turned a corner and Hayden seemed to slough off some of the weight that bowed his shoulders. She had decided that, if he didn't recognise the logical plan by himself soon, she would suggest he choose a cottage.

Ilse moved closer to the group of young folks. Despite her anger, a flicker of concern crossed her mind: Hayden didn't look himself.

Clearly, his mother was from weaker stock than her own: god forbid that unspeakable disease also had him in its maw.

On his knees still, he smiled up at Gabrielle, and Ilse clapped a hand across her mouth. For the briefest second, in her mind he had been Ronald, locked in that moment of so long ago, when he had proposed to her in that very spot.

But then Gabrielle laughed, her voice low and musical as she pointed upstairs, and the spell broke. Hayden rose, rubbing his left shoulder as he dropped a hammer to the ground, and Ilse found her anger again.

He had no right to look at Gabrielle in that manner. Gabrielle was doing the right thing, rebuilding the premises. Somehow, the ideas Ilse whispered to the girl, the notions she planted in her head, were taking root—and Hayden would only distract her.

The trio headed her way, though the younger woman made for the front door. And, for goodness sake, they had a dog with them. She liked animals, but they had their place: outdoors. Now there was a rainbow-coloured mutt stuck like glue to Hayden's leg. Dog hair would be added to the dust.

'Grab a loaf of crusty bread, too, please Sharn,' Gabrielle called after the blonde woman. 'I've made something special for dinner.'

'Yum!' Sharna yelled back from outside.

Hayden and Gabrielle moved towards the stairs, but Hayden paused, his foot on the bottom tread. He turned back towards Ilse.

Her heart skipped.

'Wait a moment,' he said, and she sucked in a tremulous breath. He saw her!

He strode towards her, and the anger she wore like a coat fell to the floor. Oh, she had missed him, it was hard to be separated from those you loved the most.

She leaned forward eagerly, anticipating his kiss on her cheek.

But Hayden walked past her.

Of course he did. She was mad to think he could do otherwise.

He reached up, above the door jamb, to where a nasty-looking black house spider had her web, the greying strands threading into a funnel-like nest behind the wooden architrave.

'What have you found?' Gabrielle called, crossing the marble floor to join him. The dog swung his head from one side to the other, as though following their conversation.

'This needed rescuing,' Hayden said, carefully extracting a fluttering moth from the silky snare.

'How pretty,' Gabrielle peered over his arm at the pale cream insect, the upper wings dotted with multicoloured, pinprick-sized spots. 'It looks like she's covered in fairy confetti. I've never noticed that before; I always thought moths were plain white.'

'Fairy confetti, huh?' Hayden grinned as he held the moth in his cupped palm at eye-level, picking each sticky strand of web free with the long, slightly spatulate fingers he had inherited from his grandfather. 'Don't know about that. But she's definitely too pretty to be spider-dinner.'

'So, you only help the ones you find attractive?' Gabrielle slanted her dark gaze up at Hayden, and Ilse caught her breath. Not that she was shocked at the younger woman's obvious flirtation; she admired self-confidence. No, her surprise was at Hayden's reaction. His eyes locked on Gabrielle's. He lowered his hand as his chest swelled, every ounce of his attention on the attractive woman beside him. She could practically feel his yearning interest, could read the admiration and hope and desire in his expression as the two of them swayed towards one another, as though inexorably drawn.

'Oh, for goodness sake,' she snapped. Hayden had no right to these feelings and emotions, passions she would never again experience *because of him*. She tutted loudly and the dog swung his head to look questioningly at her, one eye a bright blue so like Ronald's she had to tear her gaze away, refusing to be judged by him. She had every right to her anger. Except—she inhaled quickly—except wasn't she once more experiencing the alluring melancholy of those long-forgotten emotions, albeit vicariously?

She patted at her chest, her wedding ring rotating loosely on her finger as she tried to steady her pulse. But the sweet reminiscence refused to be calmed; she could recall the flowering of love, like the gradual unfurling of petals to the gentle kiss of the morning sun.

'I rescue the ones that catch my attention,' Hayden murmured.

Gabrielle caught her lower lip between her teeth, her high cheekbones flushing.

Ilse's heart danced. She may have been wrong. Perhaps Hayden wasn't distracting Gabrielle; rather, she was the woman he needed, the force who would balance and complete him, make him the man his grandfather had been.

'Besides,' Hayden smiled wryly, 'Nan taught me to always rescue moths, butterflies and bees, because they're pollinators.' He held his hand towards the door the younger girl had left open, and blew gently so that the insect lifted from his palm and headed outdoors.

He shrugged, an awkward movement with only his right shoulder. 'Nan pretty much raised me, so I always took onboard anything she told me. My brother and first sister came along pretty quickly after me, though the other two were years later. I always said Mum and Dad should've invested in a state-of-the-art flat panel TV.'

Gabrielle snorted with sudden laughter, but she didn't interrupt.

'It would have been cheaper than bringing up five of us. So, Nan took me while Mum dealt with years of babies. Nan was definitely old-school, a "spare the rod, spoil the child" type.' He grinned fondly. 'Luckily, as I got too big to be put over her knee, the wooden spoon was retired to baking use only.'

'She was good at baking?' Gabrielle asked, as though that were actually interesting.

Ilse tensed, wondering how Hayden would answer. 'Not particularly. She was more likely to serve some kind of slice made of smashed biscuits and melted chocolate. Or her favourite concoction was Rocky Road, with marshmallows and Turkish delight. She had a wicked sweet tooth. But she also made a killer wattle-seed cake. I generally made sure she knew when I was coming over to do some work in the gardens, because that would guarantee a wattle-seed cake.'

Well, at least he appreciated the cake, Ilse thought petulantly. And there was nothing wrong with her sweet tooth, she had always kept it well in check—as her waist measurement, even after three children, could attest.

'Nan was far more into gardening than cooking. She had my grandfather build all the stone walls, and she redesigned and planted the gardens—well, they're kind of ruined now. But I'm going to fix them. I owe her that much. Anyway, literally anything you could ever want to know about plants, Nan had stored away up here.' Hayden tapped his forehead.

'It sounds like you loved her very much,' Gabrielle said softly.

Hayden nodded his expression suddenly bleak. 'I did. Probably more than I've ever loved any other person. But it wasn't enough.'

'What do you mean?' Gabrielle whispered, evidently sensing the terrible truth.

Hayden closed his eyes, his words a hard, toneless grind. 'When she needed me most, I made the wrong call. I failed her.'

Ilse's knuckles stood proud as she tightened her bony hands into fists. His words had set her straight, shaken her from her silly old-lady segue into reminiscence and sentimentality. Now she remembered exactly why Hayden deserved her anger.

She had not been ready to die.

26
Hayden

The moth—or butterfly, whichever it was, he had never worked out the difference—fluttered from his hand and made a tilting, erratic dash after Sharna, who had skipped across the gravelled road clutching his keys.

In some ridiculous manner, he wanted to imagine a little of Nan's spirit into the rescued insect, envisage his grandmother heading out to the garden she so loved.

'How did you fail her?' Gabrielle asked softly.

He kept his eyes on the moth's path, even after it had disappeared. 'She wasn't well. Just a cough, didn't seem too serious, but I'd promised to take her to the doctor, to see Tay. I headed out on a CFS call first, and . . . I didn't get back in time to help her.'

He couldn't bring himself to look at the accusation and judgment that must be in Gabrielle's expression.

'She passed while you were gone?' she asked.

He nodded. The polite euphemism 'passed' bothered him. Perhaps because it didn't have the ring of finality it deserved. 'I didn't find out for ages. Then I didn't come here again. Not until . . . not until you brought me here.'

Gabrielle clutched at his arm, but for once he didn't relish her touch. 'Oh my god, Hayden, I'm sorry. I had no idea.'

'Nothing for you to be sorry about. It was my fuck-up.' His voice almost broke and he tensed his jaw angrily, fighting the aching weakness of his throat.

'But you said you were out with the fire service? Was there a fire?'

Oh, hell yeah, there had been a fire. He nodded curtly.

'Then you were working. It wasn't your fault: how could you be in two places at once?' Gabrielle said matter-of-factly, as though the strength of her assertion would prove her correct. 'You said you have siblings. Why couldn't they take your nan to the doctor?'

'Because she trusted me to,' he muttered, the emotions he'd shoved deep inside trying to fight to the surface.

Trigger gave two short barks, reminding him not to rake his fingertips against the scar tissue on his shoulder. God, he couldn't revisit this. Not out loud, anyway. So many times, in the privacy of his house, curled up on the floor hurting and broken with only Trigger for company, he had tried to deny responsibility. Blamed Simmo for ploughing the car into the fire and landing him in hospital, unconscious and on life support for weeks. Blamed his brother and sisters for not being close enough to Nan to realise she needed help. Blamed his parents for being so tied up in his mother's illness that they had no scope to think beyond their own pain.

But the truth was, he hadn't needed to attend the call-out: he'd gone to flex his muscle as the new brigade captain. And he'd cultivated a unique relationship with Nan, revelling in the way everyone else complained that she was acerbic and demanding, the fact that they couldn't see her qualities or find the humour that danced behind her stern expression and faded gaze. Not one of them knew Nan like he did.

And that had killed her.

He had killed her.

'Hayden.' Gabrielle's voice was soft, but he shook his head, automatically reaching for the reassurance of Trigger's snout as the dog nosed his leg.

'Hayden, look at me.' Gabrielle's hands, soft and smooth, cupped his face, trapping him. Protecting him from his own destructive thoughts. 'Hayden, I can imagine how hard this is for you. But you can't let it rip you apart. If your nan loved and trusted you, she would have understood.'

He shook his head, his hand clenching in the soft fur on the scruff of Trigger's neck. 'There's nothing to understand. I made a mistake. Don't you see? I should have been here, protecting Nan. But I made the wrong choice. And now I have to live with that.' His voice shook. 'And I don't know if I can.'

He had never admitted the thought outside his own head, when the temptation of an easy escape had called to him in the darkness. And now that he spoke it aloud, he knew it wasn't true.

He would carry on.

He would do it because he deserved to live with the pain and guilt: death would be a cop out.

Gabrielle's hands tightened on his face, and she stood on tiptoe. She pressed her lips to his.

'Hayden,' she breathed against his mouth, 'I didn't know your nan, but I know that if she loved you, she wouldn't want you to torment yourself like this.'

The potted aspidistra he had brought earlier in the week as a housewarming gift chose that moment to topple from where he'd balanced it on the broad, rounded end of the bannister. He forced a laugh, barely pulling away from Gabrielle, not wanting to leave the sweet balm of her lips. The kiss hadn't been sexy or seductive or wanton, but it had been everything he needed in that moment; the touch of a caring human being. 'It looks like that ghost of yours disagrees.'

Instead of laughing, he felt a shiver tremble through Gabrielle. Hell, he could feel a lot more than that. His right arm had instinctively closed around her, tightening protectively as she jumped at the crash of the ceramic pot. His left he kept at his side, his shoulder pulled away from her, his fingertips on Trigger's head. He so badly wanted to kiss Gabrielle again, but it almost seemed that would be taking advantage of her generosity. Perhaps her intention had been only to distract him from the darkness of his own mind, much as Trigger did.

Gabrielle turned towards the mound of damp, peaty smelling soil and shattered pot, though she remained within the loose circle of his arm. 'You're joking, but there's some weird stuff going on here.'

'It's an old house. Things move. And Juz has put such a shine on that handrail, I reckon a speck of dust would slide off, never mind a pot plant.' He refused to think about just how much time Juz had spent here to achieve the finish.

Gabrielle shifted from his embrace, though she caught his hand as it slid down her arm. 'It's not just that. Juz and I were talking about where to source some furniture to restore. He said there are a couple of farm clearances coming up that he plans to try. Anyway, we were standing in the old kitchen discussing it, and the door from the Ladies' Lounge slowly creaked open.'

He let his thumb run over the back of her hand, as though he were soothing her. 'Sounds like how all good ghost stories start.' Minus the bit about her being alone in the place with Juz.

'Then the door that leads down into the cellar opened.'

He ignored the rash of goosebumps that lifted the hairs on his neck. 'You said you had loads of broken windows out back?'

'Not then. This was after the glazier.'

'Then I guess you had one open. The door caught a cross breeze.'

'Maybe.' Gabrielle sounded entirely unconvinced. 'Except it wasn't really windy.'

'Your lock guy must have oiled the hinges throughout.'

'It happened three times.' Clearly, Gabrielle wasn't willing to hear reason on this one.

'I'd say the repetition proves it was the wind. What else could it be?'

She looked at him for a long moment, then drew him towards the Ladies' Lounge. They walked through the room, their feet rapping on the now-bare boards, and into the tiny original kitchen. Gabrielle pointed at a solid door. 'Does that look like it would swing in the breeze? With any amount of oil on the hinges? Anyway, even if it was blowing a gale, do you know what we found when we went down there?'

He grinned. 'Hopefully some vintage wine, but more likely dust.'

She shook her head. 'Unfortunately, no and yes to those. But also—' she paused as if for effect '—furniture,' she intoned dramatically.

He almost laughed. 'Okay, that's not exactly skeletons-in-the-closet stuff. In fact, with my wine dream shot down, it's pretty much what my next guess would have been.'

She shook her head. 'You don't get it. It was retro furniture. Nineteen-fifties stuff. Exactly what we had been discussing.'

'Well, at least it seems you have a helpful ghost, then,' he teased. He wouldn't have picked a hard-nosed business exec as the type to be taken in by ghost stories, but somehow the quirk made Gabrielle even more endearing.

He realised with a start that was exactly what she was: not only smart and sexy as all hell, but endearing with her little traits and inconsistencies. If he didn't watch out, he could be in a heck of a lot of trouble here. He thought he knew exactly what type of woman he was interested in, but Gabrielle was pushing every one of his buttons, even those he hadn't known existed.

'I'll grab those cans of paint and haul them into the lounge,' he said, abruptly curtailing the conversation.

He didn't allow himself to hope that her expression registered disappointment. With Trigger at his heels, he headed out to collect the drums of paint, pausing beneath the verandah to take deep breaths of the cold air to calm himself. He stared out towards the river, across the lawn, which was more of a paddock now. It was going to take a shitload of work to put this place to rights. Nan would be furious if she could see the tangled weeds among the roses, the overgrown lawn interspersed with muddy dead patches. The bed of prized dahlias, and the chrysanthemums which should have flowered a couple of months earlier, had become a snail-feast. Fortunately, the stone wall he had built around the jacaranda stood as firm as those his grand-father had used to border the property.

His gaze wandered towards the cottages near the wooden dock on the riverfront. He had to make a decision about them, too. First, though, he needed to make a decision about Gabrielle. Because no amount of fresh air was cooling his interest.

Hefting two of the fifteen-litre trade drums ripped at his bad shoulder, but the pain was a timely reminder of the other reason he couldn't let things go any further with Gabrielle. It might be vain, but it added to his determination.

There couldn't be a woman in his life. Particularly not one as fine as Gabrielle Moreau.

'Let me take one,' she suggested as he hauled the cans through the front entrance.

He grinned at the notion. 'How about you bring the industrial vacuum cleaner in? We're lucky, the boards are already oiled. They must have been stripped at some stage. With a bit of a clean-up, they might look all right. Or, if you prefer, we could give them a light sand and another coat.'

Gabrielle looked towards the lounge, pressing a hand against her chest. He'd noticed she frequently did that, as though massaging away a pain, or perhaps connecting with something deep inside her. 'I think they look nice as they are. Distressed but not grungy. What do you think?'

'Not my place,' he said, stacking the drums against the wall.

'But I value your opinion.'

More than Justin's? he wanted to ask, knowing the rivalry was juvenile—but it was hard not to feel that if he couldn't have her, no one should. 'I like the floor the way it is. It's more honest. If you tart it up too much, there's always a risk it'll look like you're trying to pretend it's something it isn't.'

Gabrielle frowned, twisting the ring around her little finger. She looked . . . wounded. 'That's what marketing's all about. And, sometimes, hiding what lies beneath is the only way to make something acceptable.'

His hand flew to his shoulder.

She *knew*?

'But I agree with you,' she continued. 'We'll leave the floors. Where on earth did you find an industrial cleaner?'

'Hired it,' he said shortly.

'You really think of everything. I would probably have bought a brush. Or, you know, have splashed the cash and hired a carpet cleaner . . . If I could find someone who'd turn up.' Her wry grin invited him to have a shot at her tendency to buy her way out of trouble. 'I'd be screwed trying to do this without you.'

The warmth in her tone made him question his assumption. Taylor had warned him about being too sensitive, developing a dependency on his need to head off any sympathy or judgment. Gabrielle didn't know his secret, at least not that one. 'I'm sure your ghost would help you out,' he joked, trying to recapture the easy humour they had shared moments earlier.

Gabrielle clapped her elegant hands together. It was hard to tear his eyes from them, remembering their soft touch on his face. 'Speaking of our ghost, do you want to see the furniture we found?'

He had zero interest in furniture, but the thought that Juz had already shared the exploration with her sparked his competitive side. 'Sure. Did Juz bring it up?'

'No, we left it in the cellar until we have somewhere to put it.'

'I'll shift it for you when you're ready.' Lucky Sharna wasn't here; she would have been sure to take the piss out of him for his need to make himself indispensable.

'It's going to take the four of us to carry some of the pieces,' Gabrielle warned.

A jolt of happiness flashed through him, as though her considering the four of them a team, friends, actually counted for something. 'Okay, I'll take a look when we have a break. But we'd better get a move on here. The lads have agreed to come out and help paint once you choose colours, but we need to get the prep work done first. Then we'll be able to knock it over in a weekend.'

'A weekend?' Gabrielle sounded astonished. 'How many "lads" is this?'

It was his turn to be surprised. 'The footy team. Blokes from the CFS. Couple of other mates. The regular crowd— Luke, Juz, Matt. Some of the girls, too, though I reckon Taylor needs to take it easy. And Roni will have her hands full with the kids.'

'You're friends with that many people?'

'You're not?' He refused to believe she didn't have a huge circle of hangers-on.

Gabrielle shook her head. 'Not so much friends, more acquaintances. Certainly not to the level that they'd do me a favour like painting an entire pub.'

Hayden appreciated solitude, but he couldn't conceive of a life that didn't include the mates he'd known forever. And he couldn't imagine how lonely Gabrielle must feel. He might choose to avoid human contact, but he always knew where to find friends when he wanted—or needed—them.

He shoved down the urge to promise Gabrielle he could

offer what she was missing. It would be a lie, anyway: he didn't need any more friends.

Because what he instinctively wanted from her was so much more.

He clicked his fingers for Trigger, and took a step towards the stairs. 'Well, like I said, we need to get the base work done first. We'll be less in each other's way if we split up, and Sharna can jump in wherever. Do you want to start slapping on the undercoat in the lounge, or rip out the remaining carpets upstairs?' He needed to create some distance between them, so he could concentrate on the job instead of being distracted by the way she moved, her voice, her smell. Why the hell had he ever suggested they work together? A few more days and he would have had the prep work done anyway: alone, instead of torturing himself with her proximity.

Gabrielle closed the small amount of space he had managed to put between them. 'How about you show me what you want me to do?' she said, her voice low and sultry as her dark gaze fixed unwaveringly on his.

His heart thudded against his ribs. This time there was no mistaking her meaning. She was making it damn clear she was into him, but he couldn't allow this to go anywhere. He had no interest in taking a quick roll in the hay—or one of the upstairs bedrooms while Sharna was gone.

And permitting anything more would lead to caring.

He couldn't risk that.

'I–I can't,' he stammered like a teenager.

Gabrielle moved closer, until there was only a sliver of air between them. 'Why not?'

'Because it can't go anywhere,' he groaned as she pressed her lithe body against him.

'Did I ask for a destination?' she murmured. Her thighs brushed his, her perfume enveloping him in a heady mist of flowers and musk.

His arms slid around her waist, his biceps tense as he fought the urge to crush her to him. 'Don't get me wrong, Gabrielle. I want this.'

'Then that makes two of us. It's been a while, but last time I checked, that was all that's required.' Her cold fingers slid around his neck, drawing his head inexorably down to hers. Not that he was fighting it all that hard. 'No expectations, no blame.'

If she had no expectations, he couldn't disappoint her. It was only his own heart he needed to control.

He couldn't let himself get involved.

He wouldn't.

But hell, he needed her right now. 'Just friends?'

'Really good friends,' she murmured, her breath hot against his lips.

He was only a man. He had no armour against her, not when thoughts of her had kept him awake at night for weeks, not when he wanted her so badly.

He threaded his fingers up into the back of her hair, pulling her closer.

She melted into his embrace. But her soft lips were demanding; consuming, devouring him. She tasted of musk and sherbet and sparkled like apple cider on his tongue.

27
Gabrielle

Gabrielle had never been so turned on in her life.

Hayden's arms encased her, strong and protective. Solid, as though she could trust him to be there forever.

Which was ridiculous, she reminded herself staunchly, even as she pressed closer to his hard body. She had made it clear that she didn't want anything like that.

Except she had lied, saying the words she knew he wanted to hear. She didn't have much experience of men, but enough to realise that the last thing any guy wanted was talk of commitment.

Besides, she knew her limitations. Hayden had already said he didn't care for a false veneer hiding the truth, and that described her perfectly. If there had been any chance she thought she could reveal herself to him, those words had dashed her hope.

His strong, callused fingers moved back into her hair, finding the tie and releasing it to fall about her shoulders. She tipped her head to one side as his lips traced a hot path up her neck, his teeth toying with the gold mesh net of her Paspaley circlé pearl earrings. He took a tress of her hair and pressed it to his lips. 'So soft,' he murmured. 'God, Gabrielle, you're so beautiful.'

The words plunged a spike of ice into her heart. He could never discover the truth. To distract him, she pressed closer, feeling the hard interest of his arousal.

He twisted slightly away from her, the movement of his broad shoulder allowing a cold draught to thread between them. 'Gabrielle, I—'

Trigger gave a short bark of alert from his place on the tessellated marble floor, and a heartbeat later, the sound of tyres crunching on gravel echoed through the unfurnished room.

'Sharna,' Hayden warned. Although the slow retreat of his hands seemed reluctant, and his lips lingered on hers once more, she thought she detected a note of relief in his voice.

Perhaps she was projecting her own emotions onto him. She had never been kissed as thoroughly as he had just kissed her, his touch assured, confident, practised. He didn't drown her or force her, yet his lips tasted and teased, drove her to want more, to mewl like a kitten as she tried to press herself closer, to be enfolded in his warmth and strength. And that was dangerous. She had to be so careful about taking this further, each move had to be meticulously orchestrated. Hayden might think he didn't like façades, but he'd like her less without it.

Sharna barrelled through the entryway in her usual impetuous style, but she pulled up short, looking from one to the other of them.

Hayden dropped the hand that still rested on Gabrielle's waist, and Gabrielle tucked her hair behind her ears, resisting the urge to tie it up in a ponytail again. That would make her slight dishevelment far too obvious.

'Ew,' Sharna groaned, cocking an eyebrow. 'And is there *any* chance anyone here is still hungry?' She lifted the low-sided cardboard box she carried.

Hayden ran a thumb over his lips, but it was more as though he were pressing the taste of her close, rather than wiping her away, Gabrielle realised with a flush of happiness. 'Hope you scored big at Ploughs and Pies,' he said.

'Worked up an appetite?' Sharna said mischievously.

'Yup. 'Bout ready to start on the undercoat.'

'You've finished stripping then?' Sharna lifted her chin towards the bar, laughter bubbling in her voice.

'Didn't get quite as far as I would have liked,' Gabrielle lied, entering into the spirit of the teasing.

Juggling the cardboard tray in the crook of her arm, Sharna grinned as she handed them each a paper bag. Trigger perked up, scrabbling to his feet. 'Savoury slice for you,' she said to Hayden. 'I wasn't sure if you were into them, Gabs, so I grabbed you a pasty. Sorry, Trigger, nothing for you.'

'He'll be right,' Hayden said, breaking off a portion of pastry from his meat-filled, cheese-covered slice and handing it to the dog. 'Just don't let Matt know, okay? He says Trigg is already borderline overweight.'

'Hardly surprising considering you feed him all your stuff,' Sharna reproved. 'Which reminds me, I ran into Tracey in town. She said she heard about the working bee, and she'll send out a chocolate cake, a pumpkin–sultana slab cake and a batch of scones when you're ready. Though, knowing Tracey, I reckon there'll be a lot more involved than that.'

'Tracey is . . .' Gabrielle ventured, keen to recognise the people who were, inexplicably, turning out to help her attain her dream.

Slowly, she was moving beyond considering the guest-house as a challenge, a project to set up and then set aside. Living in her beautiful apartment with Brendan, she had felt homeless and displaced. But here, even with all the minor inconveniences and discomforts, she was beginning to feel . . . at home.

'Tracey? The woman who came to meet Roni when we were in the cafe,' Sharna said. 'The hippie senior with crazy blonde hair.' She mimed a puffball around her own head. 'She's kind of Roni's surrogate mum, and definitely the best cook in town. Creams it at the CWA competitions, though Roni's set to take over from her.' She crammed hot pastry in her mouth and huffed around it, wincing, then swallowed and turned to Hayden. 'Anyway, Tracey asked after your mum and wanted to know if you or she need some casseroles cooked up? I told her the last lot she made would still be in your freezer, alongside your mum's—'

'Sharn,' Hayden groaned. 'You shouldn't have done that. I don't want her to think I'm ungrateful.'

'No one would think that, Wheaty.' Sharna was suddenly serious. 'But your mum and Tracey would have a fit if they saw how much food you toss out. It's no wonder Trigg's getting fat.'

'He's not fat. Just big boned.' Hayden's attempt to change the focus of the conversation was painfully evident.

'You don't live at home?' Gabrielle asked, confused.

He looked at her as though she were crazy. 'Not for more than a dozen years.'

'Ah.' That was both good and bad. Good, because she'd had a nagging reservation about a thirty-odd year old who still lived with his mum. Bad, because she'd begun to consider arranging something involving candlelight and lingerie. It would be easy to market the lighting as a romantic touch in the restored grandeur of the hotel—but if Hayden had his own place and she ended up there, she would have no control.

She held up her pasty. 'Is it okay if I give Trigger some of this?'

The half-smile Hayden gave her banished the wintry chill from the unheated air. 'Sure. You okay to do it on your own?'

She nodded. 'I think so.'

As she started to crouch in front of the dog, Hayden took her elbow. 'No. Don't take yourself to his level. Trigger would never do anything to you, but another dog might. You have to remain the alpha.'

She straightened and held the wedge of pastry out to the dog. His bi-coloured eyes on hers, Trigger peeled his lips back from huge canines, but took the morsel from her fingers slowly and with great care. Then he flipped it into the air, tipping his head back to catch it with a snap of his jaws, and swallowed with relish. Immediately, he fixed her with an imploring gaze.

'Well, he's got you pegged as a soft touch now,' Hayden laughed, but he sounded pleased with her progress. 'He's probably going to desert me. C'mon, Trigg, we'd better put some muscle into this. I'll haul the rest of the floor coverings downstairs. Do you fancy cutting them up, or getting started on the painting?' He offered the question to both of them, but Gabrielle felt suddenly shy. It would look obvious if she shadowed his footsteps.

Sharna jumped into the silence. 'Let's all work on the one room. It's more fun that way, and we can cross them off as we're done instead of getting bits and pieces every-where part-done.'

'Sure,' Gabrielle agreed, possibly too quickly. 'That's probably the most efficient way to do it.' Watching the muscles ripple across Hayden's back as he carried great armfuls of the old carpet out would make a dent in her work output, though.

'Uh-huh,' Sharna said. 'Efficient. Suuuuure.' She collected their lunch wrappers. 'No cake, Gabs?'

Gabrielle shook her head. 'I won't be able to bend over if I eat all that now. Should've put my Dharma Bums on instead of jeans.'

'Your *what*?' Sharna said.

'You know,' Gabrielle waved a hand at her thighs. 'Leggings.'

'The leggings I know are Kmart, but I'm willing to bet your Bums cost more than fifteen bucks.'

Gabrielle felt the flush mount her cheeks as she searched for a way to undo her words.

'I'm willing to bet your bum looks spectacular in any brand of leggings,' Hayden murmured to her.

'Ugh. Lucky I've got no interest in having you look at my fifteen-buck bum, then, isn't it?' Sharna called back over her shoulder as she headed towards the door. 'I'll just chuck the rubbish in the dumpster.'

'Quick.' Hayden reached for Gabrielle's hand, pulling her towards the stairs.

A step behind him, she was puffing a little by the time they'd raced to the top, Trigger at their heels.

Hayden rushed her into the nearest room, out of sight of the stairs, then eased her back against the newly plastered wall. 'I need another kiss to get me through the next couple of hours of Sharna's bad jokes.'

'I need another kiss to . . . get me through to the next kiss,' she murmured, stretching up to him.

'I really shouldn't touch you,' he said, planting his hands on the wall either side of her. 'I'm filthy.'

'Bit late to worry about that now,' she giggled, surprised by the lilting, girlish excitement in her own voice. 'And, anyway, I'm not much better.'

He shook his head. 'No. You're unacceptably perfect.' What should have been a compliment came out sounding a little mournful. But then Hayden gave a slight smile, slowly leaning forward until their lips met.

Gabrielle closed her eyes as his lips touched hers with the merest whisper, pausing until she parted her own. Then the tip of his tongue traced the bow of her lip, teasing until she moaned.

He deepened the kiss, one hand leaving the wall to slide behind her head, cushioning and guiding her as his tongue sought hers, tasting and tangling in an increasingly sensual dance.

Her moan turned to a groan as her knees weakened and she hooked a hand around the back of Hayden's neck for support, drawing him closer, deeper. She plunged her tongue into his mouth, the sensation unbelievably erotic.

Hayden pulled back a little. 'God, you're driving me wild,' he panted.

She giggled, a little giddy with oxygen deprivation. 'I appreciate the compliment, but I get the impression you're quite practised.' She regretted the words almost instantly; they sounded jealous. What did she care what his experience was?

He shook his head. 'No. Well, yes. But it's not the same. This is . . .' He paused. 'They were comic books and you're a Monet.' He stroked the back of his right hand down her cheek. 'All soft edges and smooth beauty.'

Now she definitely wished she hadn't spoken. Despite the time she spent perfecting them, she wasn't comfortable with any conversation that revolved around her looks. Meaning to pull him closer and silence his words, she slid her free hand up to hook under his left shoulder.

He jerked his hand off the wall and stepped back quickly. 'Sharna's coming up,' he said, although she couldn't hear footsteps on the stairs. 'I mean, not that we have to keep this secret from her.' His words sounded like a question.

'Or anyone,' she agreed. 'Though I'm not too sure what *this* is. Just friends, remember?' Except she wanted him to push for more.

'Really good friends, as I recall it,' he said, his smile returning. As though he couldn't stay away, his hands encircled her waist, his thumbs brushing the underside of her breasts through the fluffy jumper.

Considering the size of the room, it felt remarkably airless. Shame Hayden hadn't drawn her into her bedroom, which had a lock on the door.

And a bed.

No, no. She wasn't supposed to be going there. Not yet.

Almost with relief she heard Sharna's tuneless whistling as she came up the stairs.

'Seriously, she's like having one of my kid sisters around,' Hayden groaned.

'Yeah. But you're right. I don't want to be too in her face with this,' Gabrielle said. 'I don't want to . . .' she trailed off, not sure where to go with the sentence. Sharna had said she suspected Hayden knew about her orientation, but still, it wasn't Gabrielle's information to share.

'Hurt her feelings,' Hayden finished for her. 'Yeah, I know. She talks tough and likes to pretend she has the hide of a crocodile, but it's hard for her out here. And she liked you from the moment you walked in the pub.'

Gabrielle grimaced. 'I know. And I kind of made that worse, screwed it right up.'

'Determined to leave a trail of broken hearts behind you?' Hayden teased as he headed towards the doorway, giving his jeans a surreptitious adjustment.

Gabrielle stood there a moment longer, staring at his retreating back.

If she left, would his heart be broken?

∾

It took them the rest of the day to pull up the remaining carpet, wipe down the walls and vacuum the years of dust from the floorboards.

Finally, they sat down in the kitchen, the most modern part of the building. Without peer pressure insisting she pretend she had no interest in food, Gabrielle had been seduced by the large kitchen with wrought-iron pot racks hung above the huge range, and long workbenches spotlighted by the tiny barn windows near the vaulted ceiling. Even before they had officially moved in, she had experimented with a couple of her mother's favourite, slow-cooked dishes, which could be ladled out at any time of the day.

Hours earlier, she had prepared a rich red wine gravy and put a pot of boeuf bourguignon to simmer. Now only exhausted murmurs of appreciation interrupted their silence as they hunched over their brimming bowls, sopping up the juices with crusty bread.

She couldn't even pretend that every compliment Hayden uttered didn't count for five of Sharna's, that her heart didn't loop and spiral each time his gaze met hers, that she didn't press more food on him to prove that this was an area in which she shone.

Eventually, with hunger sated and energy replenished, they moved on to discussing what remained to be done inside the hotel.

Gabrielle brought the vision boards down from her room, along with the swatches of wallpaper she had chosen for the lounge and the paint sample cards she and Sharna had pored over for a couple of nights.

Hayden took notes in a scrawl that would make a doctor comfortable. 'So, tomorrow you've got the chimney bloke coming to sort out the fireplaces. Plus the plumbers will be in to do the second bathroom. Bluey reckons two days to complete the job, so done by Thursday. Assume Friday, because nothing ever goes according to plan.' He scratched behind Trigger's ear with his left hand as he wrote. 'I've got one more crack to chip out and fill in the fourth bedroom. Don't know how I missed that bugger, it's a big one. Then the prep work is finished throughout—unless you want to make the old kitchen a butler's pantry now, instead of waiting until you're up and running?' He pointed to Gabrielle's future projects board.

She shook her head. 'My clientele will be so small, there's really no need at this point. And I don't expect I'll have people staying weekdays initially, so there will be time to get jobs like that done later. It's more about having the public areas hitting just the right note. I don't want it to smell all new and painty—'

'Painty?' Sharna chortled. 'Not sure about that private-school education of yours, Gabs.'

Gabrielle grinned. 'Okay, I don't want it to smell painty *and* plastery. Is that better? Anyway, if we can get the interior done, then allow it to kind of mellow, develop a lived-in feel for a few weeks, while the gardens are brought up to scratch, it'll make the retro vibe more believable.'

'You're really not in a hurry for those guests, are you?' Hayden said. As always, he seemed bemused by her lack of concern about money. She pulled another sheet of paper from her folder. 'I've worked out a budget.' There was a first time for everything, though chances were she would never have realised the necessity without Hayden questioning her expenses. It was far too easy to fall back on a lifelong habit of never needing to check the price of anything. 'Because you guys have saved me so much on renovations, I'll be in the black far sooner than I expected. That gives me a bit of a window to let the dirt settle around here.'

'There *is* no dirt,' Sharna intoned mournfully, holding up a blistered hand. 'Who knew pushing a vacuum cleaner could be such hard work?'

'Well, about that,' said Gabrielle. 'I was thinking, because we will have this window, maybe you'd like to come and stay in the city with me for a few days?'

'You're going away?' Hayden sounded as though she'd said she was running off to Europe for a season.

She shook her head. 'Not until all the painting's done. Then Sharna could come and help me make a few selections. I can get a lot of stuff online, but some things I'd really like to see and feel. We need to pick out more soft furnishings, cutlery and crockery, and some finishing decorative touches. Plus, I figure I owe Sharna a manicure.' And she would take a chance, find someone to do her spray tan. A thrill of sexual desire ran through her: that way, there would be no need for surreptitious fumbling in the dark. She turned to Sharna. 'We deserve girl time, don't you reckon? I'm thinking a full spa day, with the works. Of course, you may have to develop a taste for champagne.'

'Oh my god, are you kidding?' Sharna bounced on her seat.

Her excitement was irresistible, and being able to do something nice for the girl who was becoming like a sister filled a need to care and nurture that Gabrielle hadn't realised she harboured. 'Not at all. We'll get a fancy hotel in the CBD; the Hilton is always hard to beat. There are a couple of clubs nearby that I used to go to—' she paused, meeting Sharna's gaze '—with my older sister. I thought you might like to check them out.'

'*Those* kind of clubs? Yes! This calls for a drink!' Sharna scooted off her seat and headed over to rummage in the fridge.

'You're not giving me much incentive to finish that painting,' Hayden said quietly, reaching across the table to lace his fingers with hers.

She ran her thumb across the back of his work-scarred, sun-bronzed hand. 'We won't be gone long. And I promise you, it will be worth it,' she said as Sharna returned with the celebratory Moscato and three enamel cups.

28
Ilse

Ilse hadn't felt this torn since the Vietnam war, when she'd had to balance her desire to celebrate the birth of her third son, with the loss of her first.

Watching Hayden and Gabrielle work together, she instinctively wanted to take pleasure in their slow courtship. Ilse adored her grandson; she longed to be happy for him.

But she was still so angry.

She had been robbed: she should be here to enjoy this time with them.

Yet, she wondered, running her fingertips across the beautifully restored surface of Opa's bar, had she still been alive, would any of this have happened? Gabrielle had first been here with another man, one who was clearly her partner, yet now he was every bit as invisible as Ilse. Had either of them still existed, surely Gabrielle and Hayden wouldn't be free to work their magic, slowly restoring the hotel to its original grandeur? If the fine linens and beautiful curtains she had installed were anything to go by, it seemed Gabrielle had both the means and intention of surpassing the original opulence of the establishment. Ilse delighted in wandering through the freshly painted bedrooms, captivated by Gabrielle's decorating touches. One room was completely finished in shades of white, the sparkling windows dressed in lace beautiful enough to rival even Oma's taste. The counterpane on the white-painted iron bedframe was cream, the throw pillows different fabrics and textures in shades of ivory. The furniture was almost-white satin birch, which Ilse remembered being popular in the late forties.

Although she had been horrified when Hayden took a sledgehammer and chisel and removed a wall between the bedrooms, now she found the open space refreshing. An opulent plush chaise lined one wall, overlooking the vista of the river. Stirling-silver accents decorated the room: a hairbrush, cigarette case and fob watch on the bleached dresser, a cocktail shaker and silver-banded fine glassware on the satin birch sideboard.

Ilse wandered from the corner suite, across the hall to two of the single rooms. Overlooking the courtyard and still of substantial proportions, these echoed the style of the fifties. One was in shades of rich blue and brown, with a vintage Hermès silk scarf framed behind glass, and leather and mahogany spoonback armchairs gathered around a low barley twist coffee table. The other was decorated in cream and timber, with walnut wardrobes and credenza. Deep tub armchairs with nests of side tables snuggled up to the fireplace, which had been exposed and the cast-iron surround re-blacked.

A second double suite had ecru lace curtains and was dressed in timber. Mahogany bedside cabinets braced the sides of the solid wood bedframe and a lovely Louis VI writing desk with an inlaid leather top, as green as Hayden's eyes, looked over the courtyard.

Really, Ilse couldn't pick her favourite room; yet for all the opulence, she would rather be in her castle. She drifted across the hall to the final double suite. In the southern corner of the hotel, it also overlooked the river and the garden with the jacaranda surrounded by Hayden's wall: the last job he had done for her. She squinted. Was the tree touched with the tiniest hint of purple yet? Jacarandas had such a short period when their branches were bereft of clothing, stark against the winter skies. The garden bed beneath the tree was overgrown with weeds, and the struggling fans of bearded iris. She sighed. What had become of the other bulbs Hayden had lifted for her? No doubt they had rotted to nothingness since she had been gone.

Ilse had no way to measure that time, except in the inexplicable lines that now creased Hayden's face, and the ravages of her once beautiful gardens.

From here she could see the almost invisible break in the wattle-tree hedge. She could make her way through the sad gardens to the wrought-iron gate hidden alongside the love-seat beneath the wattles, yet it seemed she could go no further, she couldn't reach her cottage, the one she had shared with Ronald. She had tried so many times, yet she was trapped here, in the hotel and the gardens where so many of her memories belonged.

Ducks flustered and quacked, waddling in a flurry towards the river as a truck lumbered up the limestone pebbles of the driveway. Every day more goods arrived on the verandah of the hotel, the removalists carrying items up to the freshly finished bedrooms.

Gabrielle's taste was faultless. Thoughtful touches adorned every surface, lending such an air of elegance that Ilse was almost beside herself with excitement, waiting for the downstairs rooms to be completed so she and Gabrielle could decorate them. Because it was a team effort, she had decided. Although Gabrielle's style was impeccable, occasionally she would angle an item the wrong way, or the silver failed to catch the light from the window. Ilse would perfect the arrangement and, all credit to her, Gabrielle left well enough alone.

And, of course, Gabrielle had eagerly directed Hayden and Justin as they carried up the furniture Ilse had led them to in the cellar. Ilse had yet to see what became of those pieces but, between Gabrielle's voluble enthusiasm for them, and Justin's craftsman-like assessment, she harboured no fears.

She realised she was looking beyond the delivery truck, her gaze searching through the wattle-tree screen for the road that led into Wurruldi.

She was looking for Hayden, waiting for him to come home.

Because although she was angry, disappointed and betrayed, not even the combination of those emotions was enough to destroy true love.

She would always forgive him.

29
Hayden

Hayden hadn't been joking when he said Gabrielle's plan to return to the city failed to provide him with any incentive to finish the restoration.

'We're so nearly done, aren't we?' Gabrielle's soft lilt was tinged with excitement, and guilt twisted his gut. He'd been deliberately lagging, working far more slowly than he would normally. But the thought of Gabrielle leaving to spend a few days in Adelaide with Sharna didn't sit well. He knew that Sharna deserved to go off and have a bit of fun; he simply didn't want Gabrielle to leave.

And that was bad. It was the first stage of allowing her too close, of caring too much. Worrying about how he could protect her, yet knowing he couldn't. He'd proved that with Nan and, hell, even with Mum.

If he couldn't control the world, far better he limited his interaction with it. Except he didn't want to sacrifice a minute that could be spent with Gabrielle.

'Yeah. The guys crushed it on the weekend,' he muttered grudgingly. Even he had been surprised by the number of volunteers who turned up to paint the hotel over the past two weekends. But it had quickly become clear that, although he and Gabrielle strove not to flaunt their . . . whatever it was . . . in front of Sharna, as usual, there were no secrets in Settlers Bridge, and word was out that they were together.

As together as they could be, considering they were stealing kisses and furtive embraces like a couple of teenagers behind the school bus shelter, he thought with a burst of frustration. But what choice did he have? Even covered with plaster dust and falling asleep at the kitchen table after labouring all day, Gabrielle was beyond perfect. Every damn muscle in his body might ache to take their relationship further but, despite Taylor's pep talk, he wasn't enough of a dick to put Gabrielle in a position where she had to choose between telling him to bugger off or somehow pretending she was able to overlook his scars.

Yet, despite the frustration, the sneaking around was fun in a juvenile, long-forgotten way, he thought as he watched Gabrielle balance on one foot halfway up the ladder, stretching to touch-up a splash of pale-blue paint on the pristine white cornice. Where previously he'd been quick to take relationships to a physical level—straight up, it was really all he'd had any interest in, notches on his bedpost, a bit of fun for both of them—now he had time to get to know Gabrielle on a whole different, impossibly more intimate level. And he quickly realised that discovering the nuances of Gabrielle's personality was potentially far more dangerous than discovering her body would have been.

'Don't know why you bother putting that away,' he called up to her as she dug the phone from her pocket. The damn thing never stopped ringing.

'I swear, I'm going to toss it in that can of paint in a minute,' she grumbled. Then, smooth as quicksilver she switched to the assured, businesslike tone that he had learned meant the caller was a colleague or client from her firm. The change in personality intrigued him, and more than once he had stood, paintbrush dripping on the tarp-covered floor, mesmerised as she confidently spouted PR jargon while deftly applying the renovation skills he'd taught her.

Gabrielle tucked the phone back in her pocket, catching his gaze. 'I know, I know. Turn the darn thing off, right? I swear, being a consultant means about five times as much work. Hey, Sharna,' she called as the younger girl carted a box of glassware into the bar. 'I was thinking—you said your mum put in a new bathroom last year? I'm placing an order with Sheridan for some linen today. How about I double up on some stuff? Does your mum have a colour scheme?'

'A colour scheme?' Sharna snorted. 'She's happy as long as the shade isn't cow-crap brown. But anyway, she can't afford your taste, Gabs. It's Kmart towels for us.'

322

Gabrielle leaned over the top of the ladder so she could see below the architrave and into the newly shelved library. 'She would be doing me a favour. I need to work out if bath sheets or regular-size towels are going to work out better. Plus, you know how some of the super-soft fluffy ones have no absorbency, they just kind of slide off your body? I need someone to give them a trial before I place a bulk order.'

That was a visual he didn't need: Gabrielle wrapped in a fluffy white bath towel that was intent on slipping from her smooth curves. He dropped the paintbrush into the tray and shoved his hands into the pockets of his jeans. Damn, he hadn't had this little self-control since high school.

How had he called it so wrong when Gabrielle first walked into The Settlers bar last autumn? Despite a tendency to use her apparently inexhaustible funds to make things right—for everyone—she was so far from up herself.

'In that case, that sounds awesome,' Sharna called back through. 'I'm sure Mum would be happy to give you written feedback, if that's what you want. By the way, how did you go with Sam?'

'Sam at Ploughs and Pies?' he asked, feeling a little left out of the conversation. It was bad enough Sharna got Gabrielle to herself all night, he didn't want to be excluded during the day as well.

Gabrielle handed her brush down to him. 'Can you load me up? Save my legs.'

Hayden reached up for the brush, taking the opportunity to run his other hand up the back of her thigh. 'These legs?'

She giggled, but darted a guilty glance at Sharna. 'I spoke with her yesterday. She said she doesn't bake her stuff, but gets it in from some bakery in Murray Bridge.'

'I know the one,' he offered. 'It'll be McCue's.'

'Yeah, that's what she said.'

'So, you'll arrange for them to supply you?' Sharna had turned up the music on her phone and bellowed over it.

'Kids.' Gabrielle quirked her eyebrow as he handed the brush back. 'No, I'll buy through Sam so she can make a bit out of it. Otherwise, if my guests only eat here, it takes money out of Settlers. Plus, Sam's going to hook me up with Tracey for some authentic local food.'

'I could have hooked you up.' Sharna sounded a little sulky, as she did each time Gabrielle forged a new relationship with one of the locals. Which was frequently. Despite the fact that it should have been impossible for her to fit in with the tightknit, laidback country town, Gabrielle had a knack for winning people over. Him included.

He stared out the open doorway, his gaze lighting on the stonework around the jacaranda tree. The last place he had seen Nan. He deliberately poked at the memory, forcing himself to remember his promise. And his failure.

He might not want Gabrielle to go back to the city, but it was time to put some distance between them. He had been using Sharna as a physical buffer, but he needed space to get his head straight. He couldn't afford to allow himself to care. Nan had taught him that love meant loss. So he had to end this, before his feelings for Gabrielle ripped him apart.

'Penny for them?' Gabrielle climbed down the ladder and dropped her brush in the tray alongside his.

'Tight-arse. Worth at least a buck.' He forced a smile.

She dug in her pocket and pulled out a gold coin. Pressing it into his palm, she used the movement as an excuse to thread her fingers through his. With a darted glance at Sharna, who was stacking glasses on the shelves behind the newly polished, glowing timber bar, she tugged him towards the corner of the foyer. 'Are you thinking about your nan?'

'Why do you say that?'

She smiled sadly. 'Sharna calls that your thousand-mile stare, which sounds sexy as hell, but it breaks my heart because you look so lost.'

'Not lost.'

She placed her palm against the side of his face. 'Your pain doesn't have to be spoken aloud for friends to hear it.'

So much for his attempt to distance himself emotionally. She could see right into his soul. 'Really good friends,' he corrected, trying to deflect.

'Really good friends,' she nodded. Then she took a deep breath. 'You know how I said that I understand how you feel? That's because, when my sister died, I figured it was my fault.'

He went completely still, even his pulse seemed to stop.

Gabrielle licked her lips. 'We were twins. We *are* twins; I don't think that Amelie can ever be past tense for me. Amelie always had low self-esteem and as she grew up that became clinical depression. Yet, even though I felt her pain,

I didn't realise how bad things were. I didn't realise how messed up she was. I guess half the time I was too busy being a teenager and focused on myself; and the other half I resented her, because I figured she was putting it on to get our parents' attention. The three of us girls were always competitive, but being a twin can be extra hard. It's like it's impossible to stand out, at least in a good way.'

Tears darkened her eyes to ebony, and he slid a hand to cradle the back of her head, as though he could take some of the weight of the memories from her. He knew better than to speak.

'By the time she was fourteen, Amelie was using alcohol. Then she turned to relationships, as though having a guy would validate her existence. I found out later that one of those low-life morons was abusive. Verbally, physically, mentally. So, to cope, she switched from her meds to illegal drugs. And one kind was never enough; if one drug made her feel happy, or invincible, or strong, even for a moment, she figured two hits would be better. Then three. She was terrified of coming down, of facing reality.'

Gabrielle heaved a tremulous sigh, and his chest constricted. 'It was a long time ago, yet it took me forever to learn how to cope,' she said, her gaze fixed to his. 'How to mourn her without letting the guilt of not realising what she was going through and the grief of losing her tear me apart. The trick is not to cling to the pain. Allow it to transit through you, acknowledge it, but don't hold onto it.' She pressed her palm hard against her chest, that odd habit he'd noticed so many times. 'I can grieve for Amelie, but I can't let the grief *become* me.'

'I know,' he muttered. 'I'm working on it. Working through it. I'll get there, eventually, I guess.' He gave a short laugh. 'Thing is, you like to joke about this place being haunted—okay, not *joke*,' he corrected, holding one hand up as fire flashed into her eyes. She had become protective of the property. 'But my problem is that I'm haunted by unresolved issues. I don't know how to move on when I know Nan wouldn't have forgiven me for leaving her.'

'But there's nothing to forgive,' Gabrielle whispered urgently. 'You *had* to answer the CFS call. You couldn't get back in time. That's not your fault.'

'It has to be someone's fault.' His jaw spasmed as he gritted his teeth. 'Christ knows, I've tried to blame everyone else for not being here for her, but when it comes down to it, I wanted to go out and direct the fighting efforts. I'd just got my captain's helmet, and was as up myself as it's possible to get. And *I* was the one who got in the car, *I* authorised Simmo to drive, *I* trusted him—' He broke off as the confusion registered in Gabrielle's face and he realised he'd said too much. 'There's no one else to blame,' he finished lamely.

Gabrielle pulled a little away, looking at him oddly. 'There's something more here, isn't there? What is it, Hayden?'

He shook his head mutely.

Her forehead furrowed, she looked disappointed. Wounded. And that was nearly enough to crack his heart open.

'Amelie kept secrets from me, too.' He could barely make out her low, sorrowful words. 'If she hadn't, maybe . . .'

She looked up, trapping him with her demanding gaze. 'For the longest time, I thought what happened to Amelie was my fault, that I hadn't been there when she needed me. But I eventually learned that when something bad happens, you have a choice: you can let it define you, destroy you or strengthen you. Amelie let her something bad define her.' Gabrielle broke off, fisting her hands tightly, her chin wobbling. 'She deliberately ruined her body, her life, her health by taking drugs because they proved what she'd been told: that she was worthless. And, eventually, her something bad destroyed her. Hayden—' her voice quivered and the tears that had stood out in her eyes trickled down her cheeks '—please choose carefully. I can't lose you, too.'

He slid his hands down to grip her elbows. His mouth worked uselessly, failing to form the words he needed. Mainly because he didn't know what to say. How could she risk so openly sharing her feelings? How the hell should he react? 'I–I've got to get some work done outside,' he blurted, trying to turn off the portion of his brain that screamed at him that he was losing his one chance. He could come clean, tell her the whole truth, let her decide. Perhaps even tell her that maybe he wanted something more than what they had, something he didn't deserve. But any of that would tempt fate.

Unable to face her injured expression, knowing his cowardice was the cause, he whirled on his heel and strode from the hotel.

He didn't stop until the rotting planks of the dock sagged beneath his heavy tread. Trigger's nails clicked against the wood, and Hayden sank down, one arm over the dog, staring at the endless pewter-grey ribbon of the river.

Nan used to sit with him on the dock, before he'd even learned to swim, their legs dangling over the edge. It would take her forever to ease herself down—she had been old even when he was a boy—and even longer for her to stand again. But no matter how often he asked to go there, she never said no. For all she had been demanding and awkward and quick to complain, she had also given with all of her heart.

She had taught him to sit ever so still, counting the types of birds they could see in the cliffs. So now he sat, staring at the rocks and scrubby bushes tenuously clinging to the sandstone. At first, he searched unseeingly, his mind too tormented to focus; but then habit took over. His brain started to itemise what he barely noticed. Pigeons nesting in caves in the soft stone. Swallows swooping to dip water from the river. No sign of what had always been their rare prize, a whistling kite soaring high above the cliff.

He let his gaze drift down the rugged precipice, searching the willows at the base. A darter sat among the bursts of greenery, its attention intent on the water swirling slowly around the fine, pendulous branches, while a tree creeper made a gravity-defying race vertically up the trunk, foraging for insects beneath loose pieces of bark. He remembered Nan telling him that in her day they used that bark for pain relief. If he were to strip every tree, would it be enough?

A formation of pelicans cast a wide V shadow on the water, and Hayden leaned back to watch their flight. His shoulder twinged, a common occurrence as a result of the labour he'd pushed himself to complete over the past few weeks. He had avoided Taylor at the working bee, knowing she would be onto him for it. She drew a fine line between encouraging him to work to promote his mental wellbeing, and stopping him from punishing himself; she was adamant that no bargain with the Devil or God would bring Nan back. He knew that. He had moved beyond that stage of grief, where he would offer his life for hers; but that didn't mean he had finished punishing himself.

Hayden dropped his head into his hands and hunched forward, his elbows on his thighs. Trigger leaned heavily against his side. He closed his eyes to listen to the river.

Nan had often talked about the river, its endless quality, the fact that, like the river, people cling to the banks of life, clawing what they can from the mud. 'Yet,' she had said, 'soon enough, we all become the river.' At first, he had been too young to understand, irritated at her repetition. Then, after Pops died, he'd been embarrassed by her maudlin sentiment.

Now, finally, her words made sense.

They were a key. Life had no beginning and no end.

Gradually, the rhythmic song of the water unlocked his tension, released his knotted anguish and carried it away.

He stared at his wet hands as Trigger leaned in to lick at the saltiness. It wasn't the tears that surprised him. In the privacy of his grief he had shed more tears of anguish, both emotional and physical, than a grown man should be capable of.

It was the complete absence of pain.

30

Gabrielle

What the heck had she done? Why had she felt the need to share Amelie's story with Hayden, when she had managed to keep it to herself for so many years? Even worse, why had she admitted to the depth of her growing feelings for him? They had agreed they were just friends, even if that became friends with benefits. But nothing more. No emotional attachment.

She didn't realise Sharna was behind her until the younger woman spoke. 'What's up, Gabs? You look like a cat that's dragged in a flea-ridden rabbit.'

Gabrielle bit her lips together for a moment before speaking. 'I screwed up.' She gestured out of the doorway to where Hayden sat on the dock, Trigger by his side as always. 'I . . . said too much.'

Sharna followed where she pointed. 'To Wheaty? Look at it this way: if you talk too much, it'll make up for his lack of conversational skills.' Gabrielle didn't respond, and Sharna let out a soft sigh. 'Gabs, Wheaty just gets like this sometimes. Goes all quiet and distant. You have to let him ride it out his own way.'

Gabrielle closed her eyes, trying to hold back tears. She was exhausted. Weeks of unfamiliar manual labour, coupled with the mixture of excitement and terror of a burgeoning relationship, and the commitment to a business venture she had begun to care deeply about, were now compounded by the emotional toll of telling her secrets. A sob wrenched from deep within her chest. 'No, you don't understand. I screwed up. I pretty much told him I like him. Like, you know, *like*-like him.' She tried to make it a joke, but sniffling and rubbing her nose with her sleeve was a giveaway.

'Aw, Gabs!' Sharna's thin arm was around her waist immediately. 'That's not exactly a newsflash. What's the problem with telling him?'

'Well, the response, for one thing,' she sniffed, jerking her chin towards the river. A magpie warbled loudly from the wattle hedge and Wheaty stood. He strode back up the paddock towards them, the dog racing excitedly ahead and back again, never straying more than a couple of metres. Gabrielle drew back into the foyer, where she couldn't be seen.

Sharna blew out a short breath. 'Wheaty's just complicated. But he's more than sweet on you. I mean, he's not taken a properly paying job since he started your renos. He's a good guy and all, but still he needs to make a living.

Instead, he's here all hours of the day and night. Plus, you know, it's not like I'm blind.' She waved a hand at her blue eyes. 'I see the two of you doing your disappearing trick together all the time. Jeez, Trigger and I have become besties because you two are so into each other.'

Hayden stopped to take a shovel from the tools he had in a wheelbarrow beneath the jacaranda tree. The sharp crack of it biting the earth rang clear on the still air.

'But when I actually told him—kind of—how I feel, he took off,' Gabrielle said mournfully.

'Processing,' Sharna said. 'You know he's got some shit going on. Sometimes it just takes him a while to get where he's headed.'

'He's not the only one,' Gabrielle sighed. She looked at Sharna, the closest friend she'd had since Amelie died. 'That's part of the problem. I'm telling him things I shouldn't. Oversharing, when I don't even know where we're going.'

Sharna snorted. 'I'm sure if Trigg and I took a nice long walk and gave you some private time, you'd find out.'

Gabrielle shook her head. 'That's just it. I *can't* go there.' She had been trying to persuade herself that once she had the spray tan she *could* go there, but it wouldn't work. She wanted more than a transitory relationship, and Hayden had been clear how he felt about façades.

'What?' Sharna's startled exclamation exploded from her. 'You're playing him?'

'Not deliberately,' she protested. 'I mean, I'm not trying to get free work out of him or anything.'

'That's the last thing anyone's ever going to accuse you of,' Sharna said dryly. 'But what do you mean you can't put out? I thought we'd cleared up this business,' she gestured between them. 'But if you happen to be rethinking it, you need to know there's no way I'll do the dirty on Wheaty.'

'No, I can't go there with *anyone*, Sharna. I'm—' She clasped her hand against her chest, screwing up the fine merino undershirt she wore beneath a chequered linen blouse, the closest thing she had to the plaid flannelette shirts of her friends. 'I'm not what you see.'

'Well, that's a relief. Because your biggest flaw is your annoying perfection,' Sharna said.

Gabrielle sagged. 'It's all marketing. Smoke and mirrors. But the product doesn't live up to the packaging.'

'Gabs, there's no arguing that you've got the packaging down to a fine art, but you're not giving Wheaty a fair shot if you reckon he's only into your looks. I mean, sure he's always had his choice of chicks; he's only ever had to give them that green-eyed gaze and there's panty-shucking going on. But he's already been there, got the macho-scoring thing out of his system. I think he's grown up now. And, to be honest, he was pretty down on you when you walked into The Settlers, simply because you looked so damn fine. He figured you'd be up yourself and high main-tenance, and there's no room for that out here. Truth is, I'd say he likes you *despite* your looks.'

Gabrielle wished she could believe that, but it hadn't been her experience. Brendan respected her professional ability but he had also loved having her as a trophy, an accessory on his arm for their colleagues to admire. Yet he'd undermined her confidence by teasing about the flaws that could never be permanently camouflaged despite the foundation she reapplied twice a day and powdered to perfection. Her nails, her hair, her clothes; they weren't vanity, they were all part of the disguise, deflecting attention from her inadequacies. Without the camouflage, she was open to judgment.

And she couldn't bear to think she wouldn't meet Hayden's expectations.

'Well, he's not going to like me at all if I don't get these paint touch-ups finished today, is he?' She forced a smile, turning back to her paint tray. 'I can't believe we're so close to being done. It's almost . . . sad.'

'Sad? Uh-uh, sister, we're off to the big city tomorrow, remember? Nothing sad in that!'

She didn't share Sharna's enthusiasm to leave Wurruldi. 'This has been fun, though, right?' she called as she shifted the ladder into the bar, where Justin had lined the walls with hip-height, routed wood panels with deep skirtings and a matching picture rail. The timber echoed the graceful, polished curves of the bar and was lifted by the lighter floor and the walls, painted in a rich cream with a deep burgundy trim near the ceiling. Darker and more opulent than the spring-filled breakfast room, it would provide the perfect cosy sitting area for colder days. 'I mean, I've never done anything like this before, but seeing the pub emerge from all that dirt and neglect has been amazing. It's transformed

even beyond my wildest dreams and sketches. Now it looks
. . . magnificent.'

'Beautiful. Even with its flaws,' Sharna said pointedly.

'Ugh. And that's what I get for oversharing with you.'
She tried to laugh it off.

Sharna gripped the opposite side of the ladder, looking
up at her. 'Gabs, you can't overshare with me. We're friends,
right? Well, that's how it works. You can say anything,
I can say anything. We don't have to agree—hell, we don't
even have to be on the same team,' she grinned to under-
line the innuendo. 'But we'll still be friends. The family
we choose, right?'

Gabrielle dropped her brush on the tarp, jumped from
the second step of the ladder, and flung her arms around
Sharna. 'Thank you,' she murmured into her shoulder.
'I needed to hear that.'

'Good. Because then you'll realise that you don't get to
criticise my choice in music anymore. And right now, what
we need to hear is some Neil Diamond.'

'Neil Diamond?' she groaned. 'Seriously, Sharna, are
you really some seventy-five-year-old hiding in a twenty-
five-year-old's body?'

'Nothing wrong with a bit of "Cherry Cherry",' Sharna
chuckled, twirling away from her.

∞

Hayden didn't come in for lunch. Gabrielle briefly argued
with Sharna over who should take him a drink and sandwich.
She won, and Sharna took the food out to Hayden beneath

the jacaranda, though Gabrielle lurked in the breakfast room, peering around the curtains to watch as Hayden massaged his left shoulder and then sat on the low stone wall, chatting with Sharna as he ate. Then she was jealous.

Every time she looked out during the afternoon—which was embarrassingly frequently—Hayden still laboured in the garden under the tree. Even from a distance, she could appreciate the improvement as he cleared the weeds and turned the ground. He disappeared for a while and then reappeared, pushing a barrow filled with manure from the mound she had noticed near the rear screen of wattle trees. He made multiple trips, on the final one carrying sacks filled with something she couldn't make out, and then spent hours crawling around the large bed on his knees, pushing whatever they were into the earth.

As evening drew close, she realised with a start that he was walking back up to the hotel. She quickly busied herself packing up the last of the painting paraphernalia, ditching the thin plastic drop sheets and the brushes into a large garbage bin rather than wash them clean. That was one 'unnecessary' expense she wasn't willing to let go of—she had quickly discovered that paintbrush handles remained sticky and gritty no matter how well they were cleaned. So, to Hayden and Sharna's laughing disapproval, she had decided they were disposable, and chucked them at the end of each day. There was something refreshing about starting the new day with a new brush: it imbued the job with potential, rather than drudgery. Much like having a fresh canvas and a clean palette, she'd told Hayden when he teased her.

'Looking good,' he said, his voice deep with hidden meaning as she bent over, mopping a few speckles of paint from the floor.

Her shoulders sagged in relief: Sharna was right, his introspective mood had passed. And, equally welcome, he was flirting with her.

'Back at you,' she grinned over her shoulder, not rushing to straighten. 'Oh my god, you're filthy,' Gabrielle said as she caught sight of him properly. Even beneath the dark stubble he kept neatly trimmed but never seemed to entirely lose, mud and grime marked his tanned skin.

His teeth flashed white. 'I'm not the only one. You're supposed to put the paint on the walls.' He reached towards her, his thumb extended as though he planned to wipe her face.

She took a quick step backward, slapping a hand to her cheek. 'That's okay, I'll get it in a minute.' When she could reapply her make-up.

He looked confused by her retreat, so she turned it into a joke. 'You forgot to lick your thumb first.'

'Gross,' he said. 'That was one of Nan's moves. Both for my face and smoothing cowlicks.' He ran his hand through the thick hair that sat in an unruly wave on his forehead. 'I was thinking: we're pretty much done here, and if you're still planning on heading into the city tomorrow—' He paused, as though hoping she would say she had changed her mind. God, she wanted to. 'We should celebrate. It's pizza night at The Overland. How about you have an evening off being chief cook and bottle washer, and I'll try to sweet talk Alex into doing us a takeaway? I'll get pizza and beer—and, yes, Moscato,' he raised his voice to answer Sharna's bleat of protest as she dragged the bin through the doorway. 'Maybe I'll hang back here a bit later tonight?'

He spoke the final sentence quietly, looking intently at Gabrielle.

Her heart quivered. It wasn't like he had been downing tools and hightailing it at five each afternoon; often they worked through until they couldn't tolerate Sharna grumbling about being starved and overworked, and then they'd head to the kitchen and eat whatever she had put on to cook throughout the day. Stews, casseroles, roasts and soups—she'd been working through her mother's repertoire.

So this was Hayden's way of telling her that tonight was different.

And she was terrified. 'I–uh—'

'Ham and pineapple for me,' Sharna yelled.

Gabrielle seized on the interruption. 'Take if from someone who's been to Italy, that is wrong on so many levels.'

Hayden looked disappointed, but she kept up the pretence of not understanding his implicit question. 'But even with ham and pineapple, pizza sounds like a great plan. There's some garlic bread in the freezer. I'll dig that out. And, unless Sharna's already found it, there's one of Tracey's apricot pies left over from last weekend.'

'Great, and I've been working on rations?' Sharna muttered, although she had been complaining only that morning about putting on weight with all the rich French food. 'Is there any cream?'

'Only ice cream, I think.'

'Suits me. Unless you want to swing past Mum's and pick up some cream, Wheaty? I'll text her and let her know.' Sharna pulled out her phone, apparently having decided cream was a necessity.

Hayden groaned. 'Well, if Trigg and I are now making a full-on shopping expedition, I'd better wash up first.'

'Yuck. Like you weren't gonna otherwise?' Sharna said. 'I'm done for the day, too. Race you for the bathroom.'

As she dashed towards the stairs, Hayden lifted his hands in question. 'But there are two bathrooms . . .'

'She prefers the one with the waterfall showerhead,' Gabrielle laughed. Her pulse accelerated as Sharna disappeared. She and Hayden were as close to being alone as they ever managed.

Hayden obviously noticed, too. He closed the space between them, his hands resting lightly on her upper arms. 'I don't like the thought of you going tomorrow. It feels like we're saying goodbye.'

Her heart skipped a beat. There was no way to misconstrue his words. He was admitting that he cared. That she mattered. 'Not goodbye. I'll be back in a couple of days. I mean, this is my home now.' A horrible thought struck her. 'You'll be here, won't you?' Why did she suddenly feel that they teetered on a knife's edge, as though these few moments might be all they would ever have? Was this how it felt to fall in love? This churning mixture of exhilaration and abject fear that, at any moment, everything could be stolen from her?

'I will. But before you go, I need to show you . . .' Hayden broke off, a scowl creasing his face.

'Show me?' she prompted.

'No. Don't worry about it, it doesn't matter.' His hands had tightened on her arms, and she could feel the tension in his body, as though he battled with himself. 'What I actually want is to kiss you. Now. But I smell worse than Trigger.'

'That's a bit of an exaggeration. Poor Trigger has every right to be offended—*he* doesn't smell bad at all,' she grinned. 'Wash up. Then I promise I'll kiss you.' That much, she could do. But first, she needed to get rid of him so she could scratch the paint off her face and fix her make-up.

'Trigg, you can stay here.' Hayden glanced at her. 'Is that okay?'

'Perfectly.'

He leaned in, stealing a quick kiss before striding towards the foyer hollering, 'Don't you use all that hot water, Sharn!'

'I hope we can get more than a couple of showers out of the unit,' Gabrielle called after him. 'I need one later, too. And I don't think guests will be too happy about paying for a cold shower. C'mon, Trigg, let's see what we can find for you.' She headed into the kitchen and donned gloves to lift the cast-iron lid of the enamelled Le Creuset casserole dish on the stove. Fragrant mushroom and smoky bacon laden steam billowed from the pot of coq au vin. She stirred the casserole, then replaced the lid and put the pot to cool on the marble side.

'That one smells delish.' Sharna padded into the room on bare feet, apparently oblivious to the evening chill.

'Better than bouillabaisse?' Gabrielle teased.

'Booyah who?' Sharna said, breaking a piece of crusty bread from the loaf Roni and the twins had dropped in and reaching for the casserole lid.

'Wait! Hot,' Gabrielle said, putting on her oven glove and removing the lid so Sharna could dip the bread into the rich red-wine sauce. 'Bouillabaisse. The fish stew.'

'Oh, that one. Ugh.' Sharna pulled a face.

'You should be glad I couldn't get the scorpionfish or conger eel,' she grinned. 'Had to make do with cod and mussels from the fishmonger in Murray Bridge.'

'You were testing even Wheaty's love with that,' Sharna said. 'But this? Yum. Now I don't want pizza. Will this keep till we're back?'

'I'll put it in the fridge for Hayden to eat while we're gone. If he comes by, that is.'

'I'm sure he'll be mooning around here looking miserable,' Sharna said gleefully, 'while we're busy partying it up in the city.'

Maybe she should warn Sharna that the city wasn't all it was cracked up to be. There were plenty of places to go, but she suspected Sharna would want to kick on. Sugar would probably be their best bet: they'd get a decent feed and the old vinyl they played would appeal to Sharna. Later in the evening the place tended to get cranking. Gabrielle hid a sigh behind her hand; she must be getting old. The notion of clubbing held zero appeal.

Her fingertips touched the paint on her cheek. 'I've just got to fix my face,' she said to Sharna.

'Bathroom in there, boss,' Sharna pointed through to the lower-level guest facilities. 'Got lost in all your real estate?'

'I need my make-up bag,' she called as she headed for the stairs. 'Keep Trigg with you, I've not fed him yet.' As usual, Sharna had left on every light switch she touched, and Gabrielle admired the welcoming glow cast by the wall sconces and ceiling pendants. The light shining through the high, frosted door panel in the bathrooms, one either side of the corridor, was a bright glare though, meaning the heater lamps had been left on. At least there would never be a problem with damp and mildew as long as Sharna lived here.

Gabrielle grasped the ornate brass door lever of the bathroom, pulling it down and pushing against the door at the same moment.

She stepped into the doorway.

And froze.

Hayden stooped over the basin, scrubbing his face with a towel.

She made a quick assessment of his broad back, the muscles sculpted and defined by years of labour, the skin deeply tanned as though he often worked shirtless.

But that wasn't what stole her breath. The back of his left shoulder, and what she could see of the front reflected in the huge, gilt-edged mirror, was a tortured roadmap of ridges and burn scars. His arm was covered in a dark blue compression sleeve.

As she stared, unable to pull her eyes away, Hayden dropped his towel into the sink and straightened, flexing his shoulders. His gaze met hers. 'Jesus, Gabrielle!' He snatched the towel up, pressing it to his shoulder as he whirled to face her. 'What the hell are you doing in here?' Embarrassment suffused his tone, his face suddenly pale.

She shook her head, gesturing behind her, still unable to take her eyes from his mutilated flesh. 'You're in the wrong bathroom.' Her fingers stretched towards his shoulder as she took a step forward. 'Does it . . . does it hurt?' she whispered.

Hayden leaned back, pressed against the basin as though he could prevent her from touching him. 'Some,' he growled, still trying to cover the burn.

'Did this happen when . . . on that CFS call-out?' The one that caused him such agony to recount. The one he spoke about in broken sentences and tight denial.

'Yes.'

'And it's why you couldn't get back here?'

'If you mean is it why I failed Nan, then, yes.'

Hayden's voice was harsh, abrasive with humiliation and guilt. She ran gentle fingertips over his flesh, her heart squeezing at the thought of the pain he must have endured. 'Does this hurt?'

'Jesus, Gabrielle, you don't want to touch that shit.' His hand clenched into a tight fist around her wrist, his knuckles as white as the hard rim around his lips.

She looked up at him. 'Why not?'

'Because it's fucking disgusting. *I'm* disgusting,' he grated out, his tone tormented. 'This is what I was going to tell

344

you about. I pretty well catfished you, Gabrielle. I pretended to be something I'm not.' He shook his head in defeat. 'But I was never going to take our *thing* any further, because I knew I couldn't risk you seeing this.'

'Couldn't risk it? Why not?' she said, although she, of all people, understood his reason.

'Because I'm fucking foul, and you . . . you're so perfect.'

'Perfect?' She stared up at him for a long moment. Her heart ached for his evident pain, but more, it ached with the weight of her emotions. Her feelings for Hayden had grown steadily, but she'd deliberately held them in check knowing that, no matter how many levels she and Hayden connected on, her flaws would be unacceptable to him.

Slowly, she took her fingers from the corrugated skin of his shoulder and eased from his grasp. She reached to the basin behind him. He recoiled, as though he thought she planned to rip the compression sleeve from his arm. Instead, she dampened her fingers by pressing them to the tap spout. Then she lifted her hand to her cheek and scrubbed hard, just above the paint speckle he had tried to wipe off. Too hard: she knew it would leave her skin reddened. But she had to remove the make-up, had to show him.

Hayden squinted, then shrugged, his right shoulder only. She knew now why he did that. 'You realise that birthmark is in the shape of a heart?' His lips quirked on one side, though he made no move to touch her.

'It's not a birthmark.' And, no, in her rush to cover it, she had never thought the five-cent–sized defect looked like a heart.

'And it's hardly a deformity, if you're trying to compare scars,' he said bitterly.

'Show me the rest of your arm.'

'Hell, no.'

She stepped back, unbuttoned her blouse and dropped it to the floor. As always, she wore a high-necked shirt beneath. She paused, taking a deep, steadying breath. Instead, it trembled into her lungs as nerves quaked through her. She had to do this now, prove to Hayden that experience rendered her less shallow than he believed her to be.

She closed her eyes, grasped the hem of the cashmere undershirt, and pulled it over her head. Cool air caressed her skin. Her hair, grown longer since she'd been here, tickled her shoulder blades.

Exposed, she should feel terrified; yet she felt . . . free.

Except she didn't dare open her eyes.

Hayden said she was perfect, but now she had blown apart his little fantasy. Would he be repulsed by the affliction that crawled unstoppably across her skin?

She threw back her shoulders and forced her eyes open, ready to deal with either his revulsion or, if he was like Brendan, his belittling remarks, designed to keep her ego in check.

'God, you're even more beautiful than I imagined,' Hayden murmured, his voice thick. He dragged his gaze from her breasts, barely covered by a lace bra, up to her face.

Confused, she glanced down. Did he not see what she saw?

Hayden reached for her. His chest rose raggedly, his lips parted with desire as he traced a work-roughened fingertip across her tanned skin. He tracked the smooth curve of her shoulders, ran his index finger from the hollow of her throat, down the centre of her chest.

She looked beyond him, checking in the mirror: yes, it was there, same as it had been since she was eighteen. The stark white patches that marred her naturally golden skin.

Hayden caught her glance at the mirror, her confusion. 'Does it hurt?' he asked quietly.

She shook her head. 'It's just a lack of pigment. Vitiligo.'

He ran gentle fingertips over the flesh. 'Does this hurt?'

She realised he was echoing her words to him.

'Not at all.'

'Only in here?' He lifted his hand to touch her temple.

She gave him a faint smile. 'Yeah. There. It started when Amelie died.'

'Stress?'

She nodded.

'You are stunning,' he murmured. His hand moved down, the heat radiating from his fingers as he traced the egg-sized irregular splotch on the curve of her breast. A smile creased lines alongside his eyes. 'You know I love cream in my coffee, right?'

Her breath fluttered through barely parted lips.

Hayden's hand encircled her waist. Slowly, he bent his head. Pressed his lips to her breast.

The breath rushed from her. She arched towards him. 'Yes,' she murmured.

31
Ilse

As Gabrielle reached for the wrong handle, Ilse lurched forward to warn her, but then froze in shock as the door swung open.

What had happened to her beautiful, perfect grandson?

His shoulder . . . his shoulder . . . She reached to touch him, but dismay rippled through her as she recognised the torment and despair in Hayden's face, the agony in his movement as he tried to retreat from Gabrielle.

Seconds spun by, an eternity where she couldn't move, couldn't hear, could only stare at the damage that ravaged his flesh. Then Hayden's harsh bark cut in: *'If you mean is it why I failed Nan, then, yes.'*

Failed her?

Her heart squeezed, the agony worse than on that final bittersweet summer day. Because she realised now that it wasn't grief that had broken her heart, but the unstoppable ravages of time. Yet, such a foolish old woman, she had manipulated Hayden into believing he was responsible for her and, even worse, allowed herself to harbour such a sense of betrayal, to feel so cheated, that Ilse failed to see his pain.

And then she dared think she could bestow her forgiveness, as though she had any right to punish him in the first place.

'Hayden,' she murmured brokenly. 'It wasn't your fault. It wasn't the fire, it wasn't something anyone could prevent. It was life that failed me. And that makes me sad. Sad that I had to get old, sad that I missed my card from the Queen by only a few weeks. Sad to lose all I've built here. Above all, sad to leave you. But it was never your responsibility to change my destiny. Remember, eventually we all become the river.'

Hayden's face contorted with self-loathing, and the sob welled in her chest as she backed from the room. Guilt was a burden a man his age shouldn't have to carry; it would leave him embittered for the rest of his life. She knew what loss could do, how one became afraid to show love, knowing it would hurt more when it was torn away.

She fled down the stairs, but there was nowhere to run, no escape.

The place she had treasured would now be her prison.

The agony of the grandson she loved above all others, her jailer.

32
Hayden

He slid his right hand around Gabrielle's back, using his arm to crush her close, revelling in the feel of her naked flesh against his. Still he kept his left shoulder twisted away from her, but she turned in his embrace, pressing a soft kiss against his mangled flesh.

Tears thickened his throat, but he had no time for them. Hayden had imagined this moment—no, that wasn't true. He hadn't dared imagine this moment, knowing it could never be. Instead he had fantasised. Fantasised about the woman who was now a reality in his arms.

He drove his fingers up through the back of her hair, gently pulling her face away from his ugliness. Above the lacy bra, the mottled patches, white on tan, highlighted the curve of her breasts. 'You are so beautiful,' he breathed.

Her face twisted in what looked like denial. 'It's all a façade. You know that, now.'

'No,' he said. 'You're beautiful . . . you're *good*. Where it counts.' He pressed his fingertips against her heart, beating frantically beneath his touch. 'Beauty is only skin deep. It doesn't count and it doesn't last.'

The truth of his words hit him. He had always known it, really, but somehow, tied up in his own self-loathing he'd lost sight of the fact. Mum's mastectomy should have cemented his knowledge; she had never changed her character simply because of her altered appearance.

As much as he could admire Gabrielle's physical beauty, that wasn't what he had fallen in love with.

In love.

How was it possible that the thing he desired most in life was now in his arms? He pulled her closer so he could press his lips to hers.

Her mouth opened beneath his, hot, welcoming and wanting, and her arms wound around his neck, dragging him down. As though he wasn't already drowning in his desire for her. Her tongue chased his, as demanding as he could ever wish it, and she thrust her barely covered breasts against his chest. Her nipples punched against his muscles, and he growled his desire.

She giggled into his mouth, lowering her hands to work on the fastening of his jeans. 'I want you, Hayden. I've wanted you since . . . well, since you blew me off in The Settlers. When I figured you were a challenge.'

He had never met a woman who was so direct; most had been happy for him to make the play. But the assertiveness suited Gabrielle. She was professional and educated and knowledgeable—and, hell, she was undeniably hot. 'Not so much of a challenge. I blew you off because I knew you were too good for me. That I could never have you,' he said between kisses down the smooth column of her neck. Beneath the paint and turps, she smelled sweet and flowery.

He wanted to kiss further, to explore her skin with his mouth, but at the same time he didn't want to release her, he wanted to hold her in his arms forever.

Forever.

The realisation hit him. Gabrielle was the woman he had waited for. And there was nothing to be gained by playing it safe, delaying telling her. 'Wait.' She had his belt undone, but he stilled her frantic hands on the stud of his pants. 'I have to—'

'Guys?' Sharna's voice rang from somewhere down the long corridor. 'I'm freaking starving. If you've got something other than pizza on the menu, at least let me know, and I'll get stuck into this French stuff.'

'I swear I'm going to put that kid up for adoption,' he groaned as Sharna's footsteps drew nearer.

Gabrielle sighed. 'Bit of a mood killer.'

'Hardly that,' he murmured, pressing his hips against hers.

She gasped, desire flaring hot in her dark eyes.

How could he tear himself away, even with Sharna right outside the door? 'She's an adult: we don't have to keep this secret, you know.'

Gabrielle screwed up her nose, inviting a kiss. 'It's not like she doesn't know. But let's keep it toned down a bit until after she's had this weekend away.'

'You still have to go?' It wasn't as though he had nothing to do; he had jobs backed up for weeks. But he didn't ever want her more than fifteen minutes' drive away. Even that seemed too far, though he had a sudden idea how he could fix that problem.

He scooped up her blouse from the floor and draped it around her shoulders. As she quickly buttoned it, he reached behind her, opening the bathroom door. 'Anyway, like I was saying,' he said without missing a beat, though he did smirk at Gabrielle, 'I have a suggestion about those outbuildings you want to fix up.'

Sharna slammed her arms across her chest, though she was laughing at him. 'I'm supposed to believe you two are holed up in here talking business? Shirtless, Wheaty?'

'Can't a guy get hot and sweaty?'

'Evidently.' She pursed her lips, and he caught the quick dart of her eyes to his burns.

'Working in the garden, I meant. Get your mind out of the gutter, young lady. Anyway, those buildings, Gabrielle . . .'

She had stayed facing him, her cheeks flushed though her eyes danced with mirth. 'What about them?' she asked, not managing to keep the hiccup of laughter from her voice.

He became suddenly serious. 'I'd really like it if the middle building, the castle, can stay as is. It was Nan's special place. Pops built it for—'

'Done,' Gabrielle interrupted as he tried to find the words to make his case.

'Done?'

'Done,' she nodded. 'It stays as it is.' She turned and walked out of the room past Sharna, headed for the stairs.

He shook his head in slow wonder. 'Are you always this easy to get on with?'

'Rarely.'

'Belt,' Sharna said, nodding at the flapping leather. He grunted, buckling it as he dashed after Gabrielle.

The heart-shaped mark on her cheekbone lifted as she glanced up at him. 'I have a good business head—'

'And a real hard arse, I bet,' Sharna chimed in.

He fought the urge to check the statement for himself. His hands hadn't had the chance to explore nearly far enough. Instead, he placed his palm in the small of Gabrielle's back as they reached the stairs.

'—but some things are more important than business,' Gabrielle continued. 'The buildings have more value as your memory than they'll ever have as accommodation.'

'Well, I do have a counter proposal,' he said. 'The cottages on the river front. You mentioned purchasing them to do up as extra accommodation.'

'I did,' Gabrielle's tone was all business, now. And he had a sudden urge to see her in a suit, at her corporate best. And to see her in her pyjamas, mussed in the morning. And to see her naked, in his arms.

Hayden shook his head, recollecting his thoughts. 'The nearest cottage, the largest one, is mine. It was the ferry master's cottage that Nan and Pops lived in. She left it to me when . . . when . . . She left it to me.' Damn, the word still didn't come easily.

'Oh?' Gabrielle hiked an eyebrow.

He nodded. 'My uncle owned the hotel until thirteen years ago, and Nan figured that his kids will eventually get a share of the family money from when he sold it. So she left the four cottages and the shop to me and Rob and my sisters. I can't promise they'll be interested in selling. At least, not outside the family.' He took a breath, then plunged on. 'I'm proposing—'

Sharna squealed, and he speared her with a glare. 'A business partnership. You have the public relations and promotion side handled; I have the building skills. If you think Wurruldi can be a successful venture, I'm in.'

'You want to turn the cottages into bed-and-breakfasts?' Gabrielle said, slow delight growing on her face.

'Some of them. Maybe we should keep the ferry master's cottage aside, though. In case you ever get tired of living in your hotel.' And wanted to move in with him, though he wasn't ready to run that by her just yet.

'Inn,' she said. 'I've decided it should be called an inn.'

'Posh,' Sharna agreed.

'That, and it does away with the issue of not having an ensuite for each room. I think the expectations of an inn are a little different. I can put a spin on it being quaint, old world. And that way I can let more rooms, and actually generate a positive income.'

'The Wurruldi Inn.' Hayden cocked his head, tasting the words. 'The vowels kind of run together, though.'

Gabrielle twisted her lips. 'They do when you say them aloud. I hadn't tried that. Does Wurruldi mean something? Or is it a person?'

'It's Ngarrindjeri for wattle seed,' he said.

'The kind your nan put in cakes?' Gabrielle asked.

Like the Grinch in the books Nan read him, his heart grew three sizes. Did Gabrielle remember every passing remark he made? 'Yeah, the same. She collected the seeds from the trees she planted around the border. Well, not the same trees that are there now; they're short-lived, so I guess these are about fifth or sixth generation. But they self-seed well.' He chuckled. 'Though you wouldn't believe that if you saw the price of wattle seed online.'

'And the hotel is named for the trees?'

He shook his head. 'No, the town is. My grandparents originally named the hotel The Wegener Herbege, but that went by the wayside in the early nineteen hundreds, thanks to the war.'

'Anti-German sentiment? Happened in a lot of places in South Australia,' Gabrielle said, but it seemed her mind was elsewhere. She frowned a little, then added slowly 'So, wattle seed is a popular culinary item? I have an idea . . .'

'This is your marketing kind of stuff, isn't it?' Sharna said excitedly.

Gabrielle nodded. 'There could be an opening for some value adding. Wurruldi Inn Wattle Seeds. Maybe there are other local delicacies, things we can add to make an exclusive range, build our brand?'

Our. He liked hearing that.

Sharna nodded enthusiastically. 'Wurruldi Inn—no, wait. What about . . . The Wattle Seed Inn?'

'Oh my god.' Gabrielle stared at her. 'That's too perfect. The Wattle Seed Inn.'

Sharna jumped down the last two steps. 'Junior marketing exec right here. Any time you want to cut me in on the whole deal, that'll be sweet.'

'I'll have to talk to my partner.' Gabrielle flashed her dark gaze up to him.

Her partner. He wanted to make that title permanent.

∽

Despite every hint, Sharna stayed up with them, her attention on Gabrielle's laptop as she switched between checking out the city hotel they were booked into, and researching cottage-style guesthouses so she could hone her new marketing talent.

Though Hayden wanted Gabrielle to himself, Sharna hadn't looked this happy since . . . well, never. So, he called it a night and headed home.

He was back at The Wattle Seed Inn before dawn, telling himself it was so he could get some work in. Fortunately, Gabrielle saw him from her window, waved and appeared at the front door within seconds, pulling on her jacket. His heart leaped at the way she didn't hide her eagerness to see him, and, hand in hand, they strolled through the pre-dawn calm.

The river was wreathed in mist, perfectly still as though it waited for the first touch of the sun to wake it. A kookaburra chuckled at their fascination with the crystals that slid down the naked willow branches to drip into the dark water, the ever-expanding ripples stirring the silk surface. Hayden pulled Gabrielle closer as they watched the river come to life. As moments passed, more birds woke, their whistles and chirps resounding off the timeless cliff that slowly came into sharp, stark focus as the curtain of night inched up from where the water caressed the rock.

Unfortunately, they had only minutes before the weather woke and forced them to race, laughing, across the large expanse of now closely mown grass between the dock and the inn. Every step he took, Hayden was aware that this was how he wanted to spend the rest of his life: he wanted Gabrielle's hand in his, he wanted her quiet appreciation of the living art to meet his love of the country, he wanted her to share her thoughts and feelings.

His world wasn't perfect, he still had shit to deal with; but this was perfect enough. This moment, this woman, this place, were all he could ever want.

∽

'It's only a couple of nights.' Gabrielle leaned over the open door of her Audi, on tiptoes to stretch up for a last kiss. 'Forty-eight hours, tops. We'll be back on Sunday.'

'Better be.' His hands cradling her face, he caught her bottom lip between his teeth and bit down on it gently until he heard the gasp of her arousal. 'And if you want to accidentally leave Sharna there for a few more days, that'll be fine. Failing that, I'm going to give my place a spruce-up in case we have to retreat there.'

'Believe me, even Trigger's rug and the back seat of my car are looking pretty inviting. There are some nice parking spots up on the clifftop,' Gabrielle laughed up at him.

'I don't need any scenery. Not more than this, anyway.' He pressed his lips into her hair.

They both jumped as Sharna leaned across from the passenger seat and tooted the horn. 'How can I do the whole are-we-there-yet thing, if we never leave?' she asked. 'Come on, you two. The quicker we go, the quicker we get back, I promise.'

'Okay, you go be adorable with our kid,' he said to Gabrielle as she dropped into the driver's seat. Stooping to see past her, he scowled at Sharna. 'And you ask Gabrielle what I said about having you adopted out.'

As the convertible disappeared behind the hedge, he headed up the side path of The Wattle Seed Inn with Trigger at his heel. He and Juz had painstakingly pressure-cleaned the sandstone walls, and now they glowed with the soft peach and apricot tones of the river cliffs he had admired with Gabrielle that morning.

He carefully stepped over the tufts of mondo grass that Tracey and Roni, along with the kids, had planted in the gaps between the paving, his footsteps slowing as he crossed the rear courtyard, the pavers swept clean by Taylor and her crew.

He pressed his palm against the solid wooden door to the castle, and took a deep breath. Entering the room would be the closest he had been to Nan for over a year, and his emotions were hard to define. A reluctance to see the room empty warred with a yearning to seek the familiar.

To his surprise, the room enfolded him with a sense of warmth and homecoming, as though Nan were still there. Her favourite garden magazines were scattered across the table, open to a page on treating rose rust with milk spray. A packet of Haigh's Rocky Road lay on the dresser, the open end of the plastic wrapper neatly folded under. Garden clogs, always brushed clean of mud, and blue-flowered gloves were on the corner of the stone bench that ran beneath the back window.

Skirting the mismatched pieces of furniture, he crossed to the gramophone. He turned it on and lifted the needle onto the LP carefully, like Nan had shown him a hundred times.

As the nostalgic strains of Glenn Miller's 'Moonlight Serenade' filled the room, he lowered into the chair that had been his grandfather's, and then his own. 'I'm sorry,' he whispered to the empty seat opposite. 'I'm so sorry, Nan.'

Trigger at his feet, he closed his eyes and let the music wash over him as the room settled into place, wrapping him in the safe familiarity of remembered peace. Instead of the pain he had for months felt at every thought of Nan, there was warmth, a sense of completeness, as the castle that had been her stronghold in times of joy and grief embraced him in its healing cocoon.

A breeze rustled through the potted gardenias he had placed outside the door. Although they wouldn't flower for months yet, a faint perfume wafted over him, a soft breath caresseing his hand and his heart, gradually easing the tightness and softening the emotional numbness he had worked so hard to cultivate. As though someone whispered the words to him, untwisting the tortured emotions and denial he had lived with for more than a year, finally he understood: there was no point wishing for a cure for his PTSD. The events of his life meant it was now an integral part of him, as was grief and loss and regret. But if he managed the symptoms, he would be a whole man again. Strong enough to risk moving ahead with his life. With Gabrielle. There would always be the fear of loss, but it was loss that gave value to life.

A weight lifted from his shoulders and he took one more deep breath, releasing the last of the tension that had screwed with his mind and body for so long. He opened his eyes and pushed to his feet, glancing around as he realised the door was shut. Although only hairline cracks were readily visible, there must be a larger one somewhere, perhaps hidden by the peeling wallpaper, which allowed the fragrance-laden whisper of air to weave through the room. He would take care of that, before Nan's stuff was ruined by damp.

He worked methodically, first covering the furniture with tarps, then stripping wallpaper and chipping out and filling the few cracks, although he didn't find one large enough to account for the breeze.

While the mortar dried, he rubbed back the peeling pressed-tin ceiling, and gave it a fresh lick of paint. His shoulder ached with working at an angle, but for the first time the pain was purely physical, which made it entirely bearable. He grinned as he regarded the sticky paintbrush: Gabrielle had finally managed to indoctrinate him into considering them disposable. Tossing the brush into an empty paint pot at the door, he glanced around the room.

At the back of the potting bench, against the stone wall, he had found four rolls of wallpaper. Pulling a utility knife from his tool belt, he sliced off the pieces of thick, flower-patterned paper the silverfish had munched on. Tomorrow, with the mortar dry, he would repaper the walls.

He hadn't realised so much time had passed, and was surprised to find it dark as he dragged the tarps from the room. But, pausing at the door to the castle as he reached in to flip up the huge, old-fashioned light switch, he was satisfied with his work. The slight air of neglect had been banished, and Nan's castle now looked almost as it had his entire life: shabby and comfortable and lived-in and loved.

Trigger emitted a low warning huff. Seconds later, Hayden heard the car travelling too fast on the potholed road behind the inn. It slowed, took the corner, headed towards the river with lights flashing through the wattles, and cornered again.

Hayden closed up the castle, wiping his hands on the back of his jeans as he strode across the courtyard. The first rank of wattle trees glowed dull gold in the dusk, flushed with tiny yellow puffballs clustered between the long, narrow leaves. Nan always called the winter blooms the practise display, ready for the spring flowering, where entire bushes became a bee-filled tumble of gold.

As he reached the front of the building, a red Porsche 911 pulled up in a welter of loose gravel. A man clambered out. He used both hands to smooth his already immaculate hair, then reached back into the low car to take out a suit jacket. As Hayden approached, the guy pulled on the jacket over his collared shirt and raised a hand in greeting. 'The old place is looking good,' he called.

A vague sense of familiarity tweaked at Hayden's mind. 'G'day. What can I do for you?'

The stranger gave him a quick once over. 'Just looking for your boss. She's working you late, man.'

'She's not here at the moment,' he said, reluctant to give away any details about Gabrielle.

'Seriously?' Annoyance flickered across the man's face, and he pinched his nose a couple of times. 'I wish she'd communicate a bit better. Oh, sorry,' he thrust out a hand. 'Brendan Small. Elle and I bought the place together. I see she's whipping it into shape.'

Hayden stiffened as though a cow had kicked him in the guts. Reflexively, he shook Small's oddly soft hand. 'Hayden Paech.'

'You're the main contractor? The foreman? Elle said she's got you blokes ripping through a ton of work.'

'Guess so,' he said shortly, barely able to wrap his head around Small's revelation. The contractor. What the hell, was that how Gabrielle referred to him when reporting to the *business partner* she'd never mentioned?

Small nodded. 'Good, good. You can show me around, then. Where's my girl got to?'

'She had business in the city. And, sorry, can't show you around. On a tight deadline. You know, got a ton of work to rip through,' he said dryly.

'That's okay, I'll sort myself a room,' Small said, reaching for a suitcase in the back seat of his car. 'Best I don't drive back to the city tonight. Hit it a bit too hard, you know what I mean?' He pinched at his nose again. 'I'd probably run off the cliff.'

He was supposed to care? 'Rooms are taken,' Hayden lied. He was damned if he was letting Small inside the inn. If Gabrielle wanted to admit this guy she'd conveniently forgotten to mention, that was on her. But it wasn't happening on his watch. He clicked his fingers to summon Trigger. He needed to get the hell out of here, think over what Small had revealed.

'No problem,' Small said. 'Elle's used to sharing with me. Just point me to her room, mate.'

Hayden stumbled, but recovered, although he couldn't get any damn words out. Couldn't even formulate them. He strode to stand at the front door, slamming his folded arms across his chest. The painful tug of scar tissue reminded him that his plans had turned to shit before now.

But not this one. Not Gabrielle. He refused to jump to conclusions like a bloody teenager.

He trusted Gabrielle.

'Don't reckon so,' he said, staring Small down. 'You know how it is. Don't know you from a bar of soap, *mate*.'

Small took a step back, looking nonplussed. He glanced up at the first-floor balcony, as though he expected to see Gabrielle at the window like a captive princess.

'Give the *boss* a call,' Hayden suggested. Jesus, she was more than that, wasn't she? 'She'll tell me whether to let you in.'

Small stared at him, and Hayden met his gaze unblinkingly. 'Not much point staying here without her, anyway,' Small said eventually. 'Headed to the city, you say? Lucky I've got another hit, should get me back there.' He pulled a compact silver case from his suit pocket.

Hayden turned away in disgust, striding into the building. The inn door slammed behind him, and he forced a sardonic grin. It made a change from slamming in his face.

The Porsche engine gunned, gravel spraying noisily along the track as Small sped down the driveway.

Hayden headed to the foot of the staircase. He sat on the third step and dropped his head into his hands.

Fuck.

Trigger pushed in beneath his elbow, wet nose against his shoulder, but he ignored the dog.

'What the hell, Gabrielle?' he groaned aloud.

The scent of gardenia wafted through the closed inn, but this time it failed to soothe him. The peace he had experienced only hours ago had evaporated like piss on a bushfire; instead his mind raged with the ferocity of a burning forest, replaying every conversation he'd had with Gabrielle, searching for the moment he must have missed, the moment she told him the truth.

It wasn't there.

With an effort, he forced himself to his feet. He knew his triggers, couldn't let himself dwell on his choices, on recreating life to fit his dreams. Nothing good lay that way.

He drove too fast, intent on outrunning his demons, forcing his attention to the narrow, dark roads, rather than trying to untangle the truth.

But his brain wouldn't leave it alone.

Small was lying.

Had to be. Because otherwise, Gabrielle had pretended to be something she wasn't, someone she wasn't. And he couldn't let himself think about when that had happened to him before, when Simmo had fooled them all.

His hand moved to rub his left shoulder, but he dragged it back to the steering wheel.

As the ute bounced over the cattlegrid, he told himself that Small was full of shit, that there was no way Gabrielle had steered him wrong; she had been open and honest and engaged and . . . everything he could want. But there still remained the odd sense of familiarity Small had woken in him.

Letting himself into his empty house, Hayden dropped onto the bed fully clothed and patted the mattress. Trigger settled next to him.

For five minutes, he fought the temptation to drag out his phone, but then he gave in and stared at the blank screen. He wouldn't hassle Gabrielle, wouldn't call her when she was out for a girls' night with Sharna. He would just send a text to update her on the work he'd done today.

He hit send, then, hating himself for giving in to the compulsion, to the need for reassurance, he thumbed onto Gabrielle's Instagram account.

He'd been through it before, there was nothing he hadn't seen.

He should leave it there.

Instead, he moved on to the *Small & Sassy* account she frequently tagged.

Before the screen even came up, dread washed through him. *Small.* Why hadn't the name registered?

Each post punched him in the guts.

Small had seemed familiar not only because of the business name, but because he featured, always looking like some damn aftershave model, in the company posts.

With Gabrielle.

So many posts.

Going back years.

The bastard had known Gabrielle basically forever.

Fuck.

Hayden threw his phone onto the bed. He wasn't in the right headspace to deal with any kind of dishonesty, with anyone who wasn't what they seemed. While Gabrielle might not have actively hidden Small's existence, she had also never mentioned that their new partnership was going to be some kind of three-way.

With a guy who reckoned he was sleeping with her.

The last time someone lied to him about their intentions, it had nearly cost him his life.

And it had killed Nan.

Betrayal churned in the pit of his stomach, acrid and bitter in his mouth. He hauled himself out of bed and cracked the bottle of Bundy that had been gathering dust on top of the fridge for over a year. He knew alcohol could tip him over the edge, erase the filters that kept him out of the black pit of PTSD.

He also knew it could blank the pain, if only for a little while.

∾

The light on his uncurtained window screamed late morning when he woke, though it took him a moment to work out it was Saturday. The tangled bedcover suggested nightmares he didn't recall, and Trigger whimpered from alongside the bed.

'Sorry, mate.' Hayden staggered to the door and opened it, the gust of cold air searing pain behind his eyes. His mouth tasted like the bottom of a chook yard and his head throbbed. But he'd made it through the night. He blearily recalled getting a text from Gabrielle, but he hadn't answered. Hadn't trusted himself to.

Or—hell, had he? He lurched back to the bedroom, snatching up his phone.

No sent messages.

Tossing aside the phone, he headed to the bathroom and stood under a cold shower, trying to get his head straight. He had a habit of catastrophising: it was part of the PTSD, anticipating the worst, letting the shades of grey and black overcome the light. Yesterday, he'd fallen back into the pit of hopelessness and distrust he'd spent so many months trying to clamber out of. Taylor would rip into him for adding alcohol to the mix, and tell him he needed to limit the triggers that could throw him off track.

But he knew the truth: he'd been weak, allowing his mind to lead him into darkness, then drinking himself stupid to stop the pain.

He needed to learn to keep shit to the bare facts. And the facts were, he was being a jerk. Gabrielle would have an explanation for her omission about Small's partnership. And for that bastard's bullshit about sharing her bed. In any case, she was entitled to a past; it wasn't like he didn't have one himself. It was just that jealousy was new to him, but he would learn to deal with it. As long as Small kept well out of their lives.

He dressed quickly, aware of the rain slanting against the windows, the wind keening around the edges of the shearer's cottage, trying to find a way in. Despite the weather, he would head back and get in some more work on the gardens. An apology to Nan for letting them get out of hand, and to Gabrielle for doubting her. Though it was late in the year, he'd planted Nan's precious Dutch iris beneath the tree, hopefully in time to coax a few spring blooms from them. He remembered the gardens had always been a riot of warmer weather colour, so there must be more bulbs tucked safely in the cold soil beneath the overgrown lavender and rose bushes along Pop's stone walls. If he cleared the beds, gave the roses a late prune and used a frost cloth to protect anything else he risked cutting back, the late spring display should be perfect for the opening of The Wattle Seed Inn.

Physical labour always helped: he had become practised at avoiding the chaos of his own thoughts.

∾

It was dark by the time he packed up the tools. He had repaired a couple of Pop's stone fences, cleared a heap of flowerbeds at the front of the inn and broken the cement-hard earth beneath the roses and lavender to allow the last of the rains to penetrate.

He whistled for Trigger, even though the dog was, as always, only a couple of metres from him, blending into the shelter of one of the patchworked walls. 'Good dog.' He ruffled the Australian Shepherd's ears and Trigger snorted happily, cocking his head to fix Hayden with an ice-blue stare as he gazed out across the property, towards the time-less, imperceptibly flowing river. The magpies had settled in the gums beyond the wattle hedge, their evening song quieting to the odd ruffled disturbance. Wood ducks called across the wetlands. The night-scented breeze blew in from the river, sharp and fresh.

Just like when Nan was here, the place had soothed him, eased his confusion and made sense of a world that sometimes seemed bleak. He should have come back here a year ago. But maybe it hadn't been time, then. Maybe he'd needed Gabrielle to be here, too.

He pulled his wet Driza-Bone closed against the chill. Time to head home and grab a hot shower and something to eat, in the hope it would chase away the remnants of the hangover that had pounded in the back of his skull all day. Once he'd shifted that, he'd give Gabrielle a call.

The thought of hearing her soft, slightly-accented voice finally brought a smile to his lips.

33
Gabrielle

Without the familiar dawn chorus of magpies over the Murray to wake her, Gabrielle slept in. It had taken her a while the previous afternoon to shake the slight melancholy caused by leaving Hayden and the soothing surrounds she had become accustomed to, but Sharna's enthusiasm for their first night in the big city had eventually become contagious. After shopping through the afternoon, they had dinner at Luigi Delicatessen on Franklin Street before heading over to Sugar nightclub on Rundle.

Today, it seemed even Sharna's enthusiasm had waned a little. Her hair mussed like a haystack and panda eyes smudged halfway down her freckled cheeks, she groaningly emerged from beneath her bedcovers. She scrabbled for her phone on the bedside table and squinted at the screen.

'Oh my god, I'm so sorry, Gabs. We're supposed to be finishing the shopping.'

Gabrielle poured them coffee from the pot she'd had sent up. 'I needed to sleep in, too. It's been a long time since I've been caught out at three a.m.' She was sure they would have been even later if Sharna had realised the nightclub was open till four. 'Anyway, we'll fit in a couple of places before the spa, but it's really not important. I can order everything else online.'

'But what if it's wrong?' Sharna's face crumpled.

'Then we'll hope your mum has plenty of room for new stuff,' Gabrielle grinned, adding milk to the coffee and passing it to Sharna. 'Come on, get this in you. At this rate, I'll think you're a one-hit wonder and you don't want to go out tonight.'

'Oh, I definitely want to,' Sharna said quickly. 'Just pour that whole pot of coffee into me, okay?'

While Sharna drowned her aching head in the shower, Gabrielle checked her phone again for messages from Hayden. Only the one last night, saying he'd almost finished fixing the castle. Knowing that he would be happy made her feel warm inside and had her grinning into the empty room. She longed to call him, to make conversation about not much of anything, but they weren't at that point. Not yet, anyway. And she didn't want to come over as clingy.

But she did allow herself to send just one text, a quick note to say she couldn't wait to see what he'd done. Of course, she meant she couldn't wait to see him. She hesitated, then added a kiss. It was weird, she would kiss him at the drop of a leaf, but actually putting the 'x' on screen seemed like signing a deal.

One she was perfectly willing to stand by.

∾

By the time they finished at the spa late in the afternoon, Sharna was feeling better, though Gabrielle suspected it was a false caffeine high.

'No, I'm just super relaxed,' Sharna declared, caressing her face with her fingertips. 'At this rate I'll look too young to get in the club tonight. But,' she added, shooting Gabrielle a stern glare, 'this time dinner's my shout.'

'It is definitely *not* your shout,' Gabrielle replied firmly. 'I owe you more than I can ever repay.'

Sharna grinned. 'I did kind of deliver you Wheaty on a platter, didn't I?'

Gabrielle laughed. 'Speaking of,' she said, pulling out her phone, 'have you heard anything from him? I've not had anything since last night.'

'He's as non-communicative by phone as in person?' Sharna rolled her eyes. 'Shocker.'

Gabrielle dropped the phone back in her bag, pulling a rueful face. 'True enough.'

'Aww, look at you, all love eyes like a little puppy! You do realise it's only been about twenty-four hours, right?'

Gabrielle flushed. 'I know.' She turned towards the Louis Vuitton on the luggage rack. 'Hey, seeing as we've perfected the hair and you've got the nails, do you want to get really done up tonight?'

'If you mean clothes, not drinking, I only brought another shirt to go with my jeans.'

'But as usual I have a *ton* of stuff.' Gabrielle unzipped the case. She didn't miss the chic, expensive lifestyle, but Sharna would enjoy the change. 'Cocktail dresses and heels? We're never going to get to wear them in Settlers or Wurruldi.' She held several suit bags towards Sharna. 'You pick. We're about the same size, nothing a belt can't fix.'

'Are you serious?' Sharna said as she unzipped the first bag. 'Even I recognise this brand.'

Gabrielle stroked the fabric. 'This lot needs a last hurrah before I tuck them way at the back of a wardrobe. And you need to point me in the right direction to pick up some of those work boots; we have to tackle the gardens once we get back to The Wattle Seed Inn.'

The thought of a new project, manual labour where she actually achieved something with her own hands, shot a thrill of anticipation through her.

And never had she felt more excited about a clothing purchase.

∾

Apparently oblivious to the absurdity of pocketing balls while wearing a cocktail dress and red-soled heels, Sharna hit the pool tables as soon as they got to Sugar a couple of hours later.

Or maybe her friend actually had it all worked out, Gabrielle mused, noticing the attention that followed Sharna as she sashayed back to the bar after a few games.

She flung an arm around Gabrielle's shoulders, stealing a drink from her glass.

'That's a dry white. You won't like it.'

'Tonight I love everything!' Sharna said expansively, setting the glass down and taking Gabrielle's hand to tug her towards the dance floor. 'Especially you. But you already know that.'

'And you know I love you, too,' Gabrielle laughed, her arms above her head as she surrendered to the music. It was true. She loved her sisters because they were blood, but Sharna was somehow more important: she was a friend by choice.

'I have to tell you something, though,' Sharna said, her tone suddenly serious.

'What?' Gabrielle froze, ignoring the gyrating bodies surrounding them.

'Your moves suck.'

'My moves? I wasn't making a move.'

Sharna grinned. 'Dance moves. You suck. I'm so happy you're actually bad at something.'

Gabrielle grabbed Sharna's hand, spinning her around. 'I'm not only bad at it, but so far out of my comfort zone you wouldn't believe.'

'Why are you out here, then?' Sharna gasped, clutching at her for balance.

Gabrielle swept Sharna's hair aside so she could speak in her ear. 'Protecting you. You're the hottest thing out here and Hayden said I have to look after you.'

Sharna wrapped her in a fierce hug. 'Well, don't take this wrong, but can you bugger off now?' she murmured, then tilted her head towards a statuesque blonde making her way purposefully towards them.

Gabrielle smushed a kiss on her cheek. 'You know where to find me.'

'Propping up the bar and staring longingly at your phone?' Sharna teased.

'Something like that,' she sighed, a thrill of anticipation deliciously flavouring her melancholy. Only a few more hours until she could go home. To Hayden.

Although his lack of communication disconcerted her, she knew it was because she was accustomed to colleagues who lived their lives attached to their phones and social-media accounts. Hayden was more . . . *real* than that. But this relationship was so new, so raw, she hadn't been prepared for how vulnerable she would feel.

'What's a nice girl like you doing in a place like this?'

The voice was comfortably familiar and Gabrielle swivelled on her bar stool, welcoming the distraction from constantly checking her phone. 'Brendan.' Her eyes travelled to his entourage. 'Hey, all. How did you lot find me?'

One of the girls waved her phone. 'You were tagged in an Insta post on your hotel account.'

'Ah.' Sharna had been going snap happy all weekend, but Gabrielle hadn't realised she was using their official account.

Amid the flurry of greetings and air kisses, Brendan leaned over the bar. 'Flaming sambucas by five,' he called to the bartender. 'And keep them coming. We have to drink to Elle surviving the wilds and returning to us. Believe me, I've just been out there, and she deserves a toast.'

'You were out at Wurruldi?' She accepted the drink— although she sipped it and didn't inhale the vapours the bartender trapped beneath the second glass. 'What for?'

'Do I need an invitation to see my partner?' Brendan checked his reflection in her half-empty wine glass. There could never be enough mirrors in the world to satisfy his vanity.

'Not at all. But you could have saved yourself a drive if you'd called.' She tapped her phone.

'Well, it's not a mistake I'll make twice,' he said. 'Looks like you've torn the place apart. What the heck are you doing there?'

With a vague surge of amusement, knowing details were the last thing he truly wanted to hear, Gabrielle launched into a comprehensive list of the improvements and repairs they had made on The Wattle Seed Inn, sharing her new-found fascination with load-bearing walls, septic tanks and grease-traps as Brendan looked increasingly bored.

Hayden would have sat up all night discussing her plans.

It was funny; it had only been a few weeks, but she felt she had changed, grown. Brendan, however, was the same as always.

He reached over to put a hand on her knee. 'I've missed you, Elle.'

He'd taken a little something extra before coming out. He kept pinching his nose and wiping the sheen of sweat from his tanned forehead. She tapped a finger against her nose. 'I can see you've been trying to dull your sorrow.'

He removed the trace of white powder with a final swipe, and grinned at her. 'Keep telling you, it sharpens the edges. I'm honing my advantage.'

Gabrielle sighed. They were such vastly different people, it was inconceivable they had been together for so long. Yet Brendan would always be part of her life, not only as a partner, but as a friend. And, although she was unspeakably sad about the choices he made, he had his own path to follow. She knew his claim of missing her was only good until the next girl caught his eye, the next challenge replenished his creative well, or the next drug filled his need for sensory overload.

Brendan gestured at the shot the bartender had lined up. 'To the renovation queen,' he suggested. 'It seems you've found your passion.'

She waved away the drink. 'Not for me, thanks. I'm watching out for a friend.'

'A friend?' Brendan hiked an immaculately groomed eyebrow. 'Not a great friend leaving you sitting at a bar all alone. Where is he?'

'She's the cute strawberry-blonde right in the middle of that crowd.'

'Ah.' Brendan's blue eyes gleamed with appreciation as he looked towards the dance floor. 'She? That explains a lot.'

'Like what, Bren?'

'Your protracted temporary disappearance.' He lifted his chin towards Sharna. 'Obviously, *that's* not something I can compete with.'

It was reassuring to know he never changed; as usual, everything was about him. 'Not temporary,' she said. 'And not a competition.'

'Dying!' Sharna announced dramatically as she elbowed between them. 'Yours, Gabs?' She reached for the wine Gabrielle had left on the bar when Brendan showed up.

'You must be Gabrielle's new . . . friend.' Brendan adopted his drop-your-panties voice, evidently warming up to the challenge.

Sharna turned to him, spearing him with her direct blue gaze. 'And you are . . . hitting on my girl?'

That wasn't going to help his misconception, but Gabrielle didn't care.

Brendan shot her a devilish smile. 'Chatting with my fiancée.'

'Ex,' Gabrielle rolled her eyes. 'Brendan, Sharna. Vice versa.'

'So, you're a regular, Sharna?' Brendan continued smoothly. 'Elle and I don't usually hang here. Apparently, Mandy does, though.' He gestured towards a slim woman with an asymmetrical carmine bob. Gabrielle recognised her as an intern with one of their competitors. Brendan must be on the hunt for inside information. And he was blatantly trying to drive a wedge between her and Sharna, but it didn't bother her in the least: she knew now that it would never happen.

'Hey,' Mandy smiled at Sharna. 'You are definitely *not* a regular here, or I would have noticed you. You have to teach me how to do that thing with your hips.'

'Do you mean with my hips or with your hips?' Sharna grinned, completely at ease. 'Come out on the floor. Either way, we'll make it happen.' She started back towards the dance area, phone held above her head as she snapped photos, but then she paused and turned, her face suddenly serious. 'All good, Gabs?' she inclined her head towards Brendan.

Gabrielle waved her off. 'All good. Have fun.'

'Want that other drink now, *Gabs*?' Brendan chuckled. 'Looks like we both struck out there.'

'Wine, thanks.'

'So,' Brendan said as he signalled the bartender. 'I've been thinking.'

'Painful?' she muttered.

He took her jab without a blink, and she knew his focus had flipped, like a light switch, from claiming he had missed her to being intent on a new project. No woman would ever be the most important thing in Brendan's life. 'If you're done with your premature midlife crisis, maybe it's time to think about coming home. I'm in talks with a boutique chocolate manufacturer.' He paused to down his shot. 'She's already got quite an export portfolio, produces a premium artisan product, sounds right up your alley. Solid business, been around for a decade. But that's just the thing: it's solid, not innovative. She realises that and is keen to get your skillset on board and rebrand. In fact, I've arranged for her to drop in here later tonight, so it's the perfect chance to make a connection.'

'This is really why you were chasing me down at Wurruldi? To talk me into taking on this account?' Despite her vague annoyance at his trespass on her private world, it was rewarding to reach a point where clients sought her out.

'Got me,' he grinned, not the least embarrassed at being caught out lying about having missed her.

'I assume you have a pitch ready?' She knew he would. Personal failings aside, he was a savvy businessman.

'Sure.' Brendan threw an arm around her shoulders, drawing her close so she could hear him over the music and crowd.

She leaned into him, her business persona sliding into place. But then she pulled back. 'Just to be clear, Brendan, I'm your silent partner, and I'll work as a consultant, like I promised. But I'm not coming back to the office, and I'm not coming back to the city.' She smiled slowly as she thought of Hayden and The Wattle Seed Inn. 'Because you're absolutely right. I have found my passion.'

34

Hayden

As he bumped up the driveway in the dark, Hayden made out Justin's white Toyota HiLux parked in front of his house.

'Mate,' he said as he climbed out of his car and reached into the back for the bag of Pop's stone-working tools. He wouldn't risk leaving them anywhere, not even out at Wurruldi. 'What's up?'

'Nothing,' Justin replied. 'Just checking in. Thought you might have time to go over some sketches?'

'Sure. You eaten?'

'Yep. But you go ahead.'

'The winery job?' Hayden asked as they headed into the messy lounge room. Damn, he'd meant to get this cleaned up before Gabrielle was back, in case they couldn't ditch Sharna. He'd do it before he crashed tonight.

He grabbed a meal from the freezer—Gabrielle had left him food at The Wattle Seed Inn but, though she was an awesome cook, he knew that eating without her company would rob the food of flavour—and added a can of baked beans on the side, in lieu of vegetables. He whacked it in the microwave while he fed Trigger, then he and Justin pored over the sketches, making minute alterations that would have been impossible for a less-talented craftsman to carry out with a knife, let alone a chainsaw.

Near midnight, he shut the front door behind Justin, his hand already in his pocket, dragging out his phone. He swore impatiently as he saw it had yet again quietly died sometime during the evening. It had never bothered him before, but then he hadn't cared much about keeping in touch with anyone. He headed into the kitchen to put it on the charger, and the flashing microwave reminded him he'd forgotten his meal. He ignored it and hit the shower: it wouldn't kill him to miss another meal, but if he had to wait much longer to speak with Gabrielle, that might do for him.

Finally he dropped onto the bed, simultaneously logging into his phone, his body aching with the weary sense of accomplishment that guaranteed a good night's sleep.

Gabrielle had sent a message around lunchtime, signed with a kiss. He grinned, running his thumb over the 'x'. Who cared that they weren't teenagers? She'd sent another text in the evening, detailing what they'd been up to during the day, including that they hadn't breakfasted until lunchtime because Sharna was so hungover. He couldn't help but smile as he rubbed his still-aching head. It would be a long time before he would go near Bundy again.

He checked Gabrielle's Insta feed, which hadn't been updated. Then The Wattle Seed Inn's.

It looked like Sharna had outgrown Moscato. Along with blurry photos, often showing only part of a hand or leg, were snaps of fancy meals and vividly coloured cocktails. He would have to warn Gabrielle. Until today, the business account had consisted of carefully curated images: tranquil river sunrises and raindrops clinging to branches, lush fabrics and close-ups of intricate wooden detailing.

He scrolled the pictures, Trigger side-eyeing him as he snorted with amusement. Sharna was really rocking it; they would be lucky if she didn't move to the city after this. Gabrielle looked stunning in every picture. Of course. Though she should be freezing in the high-necked, short-skirted number, the length of her tanned thigh as she leaned back against a bar stirred his interest despite his pounding head.

He flicked to the next photo, then jerked upright. Brought the phone closer to his face.

Gabrielle *would* be freezing—if it wasn't for the guy's arm around her shoulders.

A guy who, from the back, looked remarkably familiar.

Hayden took a screenshot and sent it to Sharna. *Who is the dude?*

It was twenty minutes before his phone pinged in reply. Twenty minutes he spent pinching the blurry screenshot, enlarging it as though he could see more clearly through the sea of waving arms and dancers that crowded the frame.

Assuring himself that it didn't matter if the picture was of Small, he was only Gabrielle's business partner.

Wassup Wheaty?

He ground his teeth and sent the picture to Sharna again. *WHO. IS. THIS. GUY????*

Another ten minutes. *Is fiancé. Thinks he's god's gift.*

WTF Sharna?

He tossed the phone aside before it snapped in his fist. Lunged out of bed and paced the room. Snatched up the phone again to dial Gabrielle—but what the hell should he say?

He called Sharna instead. She didn't pick up.

He slammed his left hand against the wall as he clutched the phone to his ear. Pain blazed through his shoulder.

The phone rang out again and again and he let it fall, slumping onto the edge of the bed. 'Jesus,' he groaned, his head in his hands, gouging his fingers through his hair. He'd known this would happen. Known that love only led to loss.

But he had expected to have a little longer. If he'd let himself think about it, his fear would have been that Gabrielle would find someone better. Someone whole. Not that she already had someone and he was just a side game. *The foreman.* A bit of rough to contrast her educated, urbane, unscarred, mentally-sound and no-fucking-doubt wealthy fiancé.

Trigger nosed at his leg.

'Get away,' he growled, pushing at the dog.

Trigger looked up at him with the mixture of reproach and adoration only animals could manage.

He relented and reached to fondle the dog's ears, twisting so he could see Mum's light across the paddock. Hell, but he wanted to go and talk to someone. Not Mum, though. Beyond her maternal outrage, she would have nothing useful to say. No, it was Nan who had raised him, Nan who would have had advice. She would, in her pragmatic, straightforward fashion, set him straight. Tell him to pull himself together.

He'd tell her that Gabrielle wouldn't do this, that there had to be some mistake.

And she would warn him that he was living a fantasy and that he had to learn to deal with what was solid and tangible and real, like stone. Not with passing promises and delusions.

But he could never speak with Nan again.

Yet she was right: why the hell had he allowed himself to be seduced by Gabrielle? By the promise of being normal. Gabrielle was a spin-doctor, a master of public perception. Had she marketed herself?

He slammed his head back on the pillow, barely missing the wall. Christ, had the whole thing been a ruse, a plan to get hold of the cottages? She'd mentioned weeks ago that she was keen to buy: had opened the door right then for him to offer to broker a deal. Instead, he'd said they would never be sold. So, she had worked another angle.

He shoved up and retrieved his mobile from the floor. Studied the picture again. Gabrielle was definitely leaning in to Small's embrace, their bodies melding with an easy familiarity.

Fuck.

He tossed the phone. The remainder of the previous night's bottle of Bundy rolled across the bed. He drained the last inch, then flung the bottle. It hit the floor with a heavy thud. Trigger whimpered. 'Up, boy.' He patted the bed, threw his arm over the dog and buried his face in the thick, mottled fur.

Afremov.

His heart cracked, and he let the wrenching sobs tear up from his gut. Why the hell not? What kind of man was he, anyway? Not enough for Gabrielle. She had seized on his pathetic need to believe someone could want him despite the way he looked, that his life could return to normal, that he deserved to be able to overcome the pain and betrayal and self-loathing. And she had used him.

35
Hayden

Hayden woke to Trigger's bark as a car pulled up at the front. A quick hammering of fists. The door had already shoved open to admit a frigid blast of air as he managed to stagger to the lounge. His blood chilled. 'Sharna? What's wrong?'

'Nothing,' she said airily, pushing past him. Then she waved a hand in front of her face. 'Jeez, Wheaty, what the heck? I didn't think this place could get any worse, but you've totally funked it up.'

How could she act like nothing had happened? He glanced at the old clock above the fridge. It kept shit time, but before he had Trigger he'd come to like the rhythmic ticking, the semblance of life in his home. It must have stopped. 'What time is it?'

Sharna pointed to the clock, evidently so he would notice her painted nails. 'Near three. Didn't you learn to tell the time back in school? Oh, wait, still using sundials back then?'

'Funny,' he muttered, crossing to the lounge and dropping into his seat. There hadn't been enough Bundy in the bottle to account for the way he felt, but the night had been fractured by nightmares and flashbacks, with Trigger whimpering and licking wetly at his face as Hayden wrestled his demons. And lost.

'Dude, you really look like crap,' Sharna said, bouncing onto the couch and curling her legs under her. 'You caught something?'

He looked at her disbelievingly. 'And you look fantastic,' he said, unable to keep the sarcasm out of his voice. 'Like the cat that got into the dairy. Have fun, did you?' He'd have to wean her from Gabrielle, before she got hurt, too.

'Absolutely. Best time ever. Gabs dropped me off here so Mum can pick me up, see my new cut,' she patted at her hair, which looked the same to him. 'She said she wasn't coming in because she looks like shit. Like she ever could,' she scoffed.

He didn't want to think about that. 'Hard night, huh?'

'Hard morning, too! We didn't get in till five.'

'I'm sure Small appreciated all that time with his fiancée.'

'What?' Sharna scrunched her freckled face in question.

'Small. Gabrielle's fiancé. I had the pleasure of meeting him on Friday, when he introduced himself as her bed-sharing business partner.'

'Oh, you mean Brendan,' Sharna said. 'Yeah, what a wanker.'

He was thrown by her scathing assessment. 'What does Gabrielle see in him, then?' He needed a drink. The gentle tick of the clock was the crack of a .22 rifle.

'Absolutely nothing, obviously.' Sharna stretched her hand, admiring her nails. 'Hey, I need coffee. You got milk or has it all gone off again? I'll see if I can catch Mum before she leaves, get her to drop some.'

'Might be some in the fridge. Grab me a water, will you? My head's killing me.'

'No milk,' Sharna returned with two glasses of water. 'Do you want me to find you some aspirin, or something?'

He shook his head. He should shut up, leave the subject alone, but he was like a dog with a bone. 'What do you mean, Gabrielle doesn't see anything in him?'

'I mean, he wouldn't be an ex if she saw something in him. Like, no guy's ever going to dump *her*, right? She doesn't talk about it much, but she was obviously the dumper, not the dumpee.'

'What the hell are you talking about?' The headache had become a deep, gut-cramping sickness, the kind he got after an attack, when adrenaline and cortisol flooded his body and then fled, leaving him exhausted.

'The ex. What are *you* talking about?'

'Her fiancé. Small.'

'You mean *ex*-fiancé.'

Sharna was starting to look irritated, and he knew that he was ruining her high, that she expected him to ask for details of what had been, at least for her, obviously a great weekend. But he couldn't shake his focus. 'Ex as of when?'

'Months ago, at least.'

'But . . . you said he's her fiancé.'

'Jeez, Wheaty, have you lost the plot, or what? I said *ex*.' A car horn tooted outside. 'That'll be Mum. Too late for the milk order.'

'Wait.' He staggered to his feet and found his phone. His head was about to explode. 'Look.' He pulled up her text triumphantly. 'You put "is fiancé".'

Sharna frowned at the screen for a moment, then grinned proudly. 'Speech to text. By that time of the morning, I was slurring something fierce.'

'*Is* fiancé . . . *ex*-fiancé?'

'You got it, Einstein.' The car tooted again. 'Sorry, gotta run. You sure you're okay, Wheaty?' Her usual flighty movements slowed, her face serious. 'Do you want me to call Tay? You really do look like crap.'

'Just a headache.'

He headed for the bathroom as she left, bending over the none-too-clean bowl. His shoulder ripped and tore as he vomited up the last of the Bundy. Hell, he hadn't lost Gabrielle at all. But, released by the PTSD, the darkness was in him and he couldn't expect Gabrielle's love to somehow save him. How could they be together if his insecurities made him doubt her commitment within minutes of her leaving?

The pressure increased in his head until he was certain blood ran from his ears. He dragged himself through the tiny kitchen and collapsed on the old lounge.

∾

The chime of the phone woke him, and he forced his eyes open. Trigger had climbed up beside him at some stage, so he must have been thrashing about in his sleep. He stretched for the phone, wincing at the tension in every muscle. Each sinew and tendon felt ready to snap.

In case you didn't realise, I've found a foster home for the·kid for the night. Built up the fires, so the inn is toasty warm. Come whenever you want . . . xxx

He clutched the phone against his chest, the welter of relief almost overpowering the darkness that churned like a cement mixer full of gravel inside his skull. Gabrielle was as she had always been—sweet, kind, generous and funny. Any fuck-up had been only in his own warped mind— but in future he would pay more attention to Taylor's insistence that he avoid the anxiety that triggered him to self-destructive behaviour. He should have had the balls to ring Gabrielle immediately and ask her what the deal was with Small, instead of trying to suppress his emotions through work, letting them build up until he couldn't handle them.

He would go to Wurruldi as soon as he'd kicked the blinding hangover that was a hallmark fallout of the attacks.

∾

The worst of the pain had passed when he next woke, the phone still tight against his chest. Gingerly, he pushed himself upright and flicked on the phone screen. Two a.m.

Too late to go to Gabrielle? But she had to be wondering where he'd got to. He opened his messages. Three. Each from Gabrielle, the first two asking when he was coming, saying she'd overheated the room and now had to strip off. The third saying she'd spoken with Sharna, who said he was under the weather. She signed that one off with a sad face and kisses. Warmth spread through him at the realisation: it was never going to be too late to go to her.

Fifty minutes later, he and Trigger headed down the steep, winding cliff road, then across the wetland flats towards Wurruldi. Anticipation chased the last vestiges of his headache away, and he shifted restlessly in the bucket seat. Alongside him, Trigger whined, his head cocked and nose jutting sharply forward, as though he too were eager to arrive. Hayden shook his head. 'Sorry, mate, but you're going to have to sleep in the hallway tonight. I don't think we need an audience.'

He had never before been this excited to be with a woman. He was going to have to make sure to slow things down, show Gabrielle the adoration she deserved. Though, the way he saw it, they had an entire lifetime ahead for him to practise that.

As he passed the town sign for Wurruldi, he noticed all the lights in the inn were on. Gabrielle must still be up. Waiting for him.

He drew up at the front of the building, not bothering to lock his ute as he dashed through the light drizzle to the heavy front door, and used his key to let himself in. It was unusual to find anything locked out here, but he was glad Gabrielle had clung to her city roots in this, at least.

Trigger's claws skittered across the marble and he dashed upstairs without waiting for a command. Hayden didn't bother to reprimand the dog. Instead, he took the stairs two at a time. He hit the hall at close to a run. The smell of the open fire tainted the air and his pace broke, memory slapping him in the face.

He thrust it aside.

Trigger had dashed down the long timber-panelled corridor, lit only by a pair of richly glowing sconce lights. He whined at the far end, scratching at Gabrielle's closed door.

The air smelled more strongly of smoke here, but Hayden brushed the thought aside. He wouldn't let his memories ruin this moment.

He rapped on the doorframe. As he glanced down for the handle, he froze. A ghost curled from beneath the door, a wraith of smoke. Fear and memory prickled up his spine. His mouth flashed dry and his heart enlarged. He shook his head; he was imagining the smoke.

Trigger barked sharply. Raked deep grooves in the door with his paw.

Jesus.

Even if he were imagining phantoms of his own terror, the dog wasn't.

Hayden's training kicked in. He flicked one hand across the metal door handle. Cold. Good.

He raised his left arm to cover his nose and mouth. Grasped the knob with his right hand. Cracked the door.

Smoke billowed out, more terrifying than any nightmare.

Memory rushed in. The flames leaping around him; the dashboard buckling with the nightmarish ripple of a flexing monster; his skin melting against the passenger-side door. The explosion of glass, the impossible rush of heat when he was already being incinerated in a hellish furnace. The searing pain, the crushing pressure in his lungs, the certainty of death. Simmo's face distorted with maniacal glee, backlit by dancing embers in the premature darkness beyond his window.

As flesh slid from his shoulder, exposing bone, he swivelled towards the back seat. Gabrielle sat there, her beautiful face stark with fear—or revulsion?

'Gab—' he choked out.

No. Gabrielle hadn't been in the car.

He was hallucinating.

She was here.

He dropped to his knees, vainly seeking clearer air near the floor. His mind whirling with horror and agonised memories, he tried to recall the layout of the room. Paralysed by fear, he drew a mental blank.

Trigger pushed up alongside him, emitting short, frantic yips.

'Trigg. Go find Gabrielle,' he gasped.

The dog whimpered but crept into the room, and Hayden lurched to his feet, bending to grab Trigger's harness. He shoved the fear down. He had to get to Gabrielle; she could never know the pain he had become too familiar with.

Deep within the functioning portion of his brain, the part still able to rationalise rather than act purely on instinct, he registered the lack of heat. But the fact refused to make any sense. Where there was smoke, there was fire.

His greatest fear.

No. Losing Gabrielle was his greatest fear.

The impenetrable smoke thickened, the gust of air from the open door stirring the roiling cloud. His throat raw, his lungs burning, he backhanded the tears streaming down his face as he strove to see through the reeking breath of green wood.

His knee hit furniture and he groped with his right hand. The bed.

Releasing Trigger's harness, he worked his way up the mattress, pawing frantically at the covers as he tried to find Gabrielle's slight form in the massive bed.

He touched unresponsive flesh. Found an arm. Pulled the body towards him. 'Gabrielle. Gabrielle,' he panted frantically. He couldn't be too late. Not again. He had to get her out of there.

He stood, her limp form cradled in his arms. The smoke seemed less, higher up, despite both training and experience telling him it should be otherwise.

Which meant Trigger was still in the thick of it. 'Trigg. Here boy,' he choked. The dog didn't respond.

He wasn't leaving behind the animal who had saved him so many times over the past eighteen months. Hayden lifted Gabrielle over his right shoulder and bent to fumble desperately around the base of the bed. Located a pile of fur. One hand steadying Gabrielle, he wrapped his left arm around the inert animal. Tensed, and lifted him, the dog drooping lifelessly in his grasp. Then he staggered towards the door.

Smoke filled the corridor. He stumbled towards the stairs and down, not stopping until he reached the entry hall. Chest heaving as his body fought to return oxygen to his blood, he slammed to his knees and dropped Trigger in an untidy heap of mottled fur, freeing his arm to support Gabrielle's head as he lowered her to the cold tiles.

'Gab—' He broke off, coughing and retching blood from his previously traumatised airways. 'Gabrielle?'

She lay as pale as sandstone, as still as a monument to grief.

No, there could be no more ghosts here, no more tragedy.

He dug in his pocket for his phone. Trigger whined but scrambled to lie on his belly, his nose pushed against Gabrielle's immobile body.

Dialling triple zero, Hayden hunched over Gabrielle, willing her to breathe. He knew CPR, but could barely force oxygen into his own tortured lungs.

Gabrielle moaned and his heart leaped. Or cracked.

He dropped the phone, cradling her head between his scarred hands. 'Gabrielle? Gabrielle, come back to me. I got here in time.' His voice broke and he bent low to whisper against her cheek. 'I won't lose you, too.'

36
Gabrielle

Her head pounded and her chest ached. But she was in Hayden's arms, and that was all that mattered.

In fact, Gabrielle hadn't been out of his arms since the moment she regained consciousness, lying on the floor of the entry hall.

Her recollection of events was fuzzy, but she knew that Justin had arrived, slamming through the front door and dropping to his knees beside them. His face taut with concern, he'd asked over and again whether they were okay. Sharna had been hot on his heels, Taylor and Luke not far behind.

After assessing them, Taylor called through to cancel the ambulance, which had to come from Murray Bridge. 'I'm sending you to the Royal Adelaide tonight, though,' she said sternly, placing a pulse oximeter on Gabrielle's finger. 'Both of you, Wheaty,' she added. 'You need a new set of chest X-rays, and Gabrielle's going to need a blood count and metabolic panel done. Do you know how long you were inhaling smoke, Gabrielle?'

She shook her head, shuddering at the dagger of pain. 'I went to bed early to wait . . .' She choked, trying to control the spasm as her lungs cramped.

'To wait for me,' Hayden finished. 'But I didn't get here until three.' His jaw tensed and she could see the guilt in his eyes.

'Trigger?' she whispered, her heart squeezing as she realised she hadn't seen the dog. There was no way Hayden would be there without his faithful companion.

'Matt came to get him.' Hayden stroked her hair. 'He's taken him out to The Peaceful Paws, where he can keep an eye on him.'

She tried to struggle upright. 'He's hurt?'

'He may have chucked up on your floor a bit. Lucky we'd got rid of the carpet.' Hayden tried to joke, yet the deep grooves in his face, darkened by soot, showed his torment. 'But he's fine and Roni will spoil him rotten.' Shifting back on the soft floral lounge in the Breakfast Room, he pulled her closer, crushing her against his chest. 'What's not fine is my heart. Jesus, Gabrielle,' he murmured. 'I came so close to losing you.'

'Who knew green wood could be so smoky?' she wheezed, her airways scratchy. She regretted the words the moment she uttered them because, better than anyone, Hayden knew. 'I'm sorry.' Tears blurred her vision. 'I'm so sorry you had to face that because of me.'

'Face it? I'd walk barefoot through fire for you, Gabrielle,' he said firmly.

Her heart clenched. She loved this man so much. It was sudden, it was unexpected and it was fierce. But she knew it more certainly than she'd known anything in her life.

'It's not only that the wood is green,' Justin said. 'Your chimney isn't drawing. Who was the bastard you had service the fireplaces? I'll sort him out tomorrow . . . today,' he corrected, with a glance at his phone.

Sharna hovered nearby, holding a glass of water. 'But Gabs is going to be okay, right, Taylor?' she asked anxiously.

The doctor nodded. 'Should be. It was wood smoke, nothing chemical. I'll order a bronchoscopy, too, but I'm sure the tests will come back clear.' She moved the stethoscope to once again listen to Gabrielle's lungs, squinting and shifting the cold bell on her exposed flesh.

'But the inn . . . is there damage?' With Hayden and Trigger safe, Gabrielle could worry about her other love. Although she could always rebuild, the hotel had a soul, a presence. She couldn't lose that.

'Just a bit of a stink,' Hayden said. 'Maybe we'll have to take the curtains down, hang them outside for a while, but it'll air out. Don't worry about it, Gabrielle. We'll sort it.'

As he bent to kiss her cheek, oblivious to his friends—*their friends*—Gabrielle realised that the flaws on her face and chest were visible to all.

And she didn't care.

Epilogue
Ilse

The hotel—The Wattle Seed Inn—was magnificent. Undeniably finer than it had ever been.

Gabrielle not only had an apparently bottomless purse, but a deft touch, and she'd created a seamless blend of opulence and beauty throughout. Her choice of paint colours, while not the safe white Ilse would have selected, was perfect, and the wallpaper, well . . . Ilse drew her fingers down the textured paper as she gazed out through the window of the Breakfast Room.

The heavy, drooping heads of the rose bushes partially blocked her view, but by standing on tiptoe she could see beyond the burgeoning border. Dutch iris bloomed in the walled garden beneath the jacaranda, their structured, spear-like leaves the perfect counterpoint to the wild explosion of fragrant lilac blooms on the tree, which would soon give way to delicate, lacy leaves. Stylish teak sun loungers dotted the manicured lawn around long trestle tables set with pristine white cloths. The cars had been arriving for the past hour, ranking on the neatly raked white gravel to the left of the horse trough and hitching rail. Dressed in their best—which, of course, failed to rival the elegance of her own time—guests disembarked, holding boxes and containers they carried to the tables.

In an open-necked lavender blouse and cream culottes, Gabrielle was distinctive, directing the setting of the gracefully appointed tables with the flowered scone plates and Oma's three-tiered stands. Hayden wouldn't be far away.

Ilse moved closer to the window. This was the best time of year in the garden, the rampant colour of spring making endings and death nothing but an impossible myth. With the grandeur of gardenia-hedged beds of burgundy iris interspersed with the flighty fun of freesias and sparaxis in a kaleidoscope of colours, the view reminded her of the effervescence of the Renoir above the fireplace, *Luncheon of the Boating Party*.

That was another of Gabrielle's touches of which Ilse heartily approved: stylish prints and paintings adorned the walls, and she had witnessed Hayden and Gabrielle's joy in choosing them together.

Ilse had primly prevented herself from witnessing their other joy. No one needed their nan to know what went on behind closed doors. But she remembered that happy, self-satisfied glow herself. The light that came only from true love.

As happened so frequently, the thought of love awoke the longing in her own heart . . . *Ronald*. How was it possible that she could be both so joyous and so melancholy? How could she miss him now as much as she had on the day he left? Why did that pain never ease?

She would take another visit to her castle, she decided, before anyone else arrived. She didn't want to miss a moment of the party, but the castle was a balm to her soul. Hayden had renovated the room perfectly, fixing the tatty pieces of lino and dangling wallpaper. The nice young carpenter refinished the wooden furniture, and Gabrielle cleaned the room. She placed a fresh vase of flowers in there each week, often chatting as she did so. 'The roses have started blooming, Ilse,' she would say. Or, 'Hayden tells me the perfume of gardenias is your favourite.' Sometimes, the flowers weren't even from her own garden, despite it flourishing under Hayden's touch, but were exotics Gabrielle bought specially for her.

As she thought about the room, so she was there. It seemed she had finally worked out how to manipulate the apparent perks of this non-existence. She ran a finger over the gramophone, smiling at the record on the turntable, 'Moonlight Serenade'. Sometimes, Hayden and Gabrielle came here to be alone together. And she allowed them. They were so very busy working, either on the outbuildings that Hayden was painstakingly almost demolishing before rebuilding—one of them as an art studio for Gabrielle to pursue her passion for creation—or on the cottages they were restoring for guest accommodation and, as she knew, the castle had a soothing magic. Perhaps Ronald had built it into the stone. She stroked the bench pensively, her mind filled with memories of her handsome husband and of the years that had fled too swiftly.

The heavy, honeyed scent of the golden wattles, now in full yellow-fluff-covered bloom, filled the room as Gabrielle entered. 'We can't disappear at our own opening,' she laughingly remonstrated as Hayden shut the door behind them.

'We won't.' Hayden set his strong, capable hands on her waist. 'But I need a kiss.'

'Like you don't kiss me in front of everyone, at every opportunity,' Gabrielle giggled, reaching up to link her hands around his neck and pull his lips down to hers.

Hayden kissed her deeply, and Ilse politely looked away, although she smiled softly, her heart full of love for her two young people.

His arms still around Gabrielle, Hayden drew his head back. 'Very nice. But not exactly what I wanted.'

Gabrielle pouted, stepping back with her hands on her hips. 'Oh, so now I don't rate?'

'I mean,' Hayden scrubbed a hand through his short, dark hair, tousling his cowlick and looking unusually uncertain.

Ilse clasped a trembling hand to her heart. Oh, she knew her grandson.

'I mean, I want a kiss after—' Hayden dropped to one knee, producing a tiny jewellery box from his shirt pocket '—after I ask you . . . to marry me.'

Gabrielle pressed her lips tightly together. Her dark eyes glistened like the river. 'Then ask me,' she finally whispered. 'And kiss me.'

Tears poured down Ilse's face but, finally, they were tears of joy, overflowing from her full heart.

A strong hand closed over her own, the palm work-hardened, the fingers long and spatulate. A touch she had not felt for, oh, so very many years. A touch she knew she would never again lose.

For the last time, she closed her eyes.

Peace blossomed within her, absolute serenity expanding her soul as she drifted, golden pollen in the breeze, to become one with the gardens, the rocks, the trees . . . one with The Wattle Seed Inn.

She sighed, and her breath became ripples on the endless river.

Acknowledgements

First and foremost, my thanks go to my publisher, Annette Barlow, who responded to my first draft of *The Wattle Seed Inn* with an unequivocal 'I absolutely love this', thereby inducing a few tears and ending five weeks and one day of nailbiting for me. Not that I was counting, or obsessively checking emails or anything like that!

To my editing team, *The Three C's*—Courtney, Christa and Claire. Between them they pull my story straight, deal with my many mistakes and continually check my tendency to throw 'factions' into the blend. For those who don't know the term, 'factions' are my family failing: Dad and I tend to blend fiction with fact and then share the conclusion with such a great degree of believability that we forget we invented it in the first place. I guess that's what happens when you're a storyteller, right Dad?

Courtney Lick is nothing short of a blessing. Not only does she have a knack for taking my convoluted half-page of work and replacing it with a single sentence accompanied by the notation 'or, how about something like this?', but she is a truly caring and compassionate colleague who both advocates for my work and supports me on a personal level. I would be lost without her direction, guidance and humour. Heck, she even thinks I'm funny sometimes. My kids would disabuse her of the notion, but what do they know? Courtney, if you ever need a character reference— or are available for adoption!—I'm sticking my hand up.

Nada Backovic has again produced a gorgeous cover— despite all my meddling, which everyone managed to stoically ignore. I probably should have mentioned at some stage that I basically failed art and have no concept of perspective or colour combinations.

My thanks to Cherry Getsom at The Rural City of Murray Bridge, who answered an eleventh-hour plea for help over the Christmas break and provided substantial data (because I don't *always* rely on 'factions'!) regarding development laws.

My gratitude to the readers, bloggers and librarians who made my previous book, *The Farm at Peppertree Crossing*, a success. Your reach is far greater than my own, and word of mouth is the greatest sales tool. I appreciate every positive mention you made to your followers and friends. Notably, but not exclusively, special thanks to outspoken supporters Craig and Phil at Happy Valley Books Read, Len Klumpp, Veronica at The Burgeoning Bookshelf, Helen Sibbritt, Claudine Tinellis at Talking Aussie Books and Debbie Berens.

On a very personal note, my love and respect to my dad. A few months back, Dad said something along the lines of how he is awed and proud that I recreated my life, changing careers midstream—okay, he may have said something less sensitive like 'changing jobs at your age', but let's just stick with intention! I was kind of gobsmacked because my memories of Dad have him driving trucks in a quarry, roaming the countryside as a ranger, sitting in a government office wearing a business shirt and cravat, managing the world's best interactive farm museum—which included driving a cart harnessed to a massive Clydesdale—braving the elements as a rural postal contractor, running a model aircraft shop and . . . oh, yeah, being my Dad. So, I guess I was set a pretty good example of being unafraid to chase dreams. Thanks, Dad.

And, finally, with a degree of sadness, my thanks to 'The Kid', my daughter, Taylor. *The Wattle Seed Inn* was born on one of our many road trips when we passed a small, rundown country pub and realised there had to be a story hiding behind the shuttered windows. We doubled back, took photos and spent the rest of the journey brainstorming. Why the sadness, then? Because Taylor is seventeen and on the cusp of launching into her own life, starting by studying a double degree focused on politics and law (I kid you not. She's a weird one). I'm always very aware that any story we brainstorm, any idea we discuss, any project we argue about (and we do argue!), may well be the last.

As always, life is made of bittersweet moments that create enduring memories.

The River Gum Cottage

Sometimes, home isn't a place: it's a feeling.

Lucie Tamberlani had it all: a business manager with a passion for naturopathy, she was set to take over the bookwork at the family strawberry farm in South Australia. But the unexpected fallout from a relationship sees her flee to Melbourne, raising her daughter alone. Summoned back to the farm after her father's death, Lucie must find a way to deal with not only grief, guilt and the betrayal that forced her away—but the fear of losing her daughter.

Jack Schenscher is doing it tough: caring for his aged grandparents and managing their wheat farm while simultaneously pursuing his passion of sustainable eco-farming on his own acreage leaves him with little time and even less money. With the death of his business partner, he could lose all he has worked toward. Yet when he meets Lucie, can he set aside one passion for another?

Both Lucie and Jack must discover that home is wherever the heart is.

Read on for the first chapter of
The River Gum Cottage

1

Lucie

Sometimes, she wished him dead.

It usually only happened in those hazy, sleep-drugged moments between dragging herself from her dreams and the start of her day, though. Once she was awake, her emotions were generally more rational.

But awake or asleep, there was no arguing that if he was dead, she would hurt less.

Lucie squeezed the crystal pendant strung on a leather thong around her neck. The quartz—for destroying negative energy while storing positive intentions—would need cleansing next full moon: it got a pretty hard workout whenever she thought of her father.

She eased out of the back door of the two-storey townhouse, letting it close quietly behind her so as not to wake the sleeping household. The tiny courtyard was bathed in a peachy ruddiness she told herself was sunrise, though she knew it was more an ambient glow from the Melbourne city lights.

As the ivy swallowing the garage rustled, she flinched, then hissed, 'Scat, cat.' Her neighbour defended, with a wooden spoon, a lot of gesticulating and what were very probably Italian curses, the black tom's right to roam the entire suburb, so Lucie kept the four-year war strictly between her and the cat.

The tom shot straight up the smooth bark of the magnolia and sat on a naked branch, glaring balefully down, his tail swishing.

'Don't jump onto the road, stupid,' Lucie muttered, moving away so the cat wouldn't dash onto the street. She drifted her hand across the potted lavender to release the early morning scent. Nearby, the fruit on the mandarin tree glowed like Chinese lanterns, so small that, with a bit of a stretch, she could fit three in one hand. Which meant the tree would yield only six handfuls of citrus-flavoured nostalgia, Lucie decided with a quick count. She couldn't expect a three-year-old potted tree to do much better, even though she moved it around the courtyard with the rickety trolley purchased online, finding shelter from the worst of the frosts. Not that Melbourne frosts were anything compared to those back home on the farm nestled in the Adelaide Hills. There, the birdbath tucked beneath the skeletal winter fingers of the cherry tree along-side Dad's favourite mandarin regularly froze over until after midday.

Lucie hesitated. Would visiting this memory be a pathway to old hurts? Tentatively, she allowed the images to trickle in: her breath steaming the air through mitten-wrapped hands as Mum lifted her up to check whether the slivers of pale, buttercream sun threading through the branches had melted the ice in the stone bowl, releasing the flowers and fruit they had arranged in it the night before.

The reminiscence was sweet, safe. Yet, like pressing on a bruise, she couldn't control the urge to push further, to rummage around in memory until she made herself hurt. She found a wound instantly: her feet sliding back and forth in wellington boots and her hand in his, skipping beside Dad as he strode across the dirt yard surrounding the neat double-brick house. Beyond the corrugated iron sheds, row upon row of identical mounds stretched across hectares of paddock. As they reached the nearest furrow, Dad thrust strong fingers into the dark loam, checking whether the soil was warm enough to nurture his precious strawberry seedlings. Then, his work-roughened hands cupped around hers, they would bed a tiny, three-leaved plant in the mound of crumbly earth, chanting a silly rhyme Dad had made up.

Snug tight little plant.
God the rain and light will grant.
Sun will shine, you'll grow fine,
And one day you'll be mine.

Tucking the plant in a nest of hay, they moved thirty centimetres along the row that stretched up a rolling hill to a horizon hazed with the shadowy giants of silver gums. Dad's hands guiding her, they eased the next plant into place. Sang the song. Then onto the next. And the next. Countless hours spent together in the ice-tipped sunshine, working the rows until an entire field of small, lime-coloured leaves waved in the chill breeze.

The memory itself didn't hurt: the pain lay in the contrast to the betrayal that came later. Though they had grown apart, Lucie had never expected her father to turn his back on her.

She dug a thumb into one of the tiny mandarins, then smoothly shucked the fruit. She crushed the fragrant, dimpled peel and inhaled deeply. The tangy scent wasn't the only reason for the film of tears that blurred her view of the courtyard: even after more than four years, home-sickness snuck up on her sometimes. Rural South Australia and suburban Melbourne had few similarities, but shared fragrances often evoked her unwanted memories.

The crescent moon of fruit puckered her lips as it exploded in her mouth. She grimaced, swallowed the excess saliva, and then squashed another segment against her teeth. There was a perverse pleasure to be found in mixing the sour juice with the false sweetness of her childhood memories.

She tossed the peel into the terracotta pots of oregano, basil and chocolate mint—which never tasted any different to regular mint, but she lived in hope—near the back door. The smell of citrus was supposed to keep the cat from spraying the herbs. Feline pee wasn't the kind of organic she

coveted, and it would be nice to use her produce
imagining a hint of ammonia in everything she p

An egg-shaped patio chair swung from a bra
the wall, the wicker spangled with dew crystals su
on delicate webs. She edged onto the seat, carefu
destroy the spider's work. From here her tiny garden
a little larger, her boundaries less constrained. The
sun peeking between the magnolia branches held a p
of the summer still months distant, although Mel
never seemed to match the unrelenting dry heat of Ad
At Blue Flag Strawberries, in the hills to the east
city, spring sunshine would herald an early ripen
the berries, along with the anticipation of an ext
cropping season.

Lucie gave a sharp grunt, annoyed with herself for l
her mind wander there again. Even after all these y
she related every quirk of the weather to what wou
happening on the farm. She piled the three mandari
her lap and reached into the pocket of her dressing-g
The powder-blue velour hung in a loose flap where
stitching had torn free. She had been using the same
for more than a decade, addicted to the soft, slightly th
bare reassurance of the well-washed material. A few y
back there had even been a stage when she had practic
lived in it, adding trackpants and a long-sleeved t-shi
the depths of winter. The oversized pockets were alw
stuffed with her life and had, over time, housed everyth
from uni textbooks and late-night study snacks to b
bottles and tiny, powder-fragranced nappies.

without
lated.
cket on
spended
not to
seemed
watery
promise
bourne
delaide.
of the
ing of
ended

etting
years,
ld be
ns in
own.
the
robe
ead-
ears
ally
t in
ays
ing
aby

tips brushed crumbs hiding
re locating an envelope. She
miliar handwriting. No return
er hard, as though the delib-
ided not only the letter's right

thing but a dry recount of local
r happenings in her hometown
e fact that the lifeless depiction
professed to have a love of the
m more of a betrayal, as though
to make home less inviting. The
wanted to think this was a delib-
uldn't miss Chesterton so much.
her had other explanations.
thumb and forefinger against the
existence. Collecting the mail from
of Keeley's favourite jobs, but the
hadn't mentioned the arrival of the
had found it this morning among the
ocks in the entry hall when she came
first cup of tea of the day. Saturday
tual. With a long commute to the office,
rushed to relax and enjoy the steaming
erbs she had dried the previous year. She
tea as soon as she woke, leaving it to
en bench while she took a few precious
herself in her small garden.

The roller door on the neighbour's garage, whi[ch] a rendered-cement wall with her garden, rattled an[d] ously ground open. Seconds later, Mrs A revved out of her old Volvo. The ghost departed in a cl[oud] blue smoke that drifted across the courtyard, and waved aside the burning oil, returning her attentio[n] the envelope.

As always, it was postmarked from Settlers Brid[ge] Mum chose to bypass a half-dozen villages, most wit[h] their own postal agency, to drive more than forty kilometre[s] to send her mail from a town so tiny that the post office doubled as a general store, tripled as a lottery outlet and quadrupled as a dry-cleaning agency. Lucie suspected only letters to her were dispatched from Settlers Bridge. No one there knew Mum: they wouldn't ask where Lucie was or what she was doing these days.

She had only been to Settlers Bridge a handful of times— for the district agricultural show held in a paddock on the outskirts—and could barely remember the place beyond the smell of fried donuts, battered hot dogs, fairy floss and overheating grease from the labouring fairground rides. She would have forgotten the riverside town entirely except that Jeremy had said he had lived there for a while. She remembered everything he had ever told her: of course, she'd had more than four years to relive each of their conversations, dissecting what was said . . . and what had been left unsaid.

As always, she pushed thoughts of him from her mind. It was enough to have lost Dad; she didn't need to dwell on Jeremy.

townhouse, scaring a tiny

echinacea she was coaxing

it before next winter's colds

groaned at the inevitability of

me for the battle over the Saturday

ume and, as always, there would be

solution according to Keeley: pancakes

e moderation.

now light and fluffy, pancakes left a bitter

e's mouth—because they should be served with

es and vanilla-bean cream.

he hadn't touched a strawberry in years.

last vestige of morning tranquillity vanquished, Lucie

ved a sigh and slit the envelope with her thumbnail.

he slowly stood up from the swinging chair, skimming the words that marched across the page with a decisive, spiky abruptness.

The paper trembled from her suddenly numb fingers. Drifted to the ground like a leaf, the grace at odds with the panicked hammering of her heart.

All oxygen abruptly sucked from the air, the blood thundered in her ears.

Her legs gave out.

Her lips moved wordlessly. No.

Frozen fingers inching back towards the letter, she crept up on the news, rather than confronting it.

Her mother's impersonal writing wavered before her eyes. Disjointed sentences with large areas blacked out, although

Lucie couldn't tell whether that was in her head or
page: ... *heart failure ... instantly fatal ... funera*

No. No one sent this kind of news in a letter.

Mum was lying.

Had to be.

Because Lucie wasn't one of those girls who fled
farm, vowing never to return once she'd had a taste of c
living. No, Lucie had always promised herself she wou.
go back.

One day.

As soon as Dad forgave her.

on the
...

the
ty
d